HONOUR AMONG MEN

Inspector Green Mysteries

Do or Die
Once Upon a Time
Mist Walker
Fifth Son
Honour Among Men
Dream Chasers
This Thing of Darkness
Beautiful Lie the Dead
The Whisper of Legends
None So Blind
The Devil to Pay

BARBARA FRADKIN

HONOUR AMONG MEN

AN INSPECTOR GREEN MYSTERY

Publisher: Kwame Scott Fraser | Editor: Allister Thompson
Cover designer: Karen Alexiou | Cover image: shutterstock.com/alsamua

Library and Archives Canada Cataloguing in Publication

Title: Honour among men / Barbara Fradkin.
Names: Fradkin, Barbara, 1947- author.
Series: Fradkin, Barbara, 1947- Inspector Green mystery.
Description: 2nd edition. | Series statement: An Inspector Green mystery
Identifiers: Canadiana 20220257280 | ISBN 9781459751064 (softcover)
Classification: LCC PS8561.R233 H65 2022 | DDC C813/.6—dc23

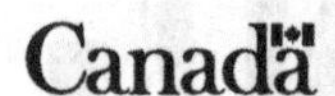

We acknowledge the support of the Canada Council for the Arts and the Ontario Arts Council for our publishing program. We also acknowledge the financial support of the Government of Ontario, through the Ontario Book Publishing Tax Credit and Ontario Creates, and the Government of Canada.

Printed and bound in Canada.

Dundurn Press
1382 Queen Street East
Toronto, Ontario, Canada M4L 1C9
dundurn.com, @dundurnpress

ONE

November 2, 1992. Annapolis Royal, Nova Scotia.

Today I finally did it. Put my name in for a peacekeeping tour overseas. Danny's been bugging me for weeks to volunteer so we could go together. Do our part for peace and see the world. Easy for him to say. For him, our reserve unit is the most exciting thing in his life, but for me it's just a way of making money to pay for college.

"There's more to the world than sheep farms," says Danny. "You never even been outside of Antigonish County!" Which is unfair. I went over to Prince Edward Island only last month to check out their vet school. I don't want to end up like Dad, working fifteen-hour days in the barns and up to his eyeballs in manure and debt.

Anyway it's the animals I like. The new lambs you help into the world, the old dog at your side no matter what. But the cost of vet school blew me away. Even if I get in — and that's a big if — I'd be up to my own eyeballs in debt before I'm through. That was what did it. I looked at the sign-up forms, did the math, and figured by the end of the six-month tour, I'd have enough money to pay for vet school and maybe even marry Kit. And Dad's proud of me that I'm going off to work for peace.

Kit is another story. Tryouts are in less than a month. There are probably thousands of reservists trying to get in, so my chances are slim, but if I pass the screening, I ship out right after New Years. What do I tell her? Wait for me? What's six months in the big picture of our lives?

***

DAYLIGHT LEAKED THROUGH the jagged rip in the blind and lit the dust in the tiny room. As it worked its way behind Patti's closed eyelids, she cursed and rolled over to face the wall. The bed springs shrieked, and her ratty quilt fell off.

She yanked it back around her, shivering. The goddamn sun was getting up earlier now, but it sure as hell wasn't bringing any warmth with it. The April wind swept across the top of Citadel Hill and down Gottingen Street to rattle the solitary window of her third-floor walk-up. It whistled through the cracks in the aging clapboard and swept down the chimney of the boarded up fireplace. The landlord was on such an economy drive with the heat that even the cockroaches had moved out.

April 9th. Patti felt a wave of despair. It sapped the strength from her limbs and the breath from her lungs. Ten years. Ten years to the day since Danny died. And look what she was reduced to. No fucking pension, no little house and curly-haired kid, no respect or sympathy. Just a throw-away life.

Bitterness rose up on cue, in the familiar dance of feelings that had kept her company these ten lonely years. Sure, she had her job, with its endless days of breathing dry-cleaning fumes and taking crap from bitchy housewives for stains that wouldn't come out. She had the happy hour gang at the Seaman's Watch on Friday nights. But it wasn't supposed to be like this.

After Danny died, she'd thought things would eventually get better. She'd loved him, but face it, he hadn't been the easiest guy to get along with at the end, and she'd assumed someone new would come along. She'd expected Danny's friends to rally around her, help her out, start a fund or something, then maybe one of them would even step up to the plate.

But the truth was Danny didn't have any friends. Not by the end. Drinking buddies was all, and she'd learned what they were worth. "Didn't see nothing, didn't hear nothing," never knew a thing that went on that night. They'd melted into the woodwork, leaving her to sort out the whole mess of his life by herself. Even his family had come and gone from town so fast that she'd barely learned their names. They'd brought with them a photo of Danny for the wake. Dressed in his reserves uniform all ready for parade, with his hat on square, his eyes set straight ahead and just the tiniest smile on his playful lips.

Looking nothing like the Danny he'd become those last months.

She'd wanted to feel a connection with them, to find a hint of Danny in them, but they were strangers. And after the funeral, they'd gone back to Cape Breton, sad but resigned. Like they'd lost Danny years ago.

"What about all his things?" Patti had asked on the morning after the wake, as they all slumped over coffee in the Tim Hortons on the way out of town.

His mother was a stick of a woman with basset eyes and ropes of muscle along her arms. Her eyes drooped further. "Is there much?"

Patti shook her head. Judging from the way Danny had borrowed off her in the last three months, he hadn't a penny to his name. When he'd been laid off for the winter, he hadn't even bothered looking for another job.

"Then you keep it, dear. I'm sure Danny would have wanted you to have it."

Danny didn't expect to die, she'd wanted to snap back, but she held her tongue. They were all in shock, all bumping around blindly in the dark.

Truth was, there wasn't much worth having in his little basement apartment off the harbour. He'd never invited her there, because he said it smelled of booze and piss, so she was surprised by how neat it was. Danny's last few months had been a mess, but his shoes and clothes were all lined up, his old enamel sink spit-polished and his blanket stretched tight across his bed. Once a soldier, always a soldier. She'd buried her face in his jacket, inhaling his scent of sweat and lemon spice aftershave. Neatly stowed under his bed, she found a kit bag full of books, souvenirs and letters from herself and his mother, all upbeat and cheerful with news from home. There were photos of himself with his company overseas, soldiers grinning ear to ear with their guns and their makeshift bunks.

For hours she'd sat on his bed, poring over the photos and letters, reading back in time to a Danny she barely remembered. Young, naive, cocky, setting out on his first grand adventure. Then she'd packed up the bag and brought everything back to her own place, thinking she'd send it on to his family some day, when she could put all this behind her.

But now, hugging the quilt around her to fend off the cold and the ache inside, she realized that time had never come. Instead, she'd been stuck in limbo, waiting for answers. For justice. Maybe even for a chance at revenge. But against what? Against the big, faceless public bureaucracy that had robbed Danny of his life? Or against an enemy much more specific. With a face, surely a name …

Something thumped against the front door at the bottom of the stairs. A dog barked. She rolled over, opened one eye, and squinted at the clock. Seven twenty. The kid from down the street had just delivered the Halifax *Sunday Herald*, and if she didn't hurry, the asshole from downstairs would steal it so he could read the comics. It was her one pleasure on a Sunday morning, when she didn't have to rush to work. When she could brew a proper cup of tea, snuggle up in bed, and check her weekly horoscope to see if her luck had changed.

She pulled Danny's old jacket over her pyjamas for the trip down the chilly staircase to the front door. The door on the landing opposite was just opening when she snatched up the paper. It slammed in her wake as she dashed back upstairs.

The headlines were the usual crap. Another suicide bombing in the Middle East, another refugee crisis in Africa, more hype from Ottawa about still another useless election campaign. She tossed the paper down on the table in disgust. Why should anyone even bother to vote? The world was going to shit, and there wasn't a fucking thing the little guy could do about it. Danny was right about that.

She made her tea, opened her package of half-priced cinnamon buns, and paged through the paper in search of her horoscope. She didn't know why she bothered. It was all lies too. Lies and contradictions. Yet for one brief moment, facing a brand new day, sometimes it gave her hope.

A moment later she stopped, her eyes riveted to page 10. She read, reread, until deep inside a flicker of triumph began to grow. Maybe this time her luck was about to change, she thought, as she shoved aside the paper and headed for her closet.

TWO

IT WAS PAST midnight when Twiggy squeezed her bulk through the gap in the bushes and slithered down the slope towards the darkened gully, guided more by feel than by sight. Three days' worth of old newspapers were tucked under one pudgy arm, and a battered garbage bag dragged along behind her. She held her bottle tight in her hand, but most of the rum was already singing through her veins. The soggy ground was slippery, but at least the ice had melted, and below her she saw the black water glisten in the aqueduct as it drifted slowly towards the old pumphouse.

Twiggy felt laughter bubble up inside her. April was her favourite time of year, when the squirrels and the leaf buds began to appear again. When the sun warmed the frozen ground and beat down on her secret hideout. After six years on the streets of Ottawa, she knew all the best spots — the ledges under the bridges, the back doors and vents of the indoor parking garages, the window wells of old office buildings. And best of all, this hidden sliver of trees and water running through the city core almost within sight of Parliament Hill. Cars whizzed by on the roads up above, but only a few regulars knew the old aqueduct existed beneath the canopy of trees. Twiggy had hoped it would stay that way, but every year the bulldozers and backhoes ripping up the Lebreton Flats rumbled ever closer to this little corner of history.

She'd had enough of her fellow man after a winter of stinky, crowded shelters, noisy drunks, paranoid psychos and ridiculous rules. She'd been waiting all month for the moment when she could finally return to her cubbyhole near the water's edge, spread out her belongings in the shelter of the graffiti wall and settle in for the summer. Her living room, she called it, complete with wall paintings from the most renowned street artists.

During the summer months, she had her regular panhandling spot next to the Tim Hortons on Bank Street, just a few blocks away. She had a special deal going with the day manager, who gave her day-old doughnuts and newspapers at the end of each day in return for her not crowding the door and for being polite and respectful to his customers. He said he'd rather have a friendly, middle-aged woman sitting quietly against the wall than a surly, in-your-face punk with piercings and tattoos all over the place. She usually made a pretty good haul during the tourist season.

Earlier that evening, she'd got a full meal at the Shepherds of Good Hope before linking up with a couple of friends to pool their take and party a little. She'd even had a little snooze in the side doorway of a hotel before some security guard kicked her out. So she was really groggy when she finally stumbled down the ravine toward her favourite spot in the shelter of the graffiti wall. The moon was high, and the looming silhouette of a steam shovel shimmered in her vision like a massive insect ready to scoop up her private paradise. So close now! Above the gurgle of the water, there was no sound. No giggles of stoned teenagers, no grunts of hurried sex or wails of homesick drunks.

Twiggy wavered dreamily along the stone embankment until her foot hit something solid, pitching her forward onto her face. Her fingers encountered hair. Masses of long, tangled curls and cool, doughy flesh. She jerked back in panic and groped the length of the body, feeling high boots and denim stretched tight over a boney ass.

Some little whore had passed out cold, half dangling in the water.

"Lucky the little bitch didn't fall in," Twiggy muttered, staggering to her hands and knees. She tried to drag the girl farther from the water, but in the end could only budge her a few inches. In disgust, she hauled her garbage bag up to the shelter of the wall, shoved the wad of newspapers under her and collapsed with a grunt to fall asleep.

The cold woke her just after dawn. Pale sunlight speckled the ravine, and the morning rush hour was just revving up. Frost had settled onto the ground, and her breath swirled white around her. She curled herself stiffly into a ball, trying to warm up as she gathered her rum-soaked thoughts.

Jesus, was her first thought. She'd jumped the gun. It was still too fucking cold to be sleeping outdoors. Tonight she'd have to grit her teeth and go back to the women's shelter. No one in their right mind was out here this early in the spring. No one except …

A vague recollection fluttered down, like a forgotten leaf from a barren tree. She rolled over and lifted her head to peer at the body by the water. Saw in the daylight that the woman was still there. Blond and long-legged, but scrawny as a chicken and wearing a man's old jacket. She was curled on her side with one hand flung out and her face tilted towards the sky. A fine layer of frost had settled on her cheeks and eyelashes, and not even the faintest puff of white mist drifted between her parted lips.

***

Inspector Michael Green eased the clutch out and inched his car eastward in the bumper to bumper morning traffic along Albert Street. Up ahead, the light at Booth Street turned red yet again. A long line of buses snaked along the transitway, waiting to turn left onto Albert Street. Green craned his neck to search for any signs of obstruction and spotted flashing red lights through the brush on the north side of the street.

As he drew closer, he saw a uniformed police officer directing traffic and a police vehicle blocking access to the municipal parking lots on the north side, throwing hundreds of downtown commuters into confusion. Lined up on the back street behind the parking lots were four squad cars, two unmarked Malibus, an Ident van, and a black coroner's van. Just beyond the official vehicles, the land fell away to a scruffy mix of trees, construction fencing and neglected scrubland that surrounded the city's old aqueduct. The entire parking lot, scrubland and aqueduct were cordoned off with yellow police tape.

Green hesitated. This was obviously a major incident. The coroner's van meant there was a body, and the sheer number of officers suggested the cause of death was far from clear. All crimes against persons fell under Green's command, and even though he had a team of major crimes detectives to handle the frontline fieldwork, he could never quite trust they actually knew what they were doing. Especially since Brian Sullivan, his oldest friend and the backbone of the Major Crimes Squad, was off playing Acting Staff Sergeant in strategic planning, and CID's new superintendent Barbara Devine was trying to control every dime and man-hour expended, so that her stats would look good in the annual report.

At this very moment, in fact, Barbara Devine was probably pacing her colour-coordinated office, tapping her red fingernails on folded arms as she waited for him to show up for his weekly report. That image alone began to shift the scales in favour of checking out the scene. Then he spotted a young woman with a cloud of frizzy red hair and a hideous black and white checked suit clumping down towards the water's edge.

The sight of Detective Sue Peters was the final straw.

He pulled out into the opposing lane and jumped his car up onto the curb, ignoring the outraged looks of the other drivers and thankful for the Subaru's all wheel drive. He drove along the grassy verge until he reached the parking lot, then clambered out of the car. Logging in with the startled officer guarding the scene, he ducked under the cordon and slithered down the frost-slicked slope. Sue Peters swung on him in surprise. Her green eyes danced irrepressibly.

"Good morning, sir!"

He nodded to the group clustered by the water. "What do we have, Peters?"

"A body, sir. Looks like a working girl stayed out too late."

Green shot her a scowl, bristling at the flippancy in her tone and the haste of her conclusions. The body wasn't even out of the scene. He prayed someone other than Peters was in charge. "Who's lead?"

The dancing eyes faded slightly. She nodded toward the parking lot. "Bob Gibbs. He's up at the car."

"Do we have an ID?"

"She had no wallet or purse on her, sir. But Gibbsie's running her specs through the system, and maybe Missing Persons will come up with a match."

Green raised his head to scan the scene. As he'd expected, there was no sign of any of the NCOs from Major Crimes. A brawl in one of the Byward Market clubs two nights ago had resulted in the stabbing of two college students in a room full of underage witnesses, who had scattered before the police arrived, tying up a dozen detectives in the search to track them down and leaving enough prints and blood spatters to keep the entire Ident unit poring over their microscopes for a month. There were precious few resources left over for this luckless Jane Doe, and with Barbara Devine clutching the purse strings, Green feared there was little chance of more.

The one positive was the presence of Sergeant Lou Paquette, an Ident officer who drank too much and whined too much, but who'd lived and breathed forensics for over twenty years. He was crouched by the stone bank, snapping photographs. When he moved aside, Green glimpsed a lanky figure on his knees beside the victim, his wild white mane of hair tumbling into his eyes. Green's pulse quickened. Dr. Alexander MacPhail was the region's senior forensic pathologist. What had prompted Gibbs to call in the big guns?

Green took a quick breath to steel himself before heading over for a closer look. He loved the thrill of the hunt, but quailed at the gut-churning stench and gore of death. Images of splattered brains and amputated body parts crowded his subconscious, clamouring for memory whenever he approached another death. Three years behind a desk had not improved his defences either.

To his relief, the victim looked almost peaceful curled up on her side on the cold stone bank. Her eyes were half shut, and she had no apparent marks on her. A working girl, Peters had concluded, but at first glance Green didn't think so. She looked thin and sick, as if she'd taken a beating from life, but her clothing had been chosen for warmth rather than titillation, and her porcelain-white face had not a trace of make-up. Crow's feet were beginning to tug at the corners of her eyes and her matted blond hair was shot with grey.

MacPhail was bent over her, inspecting her face with a powerful flashlight.

Green crouched as close as he dared. "What can you tell me?"

MacPhail cast him only the briefest glance of surprise. "This is an interesting one, laddie," he announced in his customary Scottish boom. Green had never known the man to whisper, even in the presence of the most heart-wrenching death. MacPhail waved his beam. "See the colouring on this side of her face?"

Green forced himself to study the woman's face carefully. Where the frost had melted, beads of moisture clung to her lashes and to the down on her cheeks. But beneath the waxy pallor of death, he saw what MacPhail meant. Faint red blotches discoloured one side of her face.

"She's been moved some time after death," he said.

"Aye. Now the lass who found her ..." MacPhail cocked a brow towards a group of people clustered at the base of the graffiti wall. In the middle sat a familiar figure with a mop of stringy grey hair and a paramedic's blanket draped around her massive frame. Calling her a lass seemed a stretch. Nonetheless, MacPhail continued with no trace of irony. "She says she tripped on her last night in the dark."

"That would be enough to dislodge her, certainly." Considering the weight differential, Green thought.

"Aye." The pathologist's blue eyes twinkled briefly. "But not to roll her over. I'll know more when I can check the lividity in the rest of the body. However, my considered opinion, based on having seen a few corpses in my day, is that she was dumped."

Green glanced at MacPhail sharply. The pathologist made no attempt to suppress the broad smile that cracked his features. So that was why Bob Gibbs had called in the big guns. Sharp boy, Green thought with a twinge of pride. "So we're talking what?" he said. "Murder?"

"Or a simple cover-up. She could have OD'd, and her friends didn't want the police snooping around their hangout, so they brought her out here. Pretty isolated this time of year."

Green glanced around at the surroundings. MacPhail had a point. Lebreton Flats had boasted a colourful history of sex and wild times since the years when fur traders and lumbermen first ran their goods down the Ottawa River in the late 1700s. But in the past fifty years, the area, which sat virtually in the shadow of Parliament Hill and constituted some of the choicest urban real estate in the country, had gone to seed while politicians and bureaucrats bickered about what to do with it.

During that time, street people and squatters had filtered in, bringing sex, drugs and booze to the decrepit shores of the abandoned aqueduct. Recently, though, construction had begun to clean up the Flats for fancy condos and museums, and now the Flats were crisscrossed with construction fencing. Heavy machinery sat idle amid piles of dirt, and in the middle sat the old stone pumphouse through which the aqueduct ran. But above the pumphouse, tucked in below an old wall and invisible from the street, a little pocket of trees still formed a natural hangout. In summers past, the area had been popular with transients and street artists, who had painted the wall with huge, colourful images. At this time of year, however, with the ice barely gone from the shoreline, the street trade would be nonexistent. Whoever brought the woman here had probably hoped she'd go undiscovered for days.

"Can you give me a preliminary cause of death?"

MacPhail shone his flashlight at the victim's nose and mouth. Pinpoints of red dotted her eyelids and some water clung to her upper lip and the corners of her mouth.

"Drowning?" Green ventured.

MacPhail frowned as he probed the woman's neck. His tone was distracted. "Possibly. I need to get her on the table to be sure. Paquette's taking samples of the water to compare with her lungs, and I'll need a thorough tox screen. From the looks of her, I'd say she hasn't been putting too many healthy things into her body for the last while."

Green studied the woman's clothing. Her long, narrow feet were encased in a pair of worn leather boots, and her faded jeans fit neatly over her thin hips, as if they'd been made for her. Only the jacket, a man's khaki parka which hung down over her fingertips, looked out of place.

"I guess she probably picked up that jacket from one of the missions. Or traded another one for it."

MacPhail was bagging the hands and he barely paused to glance at it. "That's military issue for both men and women."

Green perked up. A lead. "Any idea what regiment?"

MacPhail moved the hood aside. "No sign of a regimental insignia, but it's standard army. Mind you, it's known some years. It could have been passed around like a paper bag at a temperance rally, so it's pretty cold as trails go."

"Still, it's a trail." Green turned to find Sue Peters at his elbow, clipboard in hand.

"You want me to contact the military, sir? See if they have a soldier gone AWOL from CFB Ottawa?"

"No." Green scrambled for a safer assignment to occupy her. With only a few months of Major Crimes under her belt, Peters still had all the subtlety of a charging rhino, and Green shuddered at the thought of the military in her sights. Spotting Paquette, he gestured towards him. "As soon as Ident gets a good photo of the deceased, start showing it around on the streets, including the shelters, Byward Market and the Rideau Centre. Someone should have seen her."

"Do you want me to ask about pimps too, sir?"

Green bit his tongue. Jeez, she was going to screw up even that. "Stick with the victim, Peters. Find someone who's seen her, or knows who she's been associating with."

"Who should I report to? I mean … are you running the case?"

Green hesitated. As he stood at the edge of the crime scene, breathing in the scent of excitement and the urgency of death, watching the ident officer combing the grounds and the pathologist circling the victim, he felt the old passion for the hunt. People suffered, people died, and all he'd ever wanted to do was to track down the tormenters and bring them to account. Nothing thrilled him as much as making the bad guys pay. But now, in the larger, amalgamated police service, he was a middle-management bureaucrat, trapped between the field officers who wrestled with flesh and blood suffering and the senior officers, whose main battlefield was the committee rooms and ledgers of Elgin Street Headquarters. He'd stopped off here because he couldn't resist the call of the field, but he belonged, even at this moment, in Barbara Devine's office.

Yet there were elements in the case that could use an inspector's touch. He dredged up his best bureaucratese. "Not directly. It's Gibbs's case. He'll keep me apprised."

MacPhail straightened as he watched the redhead bound eagerly towards the road. Merriment shone in his eyes. "Not directly? You'll be getting your nose indirectly in, then?"

Green laughed. "Well, inquiries with the military can be delicate. Those army guys love their ranks."

***

January 15, 1993. Winnipeg, Manitoba.

Man, it's cold out here. The wind whips off the prairie like a nor'easter coming off the sound, so cold we can hardly do manoeuvres. We're mostly doing weapons training and PT, and the sergeant major's working us so hard my legs feel like they're going to fall off. He says we only got two months to get in shape, and there's going to be some of us won't make the cut. There are guys here from all across the country, a lot of them weekend warriors like me, really excited to be on their first tour. My platoon commander's a captain from the Princess Pat regulars who they call the Hammer, because he comes down hard if you mess up. They put Danny and me in the same platoon, but we're in different sections so we won't get to work together much. Your section's kind of like your family, you rely on them.

My section commander's a sergeant from Winnipeg on back-to-back rotations to Yugoslavia. He's been telling us horror stories about the shelling and the sniping going on all the time. But that's mostly in Sarajevo, and we're going to be escorting convoys and protecting civilians in Croatia, which is a little horseshoe-shaped country that curves through the mountains and down the Adriatic Sea. Maybe Danny and I can go to a Greek island on our leave. Far cry from the North Atlantic. This is our first taste of real action, and I sure hope we both make the cut.

THREE

GREEN WAS ALREADY formulating a battle plan for the military as he walked back towards Gibbs's car, but at the last minute he detoured over to have a quick word with Twiggy. The uniformed officers had obviously decided they had gleaned all the information from her that they could, for they'd left her sitting on the ground by herself. Some thoughtful officer had brought her a cup of hot coffee and a cigarette, which hung from the corner of her mouth. She cradled the coffee and pretended to be engrossed in her paper, but she was rocking slightly as if to soothe herself. At the sight of him, her lips stretched around the cigarette in a jagged but affectionate smile.

He extended his hand. "How are you doing, Twiggy?"

She squinted up at him through the smoke. "Well, well, Mr. G," she said, her voice rattling through the phlegm in her throat. "Been awhile. What is it now? Superintendent? Chief?"

He feigned horror. "God forbid! Inspector, and that's as high as I plan to go. I have a fear of heights."

She chuckled, thrusting her thick tongue through the gap in her teeth. It seemed to Green that she'd lost a few more since he'd last seen her. "I don't see your buddy around much anymore either. Sully. He retired or something?"

"Just off on another assignment. And we got a great big city to take care of now, so we don't get down onto the street as much as we used to." He eyed the soggy ground beside her. She had spread out some of her newspapers to sit on. Without hesitation, she laid out the one she was reading, and he eased himself gingerly down beside her. The reek of booze and body odour almost made him gag, but he kept his expression friendly.

"So," he said gently, "this must have been an unpleasant surprise for you."

Twiggy shrugged. Green had known her since she'd first hit the streets, and he knew the reason, yet only a slight wobble in her chin betrayed the pain she must have felt. For Twiggy, like himself, dead bodies stirred up one memory too many.

"Not the first time," she said. "Won't be the last. Some day it'll be me."

He didn't insult her by arguing. In truth, he was surprised she was still around. She was an alcoholic, a smoker and a diabetic. The only reason her heart and lungs hadn't collapsed beneath the abuse was that she'd inherited the constitution of an ox. And the bloody-mindedness to match.

He stuck to the facts. "Did you know the woman?"

Twiggy's eyes peered shrewdly through folds of fat. "Didn't get a good look first time round, and wasn't about to take another."

"Still ... did she look familiar?"

"Like you said, it's a big city."

"But you've seen a lot of it."

She chuckled. "Not so much recently. My knees don't like to travel. But she wasn't from around this part, that much I'll say."

"Did you see her arrive?"

"She was already here."

"Already dead?"

"Maybe. It was dark, and I didn't notice."

"Was anyone else around here last night?"

She shifted restlessly, wincing at the stiffness of her joints. "Mr. G, your cops already asked me all this. They took notes up the ying yang. Now I gotta go before I lose the best part of the day."

Green pulled his wallet from his inside jacket pocket. "It's just that sometimes, after the shock wears off, witnesses remember more details."

Twiggy's eyes flicked to his wallet before travelling up the slope towards the buildings on Bronson Avenue. She poked her tongue through her teeth. "I might have seen her earlier. With someone."

"Man or woman?"

She stared into the distance, worrying her teeth with her tongue. "It was just a vague impression. I saw more the jacket than the woman."

"When was this? The same night?"

"Maybe, maybe not. The nights all blur together, you know?"

"What were they doing together? Did it look like drugs? Soliciting?"

"I just remember them on a street over there, outside some fancy place." When she pointed a stubby, yellowed finger towards downtown, Green noticed an oozing sore on the finger where the skin had cracked. "Talking."

"Hear anything?"

She cast him a disdainful look before stubbing out her cigarette and beginning her struggle to rise. Green reached to haul her up, then extracted twenty dollars from his wallet. "Treat yourself to a proper breakfast, and check that finger out at the clinic." He extended his card with the money. "And Twiggy, you be sure to call me if you remember anything more."

A jagged smile lit her doughy face as she plucked the bill from his hand. "Sure thing, Mr. G. My memory's a funny thing these days."

***

Actually, Twiggy's memory was still remarkably sharp for details that were important to her survival. Such as the whereabouts and activities of all strangers who came into her personally declared sphere of operation.

She waited till Green had disappeared around the edge of the wall before she made her move. Stuffing her newspapers under her arm and dragging her garbage bag behind her, she struggled up the muddy slope and headed to the seat in the nearby bus shelter. There, shielding her actions from the suspicious eyes of the police officer guarding the scene, she emptied her garbage bag onto the bench beside her. She pawed impatiently through the crumpled bedding and the pile of smelly clothing, picked up a small cardboard box and pried off its lid. Inside were two pairs of homemade bead bracelets and a gold ring now much too small for her swollen fingers. They were remnants of another lifetime, kept only because they were worth more in memories than in cold hard cash.

She frowned at the inside of the box. Too small. She groped through the clothes for a better hiding place, but everything was damp and stained. As a last resort, almost reluctantly, she picked up the two books that had weighted down the bottom of the garbage bag. One was a paperback picked up at a church rummage sale for 25 cents. *If Life's a Bowl of Cherries, What am I Doing in the Pits?*, by Erma Bombeck. Bombeck had been dealt one of life's crappier hands but had risen to fame and happiness, only to be struck down by a fatal disease at the height of her success. Twiggy had been unable to resist the irony, and indeed, Bombeck's humour had brought her through many a desolate night.

But the paperback wasn't big enough. Not for what she had in mind.

The second book was a thick hardcover tome with gilt lettering and a splintering spine. *The Collected Works of Charles Dickens*. Twiggy picked it up and let it fall open naturally to reveal the treasures that lay inside. Two photos, lovingly preserved against the crush of life on the streets. Like the jewellery, they were remnants of another lifetime. Carefully, she tore the newspaper along its crease and folded the page into four. Flipping to a fresh spot, she tucked the small square between the pages of the book.

Another remnant, valuable not to her past, but perhaps to her future.

***

After Green left Twiggy, he headed up to speak to Detective Bob Gibbs. He opened the passenger door and slipped in just as the young detective was lifting his coffee cup from its holder. Gibbs started, spilling coffee all down the front of his impeccable white shirt. His Adam's apple bobbed as he searched for his voice.

"Sorry about that, Bob," Green said, rescuing the cup and setting it down. Bob Gibbs had many talents, but a confident disposition was not one of them. Still, in the current state of CID, you had to take the good with the bad. He glanced at the screen on Gibbs's laptop. "How's it going?"

Gibbs found his voice. "It's still early, sir. How … how did you know …?"

"I was just driving by. Any luck with missing persons?"

"It's no one local, at least recently. But I've asked MisPers to check Quebec and Ontario."

"There may be a military connection."

Gibbs blinked in surprise, and a faint flush crept up his neck. "Are you … should I …?"

"It's your case, Bob. I'm heading to the office to meet with Superintendent Devine. But because of the military line of inquiry, I'd like to be kept in the loop."

A shout from down by the water interrupted any reply Gibbs might have attempted. Green peered out of the car window and saw an officer gesturing towards the water at the base of the pumphouse wall. Green and Gibbs got out of the car for a better look and saw Lou Paquette striding over towards the spot, cameras bouncing, yelling at them not to touch anything. Without a moment's hesitation, Gibbs and Green hurried back down the slope, reaching the scene only seconds after the Ident officer. The young uniformed officer who'd made the discovery was on his knees, leaning out over the water, oblivious to the damp seeping into his pants. A strange pink mottled object lay in about four feet of murky water.

"I think it's a purse, sir," he said. "Looks like it got stuck on the lip of the culvert."

Paquette was already chasing everyone away so that he could photograph it. Gibbs and Green waited patiently with the others until he had completed the photos and had fished the purse out into a large plastic pan. Water oozed from it as it gradually deflated. It was large enough to carry a small tank, Green thought, but it was hideous. Something even his wife Sharon, with her practical streak and her sense of humour, would have left on the rack. Shiny black vinyl with big, floppy, pink daisies stuck all over it.

Paquette pried open the clasp, methodically removed the contents and laid them beside it in the pan. A hat and scarf, two lipsticks, a glasses case, a half-eaten pack of Dentine, half a dozen cheap pens, black gloves, an empty Tupperware container, a hair brush, bits of sodden paper, and three large rocks.

Paquette hefted these, looking perplexed.

"Could they have gotten into the purse when it bumped along the bottom?" the young uniform asked.

Another officer elbowed closer. "The clasp was shut."

Green stepped forward and pulled on a glove before picking up one of the stones. It was heavy. Not something a woman would be eager to lug around in her purse. It was grey and irregularly shaped, certainly not chosen for its beauty. He studied the rocky shoreline thoughtfully. Similar grey stones of all sizes poked through the mud.

"The killer put them in there, hoping to make the purse sink," he said.

Paquette's shrug was non-committal. Green knew the Ident officer was not fond of theories, only of evidence he could lay his hands on. Evidence won cases in court.

The second officer peered over Paquette's shoulder at the pan. "Wallet's missing. Looks like there's no ID whatsoever. Who's to say it's even the Jane Doe's?"

Paquette had begun poking in side pockets, removing more soggy bits of paper. At this point, he glanced up. "It's not been in the water very long. The fabric's not degraded, the vinyl's still shiny and the print on these papers is still pretty clear."

Green looked at the sixty odd feet between the purse and the body. "It's hers. The killer took all the ID out, weighted it with rocks, and tossed it into the water, probably hoping the current would carry it farther away. Which was a risk, because he had to know we might find it. He must have thought it was a greater risk to carry it with him."

The second officer snorted. "Yeah. Like what guys's gonna walk down the street carrying that thing?"

Green turned to give the officer a closer look. Constable Jeffrey Weiss, his tag said. He was dressed in a casual sports jacket with his tie trailing loose and his blond hair curling over his collar. He had high, Slavic cheekbones, and beneath the peak of his jauntily set baseball cap, his blue eyes stared back, almost in challenge. Green had seen that look before. Cocksure and cynical, the mark of a lousy cop. Yet there was an intelligence in the man's gaze that gave Green pause. An instinct for the job, which could not be taught.

Green turned back to the purse. "Lou, can you dry out the pieces of paper? Maybe one of them will give us some answers."

Paquette gave him a long, exasperated stare. "Gee, I thought I'd just chuck them. I suppose you want these answers like yesterday? When I've got a whole scene to process."

Green chuckled. "Bob here is in charge of the case. I'm sure you'll get it to him as soon as you can. After all, it'd be nice to know who she is. It helps the investigation no end."

FOUR

THE TRAGEDY OF Jane Doe's death yielded one dubious bonus. When Green finally made his appearance in Barbara Devine's office, she was so distracted by this new crisis on her turf that she forgot most of the tedious items on her agenda.

"Three murders in less than a week, Mike! Last year there were eight in the whole year. Ottawa is the laughingstock of the criminal world. While our politicians squabble about funding tulip festivals and light rail projects, the drug lords and the pimps are moving in and setting up shop. What are your drug squads doing? And Vice? Selling tickets to the show?"

She had shut the door to her third-floor office and closed the blinds on her fabulous view of the turreted museum across the square — sure signs that their meeting was not for the public eye. Or ear. She perched on the edge of her chair, the wings of her black lacquered hair skewering the air, and as she built up steam, her face grew almost as crimson as her nails.

Green leaned back in his chair with deliberate calm. "It's too early to classify this as a homicide, Barbara. MacPhail's doing the autopsy tomorrow. But in any case, there's nothing to suggest drugs or prostitution."

"Then you find it, or wrap this case up before the six o'clock news. If it's her lunatic husband, nail him before the women's groups have a field day claiming the streets are not safe. If it's drugs or vice, I want ammunition so I can go to the Chief for funds. Who've you got leading the investigation?"

"Detective Gibbs."

She stared at him in disbelief. "Gibbs is afraid of his own shadow."

Green checked his own flare of anger. "The senior guys are all on the Byward Pub murders." At your insistence, remember, he thought, but kept it to himself. He wanted to escape with as little meddling from her as possible. "Gibbs has nearly three years in Major Crimes, and he knows what he's doing."

"Then I want you checking his every move, as I will yours."

It took him half an hour to talk her down sufficiently that she remembered the rest of her agenda, so it was well past noon when Green emerged from her office. He had a splitting headache and a roiling stomach that rebelled at the least thought of food. He paused for an ill-advised cup of coffee before heading to his office.

He had barely settled down to pry the lid off his coffee when Paquette marched into his office with a plastic evidence bag in his hand. His thick brows were set in their customary frown, but his eyes betrayed a flicker of excitement as he laid the bag down on Green's desk.

"Gibbs figured you'd want to see this."

Inside the bag was a small ticket stub from VIA Rail. Even though it was faded and creased, Green could clearly see that it had been purchased in Halifax two weeks earlier. Halifax was a good fifteen-hundred-kilometre, twenty-four-hour train ride from Ottawa, not a trip one would make on a whim.

"I found it in one of the small zippered pockets," Paquette said. "Our guy obviously didn't notice the pocket when he cleaned out the purse."

It was probably dark, Green thought, and when you've just murdered someone, you're not usually at your sharpest. Thank God for stupid bad guys. He felt his headache fade, and he managed a genuine smile. "Thanks, Lou. I appreciate the quick work."

Lou nodded grudgingly. "Gibbs said to tell you he's already on the phone to Halifax Missing Persons."

"Excellent. Any other useful papers turn up in the purse?"

"Shreds of Kleenex, gum wrappers. The woman chewed a lot of gum, maybe trying to quit smoking. Receipts from Pharmaprix and Loeb grocery store, both here in the Vanier area in the last week, but unfortunately all paid with cash." He turned to head out the door, and paused. "Oh, and a pamphlet from the new Canadian War Museum."

Green's interest quickened. The victim's jacket had been military. One military connection might have been random, but two connections, however remote, formed a lead. He was just about to call Gibbs when the man himself loped into his office, almost colliding with Paquette on his way out. Gibbs had his notebook open to a page covered in tight, meticulous writing, and he looked so focussed he forgot to be afraid.

"Halifax MisPers has nothing, but I sent them the DOA's photo and description. And Lou said he'd run her prints through AFIS as soon as he gets them at the autopsy tomorrow."

Green nodded. Both were appropriate lines of inquiry, but they were still looking for a needle in a haystack. Besides

AFIS, the national fingerprint database, the Department of National Defence had its own fingerprint file of all Canadian Forces military personnel, but it was designed to permit identification of casualties in wartime. It would be a stretch to convince DND that the unidentified Jane Doe might qualify as a victim of war.

But it was worth a try, particularly if it could get the case solved by the six o'clock news.

More likely, though, Green suspected that his efforts to connect with the military would take closer to a week, and require official request forms in quadruplicate. In the post 9/11 world, no one was more secretive than DND, except the spooks. So he was surprised when his call was returned before the end of the day by a Captain Karl Ulrich from Human Resources at DND headquarters. Green thought the rank fitting, a captain being at about the same level of the food chain as an inspector.

But the speed of the response did not mean good news. "Our fingerprint files are not searchable," the Captain intoned, as if reading from cue cards. "Not like AFIS. Even if National Defence could authorize access in this case, we would require the individual's name and service number in order to locate the file."

"And if that information becomes available, what process does the Ottawa Police need to follow to get access?"

"Well, there's a form ..."

Of course there's a form, Green muttered privately after he'd jotted down the procedure and thanked the Captain for his help. Probably the first of many, requiring signatures from the Commissioner of the RCMP, the Prime Minister and the Governor General herself. We'd better hope Gibbs has more luck with the Missing Persons unit of the Halifax police.

***

February 23, 1993. Fort Ord, California.

Dear Kit ... Man, I'm not very good at this diary business. The padre said we should try it, to record one of the greatest experiences of our lives and maybe help us keep perspective if things get tough. But it feels dumb, so I've decided to write it as a letter to you, even though I can't actually mail it. It feels good talking to you instead of just myself.

It's been go-go-go since we got down here to do our combat training. Section attacks, platoon attacks, fighting in built-up areas. It freaked out some of the guys because they thought our mission was just going to be keeping the peace, but we're training on all these guns and practising live-fire simulations. It's kind of scary because you wonder what you got yourself in for, but, boy — does it ever get the adrenaline going. I'm getting pretty good with my C-7, and even the general purpose machine gun.

The great news is that Danny's been made 2IC of my section because the Princess Pats regular master corporal got moved out to man one of the TOWs. These are really cool anti-tank missile systems that can take out a tank at almost 4000 metres, even in the dark. The CO says we we're not supposed to have them, but we're taking them anyway. The UN doesn't really understand what's happening on the ground, he said, and he wasn't going to make Canadian Forces into sitting ducks. I'm glad he'll be in charge when we go over.

***

It was ten o'clock that evening before Green's thoughts returned to the case. His wife Sharon was working the evening shift at Rideau Psychiatric Hospital, so the challenge of feeding, bathing, and putting their rambunctious, two-and-a-half-year-old son to bed had fallen solely to him. Green spent nearly half an hour snuggled up in bed with him, reading the antics of Robert Munsch and Dr. Seuss, which had Tony bouncing all over the bed, a million miles from sleep. Green tried the warm milk and lullaby routine that Sharon used, but it still took his entire repertoire of lullabies and a back rub before the little boy finally crashed into sleep from pure exhaustion. Green brushed a kiss to his tousled head and slipped off the bed.

No sooner had Green tiptoed out of his room when the bedroom door opposite cracked open and an elfin face peered out. The pulse of rock music escaped the room.

"Shh-h!" Green whispered urgently.

"What's for dinner?"

"And hello to you too."

Hannah rolled her eyes. She was barely five feet tall and had a delicate, heart-shaped face that radiated innocence. That illusion had allowed her to get away with everything short of murder in the first sixteen years of her life, after which her mother, Green's first wife, had thrown up her hands and shipped her across the country to live with her father. In the beginning, Green and Hannah had been complete strangers, but Hannah had been living with them for over nine months now, and at least now she occasionally spoke to him of her own free will. Even if it was only when she wanted something.

"I picked up cheese blintzes from the Bagelshop," he added.

She sighed. "Figures."

He'd learned the hard way to ignore the bait. The reality was, she had her father's unerring instinct for hidden truths, and it had taken her no time to notice that, in his forty-plus years, he had learned very little about the workings of a kitchen. Deli take-outs had served him well in his ten years between wives, and at the end of a long day he rarely had the desire or energy for culinary creativity.

Feigning nonchalance, he headed downstairs. "They're in a bag on the counter. How about heating them up while I walk the dog."

Modo, their massive Humane Society refugee, was sprawled the length of the living room with her head by Sharon's chair, snoring blissfully and showing no inclination for a walk. After repeated calling, she hauled herself up and lumbered over to the door.

Modo was Sharon's dog, and like Tony, she only accepted Green's clumsy care-giving when Sharon was not around. Even so, she left the house reluctantly and paused often to look anxiously back towards the house while they made their tour around the block. Green returned home feeling thoroughly inadequate. The fragrance of cheese blintzes and butter cheered him considerably. He found Hannah in the kitchen, chatting on her cellphone and brandishing a spatula over a frying pan.

"I suppose you want salad too," she said.

"That would be nice."

"Honestly, Mike," she muttered, and returned her attention to her cellphone.

He walked up to her and planted a kiss on her blue, curly-topped head. Quickly, before she could duck away. A murmured thanks was as mushy as he dared.

He set the kitchen table for two, but once Hannah had spooned the food onto two plates, she picked up hers and headed into the living room to turn on the TV. Green opened his mouth to protest, but when the sounds of yet another *Simpsons* rerun filled the room, he gave up in defeat. She would only have sat opposite him in silence anyway, oozing resentment.

Instead he read the paper while he ate, then fed the dog and cleaned up the kitchen. Weariness began to steal into his bones. What was he coming to, when by ten in the evening he was ready to crawl into bed? He stuck his head into the living room.

"Want some tea?"

Hannah glanced at him, and he could see the ambivalence play across her face. Why was every single move between them like an elaborate dance, with him bumbling around to learn the steps?

She shrugged. "As long as you don't make it too strong, like Sharon's."

Under Sharon's exacting tutelage, Green had learned to make her version of a perfect cup of tea. He diluted it by half and carried two cups into the living room. The TV was on, but to his surprise Hannah was sitting on the floor surrounded by schoolwork. She didn't move when he placed her cup at her side. She was actually on track to pass all her courses this semester, a feat she'd never accomplished in the years of living with her mother. He stood over her, wondering if it was safe to comment. Finally, she looked up at him and, to his amazement, flashed a mischievous smile.

"Thanks, Mike," she said, then picked up her cup and book, and disappeared upstairs.

He sank onto the sofa, propped his feet on the coffee table, and closed his eyes, too tired to figure her out. Brian Sullivan's advice rang in his ears. "If you love the kid, that's going to show." Sullivan was raising three teenagers and had been giving Green a crash course in raising his own these past few months.

God, he missed Sullivan. He could barely remember a time when the big Irish lunk hadn't been right at his side, trading theories, sharing rants and dishing out his home-spun wisdom. Full of disillusionment and self-doubt, Sullivan had gone off to another department in search of that elusive promotion. Major Crimes was mostly newcomers now, none of whom remembered the old days on the streets. Or remembered Twiggy as anyone more than a fat old lady who stuck her cup in your face. And who was on a slow, deliberate march towards death.

He sat on the sofa, letting the chatter of the *CBC National News* wash over him. Campaign trail rhetoric, media overkill, yet another poll showing the Liberals trailing the Conservatives by a slim margin. Panic had not yet taken over the Liberal camp, but the mudslinging and cheap promises had ratcheted up a notch. Green tuned it out in disgust. He felt lonely, lost in recollections about Twiggy, and hoping Sharon would be home soon. But long before she arrived, he was fast asleep.

FIVE

WITH THREE MURDERS on the go, an inexperienced staff sergeant in Major Crimes, and a superintendent snapping at his heels, Green was anxious to get an early start the next morning. He left Sharon to contend with the household and picked up a bagel and coffee from Vince's Bagelshop on his way to the police station. When he arrived, however, Staff Sergeant Larocque was already out in the field, as was Bob Gibbs. But Sue Peters was parked outside his office, wearing yet another hideous suit, this one bright pink, perhaps to flatter her fire engine hair. Recently one of the female detectives had tried to encourage a more restrained palette, the result being the black and white checkerboard she'd worn yesterday.

Normally, Green never paid the least attention to fashion, his own or others. He ran a perfunctory comb through his floppy brown hair once a day, but only got it cut when it began to seriously impede his vision. His slight, five-foot-ten frame fit passably into a size 38 regular straight off the sales rack of the nearest chain store. Departmental dress code required that he wear a suit and tie, so he tried to wear one that had a minimum of stains and odours. The suits were always grey, which hid the dirt well and required no colour coordination expertise whatsoever. His male colleagues, and many of the females as well, seemed to agree that, in a job where you're likely to get puked and spat on, grey polyester was the way to go.

But Peters was oblivious. Standing by his closed office door with her notebook clutched to her chest, she was a beacon all the way down the hall. As he approached, her face lit.

"Gibbsie's tied up at the autopsy this morning, sir, so I thought I should report to you."

It was ridiculously outside departmental protocol, but Green's curiosity won out. Balancing his bagel on his coffee, he unlocked his tiny alcove office and ushered her in. Without waiting for an invitation, she flounced into the guest chair and plunked her notebook on the desk. Green saw page after page of large, clumsy scrawl.

"Do you have a summary report, Detective?" he cut in just as she drew breath to begin.

She hesitated. "Not yet, sir, but I thought you should know what I've done, so you can give me my next assignment."

"Can you give me just the highlights then? I don't need a blow by blow."

She pouted. "Our Jane Doe didn't go to any of the shelters."

He wondered how much he could trust that information, given Peters's sledgehammer interview style. "At least as far as the shelters remember."

"They'd have remembered the purse, sir. I took a picture of it with me. And she didn't frequent any of the known street hangouts either." Peters listed them off. It was an impressively thorough list.

When he said as much, she beamed. "All right," he said. "Next I want you to check the train station staff, especially —"

"I already did. Last night, and again just now to catch the morning shift. One of the porters this morning remembered the purse. Our Jane Doe came in on the Montreal train a couple of weeks ago, she didn't want any help with her bags —"

"Bags? Plural?"

"One other suitcase. More like a duffel bag. He remembers she asked him how to get to an address in Vanier. She didn't want a cab, so he gave her directions for the bus."

"What address in Vanier?"

"He couldn't remember. He figured she had family or friends there."

Green digested this information with surprise. Not only had Peters used her initiative and tracked down a very useful lead, but she must have been up well before dawn to do so, if she'd slept at all. He felt a twinge of shame.

"Very good, Peters. Put it all in your report and … have you had breakfast?"

"Yes, sir. At the train station while I talked to the porter. I bought him a cup of coffee."

"Good. After you finish your report, I want you to return to the train station. Take a street map and buy the porter lunch. Read him every street in Vanier, and we'll see if we can jog his memory."

She gave a broad smile as she slapped her notebook shut. "That's what I thought, sir. I've already asked him his lunch hour. Will you tell Gibbsie where I've gone?"

He let the nickname pass as he watched her leave. She'd no sooner clumped into the elevator than Green caught a movement in the squad room, and he looked up to see Bob Gibbs's gangly form striding through the desks towards his office, clearly a man on a mission. Green's hopes quickened.

Could it be that this unlikely pair was going to crack this case all by themselves?

When Gibbs had crowded into Green's tiny office, the unmistakable odour of death and disinfectant permeated the air. Green had been about to close the door but thought better of it.

"You've come from the autopsy."

Gibbs folded his lanky frame into the guest chair and nodded with alacrity. Green was pleased to see that he was flushed a healthy pink rather than sickly green. The young detective had only attended a couple of autopsies, but this was another sign that he was coming into his own. He didn't even bother to consult his notes.

"It was murder, sir. Without a doubt. There were big bruises around her neck and some abrasions on her arms and legs which MacPhail thinks are consistent with her thrashing about during a struggle."

"Did she drown?"

"No, sir. Death was asphyxia due to manual strangulation. There was no water in her lungs and stomach, but several of the vertebrae in her neck were crushed."

Green visualized the scene. The victim was not a small woman, and she had obviously been conscious and resisting during the assault. It would have taken a powerful and ruthless assailant to hold her down long enough to kill her. "What else did MacPhail find?"

Here Gibbs consulted his meticulous notes and began to read them off. "Victim is 167 centimetres in height, 49 kilograms in weight, estimated age between thirty and forty years, eyes blue, natural hair colour blond turning grey. Poorly nourished and a heavy smoker and drinker, but no signs of other drug use. No tattoos, scars, or other distinguishing marks. Internal exam reveals a healthy subject except for early signs of lung and liver damage. Contents of the stomach negative for food, but there were traces of scotch. Blood alcohol at time of death was .04."

"Which is probably just one drink. What did he say about time of death?"

"He was sticking by his earlier estimate. Based on ambient air temperature, body temp, frost in the ground and her early stages of rigor mortis, he estimated she'd been dead five to nine hours."

Green did a rapid calculation. "So she was killed between eleven last night and three this morning."

Gibbs nodded.

"After consuming one scotch." Green's thoughts began to roam afield, making connections. The victim was thin and sickly, but even weak people put up tremendous resistance when they're fighting for their life. Her killer would have had to be strong and determined, and he or she — more likely he — would probably have taken some hits during the struggle. Although the victim hadn't been dressed to impress, the timing of the murder, the consumption of the single scotch, and the brute violence of the crime suggested a date gone bad. Pure speculation at this point, but a direction to pursue.

"Anything under the fingernails?" he asked.

"Some fibres and dirt, sir. I took it all over to the RCMP lab."

"Any signs of sexual assault or activity?"

Gibbs shook his head. "But there was one other thing. She'd borne a child, quite a few years ago."

Green had jotted down some notes on his notepad, and he sat tapping his pen as he pondered their next move. Until they knew who the woman was, it was difficult to investigate her close associates and to track her recent movements. As he weighed ideas, he became aware of the silence that had fallen and of Gibbs's anxious eyes upon him.

"Sir? Now that it's a confirmed homicide, are you g-going to assign the case to one of the sergeants?"

Green considered his options. They were few. He had one sergeant on holiday and another tied up full-time on the Byward murders, which continued to draw media attention and to jam the phones with calls. The third had far less experience than Gibbs in homicide cases. Besides, Barbara Devine had told him to watch Gibbs's every move, which gave him an excuse to be back in the field again.

"Not at all, Bob," he said. "I want you to get back onto the Halifax police with these new details about the Jane Doe, and tell them it's now a priority one homicide case."

***

Far to the south, fog banked up over the ocean, but overhead the sky was blue and sunlight dazzled the whitecaps in Halifax Harbour. Sergeant Kate McGrath stood at the window of her Dartmouth condo, sipping her coffee and staring out over the shipyard into the harbour beyond. From her earliest childhood memory, the ocean always had the power to awe her. Chunks of pack ice still bobbed in the distance, but in the shelter of the inner harbour, the first brave sailboats were already dancing on the brisk spring breeze.

She finished her coffee, changed into her spandex running suit, and pulled her Gore-tex jacket on top. Even though it was sunny, she knew the wind and salt spray of the ferry ride would chill her to the bone before she was halfway across.

The two-kilometre run from her condo to the ferry terminal was barely enough to get her endorphins flowing, but when she stepped aboard and headed for her favourite spot at the upper bow, a sense of peace spread through her. The engine thrummed, the waves slapped against the hull, and in front of her, the City of Halifax rose steeply in a jumble of brick buildings and narrow streets towards the historic stone citadel at its crown.

She'd been right to move here after Sean's death. Not back to the craggy beauty of the Newfoundland coast where she'd been raised, but to this gentler, lusher landscape, where pain and privation weren't etched so deeply into the soul. Sean had been blasted through the front door of a farmhouse by a shotgun during a routine domestic dispute call, ending her marriage barely a year after their honeymoon. The waterfront condo had cost her almost all his insurance settlement from the Truro Police, but it had been worth it. After twelve years here, the pain of his death had been worn smooth and soft.

When the ferry docked on the Halifax side, she began the serious leg of her run, almost straight up the hillside from the boardwalk to the base of the citadel, where the sleek new headquarters of the Halifax Regional Police sprawled over an entire city block. She was always one of the first to arrive for her shift, which gave her plenty of time to shower, change and grab a snack before afternoon parade.

Today she had to fight a fierce wind as she ran up Duke Street, so that she was gasping for breath by the time she reached the station. She refused to think it might be age. Thirty-seven was supposed to be the peak of womanhood, not the early stages of decrepitude. She took a long, hot shower, grateful to be alone, and changed into her professional attire. She kept a modest wardrobe of pantsuits and blouses at the station. Simple to clean but presentable if the media or the brass showed up. Only the colours varied.

This time she selected a navy suit with a pale blue blouse to match her eyes and complement her cropped silver hair. She was feeling good. The ferry ride in the spring sunshine had been magical, and she was just returning after two days off. She'd never minded her prematurely silver hair, which lent an edge of experience when she was dealing with criminals and colleagues alike. She was an outport girl from a Newfoundland fishing cove who'd grown up in a household of salty men, and she thought women needed all the edge they could get.

After she'd finished dressing, she raked her fingers through her damp hair and headed upstairs to General Investigations. She had a few minutes before her meeting with the day shift sergeant, so she flipped on her computer to check her email. After two days away from her desk, she had dozens of messages. Incident reports, follow-up reports, bulletins, requests and notifications of all kinds. Some were general distribution, others personal.

She scanned the names and subject lines for messages of high priority or interest. Two messages from the Ottawa Police caught her eye. The first was a general distribution missing persons inquiry about a Jane Doe, and contained a photo and description. The second was directed to Criminal Investigations and was marked priority one pertaining to a homicide investigation. It included a more detailed description of the victim along with a series of autopsy head shots taken from different angles.

McGrath studied the frontal head shot thoughtfully. The eyes were half shut and the mouth gaped open, making it difficult to picture what the living woman would have looked like. Yet something in the deep set eyes and round face touched a memory. She clicked on the profile shot and looked at the slightly upturned nose and the broad forehead. She frowned at the elusive memory. How many women looked like that? It was an ordinary Celtic face, like so many on the streets of Maritime towns.

The day shift sergeant was heading towards her, impatient to hand over control. She gestured to the photos on her screen. "Has there been any action on this Ottawa request yet?"

He glanced at the screen and nodded. "It's part of uniform parade. The photos are being circulated to patrols, and they're supposed to ask around and keep their ear to the ground. We also passed it on to the RCMP to cover the rural areas. No one's had any missing persons reports that match. The Deputy Chief is thinking of making an appeal to the public, broadcast her photo and description."

McGrath hesitated. Her backlog of work still beckoned, but if her instincts were correct, this was part of a once-in-a-lifetime case that had never been solved. "Before he does, I want to check something," she said. "Let me requisition a file from archives, and then I'll be right with you."

Even with a rush on it, the file took several hours to arrive, giving her time to make a dent in her backlog. She watched as the boxes were unloaded onto the floor by her desk — stacks of statements, reports, warrants and futile leads, all neatly catalogued as she had left them ten years ago in the hope that someday she'd have a reason to come back to them. A new lead, a belated recollection or pang of conscience.

The memories of the case came back in a rush as she flipped through the pages, scanning the contents. Finally, she came to the photos. Before CDs and digital cameras, everything had been retained on colour Polaroids. There were dozens of photos of the crime scene, the autopsy, and the witnesses — at least those who were still in the bar by the time the first squad car reached the scene.

McGrath was looking for a single photo of a woman standing arm in arm with a young soldier, and she finally found it near the bottom of the pile. The woman was looking straight into the camera with her head cocked mischievously to the side and a broad smile lighting her face. The young man was sombre, his gaze fixed with purpose as if he knew the heavy responsibility that lay ahead. His features were tense, but at least they were intact, McGrath thought, which was more than could be said for the rest of his photos.

McGrath picked up the frontal photo from Ottawa and held the two photos side by side. The face of the woman in the earlier photo was younger and fuller, but ten years and a hard life would explain that. The particulars fit. Five-foot-seven, blond hair, blue eyes. The estimated age fit. Even the last detail, the evidence of an earlier pregnancy, fit too.

She packed the files back into their boxes, picked up the two photos and went into her staff sergeant's office. She laid the photos on his desk.

"What do you think? Could they be the same woman?"

He turned the earlier photo over to read the back, and his eyebrows shot up. "The Daniel Oliver case?"

"What do you think?"

He shrugged. "Anything's possible. I can't see it myself, but you were closer to the case. You're thinking this is the girlfriend?"

"Patricia Ross. The specs fit."

"Yeah, her and half of Nova Scotia's female population. We're thinking of releasing a request to the media."

McGrath thought fast. The staff sergeant was a fair, experienced officer, but he always aimed for the most efficient route from A to B, and he rarely worried about the emotional fall-out. In the Daniel Oliver case, it was the emotional fall-out that haunted her most.

"Can you hold off for twenty-four hours? Give me a chance to track her down?"

He frowned. "Ottawa needs answers ASAP. They're sitting on a homicide, Kate."

"But there may be family. Children. You don't want their dead mother's face plastered on TV to be their first inkling of the news. Twenty-four hours."

He glanced at his watch. It was past four o'clock. "Seven a.m. Take it or leave it."

She took it. Dropping all else, she returned to her desk and started to track down the current whereabouts of Patricia Ross. The address in the file proved a dead end. Not only had Patricia moved out years earlier, but the old house itself had been demolished for an office building. A Canada411 search uncovered no Patricia Rosses living in Nova Scotia, but seven P. Rosses in the Halifax area. Calls to all seven were negative. If Patricia Ross still lived in Halifax, she had no phone in her own name. Yet the province had no record of a Patricia Ross registering a marriage at any time in the past ten years.

Dinner consisted of a donair and a V-8 juice consumed at her desk while she turned to the next phase of her inquiries. Of the dozen witnesses she'd interviewed who claimed to be friends of Daniel Oliver, she was able to reach only four, but none of them had kept in touch with Patricia. Two thought she'd gone to stay with Danny's folks in Cape Breton, but when McGrath phoned, Danny's mother said she hadn't spoken to Patricia since the wake. She didn't even know if the baby had been born.

Mrs. Oliver's tone was high and querulous. "To this day I've never forgiven her. It was all her doing, Danny's troubles.

And then after he'd gone, she never even bothered to pick up the phone." Belatedly her voice dropped. "Why? What's happened to her?"

McGrath recalled that the mother's feelings had been very different ten years earlier. Patricia was to have been her future daughter-in-law, and she and the baby were supposed to make the world of difference in Danny's life. "I just need to get in touch with her," McGrath hedged. "If you do hear from her, please ask her to call the Halifax police."

There were two other official avenues of inquiry she could pursue in her search, but both the Health Department and Revenue Canada would not be accessible until business hours in the morning. She was just about to give up for the evening when her phone rang. It was one of Daniel Oliver's old friends, for whom she had left a voice mail message earlier. He had a deep drawl with a hint of Cape Breton in his vowels.

"I did run into her a year or so ago, and we had a couple of drinks for old times. Never found out where she lived, but she seemed a regular at the Seaman's Watch. They might know."

McGrath glanced at her watch. It was just past eight o'clock — peak time in the Halifax bar scene. She dived for her jacket, clipped her gun and phone onto her belt, and went in search of a partner. The Seaman's Watch was a well-known sleaze bar on Gottingen Street just a few blocks north of the police station. It attracted a prickly mix of sailors and students, as well as the whores who serviced them and the petty thugs who thought there was money to be made. McGrath knew better than to walk in there alone. She commandeered a beefy young constable who was just coming in to write up a traffic accident. Minor, he said, no injuries. It can wait, she replied and led the way to the car park.

At nine o'clock on a Tuesday night, the Seaman's Watch was already crowded. The yeasty stink of beer and sour bodies choked her as they walked in, but she stifled her grimace. A lively, inebriated band was banging out drinking songs at the end of the room, and the audience was singing along. Ignoring the leers, McGrath sought out the bartender and drew him close so that she could shout in his ear. She gave him a vague story about needing to locate Patricia for her own safety. Once he'd deciphered her request, the bartender's brow furrowed.

"Yeah, she comes in here regular like, but I haven't seen her the past couple of weeks."

"Do you know where she lives?"

He hesitated, then glanced at the table nearby, where a group of sailors were roaring lustily. "A few of the lads have taken her home, like, you know, not a regular thing, but from time to time. She's kind of a sad case, is our Patti."

You don't know the half of it, McGrath thought to herself as she signalled her bodyguard towards the table. Five minutes later, they were back out in the crisp, salty night air, armed with a street name and number. They drove slowly up the street, scanning house numbers until they came upon a tall, narrow clapboard house perched near the top of the hill. It was impossible to be sure of the colour beneath the peeling layers of grime, but McGrath suspected it had once been robin's egg blue. She rang the top buzzer. It had no name, but the sailors had said she lived on the top floor.

No answer. McGrath rang again. Still nothing, although she could hear the abrasive buzz reverberate inside. Her sense of foreboding grew.

It took an hour to locate and summon the landlord to open the apartment door. He was a familiar figure to the police, a low-level drug dealer who laundered his money through several of the less savoury properties in the downtown core. He fumed as he stomped up the stairs to her floor.

"She's one of my most reliable tenants. Clean, quiet, always pays on time. Fuck, she better not have done a runner. She knows I need a month's notice."

McGrath didn't even dignify his whining with a response. As he unlocked the door, she shoved past him into the room. It was almost bare. Only a bed, table and chair, dresser and an ancient TV with rabbit ears. On the bed were neat stacks of old letters, photos and a folded *Sunday Herald*. In the closet, jackets and pants hung on three forlorn hangers, and the dresser itself was half full of clothes. The cupboard above the sink in the tiny kitchenette still held crockery and pots. McGrath ducked into the bathroom. The shampoo and soap were still by the tub, but her toothbrush was gone. So was her purse.

Patricia Ross had gone away, but she had intended to come back again.

McGrath returned to the main room to find the landlord rifling through the Sunday Herald. "Don't touch that, please!"

He tossed the papers down sulkily. "Just seeing if she left me a note."

The papers fell open to an inside page, half of which had been torn off. McGrath looked at it curiously. Page 10, which was full of local news. She hunted briefly through the rest of the paper, but there was no sign of the missing page. "Did you tear this?"

He scowled as if affronted. "It's two weeks old! The kid downstairs probably took it. They fought all the time about that."

He could be right, she thought. A torn page didn't mean much, although it might be interesting to check its contents.

"When was the last time you saw her?"

He scanned the room, then shrugged. "She brought April's rent to my office three weeks ago."

McGrath unfolded the photo of the dead Jane Doe and held it out. "Do you recognize this woman?"

The landlord glanced at the photo and to his credit, he blanched visibly in the dingy apartment light.

SIX

April 6, 1993. Zagreb, Croatia.

Dear Kit ... We're in the airport waiting for our ground transport, so this is my first glimpse of the country. Zagreb airport looks like any other modern airport. I don't know what I was expecting — snipers, tanks and big craters in the ground from mortar fire. But there's nothing but wall to wall peacekeepers in the pouring rain. It's wet and cold, but everybody's excited.

April 10, 1993. Pakrac, Sector West, Croatia.

We're at our position now and getting dug in. Our section house is a bombed out farmhouse in the middle of a field. There's mud everywhere from the winter rains. We're all pitching in, learning the jobs from the 3 Pats who are leaving. Today I did six hours at the hot dog stand. That's what they call a checkpoint. It can be boring, you sit there and search each vehicle that comes through, write down the licence plate, who's in it and where they're going. Sector West is a UN protected area with a Serb side and a Croat side, and the ceasefire line in between runs right through the Canadian Battalion's area of responsibility. The CO says they put the Canadians in the toughest spot because we're the only UN peacekeeping battalion that has the equipment and the training to do the job.

Anyway, there aren't supposed to be any weapons inside the UNPA, but both sides are always trying to sneak them in, and it's our job to stop them. Sometimes we have a translator but a lot of times we just use hand gestures and it can get pretty funny. Us pointing go back and them pointing forward. There's a Muslim kid Mahir from the nearby village who knows some English, so we use him when he's free.

April 15, 1993. Sector West, Croatia.

Dear Kit … The past couple of days we've noticed this dog hanging around the woods near the hot dog stand. She looks like a border collie and shepherd mix with sores on her legs and her ribs sticking out. Mahir says she belonged to a Serbian family who abandoned their farm. She was so spooked it took us three days to coax her to come near. Today we got her in the APC and took her back to the section house, and tomorrow we'll build her a dog house. She'll probably end up sleeping with us, but Sarge says when the Hammer's around, she'd better stay in her kennel. Rules are rules, after all. I'm looking for a good name for her.

May 1, 1993. Sector West, Croatia.

Good things and not so good. Our dog's been gaining weight steadily and the platoon medic treated her sores with antibiotics. Sarge swore him to secrecy. I swear she's the smartest animal I've ever met. She knows about fifty English words already, more than the Croatian kids we're trying to teach. I've named her Fundy. The guys tease me about my new girlfriend, but I don't mind.

She's no competition for you, but she reminds me of home.

Today our section did patrol, which is more interesting than the hot dog stand. We drove all around the countryside in the APC checking for weapons caches and looking for troop movement. The countryside's green and beautiful, but a lot of the villages are destroyed, and hardly anyone lives there anymore. Everything is bombed to hell. One of the patrols came across this Serb village where there were no people, just stuff left on the ground, like sneakers and kids' clothes. Word is there's a mass grave there, but we'll never know. Kind of creepy, that only half a klic away, everyone's just carrying on.

***

AFTER GIBBS HAD sent his priority request to Halifax earlier that day, Green dispatched him to meet up with Peters at the train station. Peters had proved that she had more detective instincts than Green had initially thought, but he didn't trust her not to get carried away when those instincts took her on the hunt. He recognized the danger signs of over-exuberance bordering on obsession, because he'd been there.

Besides, if she was going to go poking around in the low-cost accommodation facilities in Vanier, she'd better not go alone. Vanier had proud, francophone working class roots, but like many inner city neighbourhoods, it was now an uneasy mix of immigrants, transients, drug addicts and the working poor. Crack houses stood side by side with the modest woodframe cottages of the founding families.

Green himself spent the rest of the day managing the developments in the Byward Club investigation, which was fast deteriorating into a circus of lying teenage brats, irate parents, and their threatening lawyers. Fortunately, they kept Barbara Devine so busy that she had little time to agitate about the murder of an unknown, unlamented Jane Doe. Not even the women's groups seemed interested in taking up the cause.

By five o'clock, Green's patience was expired, his head ached, and he knew he still faced several more hours of diplomacy and hard work once he got home. He was just returning to his office from his third lawyer meeting when Gibbs and Peters came off the elevator from the basement car park. Gibbs moved at a purposeful lope, and Peters had to hustle to keep pace. Spotting Green, they changed course to intercept him.

"Let's get a coffee," Green said, steering them towards the stairs to the police cafeteria, although they both looked as if they'd already overdosed on adrenaline. Green bought them coffee and muffins before sitting down opposite to listen. They sat side by side, he noticed, looking very comfortable with each other.

"Any news from Halifax?" Peters asked as she added three packages of sugar to her coffee.

Green shook his head. "Did you have any luck with the porter at the train station?"

Gibbs nodded proudly. "Sue hit the jackpot on that one. Y-you tell it, Sue."

She clasped her hands and leaned forward on the table, her coffee forgotten. "Marier Street. That's the street our Jane Doe was looking for. So we drove down there and canvassed every house and building on the whole street. We found her at #296. It calls itself a motel, and it's one of those long, two-storey 1950s buildings where the clients either stay an hour or a week. She'd booked in for a week on April 11th, and she paid another week on the 18th."

"How did she pay?"

"Cash. And she registered under Patti Oliver from Sydney, Nova Scotia. There are two Olivers listed in Sydney, but neither of them have ever heard of a Patti."

"We c-could find no such person listed anywhere in Nova Scotia," Gibbs added. "Although we've still got some calls to make."

"Did she at least provide the motel with a phone number or a contact name?"

Gibbs shook his head, but before he could untangle his tongue, Peters jumped back in. "Cash, no questions asked, works fine for these guys. But we got the motel manager's permission to search the room. We found the duffel bag the porter told me about, mostly full of clothes and food. There was food on the dresser — bread, juice, tea, canned soups and beans — low-cost stuff. Everything was healthy, and her clothing was mostly clean, even if it was old. It looked like she tried to take care of herself and watch her money."

Green was again pleasantly surprised by her perceptiveness. "Any scotch?"

"No, she must have bought that at a bar."

"Or someone bought it for her. Any clues to suggest who she was or why she was here?"

Peters glanced over at Gibbs as if in silent invitation, which he accepted. "Just one small thing, sir." He reached into his jacket pocket and handed over an evidence bag. Through the transparent plastic, Green could make out a small leather box. Slipping on latex gloves, he opened the box. Nestled inside was an embossed silver disk attached to a red and blue striped ribbon. On the front was a maple leaf inside a wreath, and on the back were engraved the words "Bravery — Bravoire".

"There's a little card underneath, sir," Peters burst in, unable to contain herself. She plucked the card out and began to read. "This Medal of Bravery is awarded to Corporal Ian MacDonald for acts of outstanding heroism in hazardous circumstances, September 10, 1993."

"Ian MacDonald. Have you checked this out?"

"Yes, sir," she said. "It was awarded on a peacekeeping mission in Croatia, where he was serving with the Second Battalion of the Princess Patricia Light Infantry Regiment."

Green saw the suspense in their eyes as they waited for him to digest that information and to ask the obvious question. "So did you track down this Ian MacDonald?"

"Well, that's the thing, sir," said Gibbs, so excited he didn't even stutter. "Corporal Ian MacDonald died September 10, 1995, and we can't get anyone in the military to talk to us."

***

It was now past six o'clock, and Green was unable to rouse anyone official at DND. He left an urgent message on Captain Ulrich's voice mail to phone him the instant he got the message. Then he turned his attention back to the two detectives, who had followed him hopefully back to his office. Both were beginning to sag as the adrenaline wore off. Peters, he recalled, had now been on the job at least twelve hours.

"Okay, good work, you two. Assign the follow-up work to someone on the night shift. Let them try to locate Patricia Oliver and Ian MacDonald through the various databases. You can pick it up again in the morning."

After the two detectives had walked back to the elevator together, Green glanced at his watch and cursed. Sharon was working the evening shift again, which meant that Hannah had been in charge of the household for three hours now. Dinner was going to be very late, even if he picked up something easy from the Bagelshop again on his way home, and Tony would be apoplectic with hunger.

He locked his drawer, logged off his computer, and was just grabbing his jacket when his phone rang. He considered letting it go to voice mail, but thought it might be Captain Ulrich.

Instead, a familiar, manic voice came through the line over the background of chatter and office machines. "Mike!" The man hailed him like a long lost friend. "Glad I caught you. These murders are keeping us both hopping."

Green muttered a soft oath. This is what voice mail was for — to intercept unwanted calls from the press at the worst possible moments. Frank Corelli was the crime reporter for the *Ottawa Sun* and, as crime reporters go, he was smart and reliable. They'd known each other for four years and had helped each other out when Green needed a certain spin put out on a case and Frank needed a story. But no publicity was going to be good publicity in the Byward murders.

So he dusted off the classic departmental evasion. "Frank, you know I can't comment on the Byward case at this time. Superintendent Devine has scheduled a press conference for —"

"I know, I know. And I'll be there, duly copying down the party line. But this is the other case, and I've got something for you for a change."

Green perked up. "The aqueduct case?"

"The very one. Now you know I always play straight with you guys. You don't want something reported, I keep it under wraps. I learn something, I pass it on. Right?"

"Frank, spit it out."

There was a pause, during which Green could hear a phone ringing. "I got a call from a woman. She wouldn't give her name, just said she knew who killed the prostitute in the aqueduct, and was I interested. I played dumb, what do you mean am I interested? Well, she says, how much is it worth? Nothing, I said, that's obstructing a police investigation. You call in the cops, she says, and I'll take it to the competition. I says nobody will touch it, and she says you got no imagination. Anyway, I thought you should know you got information out there somewhere."

"Or maybe not." Whenever a major crime occurred in the city, the wackos and the wheeler dealers came out of the woodwork.

"Maybe not, but she sounded like she was holding some good cards. Not a wingnut, clear, calm, seemed intelligent. She knew the body had been moved after death. That true?"

Green said nothing. Inwardly, his thoughts raced over the scene at the aqueduct. How many people knew that detail, which had been held back from all press reports. He tried to sound disinterested. "So what did you tell her?"

Frank chuckled knowingly. "I told her to give me a day to set it up and to call me back. She wasn't happy about that, but I told her I had to get the money approved. We gotta figure out how you want to play this."

"Did you record the phone number?"

Corelli read it out, and Green put him on hold while he logged back onto his computer and searched the phone number database. His momentary excitement faded. The call had come from a payphone on Bank Street near Wellington, which was the major intersection almost opposite Parliament Hill. Thousands of people, tourists and government workers alike, passed by it every day. Green weighed his options.

"Okay, here's what I want you to do. When she calls back, set up a meeting to see what she's got. I'll have someone nearby, and we'll pick her up."

When Green finally escaped the office, his spirits were greatly buoyed and his headache gone. The case was breaking open, with new leads unfolding in all directions. He held fast to his good mood throughout yet another hectic evening as sole cook, babysitter and dog walker, and poured himself a well-deserved shot of single malt as he settled down to the eleven o'clock news. Only as he sat through the usual stories of global carnage and the endless spats on the federal campaign trail did his mood begin to sag.

Politics. It was a game too often won by opportunists and manipulators, who mouthed platitudes about the public good, but whose real passion was power. The Liberal Party, having been ousted from power after years of corruption, was pulling out all the stops to reverse the Conservative backlash. High-profile candidates for both parties were being bribed with promises of cabinet posts and plum appointments. Jubilant reporters were crisscrossing the country, stoking the flames of division in key ridings where election races were most heated. The real losers, Green thought, were the genuine good guy candidates who wanted to make a difference for their country. And the country itself.

It was no different in policing, where, once in the public spotlight, who you knew and how well you could play the game were often more important than what was right. A victory of form over substance. And we have only ourselves to blame, Green thought as he groped sleepily for the remote to shut off the latest Conservative rant. Because people like him refused even to get in the game.

Unexpectedly, the phone rang, sending a spike of fear and excitement racing through him. At this hour, a phone call almost always meant trouble.

"Inspector Green?" It was a woman's voice, curt and authoritative. "This is Sergeant McGrath of the Halifax Regional Police. Sorry to disturb you at home, but the detective down at your headquarters insisted you'd want to be informed."

Green bolted upright, wide awake and rooting on the side table for a pen. Years of hounding the duty desk had paid off. "Yes, Sergeant?"

"Good news. I believe we've identified your Jane Doe."

SEVEN

THE NEXT MORNING Green waylaid Barbara Devine the moment she arrived at her office.

"Good timing," she said as she swept past him through her door, her plaid cloak trailing. She headed for her closet. "You were the first item on my agenda."

"I need to go to Halifax."

She whirled around, her cloak in hand. "Why?"

"Because Halifax has a tentative ID on our aqueduct murder, and it may be connected to a cold case of their own."

"So get them to fax the file."

"It's several boxes. And I want to re-interview the witnesses myself, in light of our case."

She finally hung up her cloak, then paused to look at herself in the mirror. She patted her helmet of hair, denting it slightly, then moved behind her desk with exaggerated calm. Only then did she meet his gaze. "Well, you can't. You're needed here. Send Detective Gibbs, he's the lead investigator."

"Gibbs has to stay here to coordinate things at this end. Besides, he hasn't the experience to handle this on his own, and I can't spare two officers."

"Then get the Halifax detective to do the interviews for you."

"It's our case, Barbara." He restrained his irritation with an effort. Like it or not, he needed her co-operation. He held out the travel requisition. "I'll be there and back in forty-eight hours, guaranteed, and I'll keep in constant touch by phone and email."

He'd already packed and tentatively booked himself on the eleven a.m. flight to Halifax, but by the time he emerged from her office with her signature on the requisition, he had little more than an hour to make the plane. Barely time to brief Gibbs on the newest development in the case and to tell Frank Corelli that if his mystery woman phoned, he was to work through Bob Gibbs on the meeting.

Only once he was up in the air, heading east over the farmland of Quebec, did he have a chance to reflect. The truth was, he should have given the trip to Gibbs. It was his case, his chance for glory, but the lure of an unsolved homicide had proved too strong for Green. He could hear the excitement in Sergeant McGrath's voice when she talked about it. For her too, this new development, despite its tragic outcome for Patricia Ross, breathed new life into her case and gave her a chance to catch the bad guy who had foiled her for so long. She sounded like Green's kind of detective. Driven, determined and exhilarated by the hunt.

Her gruff tone on the phone had prepared him for a square-shouldered matron in a dour suit and sensible shoes. He was surprised when he emerged from the arrivals gate at Halifax airport to see a tall, slender woman wearing a tailored navy pant suit and holding a sign saying "Inspector Michael Green." She had fine silver hair and deep-set blue eyes that widened with equal surprise as he approached. He knew his deceptively youthful air and bargain basement polyester confounded a lot of people, but he wondered what she'd expected an inspector from the nation's capital to look like. A balding, fiftyish pencil pusher with a poker up his ass?

He smiled broadly as he extended his hand, thinking this forty-eight hours was going to be even more interesting than he'd anticipated.

She gave his hand a brief, formal shake. "I've arranged for lunch to be sent up to the incident room, sir," she said as she led him toward the exit. "I expect you'll want to get a look at the files right away."

Despite her formality, the mischief of Newfoundland still clung to her speech in her flattened vowels and Irish lilt. Green winced at the prospect of police cafeteria sandwiches and wilted celery sticks eaten within the windowless, airless ambiance of a police incident room. "Actually ..." he said. "I've had a rushed morning and a cramped flight. What I'd really like is a proper lunch in a real restaurant, while you tell me about the case in your own words."

She looked dubious as she approached the unmarked car sitting at the curb in the pick-up zone. "Inspector Norrich of Special Investigations is planning to join us, sir. At least initially."

Green smiled. Policing has its protocol. One inspector deserves another, even though he suspected Norrich knew nothing about the case and had much better things to do.

He tossed his bag in the trunk and climbed in beside her. "Tell Inspector Norrich that I'm in good hands and don't want to put him to any trouble. I'll drop by to keep him apprised after our meeting."

Her lips twitched, and her stiff posture eased. "Your first time in Halifax?"

He nodded. "First time east of Montreal. That's shameful, I know."

"It is. You like seafood?"

He hesitated, picturing scaly fish with dead eyes staring from the plate. "Does pickled herring count?"

She actually laughed, a musical trill that almost erased his hunger pangs. "There's a place down on the harbourfront that serves terrific crab cakes. Worth a barrel of pickled herring."

She drove for what seemed like hours through a wooded countryside dotted with lakes. Once they hit civilization, Green was struck by the bright colours of the woodframe houses. The sun shone in a cloudless cobalt sky and glistened off the harbour below. She wove past shabby warehouses and shipyards to the historic downtown waterfront, parked the car and led him onto a wooden boardwalk. She headed straight for a white woodframe restaurant at the edge of the wharf, where the owner greeted her with a huge grin.

"Crab cakes to go, Kate?"

She shook her head. "I've got a newcomer from Ontario with me, Jim. Have you got a table overlooking the waterfront?"

He led the way through the restaurant and peeked out the back door. Outside, the patio adjoining his restaurant was drenched with afternoon sun. "If you're brave, I can open up the patio for you."

A brisk breeze blew the scent of salt, fish and diesel fumes in off the harbour. Ice crystals still clung to the water's edge, but already the gulls were circling and the shops were setting out their tourist wares. McGrath cocked a questioning eyebrow at Green, and, not to be branded a wimp, he nodded.

Her formality slipped away as she settled into her seat. She waved away the menus Jim brought and ordered them both crab cakes with organic greens on the side. When they came, Green was relieved to see no fish heads. The cakes were exquisite, breaking up in his mouth like a feather light mousse. She waited until the magic of the first morsel had passed, then sat back and took a deep breath. Suddenly, she was all business again.

"Patricia Ross was the fiancée of a mechanic named Daniel Oliver."

Green reacted to the name with surprise. "Fiancée? Are you sure she wasn't his wife? She registered as Patti Oliver in Ottawa."

She shook her head. "They never got to the altar, unfortunately. Daniel was from down Cape Breton way originally, but he'd come up to Halifax in the mid nineties to find work, and he met Patricia here. But employment was sporadic and money tight, and the last winter he was having trouble keeping body and soul together. Then at approximately 12:08 a.m. on April 9, 1996, police officers responded to a disturbance at the Lighthouse Tavern on Barrington Street. The Lighthouse is a strip joint with a rough clientele, mainly sailors off the ships, some armed forces personnel ..." she smiled wryly, "and students slumming it. The staff usually handle their own disputes without calling in police. But that night the bartender himself put in the call, and when the first squad car responded, the fight pretty well involved the whole place. By the time other officers arrived and broke it up, there were four individuals wounded, one mortally."

"Daniel Oliver."

She nodded. "He was the instigator. According to witnesses willing to talk, he started an argument with another male customer. When that customer's companion came over as backup, Daniel's friends jumped in to take his side, and before you know it ..." She shrugged in distaste.

"Who was the other man?"

"That never came to light."

Green's eyebrows shot up. "You never caught him?"

She shook her head. "While the officers were breaking up the brawl, he apparently just walked out. Daniel's friends said they didn't recognize him, and the bartender said he'd never seen him before. He wasn't even a Nova Scotian according to witnesses who overheard him speak, but then they were well plastered by that hour of the night, so you know what that's worth."

"How did Oliver die?"

"Blunt force trauma to the left side of the head, the pathologist said. Caused massive intracranial bleeding, and he died four hours later in hospital without regaining consciousness."

"What caused the trauma?"

"According to the pathologist, a bare fist, driven with such force it left the imprint of knuckles imbedded in the man's skull."

Green digested this image soberly. It suggested either one hell of a strong guy, or one hell of an angry one. "Did you get any leads? Do you have a suspect but can't prove it?"

"Patricia was convinced it was someone from Daniel's past. She and Daniel and four other friends were at a table near the back. They'd been drinking for three hours by then, and the bartender estimated they'd consumed about a dozen pitchers of beer between them. The stranger walked past and Daniel called him over to the table, saying something like 'Hey, you son-of-a-bitch.' Now Daniel Oliver was a big guy, and when he was drunk, he could look pretty mean. And he was apparently yelling something about it being all this man's fault and calling him a traitor and a lying bastard. There was a lot of noise in the bar, making it difficult to hear the whole conversation. Patricia was farthest away from the shouting match —"

"So the stranger was shouting too?"

McGrath fell silent, thinking. "No. If I remember the witness statements, he was speaking very softly, almost not at all, then suddenly he came over the table at Daniel with a deadly right hook."

Green's surprise must have shown, for she grinned. "I have five brothers. All boxing fans."

"Your suspect had to have some expertise in that area too," said Green. "Or it was one lucky punch. Unlucky, if you're Daniel Oliver."

"Yes, it was one of the specs we fed into his profile, along with coming from away."

"What other facts did you learn about him? Witnesses must have observed something during the evening. Or the bartender. They usually watch the unknowns like a hawk."

"The man didn't draw attention to himself. He'd come in alone about an hour earlier, sat in the corner at the bar by himself ..." Here she paused, wrinkling her brow in her effort to remember. "Watching TV and drinking pretty heavily over the course of the hour. The man next to him struck up a conversation at one point, and the two of them got pretty chatty. When they got up to go to a table in the corner, that's apparently when the confrontation took place."

"What did this third man say about him afterwards?"

"Claimed he didn't know him, they just talked about the news on TV."

"Did you think he was lying?"

"If I recall correctly, I did. But I don't know why."

"Who was he? Local?"

She signalled to Jim and ordered two coffees. She seemed to be using the diversion to search her memory. "If I remember, he gave a fake ID. Lots of people do, when they don't want to get dragged into an ugly investigation of a bar fight.

And this was a strip club, remember. Wives and bosses might take a dim view."

"Still, couldn't he even give you the first name of the assailant?"

His skepticism must have showed, because for the first time a trace of irritation flickered across her face. "Listen, I investigated this case for months. I interviewed and reinterviewed dozens of witnesses, checked every hotel in Halifax and Dartmouth, and turned over every rock looking for the man. If he could have been found, I would have found him. We couldn't even work up a decent composite of him, because the witnesses were all so contradictory."

He held up a soothing hand, impressed by her vehemence. At that moment Jim arrived with their coffees, and they both took some time out to add cream and sugar. On the wharf nearby, seagulls squabbled over a scrap of fish, and from the harbour came the mournful blast of a distant ship's horn. McGrath sipped her coffee and shook her head slowly back and forth, as if caught up in the memories.

"Some cases just stick in your craw, eh?" he said gently.

She watched the gulls in silence a moment before replying. "It was such a pointless, brutal act. Not the bar fight. Men have been beating each other senseless since they first fermented the grape. It's just that things were starting to turn a corner for Daniel. He didn't deserve this, and neither did his fiancée."

"You said earlier that she thought the fight had something to do with the past. Did you find anything useful in his past?"

"I went through it with a fine-toothed comb. It's all in the files, but nothing jumped out at me. He was a tough, blue collar kid who was reportedly a bit wild as a teenager, but there was nothing in the RCMP or local police files.

He joined the reserves because he liked uniforms and guns, and —"

Her cellphone rang. She checked the call display and made a face before answering. Her expression was deadpan as she listened, her eyes fixed on a distant freighter being tugged into harbour. "Yes, sir, we're on our way," she said and disconnected. Tossing back the remains of her coffee, she shoved back her chair. "We'd better get back. Inspector Norrich is anxious to meet you. We can check the details of Daniel Oliver's background in the files at the station."

***

Norrich was waiting for them in the incident room, seated at a long conference table with the case files spread open around him. His massive frame overflowed the molded plastic chair, and his face had a bruised, purple hue that Green recognized all too well. When he struggled to his feet and lumbered forward to shake hands, Green detected the unmistakable whiff of booze.

"Mike! Leo Norrich. Welcome to the finest town in all of Canada."

Green tugged his hand free from the meaty grip and smiled dutifully. "You may convince me yet."

"Your first visit?"

Green nodded.

"Then you must come over for dinner tonight. Annie and I will show you what real down east hospitality is all about."

Green was conscious of Kate McGrath standing beside him. Norrich had barely acknowledged her presence, let alone included her in the invitation. The thought of a boozy, back-slapping evening on his own with the inspector and his wife made him cringe.

"That's very thoughtful of you, Leo. But judging from the number of boxes on that table, I may be here all night."

Norrich waved a dismissive hand. "Most of this is irrelevant. Witnesses interviewed five times over, who never saw anything in the first place. Or have forgotten anything they might have seen." He winked. "It happens when you're three sheets to the wind, eh?"

This time Green didn't bother with the dutiful smile. "Even so, I'd like to have a look. I've come all this way, might as well be thorough."

A scowl flitted across Norrich's florid features. "Suit yourself. I can't see why you think Patti Ross's death is connected to this case anyway. This was ten years ago, just one of those pig-headed bar fights that gets out of hand when a little pussy starts ramping them up. I don't know what things are like in Ottawa, but down here, sometimes guys just have to blow off steam. They're cooped up all winter, jobs are scarce, and they've got too much time on their hands. And truth be told, Patti's life hasn't been all smooth sailing since then either, and she's been known not to choose her company too carefully."

Beside him, McGrath bristled. Green lifted an eyebrow. "You've been keeping track of her?"

The subtlety was lost on the man. He beamed triumphantly. "I made some inquiries when I heard you were coming down. She was on welfare for a long time till she got this part-time dry cleaners job. She's been living in a shitty little one-room hole, drinking away most of what she makes." He stopped, obviously thinking he'd made his point — that a drunken welfare tramp more than asks for whatever tawdry fate befalls her.

Green moved briskly to the table to hide his anger. "Well, that's very helpful, Leo. Saves me some legwork. Now I won't keep you any longer. The sooner I get to that stack of files, the sooner I can take you up on that dinner."

"Kate will take good care of you. And any questions, you know where to find me." He pumped Green's hand again and trundled out of the room, leaving a palpable tension in his wake. Green heard McGrath exhale softly and wondered if there was a silent curse in her sigh. But she was all business as she strode over to the table.

"He could be right, I suppose," she said.

Green didn't reply. It was not really good form to tell a sergeant that her senior officer was an idiot, who would never spot a suspicious coincidence through the film of booze and prejudice with which he viewed the world. Patricia had scraped together a meagre existence for ten years since her fiancé's death, without even escaping the town in which the trauma had occurred. Then suddenly she buys a ticket to Ottawa fifteen hundred kilometres away, and less than two weeks later, she's dead. It could be simple bad luck, but the odds were long.

"She witnessed her fiancé's death, right?" he said. "She saw the man who punched him?"

"Yes, but she didn't know him. She would have given anything to see him caught, believe me."

"Then maybe something happened recently, to give her a lead on him. Someone told her something, or she discovered something." He had been sifting idly through the files, and now he glanced up, excited. "And that trail brought her to Ottawa. Either to meet the man or to find out more about him. Whatever she stirred up, someone wanted her silenced."

McGrath looked thoughtful. "If she was naive enough to confront the murderer, it's a good bet he'd kill her to protect himself. He must have thought he was home free after ten years."

Green nodded. He could feel the adrenaline of the hunt begin to race. It was only a theory, but it fit a lot of the facts. She had met the killer for a drink and had confronted him, maybe to ask for money or simply for her own satisfaction. Desperate to silence her, he'd suggested an evening stroll and led her to an isolated spot, where he'd strangled her. Green pondered the scenario. It explained the brute force and apparent ruthlessness of the murder. This killer was not only a very strong man, but he was frantic to protect his secret. Perhaps he'd decided the body was too easy to find, so he'd later dragged her as far as he could to the secluded aqueduct. It wasn't a perfect explanation, but it was the best Green could do with the facts he had.

"We're looking for a powerful, physical man," he said. "Someone Daniel Oliver knew from the past and who'd betrayed him in some way. Was Daniel involved in criminal activity? Drug dealing?"

McGrath shook her head. "He was a mechanic, although he'd been on the skids for a few months, lost his job and was on unemployment insurance. He was doing some fairly heavy drinking, but no drugs. The friends we interviewed said he was basically a decent guy."

"But his life had been on the skids, despite having a woman he planned to marry."

"Yes, that was slowly bringing him out of it. Plus the baby on the way."

Green thought about the findings of the autopsy. "What happened to the baby?"

McGrath made a sympathetic face. "It was a little boy, born early because of all the stress. He had some health problems, I think, and she had trouble coping. When I last had contact with her, the Children's Aid was taking measures to remove him from the home. I think that last loss just about destroyed her. That's why when Inspector Norrich talks about Patti's lifestyle ..." She broke off, pressing her lips together as if to censor herself.

"Yeah." Green let the contempt hang in the air, then resumed a safer line of inquiry. "So what happened to send Oliver's life into a tailspin?"

McGrath seemed to pull herself from the memories with an effort. "According to Patti, his best friend was shot in a freak hunting accident about six months earlier, and Daniel blamed himself because he hadn't kept in close enough touch. They'd been in the reserves together and served six months of peacekeeping duty overseas. They'd always been very close, but when they got back to Nova Scotia, the friend turned his back on his plans and retreated into himself."

Green's instincts went on full alert. He'd known police officers who'd done UN duty in Yugoslavia, and he knew the stresses and dangers they had faced. He knew that stress could bond a group of men more strongly that ten years together on a normal job. It could also create some bitter enemies.

"Did you interview any of their army mates? Especially those who were overseas with them?"

"Norrich did."

Green's eyes widened. "Norrich? He was on the case?"

"He was lead." She hesitated. "Technically. He was sergeant at the time, and I was a constable. I worked most of the case, but Norrich took the trip down the valley to talk to Daniel Oliver's regiment. He figured ..." She hesitated again, and Green could almost see her wrestling with propriety. "Being a sergeant ..."

"And a man."

She inclined her head slightly in agreement. "He'd get further."

"And did he?"

"No. I guess military buddies close ranks even tighter than drinking buddies. All they said was that Daniel had been an excellent soldier in Yugoslavia, even got a promotion in the field, and everyone was very proud of him. But ..." She reached for a file that lay on top of the stack. At a glance, Green could see Norrich's name at the bottom of the report. "There was something I thought didn't quite add up. Oliver had been on track for making sergeant, and moving up the ladder as an NCO. But two years after he got back from overseas, he quit the reserves. So things can't have been as rosy as they painted it."

"Not to mention the strange behaviour of his friend when he returned from overseas." Green stopped abruptly as a thought struck him. McGrath had said the friend's accident was six months earlier. Daniel Oliver had been killed in April 1996. Counting back six months yielded the fall of 1995. He sucked in his breath as another coincidence hit him between the eyes. "What was the friend's name?"

She rummaged through the files, scanning rapidly. "I know I've got it in one of my interviews with Patti. I'm sure I wrote it — Ah-hah! Ian MacDonald. Corporal Ian MacDonald."

EIGHT

May 28, 1993. Sector West, Croatia.

Dear Kit ... The APC broke down again this morning and Danny spent half the day tying the fuel pump together with wire. He's a wizard under the hood, which you have to be with some of the equipment we got. The tracks belong in the war museum! Whenever anyone in the platoon has a problem, they send for Danny. He jokes he'll be good enough to get his mechanics papers when he gets back to civvie street.

So we had a day around camp instead of going on patrol, which was a nice break. Peacekeeping is a lot different here on the ground than the politicians think. Neither side trusts the other, and they sure as hell don't trust the UN to protect them. Our platoon commander says that's because other UN battalions haven't done their job. Some of the third world ones are so poorly paid they take bribes from both sides and turn a blind eye when Serbs or Croats sneak weapons in or cleanse a village or whatever. Besides even when we find weapons, all we're supposed to do is turn them over to the local police, who probably hid them in the first place.

Don't get the Hammer started on the UN rules, because the bureaucrats have no idea how the militias, the police, and the locals are in it together. Both sides trust their own militias way more than they do UNPROFOR or any fancy ceasefire plan dreamed up in Zagreb. And each local militia's got its own commander who thinks he's the boss and he doesn't have to obey orders from his own command, let alone us. So every day we catch guys sneaking behind the lines to lay mines, and every night the two sides shell each other back and forth over our heads.

Anyway, the strategy of our battalion CO is to try to get the locals to trust us by building relationships with them, and helping them fix up their homes and roads after the bombings. Our section house is near a little village that used to be Serb but now it's Croat, although there are two Muslim refugee families, like Mahir who escaped from Sarajevo with his mother. Sarge has kind of taken her and Mahir under our wing. The kid's only fifteen, but he wants to practice his English so he does our translating. He hates the Serbs. He says when the Serbs ran away from the village, they burned their houses so the Croats couldn't use them. But I'm not sure, I think maybe the Croats torched the village to chase the Serbs away.

Lots of our guys think the whole place is just nuts, but I'm trying to learn how all this started. It's hundreds of years old and each side accuses the other of atrocities. The Serbs hate the Croats for collaborating with the Nazis to massacre thousands of them. The Croats say the Serbs took over their land and were the enforcers under the communists. And both of them have hated the Muslims since the Turks massacred and looted their way through the area during the Ottoman Empire. Five hundred fucking years ago, for crissakes. Nobody forgets.

I have to say it makes Canada look like heaven on earth. Most of our guys can't believe the bitterness, even between neighbours who've known each other for generations. So like I said, we're trying to get them to trust us at least. The Hammer thinks we have enough to do without wasting our time playing Pollyanna, but then he's the guy who has to argue with both sides each time they try to show their muscle. But Sarge got our section to build a soccer field and a jungle gym for the school in the village, and it's really great to watch the kids run around laughing. Like there's not mines all around the town perimeter and mortar fire in the distance all night. The Sarge thinks kids are where we can make a difference.

***

TWIGGY HUNG UP the phone in frustration and turned to scan the street. There was no one nearby, no one watching her. No one remotely interested in a fat old bag lady standing near the corner of Bank and Wellington Streets, almost in the shadow of the Confederation Building on Parliament Hill, an area probably crisscrossed with so many security cameras that no one would dare do her harm. The phone booth was well chosen from that point of view, although the voice at the other end of the phone had been almost drowned out by the roar of traffic, not to mention the damn bells of the Peace Tower.

She'd used up half a day's worth of quarters making the long distance call to Petawawa, only to have the stupid twit on the phone say she'd have to check with her boss. Who wasn't in, of course. Where were these politicos when you really needed them? Out on the campaign trail, kissing babies at Easter parades and shoving party pamphlets into distrustful farmers' hands.

Preaching about peace, honour and returning Canada to its respected place on the world stage. If she had a loonie for every ounce of sanctimonious crap those guys dished up …

It almost made Twiggy want to go with the *Ottawa Sun* guy. To stand for something right in this me-first-and-only world. But she was part of that world, which had never done her any favours when she'd tried to live by a higher code. So why the hell shouldn't she put herself first too? In the end, money was all that counted, and whoever was willing to come through was going to get her story.

But both sides were playing coy. Both had listened to her pitch and said they were interested, but they'd have to get back to her. Which cost her time and money every time she had to trek to the phone booth. Both had tried to get something for free too. Tried to find out who she was, where she was calling from, exactly what she thought she'd seen. Well, she could play coy too, and they weren't getting a thing until she had something to show for it in return.

She did wonder how much they could tell on their own. Could they identify the telephone booth? Were they recording the calls and analyzing every sound to figure out who she was and where she was calling from? Did they have that fancy equipment the CSI used on that cop show on TV? Naw, she decided. One was just a cheap tabloid hack, and the other a political wannabe from a two-bit country riding up the Ottawa Valley.

She hobbled slowly across the street, dragging her garbage bag as she headed towards Tim Hortons. Thinking about cops gave her a momentary twinge of guilt. Mr. G had always been good to her; she knew he'd been genuinely freaked out when her boys were killed, and he'd shown a lot more heart than the rest of the cops and doctors and lawyers she'd met in the last six years. He was one of the good guys. There wasn't really a single person alive on this planet that she gave a damn about anymore, but Mr. G came close. By rights, he deserved this information, so that he could do something good with it. Get a surveillance team, search warrant, wire tap, whatever cops did to lay their trap and catch the bad guy. Before the creep had a chance to cover his tracks.

She worried over this unaccustomed moral dilemma for the five minutes it took her to reach the Tim Hortons. Was there a way she could let him know, and still get her money? Something anonymous, maybe, that couldn't be traced back to her?

Worth thinking about, anyway.

***

Holding two plates aloft, Anne Norrich pirouetted through the kitchen door and bumped it shut behind her with her hip. Her eyes shone, and her face was flushed a hot pink to match her floral blouse.

"Ready?" she challenged.

Green steeled himself and nodded. A plate descended before him, and it took him a moment to recognize the apparition sprawled across it. He had prepared himself for scaly skin, even a fish head with shrivelled eyes, but this was far worse. A speckled red missile with beady eyes, long bony appendages, lethal claws and worst of all, feelers which draped either side of the plate and came to rest in the mashed potatoes. Green was transfixed with horror.

Norrich roared with laughter. "You should see the look on his face, Annie!"

Alarm flitted across Anne's face. "Have you ever eaten one?"

He managed to shake his head, his voice still somewhere in the pit of his stomach.

"Well," said Norrich, "you haven't lived until you've had an honest to God Nova Scotian lobster. Steamed in ocean brine, no spices or fancy sauces. Just a bowl of lemon and melted butter to dip it in." He lifted the bottle of wine which sat at his side and held it across the table towards Green. "Here, I think you need a good dose of extra courage. Then you won't notice how hard it is to get any food out of the horny bastards."

They'd started the evening with scotch and were now well into their second bottle of wine. Since Green's idea of tying one on was a second beer with his smoked meat platter at Nate's Deli, he was already seeing double. Perhaps there weren't quite as many legs as there seemed to be, he thought in a brief lucid moment, but nonetheless he held out his glass gratefully. It was the only way he was going to get through this course.

Green was not much of an observant Jew, particularly where the Kosher laws were concerned, and he loved his Chinese shrimp and barbequed pork as much as the next Jew, but he thought the rabbis were on the right track in forbidding this menace. A vision of Woody Allen chasing the lobster around the kitchen in the movie *Annie Hall* popped into his mind, and he almost choked on his healthy slug of wine.

Anne was a solicitous hostess and fluttered around tying his bib and showing him how to crack open the shell to extract the meat. When the head and some green insides spilled out onto the white lace tablecloth, she spirited them miraculously from view. With no feelers and beady eyes to contend with, he was able to concentrate on getting some nourishment.

As he struggled, Norrich regaled him with stories about growing up in a remote fishing village, where his father had been the only RCMP presence in town. The man grew to be a legend over the course of the lobster. After Norrich had popped the cork on the third bottle, Green decided he'd better steer the conversation to the case before they both sank into a stupor. He had spent part of the afternoon reading Norrich's reports on his visit to Daniel Oliver's reserve unit and had been unable to glean a single useful fact about the man. Not only was there no mention of a possible connection to Ian MacDonald's death, but there was no hint that Norrich had even asked about it. Surely there were tidbits Norrich had picked up that he'd chosen to leave out of his official reports.

Green couldn't think clearly enough to be subtle, so he plunged straight in. "I saw from the reports that you went out to the West Nova Scotia Regiment to ask about Daniel Oliver. Did you find out anything about his peacekeeping tour?"

Norrich blinked and stared at the table cloth as if trying to remember where he was. "No, it was just a routine inquiry. 'Did he have any enemies? Did he mention any conflicts?' That kind of thing. But since Oliver had left the reserves a year earlier, they'd pretty much lost touch with him. Waste of time from the investigation's point of view, but I met a great group of guys."

"Did you speak with any of his overseas mates?"

"No, but none of the regiment was overseas with him. He'd served with a battalion from the Princess Pats which was based in Winnipeg, but it had reservists from all across the country."

"What about his friend Ian MacDonald?"

"Ian who?"

"MacDonald. Served with him in Croatia. He was killed two years after coming home. He was in the same reserve outfit. Did you ask about him?"

Norrich peered at him balefully. Despite the haze of booze, he obviously sensed the implied rebuke in Green's tone. "Don't see how the hell that was relevant."

Which means you didn't even ask, asshole, Green thought. He forced himself to take a deep breath. "Why did Daniel Oliver leave the reserves?"

Norrich picked up a claw and splintered it with vigour. "He developed a serious attitude problem. He picked fights with friends, said none of them knew what the hell being in the army was all about. He was disrespectful of superior officers, derelict in his duties. The way the fellows on the base talked, if he hadn't left, he might have been in for some disciplinary action. He was becoming a disgrace to the uniform."

Green filtered his thoughts through his anger, trying for some tact. "I know a few guys who served with the UN police in Yugoslavia, and they had some trouble readjusting when they came back. And we know from highly publicized cases like Romeo Dallaire that a lot of soldiers encountered situations overseas that haunted them when they came back. Didn't Oliver's behaviour ring any alarm bells with his regiment?"

Norrich slapped the table impatiently. His plate jumped, and his cuff came to rest in a pool of grease. Wordlessly Anne jumped up, rescued both men's plates and disappeared into the kitchen. "I think all this stress stuff is a load of horseshit. It's their job, for Christ's sake! It's why they signed up, and if they don't have the stomach for it, they should just pack up and leave the job to the men who do. Last thing a soldier needs, just like a cop, is a mate who freezes up under fire and second-guesses whether he should act. It's an insult to all the brave men who've ever served their country to pander to these guys and offer excuses. Worse, it makes them doubt themselves. Makes them wonder if they've got what it takes to be a hero when the shit hits the fan. A soldier, just like you and me, has to act. Not analyze or feel or whatever other lily shit the shrinks have come up with for our own good."

His jowls quivered, and he had turned a dangerous purple. In the kitchen, Green heard dishes clattering, and he wondered if Anne was deliberately staying out of her husband's way. His own very personal outrage threatened to overpower him, and he debated the wisdom of continuing, but in defence of all the police officers and emergency workers he'd known, he tried to find a dispassionate response.

"No one questions their heroism or their ability to act when they need to. But with the guys I knew, it was the aftermath that was tricky. When they had time to think —"

Norrich slapped the table again. "The problem is Canadians are soft! We haven't had a war on our own soil in nearly two hundred years, and two generations have grown up never feeling the threat of any war. We've pampered them at home and at school. Car pools and after-four programs, and when they grow up, welfare and unemployment insurance and health care. What the hell's left to fight for? So when trouble hits, there's no backbone. Hell, most of the world sees more trauma —"

The kitchen door burst open, and Anne came out carrying a massive platter mounded with lemon meringue pie. She had a determined smile on her face, but her eyes glittered with warning.

"Enough shop talk, gentlemen. You wouldn't want a good pie to go to waste in the heat of discussions. Mike, would you like some tea? Or coffee perhaps?"

Green seized on the latter offer with gratitude. A dull ache was beginning to replace the spinning inside his skull. While they had coffee and dessert, Anne skilfully steered the conversation to harmless realms. Although Norrich continued to sputter and huff, his colour gradually returned to a dull pink. As soon as he could respectably do so, Green rose to say his goodbyes.

Norrich had been drooping over his Bailey's, and he lifted his head in surprise. "Here, I'll drive you."

Fortunately he seemed to have exhausted all spirit of argument, for he accepted Green's hasty refusal and merely propped himself in the doorway to wave goodbye as Green climbed into a cab. Cruising through the neat, tree-lined suburbs towards downtown, Green drew a deep, cleansing breath and glanced at his watch. Just past ten o'clock. There was nothing to do in his hotel room except go to bed, but it was too early, especially with his biological clock still set on Ottawa time.

Part of him longed to curl up in a warm bed and phone home, but Sharon would still be out at work, and a conversation with Hannah would last all of two minutes. Besides, another part of him was restless. Ill at ease. More disturbed by Norrich's passionate accusations than he cared to admit. Norrich was the last person who would have noticed any troubling undercurrents between the soldiers who were the pride of the nation. Green didn't relish more alcohol or more conversations with drunks, but there were places to visit and questions to ask that could only be done at night. He fished out Kate McGrath's business card and punched in her cellphone.

"Kate? How would you like to meet me for a drink? Dress for the trenches. I hear the Lighthouse Tavern is a rough place."

NINE

CALLING THE LIGHTHOUSE rough was like calling Baghdad unsettled. It didn't nearly do credit to the place. The raucous blend of music, raunch and shouting could be heard from a block away every time the door burst open to spit another drunken patron out into the street. Green and McGrath pushed through the swinging saloon doors into a dimly lit cave of scarred tables and pockmarked walls, murky with smoke and rancid with the stink of booze and sweat. A bar ran down the middle, separating the pool tables from the strip club. Serious drinkers were propped up along the bar, while others lolled around tables littered with beer, leering at the young girl on the brass pole. She was decked out in leather and black lace, just getting started on her routine.

Kate McGrath was the only other woman in the place. Fortunately, she had told Green to ditch the tie and jacket, but even with his shirt unbuttoned and his undershirt hanging out, he was in a league of his own. Heads swivelled in unison as they walked in.

"I guess there's no point in our trying to be undercover," Green muttered.

"Jeez," she replied, her hand instinctively covering her nose. "It's gone downhill even in the last ten years. It was always a blue collar bar and proud of it. No knotty pine tables or amber microbrews here. But I'm not sure even your most hard-bitten sailor out for a night with his mates would choose this place anymore."

He glanced at her. She was wearing a no-nonsense athletic jacket, jeans and walking boots, but she hung back in the entrance to the pool room, scanning the tables uneasily.

"Do you want to go?" he asked.

His question seemed to challenge her. A frown flitted across her brow, and she squared her shoulders defensively. "I'm a cop, inspector, not a date."

He opened his mouth, but before he could think of suitable words to extricate himself, she strode up to the bar and picked a stool by the wall. He wanted to say that his question was no reflection on her capability as a police officer, but merely an admission of the obvious. That they were two plainclothes officers with more brains than brawn, walking into an unknown, potentially hostile situation. Circumstances, not gender stereotypes, advised caution.

If he were honest, though, he had to admit that sex played a role. He was a bit drunk, and his defences were down. Women had always been his weakness, and tonight, after a trying evening with a lobster and a loutish host, Kate McGrath had seemed the perfect antidote. He'd invited her as much for her company as for her professional assistance with the case.

He was still sufficiently sober not to say so, however, but instead joined her at the bar, where she had already ordered a Keith's and struck up a conversation with the bartender. She cocked her head towards Green brusquely.

"Rob, this is Inspector Green of the Ottawa Police. Rob was here the night Daniel Oliver was killed."

Rob was a tank of a man with a cauliflower nose and a paunch that ballooned over his apron. He flicked Green an oblique glance from under one bushy white eyebrow, then continued pulling the pint of Keith's.

"I'm hoping you can answer a few questions for me," Green began.

"What's it to you?"

"Someone murdered Patricia Ross in Ottawa three days ago."

Both bushy eyebrows shot up. "No shit. How?"

"Strangled, by a powerful man who crushed her vertebrae like twigs. The same kind of power that killed her fiancé with a single blow," Green added, varnishing the truth a little, for he was convinced there was a connection. Someday he'd get the evidence to back it up.

Rob said nothing for a moment, then turned to a young man who was collecting empties from the counter. "Sal, take over."

He gestured the two detectives to an empty table at the back of the pool room. It was littered with bottles, but he sat down without bothering to clear them.

"This is where Daniel was hit," McGrath said as she pulled back a chair. Out of the corner of his eye, Green saw her wipe the chair surreptitiously, but his attention was focussed on the bartender. The big man's face was set.

Green's instincts quickened. "You've got something to tell me, don't you."

Rob leaned his massive forearms on the table, displaying an elaborate collage of snake tattoos in vivid red and black. He fixed his dark eyes on Green. "In a place like this, you hear things. Guys drink, they blab, they brag, and sometimes the truth has nothing to do with it. Daniel Oliver's death was the talk of this place for months. Lots of guys knew and respected him, because he was a genius with engines, and he'd seen real combat. He became almost like a legend. Guys said the man who KO'd Daniel with one punch must have been some kind of pro — a championship boxer, a tenth-dan black belt in karate. Or a special forces commando."

A roar rose from the crowd in the club section. The bra must have come off, Green thought, momentarily distracted. He resisted the urge to look as Rob paused to scan the crowd with a practised eye. Then, apparently satisfied that all was under control and that no one was paying them any attention, Rob resumed.

"We get a lot of servicemen in here, usually on two-day leaves, and all they want to do is get hammered and laid. It's a word of mouth place, like a home away from home."

Green glanced around the grubby room. His disbelief must have showed, because the bartender's eyes grew hooded. "It's going through some changes."

"So, are you saying someone recognized our killer after all?"

"I'm saying somebody got drunk and blabbed. Said the killer was military and that he and Danny had served together in Yugoslavia."

Green opened his notebook. "Do you know this witness's name?"

"Roger somebody."

Green looked across at him with exasperation. "Can you do better than Roger somebody? A last name, or an address?"

"Well, he wasn't military. Local, maybe?"

"Do you recall if this Roger was actually in the bar at the time of Oliver's death?"

"Yeah, he was at the table with Danny. Would have seen the whole thing if he hadn't been passed out on the table top."

"When did Roger report this information?"

"He didn't report it. Like I said, he blabbed it to his buddies along with a whole lot of bullshit about the army. This was maybe a year after Danny's death. I remember it was the same time as the government shut down the Somalia Inquiry, just when all that stuff was coming out about the Airborne Regiment torturing civilians on their peacekeeping assignment over there. The guys at the table were all saying the UN and the government doesn't know the half of what goes on. Roger just added his story about Danny's death to top the pack."

"So you didn't believe it worth passing on?"

Rob fixed Green with an exasperated stare that said one more snarky crack out of you and your big city snout will be sticking out your ass. "Listen, I told Norrich and —"

"Wait a minute. Norrich was still investigating the case?"

"Naw. He was in here one night drinking with some of his army friends. He thought the story was a crock."

Green glanced at McGrath, whose frown spoke volumes. The Lighthouse was hardly the type of place you want your high-ranking police officers hanging around. Keeping his expression neutral and disinterested, he flipped ten dollars onto the table and stood up. "Well, I guess we'll go see if we can find anything on Roger buried in those boxes down at the station."

She looked dismayed. "Tonight?"

He checked his watch, which read nearly midnight. He smelled a lead, but in a ten-year-old trail, a few hours was not going to change anything. He forced himself to behave. "First thing tomorrow will be fine."

***

When Green strode into the incident room at eight o'clock the next morning, however, he found McGrath already ensconced at the table and surrounded by files. Her face was haggard with fatigue and her blue eyes were bloodshot. She was still wearing the same cableknit sweater and jeans she'd had on the night before.

He grinned. "You're worse than me."

She rubbed her eyes. "I couldn't sleep. I figured you only have one more day here, and I can always sleep tomorrow."

Worry pinched her brows despite the smile on her face. Green suspected he knew the source — Norrich — but he sidestepped her unspoken fears. "I appreciate your help. Find anything?"

She shoved the files away and slumped back in her chair. "Not so far. Whatever the bartender told Norrich, it didn't end up in his official reports. Norrich probably considered the information unreliable."

"No evidence that he followed up either?"

She pursed her lips, as if to keep her thoughts to herself. "At that point it was a pretty cold case and we had a few other things on the go. Plus … Norrich got promoted out of the unit."

Green had his own theories as to why Norrich had never followed up on the tip. For one thing, it would have meant admitting he frequented the strip club, but more likely, he'd been too damn drunk to remember anything he'd been told. From McGrath's disgusted expression, he suspected it was not the first time.

He smiled at her. "You had breakfast yet?"

She looked up, her face lighting at the idea. "Oh man, I'd kill for a double shot of Columbian Dark."

He laughed. "My kind of woman." He unhooked her jacket from the door knob and held it out. "Lead on, Sergeant."

She led him on foot down Duke Street to Argyle at a pace that soon left him huffing. Her long, effortless stride suggested an athlete, and once again he cursed the long hours he spent behind his desk. Walking the dog from tree to tree around the block did not seem to be doing the trick.

The Economy Shoe Shop was a trendy bistro tucked into a block of heritage storefronts on Argyle. At eight o'clock, it was packed with workers catching their last dose of caffeine before heading to the office, and the hiss of cappuccino machines rose over the general chatter. Green breathed in the smells. Strong coffee, fresh muffins, and the buttery sweetness of croissants. His stomach contracted, and he selected a banana chocolate chip muffin, feeling virtuous for having passed on the croissants.

The shop had a cluster of cast iron chairs outside on a cobblestone patio. A brisk breeze kept most of the patrons indoors, but McGrath found a small patch of sunlight and sat down, tilting her face to the rays and shutting her eyes. A smile spread across her features as she savoured her first sip.

Arousal tingled unexpectedly through Green, bringing a mixture of idle pleasure and caution. It was just as well he was going back on the ten o'clock flight tomorrow morning, he thought, as he busied himself unwrapping his muffin.

"So," he said, "in your search last night, did you find any references in the bar to a military connection?"

She opened one eye almost reluctantly. "There were several soldiers among the witnesses. In fact, the man who was seen in conversation with the assailant — the one who gave me the fake ID — he seemed military. The precise language and the ramrod back tend to give them away. At the time, I figured he was slumming it and didn't want to be found out."

"Did he think the assailant was military?"

"If he did, he didn't volunteer it. He said they just talked about the news on TV."

Green mulled this over. In his experience, soldiers, like police, shared a kinship that they could sense a mile off. If the two men had both been military, the first words out of their mouths would have been "What's your unit?"

Maybe it had been. "Did you believe him?"

She opened both eyes and turned to face him. In the sunlight, her blue eyes were startling. They held a glint of excitement. "Not particularly, especially once I found out he'd lied about his ID. But at the time I had no reason to be suspicious, so I just let him go. I had a whole bar full of drunken witnesses to go through."

He returned her smile for an instant before his thoughts scattered again. "So now we're stuck with not just one, but two unknown soldiers. Maybe if we poke around in Danny's military service, we can get some names to go with them. Did you find out anything else?"

Her smile broadened as she flipped a page in her notebook. "I did. I found an interesting witness who was at the bar that night. In his statement at the time, he said he'd been asleep and had seen nothing. But his name was Roger Atkinson."

***

Back at the police station, McGrath set out to track down the current whereabouts of Roger Atkinson while Green put in a call to Gibbs. He relayed the information about Daniel

Oliver's murder and its potential connection to his military past, then asked Gibbs to start tracking Oliver's army associates. Normally Gibbs was conscientious and thorough to a fault, and Green knew if there was any information to be found, Gibbs would pry it loose. But this morning he sensed the young detective was barely listening.

"What's up, Gibbs?"

Gibbs's newfound confidence echoed through the phone lines as he filled Green in on his own inquiries. He didn't stutter once.

"Yesterday Detective Peters and I interviewed the desk clerk and other residents of the Vanier hotel where our Jane Doe — I mean Patricia Ross — was staying. They said she seemed to spend her time like any other tourist. She'd go out in the morning, catch a bus on the corner and be gone most of the day. They always noticed her because of that big flowery purse she carried everywhere. She had a street map, and once she asked the desk clerk in the lobby how to get to the Voyageur Bus Station and also the House of Commons. She seemed quite disappointed that it wasn't in session because of the election."

"The bus station?" Green pounced on the implication. The House of Commons was a standard destination for any tourist to Ottawa, but the Voyageur bus station wasn't. It was strictly for cheap intercity travel. "Did you —"

"Sue's going down to the bus station this morning, sir," Gibbs interjected. "She's taking the photos of the DOA and the purse to see if anyone remembers her."

Green chuckled to himself at the pride in Gibbs's tone. Pride not only in his own investigative skills, but also in his partner. Who would have thought the mismatched pair would ever gel? "Excellent. Keep me posted. If Patricia took a bus somewhere outside of Ottawa, she was probably going to meet someone important. This was a woman on a mission, I'm convinced of it. Anything else to report?"

"Yessir!" Gibbs's voice cracked in his exuberance. "The dead woman apparently made a number of phone calls from the payphone in the hotel lobby, and she received at least one there that the desk clerk can remember. It was a man's voice. We're working on getting the phone records for that payphone, which might even tell us who she was meeting."

When Green hung up, he was energized by the progress being made on all fronts. They still had no idea what was going on, but with all the promising avenues opening up, he sensed the solution was almost within reach. He was just jotting some notes in his book when McGrath burst back into the room, brandishing her notebook. Her whole body vibrated with excitement.

"Well!" she announced, tossing the notebook down on the table. "This is an interesting coincidence. Roger Atkinson's mother hasn't seen him in nine years, ever since he was offered some plum job up in Ontario. According to my calculations, this job came less than two months after he opened his big mouth about Daniel Oliver's death."

TEN

TODAY, TWIGGY DECIDED, was a make or break day. No more games or stall tactics. That resolution put some energy into her flagging muscles as she trudged up Albert Street on her way to Tim Hortons for her daily dose of caffeine and doughnuts.

The spring sun was finally warm enough to sit outside without discomfort, and she was just arranging her bulk against the brick wall when the manager opened his shop door to give her a coffee. This time as she sucked back the bitter liquid, he stood over her hesitating.

"A man was in the shop last night, asking about you," he said.

She paused, her cup to her lips. "Asking how?"

"Just asking if I knew anything about a bag lady who hangs out around here."

She frowned. Who the hell would be interested in what she was up to anymore? Her thoughts drifted to her family. Her in-laws were a write-off, of course. Way too much pain for them to ever face her. They hadn't even come to the coroner's inquest, brief and pointless as it had been. When the recommendations came down — about plugging gaps in the mental health delivery system, about increasing the monitoring of psychiatric outpatients and improving emergency response protocols to 911 calls — they had written her a very short note. *So sorry, dear. He was our son. May God forgive him, and I hope you can.* Then they had dropped out of her life.

The only blood relatives she still had were her sister and her family, but Linda kept her children under lock and key, as far as possible from their derelict aunt and the unspeakable memories she evoked. As if Twiggy herself were a symbol of all that could go wrong in their neatly ordered, middle-class world, and just seeing her, like Medusa, could bring her cursed life down upon them.

Still, maybe twice a year Linda or her husband Norm would track her down and pay her a visit. Give her some money and some clothes, bring her news of the children. Sometimes they'd pack her into the car — always with a beach towel spread over the seat, Twiggy noticed — and take her to the doctor or the dentist. Never home for dinner. You never know with curses, after all. So they would buy her a burger at Wendy's with all the trimmings and a healthy salad to match, before dropping her off at the "Y" shelter and driving back to the tree-lined crescents of Kanata, where the noise and mess of the world were carefully kept at bay.

It might have been Norm who was looking for her. "What name did he call me? Twiggy?" Or Jean, she added silently. No one on the street knew that name. Jean had died in that frenzy of madness and blood on May 10th, 2000. Welcome to the new millennium.

"He didn't give a name, Just asked about the bag lady who hung out by the aqueduct."

Alarm bells rang, ever so softly. It could have been one of her street friends, or someone she'd met in a shelter. She'd deliberately left her old self behind when she changed her life, but sometimes old habits die hard. She'd been helping a few of them learn to read, just in passing, whenever the mood struck. But they didn't always bother with niceties like names.

"Was it a street person?"

"No. He was nicely dressed, looked like he might work for government or social services. Maybe they're trying to find you to give you some money."

Twiggy snorted. Do-gooders did sometimes try to track her down, under the delusion that after what the poor soul had endured, all she really needed was a little TLC. As if the love and platitudes of a stranger could hold a candle to the love she'd lost.

She was entitled to money. Even Mr. G had tried to tell her that, although he more than anyone knew how meaningless that compensation was. Not only would she qualify for a government disability pension, but there was probably money for long-term disability through the teachers' union. But she doubted very much any of them would waste any effort trying to give that money away. Besides, they would have called her Jean. Jean Calderone. A name she barely remembered.

Twiggy drained the last dregs of coffee and as a joke, rolled up the rim. Not expecting to win a prize. What would she do with a plasma TV or a big-ass SUV? But just making sure her luck hadn't changed. Please play again, she read from the inside of the rim. She chuckled. Play again. Isn't that a metaphor for life, as it keeps kicking you in the teeth?

She remembered her resolve of that morning. She was going to play one more time, make one more big score, so that she and her friends could buy themselves one last wild fling at life. Not on the terms of the mission do-gooders or even the outreach nurses, not on the terms her sister Linda would dictate, but on their own terms. No moral obligations attached.

"Well," she said, grabbing the manager's hand to haul herself to her feet, "it's probably nobody. Maybe a reporter still looking for a story. But if he asks again, don't tell him anything. Now I'll be back, Moe, so save my spot." She chuckled as she picked up her bag and handed him her empty cup. She patted his cheek. "Got a call to make."

She turned and tromped off toward Wellington Street before he could see the slight frown that puckered her doughy face. She didn't really believe it was a government worker or a reporter. The newshounds had given up milking her tragedy years ago, and certainly there were juicier stories around now, what with terrorists and election scandals. Not to mention the three murders still hogging the headlines after nearly a week.

Could someone have seen her that night outside the hotel? Could they have put two and two together and figured out she was the person putting on the squeeze? Her footsteps faltered. She glanced around and caught the eye of a businessman waiting at the Wellington Street light. Twiggy shivered. It was definitely time to get this game over with. There was no time to mess with the people from Petawawa. Those people had been known to kill someone who got in their way. At least the reporter from the *Sun* would just try to stiff her out of fair payment.

The phone on Bank Street was occupied, so she sat on a bench in a little square and watched the business world hustle back and forth around her. People who thought they had a place to go, a job to do, and a family to support. People who thought they had the game beat. Hah.

The person on the phone hung up, and Twiggy heaved herself to her swollen feet. So many of them looked like the man Moe had described. Maybe she should use another phone. But she was here, and it was too damn hard to walk another block.

***

June 3, 1993. Sector West, Croatia.

Dear Kit ... Man, it's been nuts around here, weapons coming in as fast as we can get them out, and mines showing up all over the fields around town. It's a game of one-upmanship, and we're caught in the middle. Last night even our soccer field got mined, but Fundy barked to warn us. I think I can even train her to detect mines. She seems to have an amazing nose. Worth a try, better than being fish in a barrel.

June 15, 1993. Sector West, Croatia.

It was Sarge's birthday yesterday, so after patrol the Captain came over to our section house with a two-four of Labatts and a forty ouncer of genuine Canadian Club. First time I ever saw the Sarge get loaded and he was funny as hell. Danny and I taught the good prairie boy "Farewell to Nova Scotia," and he started tuning up all the beer bottles. He got the whole village into the act playing whatever they could lay their hands on. One of the locals plays a mean pair of spoons and another had a mouth organ. Mahir used a stool for drums.

Even the Hammer was laughing by the end and when we all played a soccer game on the field we'd built, he didn't say a word about it being a waste of time. I think maybe he just takes his responsibilities very seriously. He doesn't want us to get too friendly with the locals because there are thousands of them and only a few dozen of us scattered along the ceasefire line, and if they ever decided to take us on, we couldn't stop them. Respect and fear, the Hammer says. That's how we maintain our advantage. We're the UN. Take us on, you take on the whole world.

ELEVEN

MIDWEEK TRAFFIC WAS light on the four-lane Trans-Canada highway from Halifax across central Nova Scotia to the north shore, and Kate McGrath made excellent time. She guided the unmarked Malibu with a calm, deft hand, and pointed out the scenery as she drove. Green was surprised, and a little embarrassed, to learn that Nova Scotia had been homesteaded since the 1630s and had already fought several wars with the French and the Americans when his own Ottawa Valley had been nothing but a wilderness of lumberjacks and fur traders.

"Some pockets were first farmed by the French in the 1600s," she said, waving at the rolling hills dotted with pastures and forest. "And when the British conquered the land, the local French settlers who wouldn't swear allegiance to the King were booted out. Then masses of New England loyalists moved onto the land they left behind. There are still Acadian enclaves interspersed with the Scots. The roots of family go very deep around here."

He heard the pride in her tone. "Did you grow up around here? I thought you were a Newfoundlander."

"I am. But I started my police career up here in Truro."

"What made you move to Halifax?"

She hesitated, and a faint frown narrowed her eyes. "I wanted a change of scene. And I also wanted a city big enough for good policing opportunities. I'd gone to Dalhousie University for my degree and fell in love with the city." She paused to peer at a highway sign, then slowed to turn right onto a smaller highway.

"Loch Katrine, Caledonia Mills," he chuckled, reading the sign. "Right out of Scotland."

She nodded. "Antigonish County was largely settled by Highland Scots, and about every second family is a MacDonald."

Off the main highway, the road dipped through lush, hilly countryside covered with trees just beginning to bud. Rivers and lakes glinted through the lacy branches, and brightly painted farms clustered in the valleys. Sharon would have loved it, and Green felt a twinge of homesickness at the thought of her delight. She had always wanted to see the east coast, and he had left her green with envy yesterday morning with no more than a brief kiss and a promise to be back in two days. I probably won't even get out of the police station, he'd told her, let alone get a chance to see a beach or a fishing village. Maybe this summer, they would make the effort to coordinate their work schedules enough to take a real road trip out here.

McGrath slowed again as a narrow gravel road appeared on their right. A small sign pointed to Hoppenderry. "It should be up here somewhere," she said. They followed the twisty road for a few more kilometres, past sparse farms and rolling pastures. McGrath craned her neck and squinted against the midday sun as they approached a small lane. Almost hidden by brush was a carved wooden sign "Derry Brook Sheep Farm, lambs and fine wool."

"Here it is!" she exclaimed, turning in the lane. As they bumped down the rutted drive, a meadow opened up on their left, a startling green against the greys and browns of spring. The meadow was dotted with sheep who barely gave them a second glance, but a black and white border collie sitting by the wood rail fence watched them with a baleful stare. Up ahead a collection of buildings greeted them, including three barns painted red and a yellow woodframe house with a steeply sloped roof and a sunporch stretching the width of its facade.

The farm had clearly seen better days. The paint was faded and peeling, and the front yard was little more than a swamp of mud and straw. In front of the house sat a rusty blue pickup and a tractor with chunks of mud stuck to their tires. A pair of red dogs clambered off the porch and hobbled towards the car, barking. Otherwise nothing stirred. The curtains were drawn on the windows, and the barn doors were shut tight.

"I told you his parents weren't very enthusiastic when I phoned to say we were coming," McGrath said.

Green eyed the dogs dubiously. Despite their greying muzzles, they were still a handsome pair, with glistening copper coats and white paws. They paced in half-hearted circles around the car, with their teeth bared. "Well," he ventured, "we didn't drive all the way up here just to —"

The front door flung back and a tall, gaunt man filled the doorway, arms crossed, glaring at them. Behind him, a woman peeked around his shoulder. Neither made any move to call off the dogs.

"We could always split the dogs up," McGrath said. "You head for the shed, I'll go for the house. They look so old, we could probably outrun them."

At that moment, the woman ducked under the man's elbow with a sharp shake of her head. When she whistled for the dogs, they stopped barking immediately and stood by the car, tails wagging and amber eyes alert. Green smiled. Whoever said men were the masters of their own domain? Dogs knew better.

Green sized up the stubborn couple in the doorway. "If it comes to it, I'll take the mother. I think the father might respond better to a fellow Maritimer."

His instincts proved accurate once he and McGrath had introduced themselves. The MacDonalds may not have been happy to see them, but Mrs. MacDonald at least welcomed them into the living room and insisted on brewing a fresh pot of tea, which she served with a warm apple cake she had clearly baked for the occasion. The delicious scent of cinnamon and yeast blended with the underlay of manure and damp wool that permeated everything.

Mr. MacDonald folded himself into an aging wing chair in the corner by the door, as if for a fast exit, and fixed them both with a chilly stare. Blue overalls with frayed cuffs hung on his bony frame, and a pair of oversized sheepskin slippers swallowed his feet. His wife flitted in and out of the kitchen as if she hoped to distract them from the purpose of their call.

"Mr. and Mrs. MacDonald," McGrath began once the woman had finally subsided on the sofa. "Thank you for seeing us. I'm sure it's not easy to talk about your son —"

Mr. MacDonald snorted. "I don't see why you've got to be bringing it all up again. It's over, more than ten years past now, and we answered all your questions about the accident back then. It's all in your files, if you'd bother to read them."

"Well, it's actually about Daniel Oliver's death —"

"And we've been through all that too. We don't know anything about his murder, it had nothing to do with Ian. Ian and Danny hardly even saw each other anymore."

Mrs. MacDonald looked up from pouring tea. "Ian was back here on the farm working with his dad, and Danny was in Halifax."

"I know," McGrath said. "We're just looking to clarify a few details."

"Why?" the father said.

"There have been some new developments," Green interjected quietly. McGrath had been following the classic police interview strategy of stonewalling, but after a brief deliberation, he decided that full disclosure might work best. That, and a touch of surprise. "Daniel Oliver's former girlfriend was murdered last week in Ottawa, and when she died, she had your son's army medal in her possession."

Both parents gaped. The father uttered a small grunt, as if he'd been punched in the stomach. He swallowed convulsively before words would come. "Why would she have Ian's medal?"

"That's what I'm hoping you can tell us," Green said.

Mrs. MacDonald flushed in confusion and busied herself cutting the cake into perfect squares. "I can't imagine. We ..." Tears unexpectedly robbed her of speech.

Her husband shot Green a scowl. "We wondered where it got to. Danny must have taken it."

"When?"

"When he was here for the funeral, I suppose."

"Why?"

MacDonald raised his bony shoulders in an impatient shrug. "How should I know? Jealous, maybe?"

"Oh, but dear," interjected Mrs. MacDonald, recovering her voice, "I told you that doesn't make any sense! Danny was very proud of him."

"Doesn't stop a man," her husband muttered. "He probably wasn't thinking straight. Got extremely drunk that day."

"What did your son get his medal for, Mr. MacDonald?"

MacDonald squared his shoulders and met Green's gaze with steely pride. "Risking his life for strangers half a world away who didn't even appreciate what our lads were sacrificing for them, from the sounds of it. The town they were protecting was under fire, and Ian rescued a lot of local villagers. His company commander put him forward for the medal."

Mrs. MacDonald's eyes were brimming again. "On Danny's recommendation, don't forget. He was Ian's section leader."

Mr. MacDonald nodded grudgingly. "They were inseparable once."

Green leaned forward, his tone soft. "What happened?"

"What do you mean, what happened? I just told you!"

"I mean when Ian came home. I understand he had some trouble readjusting to civilian life."

"Who told you that?"

Green took a careful sip of tea. "He changed his plans about vet school and returned to the farm."

"And what's wrong with that? The lad hadn't been more than a hundred miles from his home his whole life. The apples and hay were just coming in, and there was a lot needed doing on the farm. I think he was grateful for the peace and quiet after Europe."

Mrs. MacDonald bent over her tea pot, her lips pursed, but Green thought he saw a tiny spasm of pain flicker across her face. He hated to add to it. "I know this is difficult for you, but I understand he was shot in a hunting accident. Was he alone?"

Mr. MacDonald surged to his feet, bristling. "I don't want you putting my wife through this! What do the damn details matter? He was duck hunting down by the creek, just like he loved to do, and the gun misfired. Danny wasn't with him, if that's what you're getting at. Danny hadn't been near the place in over a year, and if that was eating him up, it damn well should have!"

He was hunched in the doorway. His wife looked up at him, her cheeks flaming. "Angus, the detectives are just doing their job."

"And it shouldn't involve stirring up Ian's death, which was a pointless accident. The boy runs through bullets to rescue a bunch of bloody foreigners, and he ends up getting shot with his own rifle in his own backyard!"

Unexpectedly, Kate McGrath stood up and reached out a soothing hand. "Mr. MacDonald, I'm sorry to put you both through this again. To spare your wife, perhaps you and I can go outside, and you can show me where it happened."

MacDonald hesitated, scowling dubiously at Green from under a bristly black eyebrow. "I don't see any reason for him to be staying in here —"

"He can keep me company while you're out," his wife interjected, collecting her husband's tea. The cup was untouched, and a faint tremor in her hands sloshed tea into the saucer. "Since Ian's death, it's been hard for me … to be alone."

MacDonald took some convincing, but finally he snatched a sheepskin jacket off its peg, shoved his feet into massive work boots and jerked his head to summon McGrath outside. In the living room, Mrs. MacDonald sank back onto the sofa as if relieved to be rid of him and reached for the teapot.

"More tea, Inspector?"

He rose to take the chair closer to her and held out his cup. "Thank you, it's delicious."

She fussed over the cup and added a square of cake to the saucer. A frown pinched her brow, and her eyes avoided his. Green waited, sensing she was building up to something.

"That's a terrible thing about the Ross girl," she said finally. "I remember her. She came to Ian's funeral with Danny, was a big help to him. Poor lad."

"I gather the boys had a pretty rough time in Yugoslavia."

"More than many of them bargained for, that's sure."

"Did Ian talk about those times? About what went on, or about the soldiers he was with?"

"We got letters from many of them when he died. They were so proud of him." A tremulous smile played across her lips. She thrust aside her tea and struggled to her feet. "Come on, I'll show you."

He followed her through a low doorway and up a steep, narrow, wooden staircase to the upstairs hall. The ancient floorboards creaked as she led the way down a dim hall to a door at the end. When she opened it, light flooded a room barely larger than a closet. Dust motes danced in the shaft of sunlight from a gabled window overlooking the pasture. It was clearly a young man's room, with a single bed neatly made under the window and an array of homemade shelves along the opposite wall, on which were orderly stacks of clothes, books, CDs and computer equipment. On a dresser by the bed sat a large studio portrait of a young man in a dress suit. He had his father's blue eyes, poorly tamed brown hair, and a lean hatchet face that he had yet to grow into.

"That's his high school prom, the first real photo we ever had taken of him. We never dreamed it would be the last." Her eyes welled. She tugged open a dresser drawer and bent over it. Inside, he could see piles of cards bound together with elastics.

"We didn't want too many people at the funeral," she said. "Some of his reservists came, but we got cards from all across the country from men in his peacekeeping battalion."

His interest piqued, Green came to look over her shoulder. "What did they write?"

"Mostly about his bravery. Some about his way with the local people, and about how he would always lend a helping hand or a listening ear. Also his gentleness with the animals. Ian always had a way with animals. Those two duck tollers outside, Rob and Roy, he got them as pups when he came back from Yugoslavia, and he trained them completely on his own. Hours, he'd spend with them out in the field. They're old now, but they still miss him."

She picked up one of the letters, opened it, and slid out a simple sympathy card with a long note scrawled on the inside page. "From his first section commander over there, Sergeant Sawranchuk. *Ian was as steady and courageous a soldier as any commander could hope for,*" she read, "*and he was the glue of the section. He took on all tasks, small or large, and endured the many hardships and personal discomforts without a word of complaint. He preferred talk to fighting, but he was as good with his weapon as any man, and in a crisis he could always be relied on to be in the thick of things. He believed in our mission, and he hoped we were making a difference in the lives of the people over there. He will really be missed.*"

She slid the card back into the envelope and replaced it carefully into the drawer. "The sergeant was sent back home on medical leave before Ian got his medal, but at least he was kind enough to write. Oh, here's a picture of them all — his friends and the men he worked with." She drew out a photo of a group of soldiers posing around a large armoured vehicle. They were grinning and hamming it up.

Green took the photo for a closer look. The sun was bright and the shadows sharp, making it difficult to distinguish facial features, but a lab technician could probably make them recognizable.

"Do you know who they are?" he asked.

"Other than Ian and Danny, no. There's Ian ..." She pointed to a young man in the middle with his arms slung around two others. "Always surrounded by friends. He touched so many people."

"May I borrow this? I'll reproduce it and send it back, I promise."

"Oh ... it's just sitting in a drawer now. Those days changed him so much — they aren't how I want to remember him." She stared out the window for a moment with sadness in her eyes, before she seemed to pull herself back from the brink of memory. Delving deeper into the pile, she pulled out a small, austere card without the purple roses and embossed script that adorned most of the others.

"Even months later we still got cards. This was from his platoon commander Richard Hamm, promoted to major by then and stationed out in Edmonton, so it took him a while to get the news, I suppose." Her hands trembled slightly as she opened the card and held it out to Green. "He's not much for words, but what he said about our Ian ... it says a lot."

Green glanced at the card, which contained two lines of terse prose in a brusque, heavy hand. *Dear Mr. and Mrs. MacDonald, my condolences on your loss. Ian was a tireless and committed soldier whose bravery saved many lives.*

"Tireless, committed, that was our Ian. If he believed in something, he'd give it his heart and soul." Her chin quivered, and she dropped her gaze. "Nice of the major, don't you think?"

Green studied the card with a nagging unease. He'd heard many expressions of condolence in his time. Perhaps it was his imagination, but he sensed the major's choice of words was important not for what they said, but what they didn't say. No mention of a pleasure to have under my command, or an example to his fellow soldiers. These words were carefully chosen to comfort the bereaved without eulogizing the dead man. There was no warmth in the sentiment expressed; on the contrary, Green sensed a chill in his words. Yet Ian was a soldier who'd received a rare medal of bravery under the man's command.

"Was this the man who recommended Ian for his medal?"

Her gaze flickered for only an instant before she shook her head. "That was Danny. It was when the company moved down to Sector South in Croatia, and conditions were much more dangerous for them. There wasn't much peace to be kept, truth be told, and Danny had to take over command of the section. That's normally a sergeant's job, and Danny was only a corporal then, but I guess something happened to Sergeant Sawranchuk —" She leaned towards him, her eyes glittering. "Exhaustion was the official word, but that covers a multitude of sins, doesn't it?"

"I've certainly heard that the missions were very hard on a lot of men." Green steered her gently back. "So it was Daniel Oliver, not an officer, who recommended him?"

"Put his name forward, yes. Oh, don't get me wrong. They all supported it. His battalion commander, company commander, and this Major Hamm. Captain Hamm back then and probably General by now. He was that kind of soldier."

"What did Ian say about him?"

"That he was a bit of a slave driver. But then they have to be, don't they? They had their orders too. Still, with our Ian, that wasn't the way to handle him. Tell him why he should do something, point out the good in it, trust him to give it his all, and he will. Always been like that, which was something his dad had trouble seeing. This sergeant who went on medical leave, he was much more Ian's type of leader. I think it was hard on all the boys when he left. But Danny stepped in and did the best he could."

Green nodded slowly. "They were all just boys, weren't they? Thousands of miles from home."

He heard her suck in her breath and expel it in a long, sigh. "And it wasn't like in a war, where the soldiers all come back home as heroes who'd defended their country. No one knew what our lads had been through or what they'd seen. Why they couldn't stand the smell of a barbeque or a trip to the dump. Why they couldn't sleep at night or take a walk through the orchard without their gun." She gripped the card and struggled to get it back into the envelope before abandoning the effort. "That damn gun … I was his mother. I should have known."

He felt sorry for her, hovering over the abyss of her loss. He hated to tip the balance, but sensed if ever there was a time for truth, this was it. "Should have known what, Mrs. MacDonald?"

She shook her head. "He didn't take the dogs that day. The only time he left them behind."

He waited. In the silence, the distant bark of a dog penetrated the windowpane. She took a deep, shuddering breath. "His father calls it a hunting accident. He has to. To Angus, our boy is a decorated soldier and a tribute to his country. To face the truth is to dishonour his memory. Our boy *was* a hero. Nothing takes that away."

Still he waited. Barely breathing.

"But he was also afraid, and tormented and confused. In the end, he took his damn hunting rifle, left his dogs behind because he didn't want them to see, and he went down to the river marsh at the bottom of the farm. Where he propped his rifle against a tree and shot himself."

TWELVE

"THE CASUALTIES OF peacekeeping," McGrath said. "After Romeo Dallaire, the army's worst kept secret."

They were having a late lunch at a roadside diner outside Antigonish. Mrs. MacDonald had offered to make them lunch, but sensing that their continued presence there was like salt in her wounds, Green had declined. Now they were hunched over greasy fish and chips. Green doused his with more ketchup as he considered McGrath's words.

General Romeo Dallaire was the army's highest profile example of the post-traumatic stress the country's soldiers often endured after trying to maintain peace in some of the most violent and tribal corners of the world. Clearly, Ian himself had struggled with memories and fears upon his return, and on that fateful morning in September 1995, he had finally ceded defeat. Despite being recognized as a hero by his superiors and his government, he was just a boy who had faced more than he could bear.

Perhaps.

And yet …

Green wrestled to make this new piece of the puzzle fit in with the subsequent murders. Daniel Oliver had been Ian's section commander in the latter part of their rotation, and he had recommended Ian for a medal of bravery — a relative rarity in the peacekeeping ranks, where combat heroism was less valued than mediation skills. His platoon commander, Captain Hamm, had supported the recommendation, but if his tepid letter of condolence was any indication, he did not share Oliver's enthusiasm for Ian's accomplishment.

"Somehow, all these things connect to Yugoslavia," Green said eventually. "Ian's suicide, Oliver's murder and Patricia's murder. I think something happened over there …"

"Yeah, well, with Norrich handling that part of the investigation …" She paused, grimacing as she picked oily chunks of batter off her fish. "I suppose I could have a go at the West Nova Scotia Reserve Regiment myself. See if anyone knows anything."

"That won't help. We need to find out who served with them in Yugoslavia and interview every last one of them." He reached into his pocket and slid the photo Mrs. MacDonald had given him across the table towards her. "These are some of the guys in their unit. We should start by IDing them. I have a contact in army personnel in Ottawa. I'll get one of my men in Ottawa to follow up."

McGrath shoved aside her half-eaten fish and picked up the photo. She angled it to catch the light and studied it closely. A faint frown played across her features.

Green's interest quickened. "What?"

She shook her head and peered more closely. Her frown deepened. Then she tapped at one of the men in the photo. He was posed behind the others, leaning against the hood of an army truck. His helmet cast much of his face in shadow.

"This man. I can't be sure, but I think …" She looked up at him, her eyes widened with excitement. "Mike, I think he might have been the other man in the bar the night Oliver was killed. The man talking to the killer beforehand."

"You mean the guy who gave you the fake ID? And claimed he had no idea who the killer was?"

"The very one. And if you believe that, I've got a schooner full of flying codfish to sell you!"

***

The minute they arrived back at the Halifax Police Station, Green put in a call to Gibbs. The young detective sounded as if he were fairly bursting with news.

"We've uncovered another possible military connection, sir! At least, Sue — Detective Peters has. At the Voyageur Bus Station. Th-th ..." He took a deep breath as if to slow himself, and Green could almost see his Adam's apple bobbing. "This morning she took the photos of Patricia Ross and her purse to the bus station to see if anyone remembered her buying a ticket there. And ... it took two shifts, but you know Sue, she sticks to things, and on the afternoon shift she found a floor cleaner who remembered Patricia. Said she wore a hole in his floor pacing up and down, going outside every ten minutes for a smoke while she waited for the bus. And guess where she caught the bus to?"

Green's pulse leaped. "Petawawa."

There was abrupt silence on the phone, as if Gibbs had even stopped breathing. "How did you know?"

"You said there was a military connection. There aren't too many Canadian Forces bases within bussing distance to Ottawa. And Petawawa is home to a large infantry regiment that has gone on numerous peacekeeping missions." Sensing Gibbs's disappointment, Green reined in his racing thoughts. "What day did she go?"

"M-monday the 17th. Almost a week after she arrived."

And almost a week before she died, Green thought. More and more he was convinced she'd been on the trail of someone, and had stirred up a hornet's nest along the way. "Excellent work, Bob," he said. "Once we know Daniel Oliver's military associates, maybe we'll be able to determine who she went to see. Anything else come up today?"

"That reporter from the *Sun* called, sir. Frank Corelli. His witness agreed to a meet. I wanted to wait to check in with you, but I figured it was more important to get her information, so we set it up for noon today over at Confederation Park. It's a busy enough place, especially at lunch hour, that I figured our surveillance teams wouldn't be obvious. Staff Sergeant Larocque gave me half a dozen patrol officers to cover it, and I figured we'd have no trouble picking her up."

"After she talked to Frank, I hope. Otherwise, she's likely to shut up like a clam." Green glanced at his watch. Five thirty. Which meant it was four thirty in Ottawa, well past the rendezvous time. Something in Gibbs's tone suggested trouble. "How did it go?"

"She didn't show, sir. We waited a full hour, and Corelli sat in plain view on a park bench with the *Sun* open in front of him."

"Maybe the surveillance was too obvious."

"Maybe, sir, but not a single woman came near him. Or even seemed to be watching him."

"She was probably just testing his interest. Tell Frank to be ready, because I think she may call again, demanding a higher price."

"Either that or she has nothing to sell," Gibbs said. He sounded frustrated. "It may all have been just a bid for attention. She tied up a lot of resources today."

Green thought it over. He was in the incident room Inspector Norrich had provided for him, and the files still lay strewn around the table where McGrath and he had left them. McGrath was flipping through a box for her interviews with the witness who'd given her the false ID. Her eyes were narrowed with a focussed excitement he knew so well. The feeling you get when a crucial detail in the case breaks loose.

With an effort he forced his thoughts back to Gibbs's problem. Gibbs could be right; the woman could simply be a media-hungry crank. But on the other hand, she had known about the body being moved after death. To know that, she had to be one of the investigating professionals, or she had to have seen it being moved.

"I think she'll call again," he said. "So make sure Corelli's prepared."

"Will you be back tomorrow, sir?"

"Yes. My flight gets in at noon, and I'll grab a cab straight to the office. I have something else I want you to do in the meantime." Quickly he filled Gibbs in on Ian MacDonald's death and its possible connection to Daniel Oliver's murder and to their time together in Yugoslavia. He gave him Captain Ulrich's contact information at DND and asked him to try to track down as many of the soldiers in the peacekeeping unit as possible. "Starting with Major — or possibly a higher rank — Richard Hamm, who was their platoon commander. He may be out at CFB Edmonton. And Sergeant Sawranchuk, who was their section leader."

"Ask him to get photos too," McGrath interjected, looking up from her files. "And have him fax everything down here to me as well."

Once Green had hung up, he filled McGrath in on Patricia Ross's journey to Petawawa. By the time he finished, McGrath's eyes were stormy. "Patricia was tracking the same story we are. Goddamn it, if it was this simple, if we missed an obvious line of inquiry because of Norrich's stupid, macho incompetence, then I'm going to have his fucking balls for fish bait!"

***

June 18. Sector West, Croatia.

Dear Kit ... I had an amazing experience yesterday. Three of us were on a foot patrol, checking the back country paths to make sure no Serbs were sneaking weapons into the UNPA. The Serbs don't like our foot patrols because apparently the UN battalion before us just sat at their checkpoints and if they wanted to patrol, they had to ask the Serbs' permission. Permission, for fuck's sake.

So when we arrived in Sector West, our CO said no, it's not going to work like that. Our mandate is to enforce the weapons ban, and that's exactly what we're going to do. This part of the country is loaded with little off-the-map trails that only the locals know about. So we set up observation posts to do foot patrols as well as the regular APC patrols on the main road. OP patrols are out for a week at a time, just a few guys against a mess of belligerents, and I know Sarge isn't happy with the danger, but those were the orders.

So there we were, walking along, scanning the trail ahead for mines, when around the corner comes these four Serb guys, loaded to the gills — AK47s, grenades, sniper rifles, claymore mines, the works. No hunting party for sure. We told them to hand over their weapons and instead they pointed their rifles at us. You have to show who's boss with these guys or they'll walk all over you. So we raised our rifles too. Now, our rules of engagement are drilled into us. You can't initiate fire, and when fired upon you can only respond in kind. So we couldn't do anything but stare at them and wait for them to shoot first. Like that makes any sense when you're staring down the barrel of an AK47.

Anyway, Danny mutters fuck this and he shoots over their heads. They shoot back and we take cover and everybody starts firing. After about thirty seconds the Serbs turn around and run away. I started to laugh, relief I guess, and Danny's checking us out because the medic says sometimes when the adrenaline's going, you don't even know you've been hit. But none of us were hurt. I don't know if we hit any Serbs.

I was proud of myself that day. You always wonder how you're going to hold up the first time you meet the real thing. You hope you'll keep your cool and remember your training, but you don't really know. Well, when it happened, I didn't have time to be scared. I was pumped and I just acted on instinct. And we got the job done. Afterwards my legs were like jelly and I downed two beers the minute I got back to camp, but it didn't matter.

***

Green's plans to hit the ground running in Ottawa by early afternoon were scuttled the moment he woke up the next morning to a fog so thick he couldn't see the street from his second-storey window. As the taxi crept out to the airport, the cabbie kept shaking his head sagely.

"Waste of time, sir. The planes have been stacked up at the departure gates since six o'clock this morning. Not a thing flying in or out of this soup."

"When is it likely to clear?" Green asked as they pulled up at the terminal, which was still cocooned in white.

"When it feels like it. You might get off today." The cabbie's laugh was the last thing Green heard before the cab was swallowed up by the fog. For a moment Green regretted declining Kate McGrath's offer of a ride to the airport. He could have used the company, and they could have used the time to coordinate their plans of attack.

But the truth was, they had discussed everything to death already, and her company was proving a little too distracting for safety. And judging from the way her eyes had locked his when she'd dropped him off at the hotel the night before, the border into dangerous waters was very close indeed.

The airport was full of stranded passengers, but the pace of activity was leisurely. Who was going anywhere? He checked in and cleared security without difficulty. By ten o'clock he was settled at his departure gate with a coffee, trying to read the Halifax *Chronicle-Herald*. But thoughts of Kate McGrath kept drifting uninvited through his mind, crowding out the latest headlines. Her long legs, her smile that quivered ever so slightly at the edges when she'd said goodbye …

He pulled out his cellphone and called Sharon. She had the day off and sounded sleepy as she greeted him.

"Your son and I were sleeping in," she said.

He glanced at his watch and did a quick calculation. Nine fifteen in Ottawa. "Sorry, honey, did I wake you?"

"Not really. I was just lying in bed thinking I should get up. I think the entire household is camped outside our bedroom door waiting for breakfast." Her chuckle dissolved into a yawn. He pictured her in bed, her black curls tumbling in her eyes and her nightgown rumpled up around her thighs. He needed to get home.

"I don't suppose you could hold that picture till I get home?"

"Which one? Me in bed, or the kids and the dog outside the door?" She chuckled again, this time with no trace of sleepiness. "You'd better hurry, baby. Neither one will keep."

Mentally he checked off the "to-do" list ahead of him before he could cash in on the promise in her tone, but then he remembered it was Friday. "Damn, it's Shabbat," he said. He would have to pick up his father at his retirement home and bring him home again after dinner.

"Well, you know what the rabbis say. Even a quickie on the Sabbath is a mitzvah."

"A quickie wasn't what I had in mind," he replied.

"Nor was a good deed, I bet."

He was still laughing when he hung up. Their daily life was so hectic and their schedules so erratic that he sometimes feared their lives barely touched anymore. The banter reminded him of old times, and even the long, tedious wait for his flight could not dampen his hopes. His father was elderly and frail and could usually manage no more than an hour's visit for Friday dinner. The night would still be young once Green returned from driving him home.

The plane finally took off at one p.m. and touched down in Ottawa just after two in the afternoon local time. He phoned Gibbs on his way in from the airport, and by the time he arrived, the detective was waiting outside his office with his notebook and a sheaf of reports in his hands. He looked surprisingly calm and in command. This responsibility has been good for him, Green decided. That, and perhaps — amazingly — Detective Sue Peters.

"Any crises, Bob?" he asked as he dumped his suitcase in the corner of his office and looked at his desk in dismay.

It was covered with memos and pink telephone slips, which would only tell a quarter of the story. The rest would be lurking in the furiously blinking telephone voice mail box and crowding the inbox of his computer.

"No, sir. Staff Sergeant Larocque reviewed the case with me this morning and made a couple of suggestions."

"Oh good," Green said, hoping it was. The Byward Market circus must have wound down enough to give Larocque time to do the rest of his job. He nodded to the papers in Gibbs's hands. "So, can you give me the highlights?"

"Not much new from forensics yet, sir. We're still waiting on the results of the toxicology. Fingerprinting of the victim's hotel room confirmed she was there, but that's no surprise. There were lots of other prints — Lou Paquette said the room probably hadn't been thoroughly cleaned in a year — but he's got no hits on AFIS."

"Doesn't mean anything," Green said. "Our man's not your ordinary bad guy who's going to be in the system."

"We've been canvassing restaurants, bars and pubs in the vicinity of her hotel in Vanier and the Byward Market to find a witness who saw her drinking with anyone the evening she died."

"Good thinking."

"It was Detective Peters's idea." Gibbs blushed and cleared his throat. "So far no luck, but there are a lot of bars to cover."

"You've assigned some uniforms?"

"Yessir. And we've also got the regular neighbourhood officers checking the bars on their beat."

"You may need to expand the canvass to include the centretown area too. Any place that's along the route from her hotel to the aqueduct. The pathologist thought it was good quality scotch — and he's the expert — so we may be looking for an upscale bar like the Chateau Laurier or one of the downtown hotels."

Gibbs jotted a few notes in his book then flipped back, scanning as if to make sure he'd forgotten nothing. "I just called Frank Corelli from the *Sun* for an update before you arrived, sir. He hasn't heard a word from his witness. I think it was just a crank."

Green frowned. He was less convinced, but Gibbs already had enough leads to pursue without worrying about cagey media-seekers. "I'll handle Frank. What have you got from the military?"

Gibbs paged through his notes again. "Some good, some bad. Captain Ulrich was not very forthcoming. He kept talking about fishing expeditions and protecting the privacy and safety of armed forces personnel. I asked for a list of soldiers in MacDonald's and Oliver's unit, and he stalled. That's hundreds, he said, could take weeks to compile."

Green snorted. "Their computers all broken suddenly?"

"I wasn't sure how broad a net you wanted to cast, sir. Ian MacDonald and Daniel Oliver were both in the same section, which normally has around ten men in it, led by a sergeant. So I said I wanted contact info on all those men. But there are three or four sections in a platoon, and according to Ulrich, usually a platoon works as a unit performing particular duties, say guarding a checkpoint. That makes it thirty to forty men, led by a lieutenant or captain. So then I asked for the names of the platoon members and then everyone in the chain of command. He said it would take a long time, and he'd have to check with his superior, and …"

"Someone's warned them we're sniffing around," Green grumbled. His thoughts were racing. Who? One of the bartenders in Halifax with close ties to the military? Inspector Norrich? Or the killer himself, who was well enough connected to the military to be able to pull some strings?

On the other hand, maybe the military was just being its usual paranoid self, and at the first hint of outside interference, it had thrown up the walls of secrecy. That was an equally plausible explanation.

"I did get a few bits of news out of them though, sir." Gibbs was smiling now, no longer glued to his notes. "You asked about two specific men — Sawranchuk and Hamm? Gary Sawranchuk is no longer in the service; he got out in December 1995. It was a medical discharge, but Ulrich refused to provide details. Confidentiality. The man's last posting was a training unit in Gagetown, New Brunswick. Ulrich wouldn't give me his current address, but he's originally from Moose Jaw, Saskatchewan, so he may have moved back there."

"Or he may have stayed in the Maritimes," Green said. "Close enough to drop in to a Halifax bar for a drink now and then. Did you get a photograph of him?"

"Ulrich has to check that with his superiors as well, sir."

Green sighed. "I may have to have a little chat with his superiors myself." Or perhaps drag out our own big guns. Barbara Devine. He almost laughed aloud at the prospect of Devine nose to nose with some ass-covering military mandarin. "What about the platoon commander, Hamm?"

"That's the one piece of good news, sir. Lieutenant Colonel Hamm he is now, and he's on the staff of the general in command of the Royal Canadians. Posted … and this is the exciting thing …"

Green waited. He knew the answer, because he knew where the Royal Canadian Regiment was based, but this time he didn't want to deprive Gibbs of his grand moment.

Gibbs stabbed his notebook. "In Petawawa."

Bingo, Green thought. The web of clues was closing. He wasn't sure who would ultimately be trapped inside, but the excitement of the chase gripped him. He glanced at his watch. It was almost four o'clock.

"Okay!" he exclaimed, flicking on his computer. "Now get out of here and let me clear up some of my paperwork. Because tomorrow morning, you and I are going to Petawawa."

Gibbs's face fell. "Oh. Well, I — I ..."

"It's the obvious next step, Bob. Don't worry, it's your case. It's just that I know the questions to ask this guy."

"That's not it, sir. It — it's just ... Sue's already gone. I sent her up there this morning, on Staff Sergeant Larocque's recommendation."

Instinctively, Green recoiled in horror. He took a deep breath to quell it. Sue Peters may be blunt with no feeling for diplomacy or subtext, but she had proved herself to be bright and creative, and much of the progress in the investigation to date had been due to her. Green was always lecturing his men on using lateral thinking skills rather than doggedly tracking one lead after another. Whatever Peters lacked in subtlety, she sure as hell knew how to think.

Yet no amount of creative thinking would keep an inexperienced, over-enthusiastic rookie from blundering into trouble in the minefield of military culture. He allowed his dismay to focus on that.

"Without you?"

"No, sir. I mean yes, sir. I thought I should stay at the office to ..." Gibbs paused as if to regroup. "I mean, to stay on top of Ulrich and to coordinate the other avenues of inquiry. That's what the Staff Sergeant said. But Sue really wanted to go. She'd uncovered the lead about the bus trip, and she thought she should follow through right away."

"But Bob — by herself?" he said incredulously. The more he thought about the fiasco, the angrier he became. Peters was going to interview Hamm without half the background she needed to uncover his involvement, and they were only going to get one clear shot at the man. Once Hamm realized what they were probing for, the barriers would go up so high he'd be invisible.

"N-no, sir. I sent Constable Weiss from General Assignment with her."

A beginner, Green thought. *Noch besser.* Even better. "Who the hell is Constable Weiss?"

"Jeff Weiss. H … he's been with the case from the beginning, sir. He asked his sergeant to be assigned. I think he's keen to job shadow Major Crimes."

The name rang a faint, unpleasant bell. "Have I met this Constable Weiss before?"

"Yes. Well — maybe. He was down at the aqueduct the first morning, helping with the search of the area, sir. Tall guy, blue eyes and blond hair? Works out."

Green's mind rifled through his memory until it came to rest with a jolt on a face he'd barely registered at the time. It was the blue eyes he remembered. Intelligent, focussed, but cocky as hell. Fuck, he thought, just what we need, a zealous, blundering rookie detective, paired up with an entry-level officer with zero investigative skills but an ego the size of Lake Superior.

Gibbs was tugging at his tie as if in a vain effort to get more air. He cast Green a pleading look. "His sergeant says he was an experienced and level-headed street cop, sir."

Gibbs was saved from further wrath by the sharp buzzing of Green's phone. "Constable Weiss calling for Detective Gibbs," the clerk said. "He says it's urgent."

Green flipped on the speaker phone and told her to put him through. Constable Weiss's voice, when it filled the tiny alcove office, sounded neither experienced nor level-headed.

"Sir, it's Sue. Detective Peters. Something terrible's happened!"

THIRTEEN

SUE PETERS HAD been awake half the night planning her trip to Petawawa. She knew the army type inside out — she'd grown up with them — and she planned to walk a very finely balanced tightrope between back-slapping like one of the boys and allowing a peek at the merchandise. She knew she had to put in an official appearance with the local Ontario Provincial Police detachment and even with the military police on the base, but she didn't expect to learn a thing about Patricia Ross's adventures from them. She doubted the woman would even have attempted to go through official channels.

She intended to hit the bars in the cheapest part of town — if there was such a thing in a town as small as Petawawa — where the boys from the base would go for their entertainment. Where they would feel most free to talk. And where she was sure Patricia, being no stranger to the rougher side of life, would have gone to ask her questions. Even if she hadn't, her arrival in town should have sparked the rumour mill. This was a small military town; drop a blond under fifty into the mix, and surely the bars would be humming.

She had to admit that she was really looking forward to the assignment. Then in the morning Gibbsie had ratcheted up the excitement by telling her that one of her interview targets was a hotshot lieutenant colonel named Richard Hamm — Dick in the officer's mess, no doubt, and Dickie in bed — who had been Oliver's platoon commander back in Yugoslavia. She was supposed to find out if Patricia had been to see him, and if so, why. Now she was doubly glad she'd decided to show a little cleavage beneath her hot pink suit.

But then Gibbsie and the Staff Sergeant had assigned Mr. Steroids himself to be her bodyguard. A cocky prick who thought he was God's gift, and who would scare off every red-blooded soldier she tried to cosy up to. At least he had the sense not to wear his body armour and police belt, which would be guaranteed to shut the gossip line down. He was wearing instead a grey sports jacket over a conservative blue shirt, but he tucked his tie into his pocket the minute they left the staff sergeant's office. Without it, even she had to admit he made a nice package, and by the time they reached the parking lot, she had thought of a use for him. Two could play the bar flirtation game, for twice the info.

She insisted on driving, which meant she had to endure two hours of him staring down her blouse. *In your dreams, Constable. I've got a colonel to see.*

Protocol had required that the military police and Colonel Hamm be notified in advance of their visit, but Larocque had managed to be as vague as possible. Luckily, Dickie Hamm had decided they posed no threat, because he'd invited them to meet him out at his house. Fewer distractions there, he explained.

He lived off the base on Albert Street, in a bungalow overlooking the southern bank of the Petawawa River. The directions had seemed idiot proof, but with Steroids navigating, they managed to tour most of the south side of town before stumbling across the address. The fieldstone bungalow was protected by a hedge so perfectly trimmed that Peters wondered if he used a laser beam. There was no sign of the truckload of military police she'd been expecting, and instead a brand-new BMW sports van in spit-polished black sat alone in the drive. Tucked into the side yard on a flatbed trailer was a classic jewel-green MG.

Peters pulled their puke-brown Malibu in behind and was just climbing out when the front door swung open and a tall, impossibly fit-looking man strode out. He was a perfect match to the hedge and the cars. Razor-trimmed white hair, wraparound black sunglasses, and a jeans and golf shirt combo that would feed the average private's family for a month.

And the sonofabitch was heading straight for Steroids, hand outstretched and white teeth gleaming.

"Detective Peters? Dick Hamm. No trouble finding the place?"

She hustled around the car to intercept him. "I'm Detective Peters, this is Constable Weiss." She grabbed his hand before he could snatch it back. Luckily the man was quick on the draw — you don't make colonel without understanding buttered bread — and he enveloped her hand in a cool, crushing grip.

"I've got coffee on," he said, striding towards the house. "It's warm enough to sit on the deck, and the blackflies aren't out yet, so we're in luck. We have to catch these rare moments of habitable Canadian weather while we can."

When they were settled on the deck, which perched on a bluff above a bend in the river, with a pot of fabulous coffee on the table between them, Dickie Hamm removed his sunglasses and turned the full force of his ice blue eyes upon her.

"Now, how can I help you, Detective Peters? I understand this is a murder inquiry?"

Peters reached into her briefcase and withdrew the two photos of Patricia Ross taken at the autopsy. She laid them side by side on the coffee table and opened her notebook. Hamm looked at them, his face unreadable.

"Do you recognize this woman?"

"No. Is she the victim?"

"Take your time, Colonel. Have you ever seen this woman?"

"Not that I recall."

"Not recently?"

He shook his head.

"How about years ago. In Halifax."

She paused in her note-taking to watch him closely, but he gave absolutely nothing away. But then, you don't make colonel by letting the enemy read your mind either.

"Halifax," he said after a moment's thought. "That was some time ago. I doubt I'd even remember who I met then."

"When were you there, sir?"

He made a show of thinking. "I've been there three times, in fact. I did a stint as instructor at Gagetown and visited Nova Scotia on leave. That would have been between June and October 1997. I gave a talk at a joint forces peacekeeping conference in May of 2000. And I was there again briefly on a flight overseas last year."

"How about 1996?"

"I was in Edmonton in 1996, but I may have made a few trips in and out on my way overseas. I travelled a great deal in that time. What time period were you thinking of?"

"We have a witness who places you in Halifax on April 9, 1996." It was a bluff, but Peters figured it was worth a try. Witnesses could be wrong, after all. Hamm raised an eyebrow and fixed his ice blue eyes on her like he could stare right through her. She stared back, hoping her poker face was as good as his. Steroids, luckily, kept his mouth shut.

"I have no recollection of being in Halifax in April 1996."

No recollection, she thought. Spoken like someone who'd been coached by a lawyer. "Do you know a woman named Patricia Ross? Also known as Patti Oliver?"

"The victim?"

Peters said nothing.

"Neither name is familiar."

"She was Daniel Oliver's fiancée. You do remember him, I hope."

The icy stare softened, and his gaze shifted to the river. "Of course I do. Danny was an exemplary soldier, and his death was a tragedy."

"Try murder."

His lips thinned. "I understood it was unintentional. Too much drink all around."

"Maybe not. How did you hear about it?"

He flicked his gaze back to her. "The army is rather like the police force, I imagine. When death strikes one of our own, the news travels across the continent. All the way to Edmonton in my case."

"But who told you?"

"One of the other platoon leaders from that mission. Soldiers talk, you know, about who's doing what. Who's encountered trouble and who got promoted. I heard Oliver was in trouble, so I kept an ear to the ground."

"Did you contact him?"

"No." He looked back at the river. Neat trick, she thought. Commune with nature, look regretful, and avoid my eyes all in one shot. "Maybe I should have."

Peters studied her notes, taking mental stock. So far, it was the colonel three, herself zip. She ploughed ahead. "On

Monday of last week, Patricia Ross came up to Petawawa to speak to you. Do you recall that meeting?"

Dickhead laughed. "You must think me a fool, Detective. You show me a picture of the dead woman and ask if I've ever met a Patricia Ross, and despite my professed ignorance of both, you ask if I met her last week!"

Peters could feel her face flame. She tugged at her hot pink skirt furiously to get it further down her thighs. Mr. Steroids leaned in, as if threatening to come to her rescue.

"I don't think you're a fool, Colonel, and your answers were duly recorded. But people lie to the police all the time, sir. We have information that she travelled to Petawawa on the one o'clock bus to meet with you."

"Well then, she never made it here. I apologize for sounding rude, Detective Peters. I appreciate that plenty of people lie to the police, but I give you my word as an officer that I did not meet with her."

How fucking quaint, she thought, scrambling to rescue her line of questioning. "Do you have any idea why she might have been trying to meet with you?"

"Absolutely none. Not at this late date, anyway. Back when Danny died, she might have wanted to know about his tour overseas under my command. Which as I said had been outstanding. She might have derived comfort from it had she asked me. I personally promoted him to master corporal so that he could lead his section."

"Why didn't you tell her anyway, even before she asked?"

"I didn't know she existed. I did write Danny's parents." He began to collect coffee cups onto a stainless steel stray, lining up the spoons along the edge like a drill parade. "I hope this hasn't proved to be a complete waste of time," he said. "I'd feel badly if Danny's fiancée was trying to find out information about him, and I was unavailable to help."

"Where were you between the hours of one and six p.m. on Monday April 17th?"

"Monday?" He paused only fractionally. "I was at my office, in a meeting with General Stubbing and nine other senior officers and civilians. I can get them to make formal statements if that would be helpful."

Out of the corner of her eye, Peters saw Mr. Steroids jot the information down. The first note he'd taken in the entire interview. Did he notice that the guy had barely paused to think?

"Thank you," she said. "The general's statement should be sufficient."

Finally, the dickhead blinked. Or rather, set the coffee tray down with a clatter. Gotcha, she thought gleefully, and jotted the lapse in her notebook. When she looked up, he was watching her warily.

"One more question, Colonel. Where were you on Sunday April 23rd, between six p.m. and six a.m.?"

This time the slick bastard didn't even pause for breath. His alibis seemed to be right at his fingertips. "Here, with my wife. We sat in this very spot for dinner and at dusk we went inside. She to watch TV and I to deal with three hours of paperwork, after which we went to bed. I did not awaken until 0500 hours. Too late to travel to Ottawa, I suspect."

Peters made a show of glancing around, even though there was no sign of anyone else. "Is your wife here this afternoon?"

"No, Sandra works in town. Do you want her to send you a statement as well?"

"No. I'd prefer to take it myself. What is her work address?"

He realigned the coffee spoons as he rattled off directions to an address on Petawawa Boulevard. Steroids wrote down every word, and Peters stood up to leave. She thanked him for his co-operation and handed him her card, according to her detective training. As she headed back towards the car, she resisted the urge to look back. Wondering if the dickhead was already racing inside to put in a warning call to his wife. Rallying the troops, so to speak.

As she and Steroids headed towards Petawawa's main street, she took the time to observe the surroundings, looking for sleazy hangouts the soldiers would love. She was quick to discover that it was not your typical Ontario town. Almost none of its streets went in a straight line where you thought they should, and businesses seemed to be scattered helter skelter along the way; car dealers next door to banks and pizza joints, old Victorian cottages next to strip malls. Maybe it was because it had never been a town on its own, but had spread like a drunken spider's web from the big military base at its core.

Soldiers in combat fatigues were everywhere. So, surprisingly, were election placards. The drive through Renfrew County en route to Petawawa had taken them through solid Conservative blue countryside, but here in the town there seemed to be a competition of one-upmanship between Tory blue signs and Liberal red. Was it the influence of the military or of the scientists in Chalk River Nuclear Research Facility just upriver?

"It looks like a close race up here," Steroids commented, like he'd read her mind.

Peters tried to decide if it was worth replying. She was sick and tired of politics, and there was still another two weeks of media overkill before it would be over. "They're all a bunch of crooks," she said. "It blows my mind that some people still vote Liberal. How much of our hard-earned tax dollars do they have to dish out to their pals before people get the message?"

He opened his mouth, and for a moment she was afraid he was going to argue, but just then they whizzed past the strip mall housing Sandra Hamm's craft boutique, barely visible between a pawn shop and a pet food store. Peters did a U-turn, her fifth of the day, and swooped into a parking spot outside the shop. In the window was a display of painted eggs and giant twig wreaths decorated with yellow ribbons and bunny rabbits. Bit late for Easter, thought Peters, as she shoved open the door. I guess wifie doesn't share hubbie's love of precision.

But hubbie had obviously tipped wifie off, because she trotted out an alibi almost word for word the same as his, except that she specified the TV shows. *Survivor*, a gardening show, and the tape of her soap. Exciting life you lead, Peters thought as she recorded the list. The whole interview took less than five minutes.

"Well, we've learned absolutely fuck-all on this trip," Mr. Steroids said once they were back outside.

"Yeah, but now the fun part begins."

"What? Food?"

"First the bus station. Then yeah, food, and maybe even a beer or two."

"Ah, my kind of woman!"

Without bothering to explain, she tossed the address of the bus station at him and pulled out of the mall. The bus station, it turned out, was no more than a ticket booth inside a hotel at the central crossroads of the town. The King's Arms had obviously seen better days. The desk clerk did remember Patricia leaving, but not arriving, and had no idea what direction she'd come from. She recalled only that Patricia seemed excited.

"Well, that was about as useful as tits on a bull," Steroids pronounced as they came back out of the hotel.

"You'd be surprised how useful tits can be," she retorted. If the guy couldn't see the implication of Patricia being excited, he was a dead loss. Patricia must have had more luck uncovering secrets than they had.

Steroids chuckled. "Speaking of eating ..."

Ignoring him, she stood in the parking lot to figure out her next move. There didn't appear to be any obvious bar scene in this jumbled up town, but when Patricia got off the bus, she would have been on foot. Which limited the places she might go.

"We'd do better to split up and canvass all the places nearby." She pointed down the street. "You take that far side of the block, and I'll do this side, including the hotel. And while I'm driving you there, you're going to get a crash course in interview techniques. Not anything like the ones you learn in cop school."

Before she dropped him off at the first restaurant on the block, she made him ditch the sports jacket and undo another button on his blue shirt, but he still looked like a cop. She could only hope the girls mistook his steely gaze for a special forces hotshot on leave.

She drove back to the hotel and parked around the back near the railway tracks. She'd spotted a bar tucked into the back of the dank old hotel, and instinct told her that, after a long bus ride, that would be the first place Patricia would go. She tossed her pink jacket into the backseat, unbuckled her gun, and hesitated before shoving it into the glove compartment. It was bending the rules, she knew, but the Glock was too damn big to conceal in her purse. The worst she was likely to encounter in broad daylight was a lecherous drunk anyway, so she slipped her tiny pepper spray can into her purse along with her notebook. After peering at herself in the car mirror, she smeared on some hot pink lipstick and shook her frizzy red hair loose. Eat your hearts out, boys, she muttered and set off for the hotel bar.

At three o'clock in the afternoon, it was too late for the lunch crowd and too early for anyone but the serious drinkers, but nonetheless she found a bunch of rookie privates shooting pool in the corner. Their freshly shaved heads and lean, trim bodies despite the quantity of beer cans stacked on a nearby table gave them away. They hooted when she walked in, but she ignored them. Not one of them looked over twenty, and she was looking for an older crowd. The type of men Patricia would have sought out were the type who'd been around and had the war stories to prove it. Cops or soldiers, they were all the same. Old drunks only needed a listening ear and the occasional top-up to recount the horrors they had survived. Proud of the wounds and the toughness they stood for. When in fact they hadn't survived at all.

She found her man at the back of the bar, nursing a beer and scotch chaser as he watched the pool game. She walked the length of the bar and chose a stool several down from his, ignoring him. The bartender, a skinny mass of sinew and bone, was leaning against the wall, watching her. He made no move to approach.

"Give me a Blue," she said.

He shoved himself off the wall, reached beneath the bar and pulled out a can. Without cracking the tab, he plunked it down on the counter.

"I'm looking for a woman," she said to the bartender. "Friend of mine who went missing a couple of weeks ago. She said she was coming up here to see an old friend. Mid-thirties, blond going grey, on the thin side. She looks a bit rough right now. Has this big, ugly-ass black purse with pink daisies on it. She likes her liquor, so I'm hoping she's been in here."

The bartender's expression didn't change, but he lifted his scrawny shoulders in a shrug.

"Thing is," Peters said. "I'm worried about her. We've been through a lot of shit together, and she's not handling it as well as me. She might get in with a nasty crowd."

"What do the cops want with Patti Oliver?" The voice came from the corner. Gravelly from cigarettes and booze.

Peters swung around to stare at the man against the wall. For a moment she was dumbstruck. "Patti Oliver. Yeah, that's her name. Did you see her?"

"Depends."

She picked up her Blue and shifted to the stool next to him. Losing interest, the bartender wandered off towards the front.

"But you saw her. Is she all right?"

"You think I'm an idiot, lady? You come in here at three in the afternoon, as cool as you please, nice outfit, no fear. You got cop branded on your forehead. So I repeat, what do the cops want with Patti Oliver?"

Peters scrutinized him in the semi-darkness. At closer quarters, he was not as old or as far gone as she'd first thought. Amidst his wrinkled, leathery skin, his eyes were clear, and at the moment they appeared to see right through her. With a sigh, she reached into her purse and took out the photos.

"Is this the woman you call Patti Oliver?"

The man spread the pictures on the bar and bent over them in the dim light. After a long look, he shoved them away. "She's dead."

"Murdered."

"Shit."

Peters opened her notebook. "What did you talk to her about?"

"This and that. Her boyfriend that died. How she had a ticket to even the score, right here in this town."

"Even the score. Those were her words? What did she mean?"

"Beats me. She was playing things pretty close to her chest. But she was asking questions about the base, and did I know the guys who served in Croatia. And also the election. Kind of weird, that, wanting to know the background of the guys who were running. I don't follow that shit, but some of the men are pretty excited about it this time. So —"

"Hey, officer!" It was the bartender calling. She looked up to see him standing at the phone near the door. "Your partner called. He wants you to meet him outside ASAP, around the back where you parked the car."

Peters cursed. Moron, she thought, blowing my cover like that. And what the hell is this ASAP shit? Couldn't he wait till I'm done my first stop?

She shoved the photos back into her purse and turned to the guy at the bar. "Hold that thought. I'll be right back once I deal with this. And the next beer's on me."

She stomped out of the dark bar and paused, blinded for a moment by the bright afternoon sun. After getting her bearings, she headed for the car.

Muttering, "Okay, asshole, this had better be good."

FOURTEEN

June 23. Sector West, Croatia.

Dear Kit ... Only eight days till my UN leave and I can't wait to see you, hang out at the farm, watch TV, go to a movie. Man, just to take a walk down the lane without checking for mines! It's been boring here, sitting at the hot dog stand all day. The rules have changed, which is frustrating. We're not supposed to confiscate weapons anymore, we're supposed to ask the belligerents nicely if they'd like to give them up. Like that's going to happen!

So the other day a bunch of Serbs walked in and took all their rifles and grenades out of the cache we had them in, and we couldn't do a fucking thing. I thought the Hammer was going to have a stroke. He's on the radio screaming to the OC, but that's the orders from the new Sector West commander. Jordanian guy. I don't know about this multi-national idea, seems like the Canadians are the only ones who know what we're doing. So of course the Croats start screaming favouritism and they haul out their guns too. And all our hard work getting the place calmed down so you could walk around without shells flying over your heads, that's all going to be down the tubes.

On the bright side, our section beat 3 Section at soccer yesterday. Afterwards at the mess, Sarge did a little dance on the table again. From a strict religious Prairie boy, he's getting to be the life of the party. And another good thing, Fundy has made a real difference to the mines. She finds them better than the engineers, and she gets such a kick out of it. Big smile on her face and her tongue hanging out as she waits for her treat. Yesterday she was tagging along with Mahir and she spotted one buried right on the path he uses every day to get home.

***

SUE PETERS WAS being airlifted to the Ottawa Hospital on advanced life support. By the time the helicopter was scheduled to touch down at seven fifteen, Green had already been on the phone with the military police, the Petawawa OPP and the Pembroke Hospital. He'd spoken to everyone from the first officer on the scene to the doctors who had tried to patch her together. He'd briefed Barbara Devine and prepared a short statement for the press.

He knew everything that had happened from the moment Peters's battered body had been discovered inside an abandoned railway warehouse, but not a damn thing about how she got there. Constable Weiss had been nearly incoherent when questioned by the local police, and doctors had stuffed him full of tranquillizers before packing him into the back of an OPP cruiser and shipping him off to Ottawa.

By seven o'clock, Elgin Street Headquarters was teeming with people. Off-duty officers, on hearing the news, had reported in to learn the latest details, to volunteer for extra duty, or simply to be among their own. Coordination between the various police services involved had now gone up the chain of command to Barbara Devine, but when she phoned down to demand that Green come upstairs to a meeting with herself and the local brass from the military and provincial police services, he refused.

"I've got a critically injured officer landing at the Civic Campus in less than fifteen minutes. That's where I'm needed, Barbara. You guys decide how this is going to be run." He paused as he caught sight of Bob Gibbs pacing back and forth across the squad room, talking to a rapt group of detectives. It looked as if the whole Major Crimes Unit, and quite a few of the other units, had come to commiserate. Nothing was worse than an officer down. These guys needed to be involved. "Just make sure you put me on any joint task force you create."

To her credit, Devine did not protest. It seemed even she understood this was one time when bureaucracy took a back seat. Green hung up, grabbed his jacket and headed out into the squad room to round up Gibbs. Throughout the entire car ride from Elgin Street to the Civic Hospital, the young detective talked non-stop, reviewing over and over the details of the investigation to date. His speculations made no sense, but Green let him talk. Exhaustion and self-recrimination would take over soon enough.

The helicopter was just flying into view when they drove up to the landing site, which sat at the edge of a field across Carling Avenue from the hospital. In the darkness, lights and vehicles appeared to be everywhere. A circle of lights marked the landing pad, and a ground ambulance sat by the tarmac, lights flashing and stretcher ready. Green had the ridiculous thought that it would probably be faster to wheel the stretcher across Carling Avenue to the hospital on foot.

At the entrance to the landing field, a burly ground crew worker flagged him to a stop, ignored Green's badge and waved them over to the parking lot of the hospital emergency department across the street. "You'll have to check in at Admissions, sir," he shouted over the deafening roar of the helicopter. Dust and wind swirled in the air. "They'll want some information."

Green parked in a restricted area closest to the door, slapped a police sticker on the dash and led Gibbs inside to the Admissions Desk in Emergency, which was right next to the ambulance bay. Heavy metal swing doors separated the admissions area from the unloading area, however, so they only caught a fleeting glimpse of Peters's still form as the stretcher whisked by. White coats swirled around her, and a man's voice snapped out her vital signs. The flurry of activity was over as quickly as it blew up, leaving no one left to ask.

Green introduced himself to the admissions clerk and told her he'd like to speak to the doctor in charge as soon as he or she was available. The clerk gave him a brief, distracted nod before returning to her forms. The emergency room was filled with people slumped in chairs along the walls, talking in hushed whispers, reading, or simply staring into space. Several watched Green and Gibbs with idle curiosity.

They never did see an ER physician, but about fifteen minutes later, the air ambulance crew emerged from behind the steel doors and stopped by to give them a report on their way back out to the helicopter. They looked grim.

"She's going straight up to surgery, sir," said the senior paramedic. "The OR was all set up and waiting for her. But I don't want to sugarcoat it. We got her here in very good time, and she had a carotid pulse when the surgical team took her up to the OR, and those are both positives. But she's lost a lot of blood, and she sustained fairly extensive injuries to the head. Some bastard beat her up pretty bad."

Green listened with grim calm. He had already heard about the beating from the Petawawa OPP, but Gibbs's reaction stopped him from asking further details. The young man suddenly swayed on his feet, and Green and the paramedic dived to catch his arms before he slumped to the ground. With practised calm, the paramedic helped him to a chair, forced his head between his knees and ordered Green to get some water.

When Green returned with the water, Gibbs was hunched forward, clutching his head in his hands and rocking from side to side. "I should never have sent her alone. What was I thinking? I should never have sent her alone."

Oh, shit, Green thought, the self-recrimination has started already. "And maybe I should never have gone to Halifax," he interrupted. "But Bob —"

"You should never have put me in charge."

Probably not, once I saw how ruthless the killer was, Green thought, but he forced his own self-doubts out of mind. He dragged out the only platitudes he could think of. Platitudes that had been fed to him six years earlier, and rang as true and as hollow now as they had then. "Bob, these things happen. We're out there in danger every day. We make judgment calls on a wing and a prayer, and sometimes we're wrong."

"But I knew she was inexperienced. I-I just didn't have the balls to tell her no. She wanted it so bad."

"You followed proper procedure; you sent someone with her."

"Another mistake. Where the f-fuck was Weiss when this happened to her?"

Where the fuck indeed, Green thought grimly. The man didn't need to be a major crimes detective to know the basic premise of policing. Officer safety first. Never leave your partner's back exposed. Constable Weiss had a hell of a lot to answer for when he finally made it back to Ottawa, no matter what his mental state.

For now it was a waiting game. The hospital directed them to a more private room up on the surgical floor, and officers drifted in and out in search of news and moral support. As the evening dragged on, one of Gibbs's friends took him down to the cafeteria for some food and Green used the opportunity to duck outside and update Sharon.

The sky was clear, and a hint of frost clouded his breath, but he was glad of the fresh air. He shivered as he sat on the stone curb and filled her in. True to form, Sharon listened and said exactly what he needed to hear. Which was why he loved her, why he had fallen in love with her the first time he'd met her six years earlier, when she'd offered a listening ear to an overworked and overwhelmed sergeant dealing with the worst killing he'd ever encountered.

"The fact she's still in the OR is a good sign, honey," she said now. "It means she's hanging in, and they're stitching her back together bit by bit."

Sucking in the cold, crisp night air, he managed a feeble laugh. "Let's hope they find enough of the parts."

"You always said she was one tough, tenacious broad."

"But so young. So … blind."

"This is not your fault, honey. You can't control every single minute of every single case."

"But the important ones, Sharon. The ones that could get my officers killed. I should control those."

"So you've taken up clairvoyance now, besides trying to control everyone's life?" Her soft chuckle sounded through the phone, but when she resumed, her voice was gentler. "I could come down there and bring you a cup of tea. Give you a hug. Out of view of the troops, of course. On a dark street corner somewhere."

"A cup of tea and a hug would be wonderful. But I can't leave here yet. Things have got to start happening soon." He leaned back against the brick wall, picturing her tender chocolate eyes. "Sorry I missed Shabbat dinner. Did you pick up Dad?"

"Yes. He missed you, but you know how much he adores Hannah. He'd pinched her cheeks raw by the end of the night."

"He's the only one who could get away with that." He felt a bittersweet pang. Hannah had been enchanted by her grandfather from the moment she'd laid eyes on him, but then her grandfather hadn't deserted her sixteen years ago. He banished the twinge of envy; their domestic struggles seemed so inconsequential while Peters lay inside, dancing with death.

"Well, give her forty years, and you'll have earned the right too," she said.

He laughed as he hung up, his spirits lifted. Next he put in a call to update Barbara Devine and Gaetan Larocque, both of whom were still tied up in the meeting with the senior brass. When he returned to the waiting room, there was still no sign of the doctor, but there were half a dozen familiar faces. Gibbs was back, looking slightly less fragile. Perhaps some anger was beginning to take hold, for he marched straight over to Green. His jaw was tight.

"Weiss is here. Asked how she was, then walked off. Not a word of explanation. Not even an apology."

"Did you ask him?"

"I can b-barely talk to the guy."

"Where is he now?"

Gibbs nodded to a cluster of chairs at the far end of the room. Green turned to see a man leaning against the wall in the corner. His arms were crossed and his chin thrust out, as if in defiance. Green squared his shoulders and was just preparing to do battle when the swinging doors opened and two doctors emerged. They were dressed in stained hospital scrubs, and exhaustion was etched in their faces. The older, a man in his fifties with a polished bald pate and cadaverous cheekbones, introduced himself as Doctor Vargas and asked if the next of kin was present. To Green's surprise, a young man rose from the corner. He was a male clone of Sue Peters, down to the frizzy red hair and the riot of freckles across his cheeks. Beneath the freckles, he was the colour of bleached flour as he approached the doctors.

"I'm her brother, Mark Peters. How is she?"

Vargas inclined his head noncommittally. "She's a strong, healthy woman, and that's got her this far. But her condition is still critical, and it will be touch and go for the next forty-eight hours. There are a few things we won't know until she regains consciousness. If she does."

"If?"

"She's suffered significant trauma to the brain, and with brain injuries of this type, it can be weeks, even months, before we see the extent of the damage."

A collective groan rose from the officers who had clustered around to hear.

"So you're saying she could be … a vegetable?" Mark managed. His voice quavered.

"Let's get her through the next forty-eight hours before we worry about that."

Dr. Vargas went on to detail all the test results and surgical procedures they had performed, but after a while,

Green's mind glazed over. It really did sound as if they'd had to stitch her back together bit by bit.

After the doctor's departure, friends and colleagues gathered in clumps to talk in hushed tones, and Green noticed that Weiss was no longer there. Curious, he set off in search, starting with the corridor next to where the man had been standing. That corridor ended in a bank of doors, all of which were locked.

He retraced his steps and tried another corridor, peeking into rooms along the way. Linen supplies, bathrooms, offices and more doors marked "authorized personnel only." The corridor jogged and twisted at unexpected points, following the shape of the aging, multi-winged building. It came to an abrupt halt at a heavy steel door marked "exit."

Green yanked open the door and peered down a flight of iron stairs into the semi-gloom. There, sitting in the middle of the bottom stair, was Constable Weiss, hunched over, staring at his shoes. He didn't stir when Green clanged down the stairs, didn't even raise his head, but Green saw that his whole body was vibrating. Green's anger softened a touch.

"Jeff? What's going on?"

"Needed some air."

"I'm Mike Green, by the way."

Weiss gave a strangled grunt. "I know who you are. Come to tell me I'm a fuck-up, a moron, a disgrace to the uniform?"

"What happened?"

"I told all that to the cops up in Petawawa."

Green's anger crashed back. He grabbed the man's chin and jerked his head up to face him. "Listen, asshole, I don't give a shit who else you told. I'm her superior officer, and you're damn well going to tell me how you almost got her killed."

To his surprise, Weiss's eyes flooded with tears. He twisted his head away and dashed his knuckles across his cheeks. "Fuck," he whispered. "Fuck, fuck, fuck!"

"Talk to me!"

"I can't." Weiss sucked in his breath and wrestled for control. "I don't know what to say! I should have known it was a crazy idea, but she was the boss. No, that's no excuse. I should have stopped her."

"You should have backed her up!" Green thundered.

"It was a routine canvass. I thought she had everything under control."

"Canvass of what?"

"Bars, restaurants … I took half, she took half."

"Bars! Why the hell were you canvassing in bars?"

"We were trying to track the dead woman's movements. Find out what she was after."

"So you left Peters alone in bars?"

"It was three o'clock in the fucking afternoon!" Weiss shot back. "In a two-bit little town, not New York City."

"A two-bit town that might just harbour our murderer."

"Well, I — we — didn't think of that."

"You goddamn well should have!"

Abruptly Weiss sagged back against the step. Tears brimmed in his eyes again as he nodded his head up and down. "You're right, you're right. God, what a mess." He plunged his face into his hands and began to rock.

Green watched him in silence for a few minutes. Weiss's reactions puzzled him. Not the grief itself, not the guilt, not even the flashes of defensive anger. But the extremes of them all, and the erratic swings from one to another like a man ricocheting free fall from one violent feeling to the next. Was the man unstable? Or was he faking it?

Green squatted in front of him, willing him to return to the real world. He spoke grimly. "Jeff, tell me what you do know."

Weiss stopped rocking but didn't raise his head. Green waited, feeling the seconds tick by in the dank, ill-lit stairwell. Finally, Weiss heaved a deep, shuddering sigh and spoke through his hands.

"She dropped me at this bar and told me to meet her at the car by the hotel where the bus station was. There were only twelve places to canvass — the hotel, three shitty restaurants, a fast food joint, a convenience store, a couple of offices and banks. I was done my six in about half an hour, so I found the car and waited outside it for her to show up."

"Why didn't you go look for her?"

He scrubbed his face and lifted his head. His voice grew stronger. "She didn't want me to blow her cover."

"*Her* cover?"

"Yeah, we were supposed to be looking for a lost friend. In my case my girlfriend, in hers just an old friend."

"You mean you didn't identify yourselves as police officers?"

"No."

"Jesus Christ," Green muttered.

"Yeah." Weiss pressed his eyes closed. "God, am I fucked."

"You're fucked? Sue Peters may be dead!"

"I know, and believe me, if I could trade places with her, I would."

"Too easy, Weiss. Go on. You were waiting at the car, and…?"

"When over an hour passed, I started to get worried. So I went to look for her, and she wasn't in any of the places. But the bartender in the first place said her partner had called to meet her outside, so she'd left."

"The bartender said her partner called? So he knew she was a cop?"

"Yeah, apparently. Anyway —"

"Did you tell the Petawawa police about that supposed phone call? They can check it out."

He hesitated. "I don't remember. I think I told them pretty well what I've told you. Anyway, I went back to the car and that's when I noticed the smell of pepper spray. I followed it till I found her in the warehouse about a hundred feet from the car."

The OPP had already reported finding an empty cannister of pepper spray near Peters's body, but no other weapons. Her Glock had been found stashed in her car. Green pictured the young woman fending off her attacker with the only weapon at her disposal. At least the silly fool had had that; otherwise she'd be dead.

"Did you see anyone else in the vicinity? Or leaving the area?"

Weiss shook his head. "The whole place was dead. And to be honest, once I found Sue, all I could think of was the 911 call. And afterwards, how she was lying there bleeding all that time I was waiting at the car. Christ, I'm such a moron."

Green already knew that the OPP's preliminary street canvass of the area around the hotel had yielded nothing. Ridiculous, Green thought, that a woman could be assaulted at three o'clock on a workday afternoon, near the central crossroads of the town, and no one heard or saw a thing.

"We'll send our own guys up there tomorrow," Green said, then glanced at his watch. Two a.m. "Well, at first light. We'll be working closely with the local OPP, and you can rest assured we'll comb every inch of the area and interview everyone who passes through that part of town."

Privately, Green doubted the attacker had been careless enough to leave them much to go on. He didn't for one minute believe this was an opportunistic assault with a sexual intent. This was Patricia's killer; a smart, calculating man who had planned his attack with care. He had deliberately targeted an investigating cop. Either he had phoned the bartender once he knew Sue Peters was in the bar, or the bartender had phoned him with the tip. But there were two nagging questions about the whole scenario. One, was Jeff Weiss telling the truth?

And two, if he was, why hadn't the killer targeted him too?

***

When Green arrived back at the waiting room, most of the police officers had finally drifted away to work or to sleep. A couple had stayed to keep Mark Peters company during his vigil, and one detective sat beside Gibbs, who was dozing. He signalled Green to one side and asked if it was true that Ottawa was to have no part in the investigation. Appalled, Green managed a hasty assurance to the contrary before ducking outside to put in a call to the station.

Gaetan Larocque's voice gave him away before he'd even said two words. He cleared his throat anxiously. "The agreement we have is that the OPP handles the case up there, sir. It's their jurisdiction."

"And who the fuck agreed —" Green stopped himself as the answer came to him. Barbara Devine, of course, the queen of org charts and rules. Of form over substance every time. He forced himself to sound reasonable. "Okay, I'll fix that in the morning. Meanwhile you can start freeing up some officers —"

"We don't have the experienced manpower available right now, sir. Not to do a really thorough job. That's what Superintendent Devine explained."

We don't have the manpower available to investigate an assault on one of our own officers? Green thought, barely believing what he was hearing. He wanted to throttle the woman. How could she even think that, let alone justify it! Never mind that it was true, that the squad was stretched beyond reason by the three murders already on its plate. When it came to one of their own, everybody would do double duty without complaint.

But this was his problem, not Larocque's, so Green held his tongue until he could get rid of the man. Marshalling his arguments, he punched in Devine's extension and listened as it rang through the empty room. With each ring, his outrage mounted, so that by the time her voice mail kicked in, he nearly hurled his cellphone against the wall.

"Barbara," he said tersely. "No way we're staying out of the Petawawa investigation, even if I go up there myself on my own time!"

Shoving his cellphone into his pocket, he went back inside the hospital. Constable Weiss had not returned to the waiting room, but Bob Gibbs was awake. He rose and lurched towards Green at a clumsy shuffle, as if the effort to coordinate his gangly limbs was now beyond him.

"Any news about catching the bastard? Sir?"

Green tried to sound encouraging. "Everyone's working on it. It's early yet. Any news here?"

"Ident was in to take samples from under her fingernails. They were pretty clean, Sergeant Paquette said, but we need only one hair or a few skin cells to get DNA. And the g-gynaecologist was in to check for sexual ..." Gibbs broke off, his composure cracking at the thought. He struggled on.

"Whoever assaulted her didn't … There were no signs of …" Speech deserted him again, and he gulped for breath.

"That's good," Green interjected, hoping to forestall a complete collapse. "This had nothing to do with sexual assault."

Wordlessly, Gibbs bobbed his head up and down. Then his gaze shifted behind Green, and his face lit with relief. Green turned to see Brian Sullivan framed in the doorway. The big detective was bleary-eyed and dressed in a rumpled suit as if he'd come straight off a twelve-hour shift. His gaze was fixed on Gibbs, and his expression was grave. Gibbs walked straight to him, and without a word, Sullivan engulfed him in a powerful embrace. Over Gibbs's shoulder, his eyes met Green's.

"Is she dead?" he mouthed.

Green shook his head, and Sullivan tightened his grip. "She'll make it, Bob. Giving up is not in Peters's repertoire, you know that."

Gibbs drew back, his eyes red. When he raised his fist to dry them surreptitiously, Sullivan pretended not to notice. He clapped his broad hand on Green's shoulder. "Good to see you, Mike."

"I'm glad you came." Green fought an unexpected lump in his own throat. As always, his old friend filled the room with hope and confidence. God, he'd missed the man!

"How is she?"

Green glanced at Gibbs, who had slumped back into his chair. He looked drained. Beyond talk. "I could use a coffee. Let's go downstairs."

Taking a corner table in the completely deserted hospital cafeteria, Green gave Sullivan the highlights of Peters's case. The big man stretched his long legs out and listened without interruption, his eyes fixed on a distant point in space.

It felt just like old times when they were partners in Major Crimes. In the face of Sullivan's calm pragmatism, Green felt the ropes of tension in his gut slowly loosen, releasing feelings he had kept under tight lock. He twirled his coffee cup restlessly.

"The worst part of it is that I never really liked the kid."

"She was a royal pain in the ass," Sullivan replied.

"Yeah. But maybe I didn't protect her enough, didn't consider her safety enough, because I didn't like her."

"That's bullshit, Mike. You weren't even in town when she took off to Petawawa."

"But maybe I should have been. Bottom line, the kid's hanging by a thread, and we're stretched so thin that Devine has relinquished the whole investigation up there to the OPP. I told her I'd go up and do the damn case myself."

A slow smile twitched across Sullivan's lips. "I might have an offer neither she nor the Chief can refuse."

Green cocked his head. After twenty years on the streets together, he knew Sullivan inside out. Knew what that smile meant, yet he barely let himself hope.

"I'm going crazy in Strategic Planning, Mike. I could ask my Inspector for a temporary assignment back to Major Crimes, just to plug your holes in manpower and provide some experience on the ground. Under the circumstances, the brass would be crazy to refuse." His blue eyes twinkled. "That is, if you'd like some company working the streets of Petawawa."

FIFTEEN

SULLIVAN WAS ALREADY stationed outside Green's office when Green arrived the next morning. The two men had finally left the hospital at three in the morning, after deciding that Sue Peters would be better served by their being rested and ready to work on her behalf in the morning rather than maintaining a hospital vigil through the dead of night.

Green had managed only three hours of restless sleep before thoughts of the case drove him back to the office, and he was surprised to find Sullivan there ahead of him, sporting a fresh shave and a spotless suit. Green noted that in the past six months he had added a few grey hairs to his sandy blond crewcut and a pound or two to his footballer frame, but his blue eyes crinkled with an excitement Green hadn't seen in years. Before the grind of Major Crimes and the disappointments of lost promotions had worn him down.

Inside the office, Sullivan propped his size thirteen feet on the corner of Green's desk as if he'd never been away. "It's all stamped and approved, all the way up to the Deputy Chief," he announced.

"When do you begin?"

"This instant. Fill me in on the case she was investigating."

It took Green half an hour to sketch the details of the Patricia Ross case and Peters's role in it, ending with a summary of his own confrontation with Jeff Weiss. As he spoke, his doubts of last night came back to him. He shook his head back and forth. "Something is funny about that guy. I'm not sure what it is. He was hanging around the first morning when we found the body, and Gibbs says he asked to be assigned to the case. He's a cocky bastard, and I thought he was just looking for a way up the ladder, but after his utter screw-up with Peters ..."

"He's not a Major Crimes detective, Mike. Maybe he thought this was the way we work."

"They were in a strange town, going into sleazy bars, tracking a murderer, for God's sake. Did he have to be a rocket scientist?"

"Peters didn't see a problem."

"Well, Peters is ..." Green broke off, remembering the young woman clinging to life by nothing but a few hundred sutures. He left his harsh words unsaid.

"Yeah," Sullivan agreed. "So what are you thinking, Mike? That this Weiss guy is somehow implicated? That he left her to get killed? Why?"

Green shrugged. "I'm not thinking anything. I just wonder who the hell is this guy? What's his background?"

Sullivan's eyes narrowed. "So you want us to investigate one of our own?"

"Quietly. Unofficially. Nose around, maybe have a peek at his file."

Sullivan sat thinking a moment, his broad face deadpan. "Unofficially. Sure, we'll just add that to the list. Find out what Peters discovered in Petawawa, get the goods on the peacekeepers Oliver and MacDonald served with in

Yugoslavia, figure out the whole Halifax connection and how it fits in with Patricia Ross's death —"

"Which means finding out who she had a drink with here in Ottawa. Gibbs was working on that."

"Jeez, Mike. This case has more tentacles than an octopus!"

Green nodded. "And it's hard to know which tentacle to grab first, especially now that Peters and probably Gibbs are out of commission. Anyway, I can do the inquiry into Constable Weiss more easily than you. I'll just have a casual chat with his staff sergeant."

"Don't underestimate Gibbsie. You know what he's like when he's on a mission, and right now I'd lay odds he'll turn over every rock to catch the bastard who did this to Sue." He reached across with his foot and nudged Green's door open wide enough for them to see out into the squad room. Sure enough, Gibbs was bent over his computer, his eyes fixed on the screen. His suit was rumpled, and his features drooped with fatigue, but his fingers were flying over the keyboard.

After a moment, he rose, loped over to the printer to retrieve a sheaf of papers and headed for Green's office. The sight of Sullivan in the guest chair stopped him at the door. When Green explained Sullivan's special assignment to help with the Petawawa angle of the case, Gibbs looked overwhelmingly relieved. He swallowed convulsively, and his Adam's apple jumped as he struggled for words. Sullivan rescued him.

"What have you got, Bob?" he asked, nodding to the papers in his hand.

Gibbs plunked the printouts down on Green's desk. "Some information from Captain Ulrich at National Defence, sir. At least what he has so far. Photos of Colonel Hamm and Sergeant Sawranchuk, and details on some of the guys in his section. Three are still with the Princess Pats in Edmonton, two are overseas in Kandahar, and two are back in the reserves, going to university."

"Where?"

Gibbs flipped through the papers. "One at Queen's, one at Memorial in Newfoundland."

Which is a short hop to Halifax, but a long way from Ottawa, Green thought. "Well, Kingston is less than a two-hour drive, so the Queen's guy could easily do a round trip to Ottawa or Petawawa in a day. Ask Ulrich to send us the Queen's guy's photo ASAP, and we'll send the three photos down to Kate McGrath in Halifax for her to show around."

"And I'll take the three up with me to Petawawa," Sullivan said. "Sue Peters obviously stirred up someone when she was blundering around in the bars." He looked thoughtful. "Anything useful in her notebook?"

Gibbs jerked back as if hit by an electric shock. "I forgot about that! Nobody's seen it. It wasn't in her personal effects when they handed them over to us."

Green's temper flared. A missing notebook should have been a major red flag to the investigators on the scene. The look of disbelief on Sullivan's face mirrored his own, but the big detective was diplomatic. "Get them to keep looking. Meanwhile, we'd better get everything we can about her activities from that constable who was with her."

Which will be fuck-all, Green thought, since the idiot wasn't with her when she was traipsing around the bars. Suddenly a thought struck him.

He leaned forward, his instincts screaming. "The notebook was probably what the killer was after all along! He was tracking her movements in Petawawa and realized she'd learned something to make her a threat." He swung on Gibbs. "Who knew she was up there?"

Gibbs scrunched up his face in an effort to concentrate through his exhaustion and fear. He counted on his fingers. "The base commander, Colonel Lyttle. The military police captain and the OPP detachment commander —"

"And all their men, of course," Green added impatiently. "It would have been part of their daily briefing."

Gibbs nodded bleakly. "And C-Colonel Hamm. That's it, I think. Besides us."

"And who among us?" Green said quietly.

Gibbs stared at him in uncomprehending silence for a moment. "My-myself. The staff sergeant, a couple of guys on the squad."

"And Constable Weiss."

"Well — yes. Constable Weiss."

***

July 20, 1993. On some fucking road somewhere in Croatia.

We're stuck at another roadblock while the CO argues with another drunken militia leader who thinks he's a general. This has been the worst day, bar none, of the whole tour. I'd only been back from leave two days when Sarge wakes us all up at four a.m. "We're moving out, pack all your kit, because nobody knows where the hell we're going or when we'll be back." So I asked if we could take Fundy and Sarge thinks we can squeeze her in the APC, but the Hammer says not a chance. Can't be tripping over a dog when we're trying to get out in a hurry, and she might bark when we're trying to sneak through somewhere. The whole camp loves her and all, but rules are rules. Mahir says he'll take her, and I figured he'd take good care of her.

She must have been distracted by all the activity, because when the APCs started pulling out, she starts running after us. Mahir is calling her but she cuts a corner and doesn't see the fucking mine. Blew her twenty feet at least. I can see she's still alive, but the Hammer won't let me go to her. "We're on the road, soldier, he says, we're in formation and we've got twenty-four hours to get to our destination." Wherever the fuck that is.

So the last thing I see is Mahir carrying her towards his house, and I'll probably never know what happened to her. She was a brave little soldier, says the Hammer, and I want to kill the guy.

***

Sergeant Kate McGrath came on duty that Saturday morning to the news of an assault on an Ottawa police officer in Petawawa. She stared at the email bulletin in dismay. Petawawa. What were the chances that two Ottawa Police investigations were taking place in Petawawa at the same time? Nil. The killer was at it again, and this time not even the police were immune. This killer was turning more deadly and desperate with each passing day.

She thought of phoning Mike, but stopped herself. She had nothing to report and nothing to contribute to the case. What could she say? I'm sorry, and I hope you're holding up all right? That was a ridiculous luxury. Mike was probably up to his eyeballs in crises, trying to coordinate the investigation and respond to the dozens of pressures from the media, the brass and the public at large. No matter how much he might need a supportive word, that was not her place.

He had a wife, after all.

She set her jaw, squared her shoulders and forced herself to think. The best way to help him was to follow up on the case down here, where it had all begun. She felt as if she was in a holding pattern while she waited for details on Daniel Oliver's military contacts. Yet something had stirred up the case ten years after Oliver's murder. Something had happened to set Patricia Ross on the road to Ottawa. Just a tenth anniversary epiphany? Or something more concrete — an encounter, a discovery, a stray fact?

McGrath sat bolt upright. The newspaper! In all that had happened, she'd forgotten the newspaper in Patricia Ross's apartment, with its missing Page 10. It might not be much, it might just be the light-fingered tenant from the apartment below, as the landlord claimed, but it was a place to start. A thread to tug, that might unravel the entire web of secrets.

She clipped on her police belt, snatched up her coffee, and headed for the door. Back issues of the Halifax *Chronicle-Herald* were kept at the public library on Spring Garden Road, a few short blocks from the police station. The chip wagons were out in force along the street, and the air was laden with the smell of stale oil and vinegar. She had to dodge the buskers and the Tai Chi enthusiasts to get in the front door. Inside, a flash of her badge and a quick word sent the young librarian in charge scurrying to the nearby shelves where the latest issues were stacked. He returned with the *Sunday Herald* of April 9th and pointed to a long reading table. Only one other reader was there, and he didn't even look up from the notes he was taking.

The paper was full of election campaign news, most of it local, and she flipped rapidly through the results of polls and the profiles of candidate hopefuls until she came to Page 10. "Top Ten Ridings to Watch," announced the headlines, and below were brief capsules of federal ridings identified by political pundits as either traditional swing ridings or ones where candidates could pull off a surprising upset. The article profiled each riding and the main candidates in the race. In each case the journalist, whom Kate recognized as a born and bred New Democrat, had predicted a winner.

The whole article seemed rather more intellectual than the reading Kate would have predicted of Patricia, but she scanned the ridings curiously. Two were in British Columbia, which was way too far from either Halifax or Ottawa to be of interest. Two were in the Greater Toronto Area, representing the ethnically diverse communities that surrounded the metropolis. Surely Toronto was still too far away. Patricia had chosen Ottawa for a reason, yet none of the ridings were in the Ottawa area. Her hopes jumped when she found one in Nova Scotia, but after reading the article, she couldn't for the life of her see how it fitted in with old murders, the military, peacekeepers, or Ottawa.

The caption for the next riding stopped her in her tracks, however. *Military is wildcard in conservative Ontario riding.* She studied the map of the riding. It sat just beyond the northwestern extremity of the City of Ottawa, and more importantly, right near the centre of it, perched on the edge of the Ottawa River, was the town of Petawawa.

Her heart raced with excitement as she scanned the article. The riding was currently held by a hard-line Conservative and was comprised largely of rural, socially conservative voters. It was generally regarded as a safe Conservative win, and yet the journalist was predicting a tight race and a possible Liberal upset because of strong support among the military for the local Liberal candidate, John Blakeley. Who was himself an ex-army colonel and a highly experienced and decorated veteran of numerous overseas missions. Blakeley's photo showed a man with a frank, steady gaze.

"Colonel Blakeley speaks to the hearts and minds of soldiers in this riding," said his campaign manager, Roger Atkinson, reached at Blakeley's campaign office in Petawawa.

"His firsthand understanding of military issues would be an invaluable asset in the halls of power." As an interesting aside, the journalist noted, Roger Atkinson, born in Sheet Harbour and educated at Dalhousie University, brings a local Nova Scotia connection to this most exciting race.

With a whoop of joy, McGrath jumped up and got the librarian to make her a dozen copies of the page. Barely pausing to thank him, she raced out of the room with the pages shoved under her arm and sprinted back to the station. At her desk, as she punched in Green's number, she tried to catch her breath and collect her thoughts so that she could sound coherent when he answered. But after four rings, his voice mail came on. She cursed.

"Mike! Oh, damn it! I've caught a huge break. Check your fax!"

***

Leaving Sullivan to prepare for the trip to Petawawa, Green had headed over to the hospital, where Sue Peters remained in the ICU, hooked up to tubes and looking uncharacteristically fragile and still. He hated hospitals and managed to stay only thirty seconds, long enough to lose the battle with other memories from long ago, of the grey, birdlike figure of his mother dwarfed among the pillows and machines that had escorted her to her death. He'd always hoped it was painless at the end, at least for her.

But Peters wasn't going to die, he told himself over and over as he looked down at her. The doctors were promising nothing, and the nurses were gently hinting at the worst, but Green shrugged them off. She was too young and brazen to be silenced this way. She would awaken to tell the police all they needed to know, and they would nail this murderous bastard for good.

He left the hospital fired with new resolve and with a long list of inquiries to be followed up. En route back to the station, he phoned Constable Jeff Weiss's staff sergeant to arrange a meeting later in the morning.

"Good man," said Staff Sergeant Vaillancourt once Green had explained his request. "He's pretty new to General Assignment, so I don't know much about his background, but I'll bring the file. He had some problems with insubordination sometimes, but I could always trust him to think on his feet."

Right, Green thought grimly as he hung up. Like this time, *putz?* As one of the NCOs under his command, Green had known Vaillancourt for several years, but the man's police instincts had never filled him with confidence. Green suspected he would have to do some additional detective work of his own to get the real story on Jeff Weiss. Just one more small task to add to his pile. Next he phoned Frank Corelli of the *Ottawa Sun* for an update on his anonymous news source.

"Not a word since that botched meet," Frank said. "She's either a crank, or she's gone to ground. Maybe something about the set-up spooked her."

Green pondered Frank's words as he pulled into the parking lot of the station. The latter theory made a lot of sense, but even if the woman had gone to ground, he needed to find her. Now more than ever. If she really had seen Patricia Ross's killer, she might be the only person who could stop him.

As he parked, signed in and waited for the elevator, his thoughts kept drifting back to Twiggy. She had been in the vicinity at the time of the murder, she was clever enough to know how to use her knowledge to her own advantage, and she was just jaded and fearless enough to do so. Yet Twiggy, despite her relentless path to self-destruction, had an instinct for survival. Never again would she let some bastard try to dictate the terms of her exit from this world. If Twiggy had caught even a whiff of trouble, she'd be gone.

Or so he hoped. But she was also old, fat and sick. Not to mention she was up against a calculating, determined killer who didn't hesitate to target a cop. Indeed, if Twiggy did know something, Green needed to find her for her own safety as much as for her knowledge of the case. Yet Twiggy would never co-operate with any of the police officers he could assign to look for her. She hated cops, courts, judges, social workers and just about any official representative of the society that had failed her. If anyone was going to find Twiggy and get her to talk, it had to be him.

The unhappy realization came to him on the elevator trip upstairs. He really couldn't afford to take off up to Petawawa and leave all these crises simmering here. The last time he'd done that, one of his officers had nearly died.

By the time he got off the elevator, he'd decided to send Gibbs along with Sullivan instead. The young detective deserved as much. The squad room was nearly deserted, but Gibbs was hard at work reviewing reports on the canvass of downtown Ottawa bars. No doubt sifting each word for a nugget of information that might trip up their killer. Green told him to round up Sullivan and meet him in his office.

Inside his office, he looked at the pile of papers on his desk and the furious blinking of his phone. No matter how many times he checked his message box, there were always new ones. With a sigh, he flicked the machine on speaker phone so he could listen as he sifted through his paperwork. Several calls were from the media and fellow officers, asking for news or volunteering information.

Then the voice of Kate McGrath broke through, breathy and excited. Check your fax! He pawed through the papers on his desk. What huge break? Had she already ID'd one of the military photos?

Papers scattered to the floor, but no fax. He dashed outside to the fax machine and snatched up the wad of waiting papers. Cursing the office inefficiency, he scanned them until he came to the one from Kate. Not an ID of a photo, but a page from a newspaper, with several lines highlighted. He skimmed these, then the whole article, and fell back down in his chair with a thud.

Good God, what was this? Another twist? Another tentacle? How did all this fit in with old peacekeeping secrets and a ten-year old murder? Or was it a red herring, its significance only peripheral to the investigation. He was still puzzling over it when Gibbs and Sullivan walked into the squad room. Silently Green handed Sullivan the fax.

The big detective's eyebrows shot up as he read it. "Well, well, well. Politics gets into the act."

"It could have nothing to do with politics. This may be how Patricia Ross discovered the whereabouts of Roger Atkinson, who was a witness to her fiancé's murder."

"You going to warn Devine, just in case? This could get even hotter than the military connection."

Green shook his head. If they were ever going to learn anything from Blakeley and Atkinson, stealth was of the essence. Barbara Devine didn't do stealth. "Not until you've had a go at them up in Petawawa, see if you can make a connection."

Sullivan looked startled and opened his mouth as if to speak, but stopped himself. He glanced at Gibbs instead. "Can you dig up all the background you can get on Blakeley and Atkinson? I need some information before I go head to head with them."

Gibbs nodded, and as Sullivan continued to look at him, he jumped to his feet. "Now, sir?"

Sullivan checked his watch. "Now. I'll be rolling into Petawawa about two p.m., so that gives you less than three hours."

Once Gibbs had loped back outside, Sullivan nudged the door gently shut with his toe. "You're not coming with me to Petawawa?"

Reluctantly Green shook his head. "I want nothing better, believe me. But I can't justify it. We don't need two experienced field officers on this, and there's just too much happening down here for me to take off. I should never have gone to Halifax. And now, with an officer down and all the staff up in arms, they need me to be here."

Sullivan eyed him shrewdly, as if he knew what the decision had cost him. "Good call."

"I figured you could take Gibbs."

"I need him on background and file coordination. No one works those computers better than Bob."

"Well, there are several officers volunteering for extra duty —"

Sullivan slapped the desk with his broad palm, making the scattered papers jump. "I know just who to take."

"Who?"

"Jeff Weiss."

Green stared at him. Besides the fact that Weiss was a physical and emotional basket case, the man's actions were suspicious. When he said as much, Sullivan shrugged.

"All the more reason to take him. To keep an eye on him and see what he does. Plus the guy's been up there already with Sue, and he knows what they've already covered."

"So take his notes —"

"His notes aren't worth shit — he hardly wrote a thing apparently — but it should be all in his head. I think he's the perfect partner to take along."

Green mulled over the idea uneasily. Sullivan's proposal made sense, and if he hadn't already had one officer downed by this killer, he probably wouldn't be hesitating.

"Okay, get him up here," he said finally. "But Brian … Watch your back."

Sullivan reached across Green's desk for the phone and called down to the duty sergeant in General Assignment. The conversation was short and terse. Sullivan jotted down a number before hanging up.

"He's not in today. Called in sick."

"Which he probably is," Green replied with relief. "He was up half the night, in pretty rough shape."

"Still … I could phone him at home."

"Where he's probably sleeping one off. Face it, Brian, he'll be no good to you." He nodded towards his door. "Take one of the guys outside."

With a sigh, Sullivan hauled himself to his feet. "Okay, I'll take Luc Leblanc. But I'd like to meet this Weiss guy some time. Get my own read on him."

"Get in line, my friend."

SIXTEEN

JOHN BLAKELEY'S POPULARITY was visible long before Sullivan and Leblanc hit the outskirts of Petawawa. Large red billboards began to pop up on businesses and retirement bungalows amid the forest of Tory blue, announcing "John Blakeley — a Voice for You." The man's picture conveyed a mass of contradictions. His battered face looked like he'd taken on all the warlords in Afghanistan singlehandedly, and a jagged scar bisected his left eyebrow. But his thick white hair was swept into perfect place across his high forehead, and his prim smile looked like a kindly preacher trying to hustle his flock into line. Odder still, a clear, no-nonsense intelligence shone in his deep-set eyes.

Sullivan thought the eyes were likely the true measure of the man, whereas the smile and the hair were the work of Liberal Party spin doctors who thought he looked too scary in his warrior guise.

As he passed through the struggling farmsteads of the Ottawa Valley, Sullivan had to block out his own aversion to the place. The sparse, rocky landscape fostered a fierce combination of pride, independence and bitterness among those who hung on there. "This Land is Our Land; Back off, Government" warned the huge signs staked in fields along the roadsides. He should have felt pride and sympathy for the families who clung to their land in defiance of bureaucratic red tape and urban ignorance. But for Sullivan, who had grown up in one of them, it evoked memories of isolation and helplessness, drunken violence and wanton neglect. Of starving and hiding and never knowing when he was safe. He'd been eighteen and on the first bus out of town after high school before he ever felt safe.

The red Liberal signs signalled the invasion of another culture, not based on the land or the seasons, but on the military, whose loyalty depended on who had the power, the purse strings, and the vision to see the world their way. John Blakeley was one of their own.

Sullivan felt his adrenaline pump as they drew closer to their destination. Six months, he thought. Six months since he'd felt the excitement of a case, of following up leads and tracking down a bad guy. Of doing something more worthwhile than drawing up staffing plans. What the hell had he been thinking when he'd taken the transfer to Strategic Planning?

He'd been thinking about the next rung on the ladder, the next notch in his belt, the prestige and pay of a staff sergeant's rank. He'd been thinking about the exhaustion and humiliation of his twenty unappreciated years fighting society's bottom feeders in Major Crimes. He'd been burned out, pure and simple. He'd lost sight of the camaraderie and the sense of triumph when they closed a case. He'd forgotten the novel and unexpected twists of each new day. But damn it, it felt good to be back. This was why he'd become a cop, and this is where he'd always belonged.

When they turned off the Trans-Canada Highway and headed towards the centre of Petawawa, he instructed Leblanc to pull up his email on the laptop and check for

Gibbs's reports on Blakeley and Atkinson. He'd felt bad leaving Gibbs behind at the station, poring over his computer yet again, while others went on the adventure. Perhaps the trip would have been good for him.

His guilt disappeared when he saw Gibbs's reports, which were much shorter than usual. The poor kid was in shock, and in no shape for field work. Sullivan pulled into a gas station out of sight of the Blakeley Campaign headquarters, sent Leblanc out to do the fill-up and swivelled the laptop towards him. The reports were full of typos and oversights the meticulous detective rarely made, and Sullivan felt a twinge of sympathy that the young detective couldn't be home giving himself some TLC.

John Blakeley was a local boy born and bred in Renfrew in 1953, the son of an Anglican minister. He had attended Kingston's Royal Military College and graduated as a civil engineer in 1975. Last summer, after thirty years in the army, he'd retired as a full colonel, having spent the last two years on the staff of the army's top general at National Defence Headquarters in Ottawa. His military record looked impressive to Sullivan's untrained eye. Before this last stint, he'd spent two years at UN headquarters in New York, working with the UN High Commission on Refugees as an expert on the delivery of humanitarian aid. Prior to that he'd served as a military observer and as a staff advisor to peacekeeping operations in six different countries.

The perfect poster boy for the new military, thought Sullivan. He combined a soldier's discipline with an intelligence and sensitivity that allowed him to navigate the diplomatic minefield of international affairs. He'd been married twice and now lived with his second wife in a home just outside Petawawa on the Ottawa River. Gibbs had provided the address, but Sullivan figured that in the middle of a work day he'd have more luck finding the man at his campaign headquarters. Besides, he wanted a crack at Roger Atkinson as well. Perhaps even more, for as Green had pointed out, Atkinson may have been the one Patricia Ross was after.

Gibbs had had less luck tracing Atkinson's background, probably because the man was not nearly such a public figure. Reporters were all over Blakeley, but no one seemed interested in the man planning the battle strategy behind the scenes. Roger Atkinson had been born in Sheet Harbour, Nova Scotia in 1970 and had a short stint in personnel with Halifax City Hall before picking up stakes and moving to Pembroke, Petawawa's neighbouring town, in 1996. Although details were sketchy, he'd worked first in personnel and later in public relations for various transport or supply firms in Eastern Ontario. His involvement with politics seemed to start when he did some lobbying of a prominent Ottawa MP, which led to working in the man's constituency office and later on his campaign. As far as Sullivan could see, Atkinson was a nobody from nowhere who had parlayed a small pencil-pushing job into a major source of influence, with the potential to make or break party fortunes.

The two detectives found the campaign office without difficulty. It was a nondescript storefront that took up almost half of a small strip mall on Petawawa's main road, but Blakeley's workers had livened it up by emblazoning his name across the entire outside facade in massive red letters. Nice touch, Atkinson, Sullivan thought as he pushed open the glass door. Inside was a large rectangular room filled with volunteers who were hunched over lists at makeshift desks, working the phones. Lawn signs, posters, leaflets, T-shirts and party hats were stacked high on shelves around the room, all with the now familiar red and white colour scheme. Sullivan scanned the room for the man in the poster. No such luck, but a couple of private offices at the rear caught his eye, so he headed that way.

A woman leaped up to block his path. She barely reached his chest, but she faced him down like a pitbull. Her blue eyes challenged his. "Are you a new volunteer?"

Sullivan suppressed a smile. With his linebacker bulk and his frank stare, people rarely mistook him for anything but a cop, but perhaps in this crowd he looked like an off-duty sergeant major. He debated showing his badge but wanted to save the surprise for one of the men he was after. Instead he nodded towards the back.

"No, I'm here to see Mr. Atkinson."

"Oh." She shot a glance at a partially open door. "He's extremely busy. Perhaps I can help you? I'm the office manager, Leanne Neuss. And you gentlemen are ...?"

He reached for his badge irritably. "Sergeant Brian Sullivan, Detective Leblanc of the Ottawa Police. This won't take long."

Startled, the woman stepped back, and Sullivan seized the occasion to plough past her. With a perfunctory knock, he strode inside the office, waited for Leblanc to follow suit, and shut the door behind them.

The man at the desk was on the phone. He swivelled around and stared at Sullivan through bewildered eyes. Obviously not too many got past Madame Neuss unannounced. Sullivan had the impression of blond good looks that had seen too much booze and fast times. His sandy hair was thinning, his cheeks were florid, and his hazel eyes shot through with red. A second chin had begun to form beneath his jaw, and it wobbled as he gathered his features into a frown.

"Can I help you?"

Sullivan sat down and introduced himself, while Leblanc took up a position in front of the door. The man's frown transformed to alarm. He looked at the phone, which was still in his hand. "I'll call you back," he said and hung up. Plastering a smile across his face, he rose and extended his hand.

"Roger Atkinson. How can I help you?"

The man's handshake was slick and practised, but Sullivan felt a pent-up power behind the grip. On closer inspection he could see the muscles rippling beneath the man's crisp white shirt. For a pencil pusher, this guy was in damn good shape.

On the drive up, Sullivan had tried to plan his questions, but the truth was he was walking into the interview virtually blind. Despite Gibbs's research, he knew almost nothing useful about the man or his possible connection to Patricia Ross, which gave him no leverage in confronting him. And Atkinson didn't look like he was easy to push around, either. Flattery might be the best way to go.

"One of our detectives was assaulted up here yesterday," Sullivan said. "We're looking for all the help we can get."

The man pulled a sympathetic face. "Of course. Detective Peters. How is she?"

"Touch and go. She was investigating the recent murder of Patricia Ross. I understand you knew her."

Atkinson's jaw dropped then snapped shut. He made a show of searching his memory before arranging a puzzled frown on his face. "Should I? The name doesn't ring a bell."

"You're both from Nova Scotia."

Atkinson gave a dry chuckle. "Nova Scotians have invaded everywhere, Sergeant. Even I can't know them all."

"She came up here to see you last week."

"What the devil makes you think that?"

Sullivan said nothing. In the silence, Atkinson groped for his tie, which wasn't there. Finally, he shrugged. "That's certainly news to me. We didn't connect. I'm sorry I can't help you more."

Sullivan reached into his pocket and unfolded the fax of the newspaper article. "This appeared in the Halifax *Herald* on April 9th. It's the reason Patricia Ross left Halifax to come here."

Atkinson reached for the newspaper and dropped it on his desk, but not before Sullivan caught the tremor in his hand. He pored over the article long enough to have read it three times over.

"Nice plug for us," he said eventually. "Seems fairly straightforward, though. I can't imagine why it would bring her all the way up here."

"To see you," Sullivan said. "You've come a long way from your heavy drinking days at the Lighthouse Tavern, Roger, but she remembered you."

Atkinson's jaw dropped again, but this time he forgot to snap it shut. He stared at Sullivan a full five seconds before his eyes widened in recognition. "Oh, my God. Daniel Oliver's girl."

Nice save, Sullivan thought. "You were at the table with them the night he was killed."

Atkinson lowered his gaze ruefully. "In another life. My misspent youth. I was so tanked I don't remember a thing."

"That's not what the bartender says."

"The bartender? The place was hopping. I'm surprised he had time to notice a thing."

"He says you bragged it was a military man from their Yugoslavian mission who killed him."

Atkinson rolled his eyes. "If I had a dollar for all the bullshit I've dished out in bars over the years …"

"Yet right after that, you landed this cushy job near the major military base of Petawawa, and it's been nothing but upwards ever since."

The sheepish smile disappeared and the hazel eyes grew cold. "I don't think I like your implication, Sergeant. Like most men with an ounce of ambition, I wanted to go where the jobs were, and I used my contacts to land a job. Army folks move all over, which was very handy."

"Then it was just a lucky contact that landed you a job as right hand man to a future Liberal Party star?"

The man's double chin quivered in outrage. "I've worked damn hard to get where I am and I'm good at it. That's what landed me this job. And by the way, Blakeley is not just a Liberal Party star. When the Liberals win, he'll be in line for a cabinet post. The Liberal leader himself pressed his nomination, as much as promised him Defence if he could take the riding from the Conservatives. My God, do you know what that would mean to our military and to the country? To have a guy running the country's defence policy who's actually walked the walk, and knows one end of a tank from the other?"

Sullivan glanced around the room at the dozens of framed photos and press clippings that covered the walls. "He's that impressive, is he?"

"He's that important."

Sullivan rose and began to peruse the display while he planned his next move. So far, as he'd feared, Atkinson had given him nothing. Most of the clippings trumpeted the missions Blakeley had led or the famous people he'd met. Blakeley's stern, clear gaze dominated all the photos, whether as an officer surrounded by his men or as a political hopeful shaking hands with the Liberal leader. One picture in particular caught his eye. Blakeley stood in the middle of a semicircle of men, all in formal dress and smiling broadly for the camera. Atkinson was visible to one side, looking smug. And at the back, barely discernible was a face that rang a vaguely familiar bell. It had been among the many faces Green had shown him earlier in the day. But the name eluded him.

He turned back to Atkinson. "After we're done here, I'd like a word with Mr. Blakeley too."

Atkinson's proud smile disappeared. "That's not possible. He's in Ottawa."

"Oh, does he live there most of the time?"

"Oh no, no. He lives here, but his business with the defence department often brings him into the city for long periods."

"What business?"

"Consulting on peacekeeping operations, helping to draft new policies."

"I thought he was retired."

"He is. But all that expertise ... His advice is quite invaluable."

Sullivan returned to the chair. "Who was your army friend who got you the first job here?"

Atkinson blinked at the sudden change of topic. "I don't see what that's got to do with anything."

"Humour me. Was it Blakeley?"

"Of course not. I've only known him a year. It was just an old drinking buddy. No one important."

"Patricia Ross thought it had something to do with shutting you up. You say it was just a lucky contact. It would be nice to be able to verify that, and get you off my list of suspects."

Atkinson flushed and clenched his fists involuntarily.

"Before the opposition parties get wind of it," Sullivan added, to help him along.

Atkinson sputtered a protest. He cast about as if looking for an escape route, but found none. Slowly he deflated. "I don't want any trouble for him. He was just a friend, a non-com in logistical support. He tipped me off to a job with a company that was going to re-outfit the 2CMBG."

"2CMBG?"

"Second Canadian Mechanized Brigade Group — that's the group based in Petawawa." He pulled on his nose awkwardly. "It wasn't really illegal but they aren't supposed to use their knowledge or influence … He put in a good word for me."

"Why?"

Atkinson shrugged. "I fixed something for him in Halifax. Lost some paperwork at City Hall. It was nothing, but it could have hurt his career."

"A name, Atkinson."

"Terry Lawlor."

"And I can find him here on the base?"

"Oh, not now. This was years ago. He's retired now, and I have no idea where he is."

Sullivan swore inwardly. More names, more fucking twists in the trail. He leaned forward on the desk and stared the man down. "Don't fuck with me now, Roger. The truth. Did you tell Detective Peters about any of this?"

Atkinson whipped his head back and forth, scrambling to recover his shattered cool. "On my grandmother's grave, no. I never even spoke to the woman."

***

July 22. Some shithole in Sector South, Croatia.

Our new assignment. It's hotter than hell here, nothing is moving and we're waiting it out while Command finds us a suitable camp. It looks like the moon. Villages torched, big mortar holes in the ground, no trees or crops. The belligerents have tanks down here and they've dug professional trenches.

The Hammer says we're waiting for the politicians and UN bigshots to work out a withdrawal agreement, and then we're supposed to enforce it. Apparently this used to be a Serb area protected by French peacekeepers, but the Croats think it's part of Croatia, so they grabbed a bridge and a dam right under the French noses. Anyway, the Serbs were some pissed at the French, so in come the Canadians again to do the job right.

This is war, our CO says, and we're sitting right in the middle of it, so keep your head down. And by the way, watch where you step and shake out your clothes and shoes before you put them on. Lots of snakes and scorpions. I say bring the suckers on. It'll be my pleasure to kill them.

SEVENTEEN

SULLIVAN STOOD IN the parking lot outside the campaign office, scanning the street for a place to eat. He'd been up since before six o'clock, and it was now almost three in the afternoon. In the distance he spotted the familiar red script of a Tim Hortons.

"Do you suppose he was telling the truth about Sue Peters, Luc?" he asked as he yanked open the car door.

Leblanc looked across at him in surprise. "I don't know much about the case, sir, so it's hard to judge."

"On the contrary, it may give you an advantage. You have nothing to go on but his behaviour."

Leblanc was silent, gazing out at the street ahead as he considered his answer. Sullivan remembered what he had always liked about the detective; Leblanc never rushed into anything. "I think he was hiding something," he said eventually. "He avoided eye contact, he fiddled with his hands."

Sullivan nosed the cruiser into the stream of traffic on Petawawa Boulevard. "I agree. Mr Atkinson was definitely worried about something. It could just be his own butt, which would be in a sling if he brings suspicion into the camp of John Blakeley. But it's worth a closer look. So — where to next, Luc?"

"To check out Terry Lawlor, sir?"

Sullivan shook his head.

"To the King's Arms?"

Sullivan swung into the Drive-Thru, grinning. "Food. Never let yourself get worn down."

Five minutes later, loaded up with sandwiches, doughnuts and coffee, they were back on the road. "Now we check out Terry Lawlor," Sullivan said. "Find the military police headquarters on that map."

Leblanc guided them onto the base and through a series of streets commemorating famous battles. The military police platoon commander was a big man with a walrus mustache and a shaved head above a bull neck. He waved them right through to his office, only too happy to help. The assault on a member of the tribe swept away miles of suspicion and red tape. He didn't even have to consult his records.

"I remember Terry Lawlor. Eight, maybe ten years ago? He was stationed up here in the quartermaster's unit. Used to get into scrapes in the Sergeant's mess pretty regular. Harmless enough but a stupid drunk with a mouth on him to swallow a tank."

Eight to ten years ago, Sullivan thought. That fit the time period. "Where is he now?"

"Mustered out, enjoyed his retirement all of two months before he ploughed his car into a tree."

"Accident?"

The captain nodded. "Drunk as a sailor on a two-day pass. 0200 hours on a rainy night, going about a hundred klics an hour around that bend just west of town."

"You said he had a mouth on him. Was he ever in trouble for anything else? Leaking information or …?"

The captain roared with laughter. "Well, he didn't have much worth leaking. He was a bean counter in supplies.

What's he going to say? The army's ordering a thousand new dress shirts next year?"

That information might be useful to some, thought Sullivan. Overtly he acted the picture of ease, with his long legs stretched out and his chair tilted back. He chatted a few minutes longer, probing the captain's opinion of Blakeley — "real stand-up guy" — and Sue Peters's assault — "a real shame, but we get our share of guys who take it out on women." Finally, Sullivan thanked him and hauled himself to his feet with a show of reluctance. On the way out, Leblanc glanced at him curiously, but said nothing.

"So what do you think about Terry Lawlor," Sullivan asked when they reached the car.

"It's not much, but it seems to back up Atkinson's story, sir."

"Maybe. Although it's hard to see how this Lawlor guy would have the pull to land Atkinson a worthwhile job. He's a pretty small fish." Sullivan climbed into the car and revved the engine. "And that accident is damn convenient."

"You think it wasn't an accident?"

"No. Just that Lawlor makes a handy fall guy now that there's no way to check the story with him."

Sullivan sat in the car, pondering his next move. He still had to touch base with the OPP, hoping to turn up Sue Peters's missing notebook and probe their take on the local election candidates. But the picture in Atkinson's office nagged at him. On impulse he pulled up the case file on his laptop and began flipping through photos. He sifted carefully through Oliver's section members without finding anyone who remotely fit the bill. But when he went further up the chain of command, he hit a match on his very first try.

Platoon commander Dick Hamm.

Well, well, well, he thought, now there was a bigger fish. Big enough to pull a lot of strings and give a guy quite a boost up the ladder. And if there was a connection to Blakeley, who was an even bigger fish … Sullivan tried to dispute the suspicion that sprang to his mind, that Hamm and Blakeley were working together. Blakeley was a very popular candidate among the military. Maybe Hamm was just there as a supporter.

And maybe pigs fly.

"Where are we going next, sir?" Leblanc ventured once they had been sitting some time.

"Well, I was going to pay a visit to the OPP, but Colonel Dick Hamm is beginning to look a whole lot more interesting."

***

It was well past lunch time and Green's head felt like a pinball machine. Reports were flying in from various fronts so fast that he could barely keep track. Sue Peters had been the official file coordinator for the case, and although the task had been reassigned, Green suspected in reality he was the only person besides Gibbs who knew the whole picture.

Captain Ulrich from National Defence had emailed the photos of the remaining members of Oliver's and MacDonald's section in Yugoslavia, along with the names and photos of Major Kennebec, their company commander, and Colonel Thomas, the battalion's CO. He had even faxed over a chart describing the name, rank and function of everyone in MacDonald's chain of command. With one of their ranks implicated in an attempted cop killing, the military had apparently changed its tactics in favour of full co-operation with civilian authorities. Green muttered a silent prayer of thanks to the Police Chief, whose deft handling had undoubtedly been behind the change. He hoped the Chief could use the same silver tongue with the politicians if the time came.

Green immediately forwarded all the photos to Kate McGrath in Halifax, in the hope that the witnesses and bartender at the Lighthouse would recognize Daniel Oliver's killer among them. He was about to head out to his much delayed lunch meeting with Staff Sergeant Vaillancourt when Gibbs arrived at his office door, looking wan and defeated. He handed Green two short reports.

"This is all I could get on Blakeley and Atkinson for Sergeant Sullivan, sir. It-It's not much, I know."

Green scanned the meagre reports. His interest was piqued by the reference to John Blakeley's peacekeeping missions. Eight tours in six different countries. What were the odds of Yugoslavia being one of them?

"Have you sent this to Sullivan already?"

"Yessir. He needed it by two o'clock."

"Okay, but I want you to keep digging. Find out exactly where and when Blakeley did his peacekeeping tours, especially if he was ever in Yugoslavia. And I also want some background on Lieutenant Colonel Richard Hamm."

Gibbs's face fell. He propped his lanky frame against the door as if he could no longer support himself. "Well, I — I was wondering if … I'd like a few minutes to check on Sue, sir."

Green cursed his insensitivity. "Of course. I have a lunch appointment anyway." For which I am already half an hour late, he thought, glancing at his watch. He shooed Gibbs on his way to the hospital, then grabbed his jacket and headed out of the station up Elgin Street. He had chosen a small deli off the cops' beaten track, for he didn't want any curious ears tuning in. He wanted the discussion of a fellow officer to be as frank and confidential as possible.

To his surprise, Michel Vaillancourt had brought another man with him, whom he introduced as George Nelson. Both men were already halfway through heaping platters of deli sandwiches and fries.

"George was Weiss's staff sergeant when he was in uniform," Vaillancourt explained. "So I figured he'd know more about him than I do."

Nelson was a pear of a man, with a pointy bald head, three chins and a paunch that eclipsed his belt. He extended a hearty handshake, then thudded back into his booth with a resounding crash. Green looked from one man to the other thoughtfully. His vague cover story about wanting more details about Weiss's investigative experience was pretty lame, and he was surprised by both men's obvious eagerness to talk about him. With his very first comment, Nelson provided the answer.

"You're thinking Jeff Weiss might've had something to do with the hit on Peters?"

Green toyed with his menu. "Not thinking, just exploring. Why, do you?"

Nelson had stuffed his mouth full of fries, and he munched noisily as he shook his head. "Under normal circumstances, I'd say not a chance."

Green's stomach contracted at the sight of the melted cheese oozing from the Reuben sandwich. He signalled to the man behind the counter and yelled for a double smoked meat on rye. "What do you mean, under normal circumstances?"

"Regular street work. Drugs, bar fights, turf beefs — the day to day stuff. He's rock solid, got good instincts, never gave me a moment's doubt. Well —" Nelson paused to suck his fingers noisily. "He has a bit of a temper. Sometimes he'd give his sergeant a little lip, but he usually backtracked the next instant. Only a couple of incidents were written up."

"How much is a bit of a temper?"

"Enough to get him off the promotion track," Vaillancourt said ominously.

Nelson shrugged impatiently. "Just a flash in the pan. Like if somebody pushed his buttons. But what you're talking about; that would have been premeditated. I mean, to call her out of the bar and set her up like that—"

Green was surprised, then realized he shouldn't be. Details of the assault would have raced through the police grapevine like lightning.

"That's not like Jeff," Nelson continued. "He's a straight arrow and a more committed officer you're never going to see. And he wants to get ahead. Nothing wrong with that."

"But there is something, or you wouldn't both be sitting here. You're saying these are not normal circumstances?"

Nelson looked uncomfortable. He glanced around the deli as if to make sure no one was eavesdropping. The mid-afternoon crowd was sparse, comprised mainly of courthouse workers enjoying a cappuccino. No one looked remotely like a cop. Or a reporter.

Vaillancourt wiped his mouth carefully before stepping into the breach. "He did a three-month stint with the UN as a police officer in Yugoslavia."

Green stared at him, his heart in his throat. "When?"

"Fall of 1993."

"Where?"

"Mostly Sarajevo. He was doing regular law enforcement and training, beefing up the Bosnian force. It was finger-in-the-dyke stuff, trying to prevent looting, control riots, catch local thugs who didn't think the law applied to them."

Green's thoughts raced afield. In an effort to understand which peacekeepers had been where, he'd studied the map of the former Yugoslavia as it had been reconfigured in 1993. Daniel Oliver and Ian MacDonald had been with the Second Canadian Battalion, which had been deployed solely in Croatia. Nearly two hundred miles of rugged, hostile mountain territory separated them from Sarajevo. It seemed unlikely Jeff Weiss would have even met them. Unless ...

"You said mostly?"

Nelson shrugged. "He was assigned to assist in war crimes investigations a couple of times, helping the UN investigators collect physical evidence and interview witnesses. I know that stuff still gets to him."

Green's smoked meat sandwich arrived, and he was glad for the diversion. While he doused his French fries with vinegar, he pondered the possibilities. The coincidence was incredible. What were the chances of an Ottawa Police officer being assigned to investigate war crimes at exactly the same time and place that MacDonald and Oliver were posted? There had been thousands of peacekeepers in the Balkans, and probably thousands of local conflicts where war crimes could occur.

It was just a shred of a theory, and a farfetched one at that, until he had facts to back it up. He tried to appear casual as he posed his next question. "Where were these war crimes he was investigating, do you know?"

Nelson and Vaillancourt exchanged questioning looks. Vaillancourt lifted his thin shoulders in a shrug, but Nelson slapped his palm against his forehead in an effort to shake the memory loose.

"Croatia." He nodded several times. "Yup, I'm positive, because I remember when all the accusations of ethnic cleansing and mass murder were being levied against the Serbs, Weiss kept saying 'The fucking UN doesn't know the half of it. The Croats were just as bad.'"

Croatia, Green thought. Suddenly his smoked meat lost its taste, and he pushed the plate away. The coincidences were converging, but with them came more questions. What had Weiss uncovered in his investigation, and how was the military involved? His mind raced over the links he had formed so far. Something had happened in Croatia that had haunted the lives of the soldiers for years afterwards. MacDonald had killed himself, Oliver had slipped into bitterness and drink, and someone else had committed not just one but two murders to cover it all up.

These were simple country boys, Inspector Norrich had ranted that night in Halifax, unprepared for the brutality and hatred they encountered and equally unprepared for the visceral rage they might have felt in response.

What if they themselves had committed a war crime?

In 1993 the Canadian military had been reeling under the revelation of a murder committed by their elite forces in Somalia, and they were struggling to repair the damage to their peacekeeping image. What would be the worst thing that could happen at that moment? News of further atrocities committed by their soldiers in Yugoslavia would be high on that list. The pressure to suppress the knowledge and to prevent any investigation would have been huge. Certainly murders had been committed for far less.

Green's heart beat faster as the theory took shape. Yet even as his excitement grew, sober second thought began to take hold. What kind of war crime? Surely not a systematic, large scale massacre, which would have been impossible to hide. It had to be something more private. A small misstep that could easily have been buried in the chaos of battle. Was that where Weiss fit in? Had the military put pressure on him to cover it up? Who in the chain of command would have the clout to do that? Certainly not someone at the lowly section level.

Green reached for his coffee and twirled his spoon slowly in it, trying not to betray his excitement as he gathered his thoughts. In the silence, the spoon tinkled and both men watched him intently. He tried to keep his voice neutral. "So what's your guess about how Weiss could be involved with all this? You've obviously got some concerns. That he covered something up in Croatia?"

Nelson whipped his head back and forth. "Oh, no. Just this temper. Things that remind him of that time seem to set him off. I just think he's ..."

"Unstable?"

"Not usually. I mean, we all have our buttons, eh? His is Croatia."

Vaillancourt had leaned forward on his elbows, his hands folded and his forehead creased in uneasy thought. Now he shook his head slowly. "But he did ask to job shadow the Ross case, right off the bat when he first got involved in the search of the scene."

Nelson scowled. "But at that point there was no known connection to the military or to Yugoslavia. Patricia Ross looked like just another luckless hooker."

Unless Weiss already knew the connection, Green thought. And the players. He glanced at his watch, pretended to be surprised, and shoved back his chair. "Gotta run. Thanks for this. Can you do one more thing? Find out exactly when and where he was in Croatia, and anything you can about the nature of the assignment. ASAP. Off the record

EIGHTEEN

BACK AT THE office, Green pulled out the chart that Captain Ulrich had sent him of the military chain of command. If the military functioned like the police, loyalty was built from the ground up, starting with your partner and your squad. The section was the basic unit in the army. There were eight other members in the section, all of whom lived together more closely than any family did, packed like sardines into armoured personnel carriers and spending long hours together on patrol. If a breach of military law had been committed, this is probably where it would have occurred, and these are the boys who would have seen it. But who else might have known?

Sections worked closely together as a platoon, under the day to day direction of the platoon commander. Richard Hamm. There were other NCOs attached to the platoon, but all of these appeared to be more closely allied to platoon headquarters under Hamm than to the sections. There were ranking officers higher than Hamm, of course, but these would be even more removed from the frontline actions and daily lives of the individual soldiers. Hamm was the only ranking officer likely to know of their wrongdoing and capable of suppressing that knowledge.

And Hamm had been surprisingly unsupportive of Ian MacDonald's recommendation for a medal.

But if a war crime had been committed or covered up, Green was not going to get at it by going head to head with Hamm. Hamm would never admit a thing unless his back was truly to the wall. To accomplish that, Green needed ammunition. He needed to find a lowly section member who wouldn't see the harm in revealing the truth ten years after the fact, or who might be relieved at the chance to be rid of the guilt.

He yanked open his office door and caught sight of Gibbs, who was back from the hospital and deep in conversation on the phone. Green paced as he listened to Gibbs's end of the conversation.

"Thanks for trying, Karl. I appreciate your position," Gibbs said, hanging up with a sigh.

"Karl? As in Captain Karl Ulrich?"

A ghost of a smile flitted across Gibbs's weary face. "We're old friends by now. He gave me some deep background on Colonel Hamm." Gibbs glanced down at his notes. "He's fourth generation military. His father was a decorated Korean war hero, and his grandfather was an infantry platoon commander who died at the Somme and was awarded a posthumous Victoria Cross for his solo stand against the enemy. It saved most of his platoon. Quite an impressive family, sir."

Green nodded thoughtfully. No wonder Hamm had not been supportive of MacDonald's medal; he was used to heroism on a far grander scale. But the information added new clarity to the picture that was beginning to emerge. Hamm would have grown up with these family tales of heroism and sacrifice. How powerful would be his commitment to the military he loved, and how far would he be willing to go to protect it? Far enough for a cover-up? Far enough for murder?

"Sir?"

Green pulled himself from his racing thoughts.

"I'm running into brick walls on John Blakeley," Gibbs was saying. "His file is shut tight as a clam, except what they give out to the media."

Green nodded grimly, not surprised that the military's open access had slammed shut when it reached one of its gilded sons. "I guess nobody in the military wants to give the media or the opposition any ammunition to use against him."

"Even the details about his wife and his children are confidential, sir. All I could find out is he has three grown children and a wife named Leanne."

"Wouldn't want the truth interfering with a good spin. He probably had a really ugly divorce, and the children hate him." Green sighed. He wasn't sure how Blakeley fit into his conspiracy theory anyway. Although he had served on peacekeeping missions, his name wasn't listed anywhere on the chain of command from MacDonald's section to the whole battalion.

"Okay, we'll keep chipping away," he said. "But I've got something else for you to do right now. I'd like you to track down that corporal from Oliver's section who's studying at Queen's. I want him brought up here for questioning first thing in the morning." He turned to go, then belatedly he remembered Gibbs's visit to the hospital. Judging from his long face, the news wasn't good.

"How is Sue?" he asked gently.

"Alive. They did another brain scan, and there's some recovery. I suppose that's good news. I just want … I just want her to open her eyes and tell us who did this, so it will all be over." Green thought of Peters lying so still and helpless in the bed. She would hate this and would be the first person wanting to nail the bastard to the wall. If only she could. But with any luck, by the time she did open her eyes, they would have some justice for her. At the very least, they would know what had happened between the soldiers in Croatia, which would be one small step in unravelling the mystery.

In the meantime, he had to stop Sullivan from questioning Hamm until they had some concrete facts to back up Green's theory. If Hamm was the mastermind of a war crimes cover-up and the killer of Oliver and Ross, Green wanted all the ammunition he could muster before going after him. As he punched in Sullivan's cellphone number, he hoped he wasn't already too late. Hamm was one of the key witnesses Sullivan had gone to see, and he was probably in the middle of the interview right now, armed with fewer than half the facts he needed to make the colonel sweat.

Sullivan's cheerful voice came through after the third ring. "No problem," he said when Green told him to forget Hamm for now. "He's not even here. Got called down to Ottawa this morning for some meeting. He's slumming it at the Chateau Laurier, so we can catch him tomorrow. Anything else you want us to do before we head back home?"

"You could drop by the OPP to check on the progress of the Peters investigation."

Sullivan chuckled. "Already done that. They haven't made much headway, but they did uncover a couple of interesting things. You want to hear them?"

Green rolled his eyes. Sullivan had always been a tease, particularly when he knew Green was hot on the scent. Never had the teasing felt so good. "You want to direct traffic, *putz?*"

Sullivan laughed. "First, the OPP turned up an old ex-army sergeant who says he was talking to Peters in the King's Arms bar when she received the mysterious phone call. He claims he told her Patricia Ross had been asking questions in the same bar the week before."

"He seems to be keeping a bar stool warm at the King's Arms. Questions about what?"

"About the campaign, the people behind it, that sort of thing. He was a bit fuzzy. He apparently told Patricia Ross he didn't know much except that Blakeley was some military hotshot who believed in a new approach to peacekeeping. Which the sergeant apparently agreed with."

So, thought Green with a surge of satisfaction, we're on the right track with this military angle. After Patricia Ross returned to Ottawa, she'd embarked on the next step in her quest, a date with a mystery man. Shortly after which, she was dead.

"What's the other interesting thing?"

"Remember the phone call the bartender says he received from someone claiming to be Peters's partner? Well, turns out he did receive a call at approximately the right time, which came from a local cellphone."

Green sucked in his breath. "Did you trace it?"

"Dead end. It's a new line registered to a company called BA Securities, but its owner is well buried. The credit card is a numbered account."

"Did the OPP request the phone's logs?"

"Yeah, they know a thing or two about investigation up here, Green."

Green ignored the bait. "Have you got the phone number? I'll give it to our tech guys."

It was a local 613 area code and as Green scribbled it down, he thought it looked familiar. After signing off, he scrolled through the reports Gibbs and the other officers had entered on Patricia Ross's activities until he found the record of calls made to the payphone in the lobby of her Vanier hotel during the week before her death. Detectives had traced all the numbers, including one made by a cellphone with a 613 area code just the day before her death. Detectives had been unable to track down either the owner's name or the address, but the cellphone was registered to a BA Securities.

Bingo. The dots were connecting.

But what the hell did they form? And what, after days of intensive search and tons of shoe leather, did they really know for sure? He had a few suspicious names, a hint of conspiracy and cover-up, but the theory holding it all together was as flimsy and insubstantial as ever. Not one witness had seen Patricia Ross sharing a drink the night of her death. Not one witness had seen a suspicious man leaving the scene of Peters's assault. Not a single fingerprint or shoe impression had been found to tie the killer to either attack. And as for motives, the speculation about war crimes was about as improbable as blue moons.

He sat behind his desk, staring at the little piles of notes and messages that were scattered about in disarray. Had he missed something? All the crucial reports pertinent to the investigation were on computer, in a properly organized and managed case file. Yet maybe he had forgotten a little aside, not knowing its significance at the time.

He began moving the notes around, rearranging piles and discarding irrelevant notes. Suddenly at the edge of a pile, half hidden by his phone, he spotted a note he'd never seen before. It was a scrawl on a phone message slip.

"A friend called, said to tell 'Mr. G' to meet her at her art gallery at sunset."

Green stared at the message in disbelief. It was dated April 28 at four o'clock. Yesterday. "Jesus Christ!" He slammed out of his office, prepared to demand which incompetent idiot had taken it, when he realized that just after four o'clock yesterday, Weiss had called in Sue Peters's attack, and everything else had gone out the window. It felt like a lifetime ago.

Mollified, he glanced outside and saw the late afternoon sun slanting off the windshields of the cars crawling west along the Queensway. He was a day too late, but maybe Twiggy was the patient type. If she had something to tell him, she might keep going back to the aqueduct until he turned up.

***

Some day at end of July 1993. Maslenica Bridge, Sector South.

Our section just had our first night at the OP, sitting up on the top of this hill. Man, was it freaky! We're supposed to be watching this bridge to count and identify each vehicle that crosses. Now this is not a real bridge, because the Serbs blew that up when the Croats invaded, so now it's just a pontoon bridge that the Serbs lob artillery at all the time. We can hardly see it with binoculars, let alone ID the vehicle type.

Anyway, there are Serbs in the hills behind us and Croats in the valley below, and they're firing away at each other and the shells are whizzing right over our heads. Multiple rocket launchers. Whup, whup, whup when they launch. Kaboom, kaboom, kaboom a few seconds later when they land. And we're going Holy Shit! And

Sarge is on the radio, screaming to the Hammer, and the Hammer's screaming to the OC, who's down on the beach, to get us out of here. It's a miracle we all survived. On the way down, the mountain was littered with corpses. You couldn't even tell which side they were on, because they had no uniforms. We had to bag them and bring them down. I can still smell the stink on me.

***

It was past seven o'clock, and the last rays of sunlight burnished the tree tops as Green headed west along Albert Street towards the aqueduct. The police tape had been removed from the crime scene, and every single piece of trash had been picked up by the Ident officers, leaving the little hideaway unnaturally pristine. The wall paintings glinted bold red and blue in the sun, but the place was empty. Not even the stoned teens or wasted drunks had returned, as if Patricia's death still hung like a pall overhead.

Green searched for telltale signs of Twiggy's presence, but her garbage bag and her tattered pile of newspaper were nowhere to be seen. His shouts went unanswered. He climbed back into his car and tried to remember where she hung out. In the early days of her exile, she'd sometimes gone to the women's shelters or the "Y," but she'd resented their attempts to fix her life and preferred to take her chances on the open streets. She said shelters were for people who were trying to put their lives together. She had none left to put together.

Nonetheless, he phoned around. The women's shelters had not seen her, nor had the food bank or drop-in centres. With a growing sense of unease, he phoned the hospitals. It took a lot of wheedling and pulling rank, but eventually he got his answer. None of the hospitals had admitted a street woman fitting her description. It was small comfort that, had she turned up at the morgue, he would already have been informed.

The sun was just below the horizon and the streets were sinking into shadow when he remembered her reference to the Tim Hortons on Bank Street. The manager there gave her coffee, she said, better than anything the police had on offer.

Starting the car, he shoved it into gear and shot out of the parking lot through the traffic. He raced back towards downtown, did an illegal left turn onto Bank Street and parked in front of the modest coffee shop tucked between a magazine store and a shwarma take-out. The closed sign was up, but he could see someone sweeping inside. He hammered on the door and plastered his badge against the glass. The man's scowl turned to consternation as he hustled forward to unlock the door. He had a Middle Eastern complexion with a heavy five o'clock shadow and the most mournful black eyes Green had ever seen.

"I was just closing," he said without a trace of an accent. "Is there a problem?"

"Do you know a fat woman named Twiggy? She comes to your store for coffee."

"Yes." The man's eyes slitted warily. "Why? Is that a problem?"

Why did the man assume a police officer always meant trouble? Even as he asked himself the question, he knew the answer. The world had changed for this man since September 11.

Green found himself apologizing. "I'm sorry. No problem, I'm just concerned. She's a witness, and I'm trying to locate her." Belatedly he offered his hand. "I'm Inspector Michael Green."

The man stared at Green's hand, then reached forward to take it cautiously in his. When Green didn't bite, he seemed to relax. "Hassim Mohammed. And I haven't seen her today. I've been worried, because she's not a very healthy woman."

Green recorded his name and address. "When did you last see her?"

"Two days ago? Thursday. She came for her coffee, then went off. She said she had a call to make. But there was a —" Alarm widened his melancholy eyes. "Oh, no."

"What?"

"I told her about a man who was asking about her. She asked me a whole lot of questions about him — like what name he called her — and I know she didn't want him to find her."

The first fingers of fear brushed Green's spine. "Can you describe this man?"

"Dark business suit, Canadian." He paused. "I mean white. He was wearing sunglasses, he had blond hair."

"Height and weight?"

"Taller than you. Maybe six feet. Well built but not heavy. One-eighty?"

"Age?"

The man scrunched up his face and blew air into his cheeks. "Thirties? Maybe more. It's hard to tell with the sunglasses."

Green probed with a few more questions, but the description did not improve. As it stood, it was too generic to be of much help and could apply to several of the men in the case. He suppressed his frustration with an effort.

"What questions did this man ask you?"

"Did I know her, where she usually stayed, when was she coming to my place again."

"And what name did he call her?"

"None. He just called her the fat woman." Hassim's eyes had been growing larger with each question. "Is she all right? Has something happened to her?"

"At this point I just want to locate her." Green held out his card. "If she shows up, or you remember anything else, call me at that number. And I'd like you to come down to the station tomorrow to work with our police artist. We'll see if we can work up a sketch."

"Oh!" Hassim's eyes darted anxiously. "Well, the store …"

"Don't worry, Mr. Mohammed. It won't take long, and it might help us find Twiggy."

He sighed with resignation as he took the card. "She was my teacher, you know. Grade Seven. But I don't think she remembers me."

Oh, I'm sure she does, Green thought grimly. A profound wave of sadness and anxiety swept through him. But for Twiggy, that teacher doesn't exist anymore.

NINETEEN

GREEN HADN'T HAD the dream in years. It was a flashback more than a dream, so vivid that he often woke from it bathed in sweat. It began as it always did, with a call from dispatch about a reported domestic disturbance in Alta Vista, a quiet neighbourhood of winding crescents, leafy trees and sprawling bungalows. Professors, accountants and civil servants lived there, enjoying their perennial gardens and stone patios.

It was a peaceful, starlit night in May when the call came in, and the streets were deserted. Green was wrapping up a routine canvass in a nearby apartment building on Bank Street, and he was only a few minutes away. As he listened to the agitated radio chatter back and forth between the responding officers and dispatch, he could hear a woman screaming in the background. Dispatch sent more squad cars and contacted the Tactical Unit, so soon the howl of sirens filled the quiet night.

Green radioed in as he headed towards the scene. "I'm on my way in case they need CID."

When he arrived, the street was a mob scene. Cruisers blocked off the street, neighbours were hovering on front porches, shivering in their night clothes, and a dozen uniforms were deployed around the perimeter of a yard in the middle of it all. Radios barked and emergency roof lights splashed the scene with surreal red and blue.

The house at the centre of the drama was eerily still. Light shone in the upstairs windows, but the screaming had stopped. An officer was training his binoculars on each window in turn. Green edged his way into earshot.

"No signs of activity, sir," the officer said to his patrol sergeant, who had just arrived.

The sergeant swore softly. "Try phoning."

The phone rang endlessly through the house without response. The Tactical Unit arrived and used a bullhorn to order everyone inside to come out. Still nothing. The unit huddled together, planning their entry as the sergeant tried to establish how many lived in the house and who slept where. He conferred in an inaudible whisper with a man Green took to be a neighbour.

Green wandered over to a group of neighbours clustered behind the barricades, who watched his approach with a mixture of excitement and shock.

"Who called 911?" he asked.

"Several of us did." A tall, spindly man detached himself from the crowd. He was wearing striped pyjama bottoms and a terrycloth robe, which he hugged around himself. Despite it, he was trembling, and in the darkness his eyes were bright with fear. "I've already told the police what I know. Are you a reporter?"

Green shook his head. "I'm Sergeant Green with Major Crimes."

"They're a nice couple. He's a professor, she's a teacher. Never a loud word. Their boys are a handful, but they are so patient with them. Sweet Jesus, I hope nothing bad happened."

"What made you call 911?"

"Her screaming. It woke me up. Screaming 'Stop! Stop!' Sweet Jesus, such an ungodly animal howl. And the chain saw was so loud."

Green's mouth went dry. "Chain saw?"

"He has one for the brush and trees. He always keeps such a beautiful garden. And he's been helping all of us this spring, to clear out the deadwood, you know? Oh … God."

As much to keep his own wild imagination at bay as to keep the man focussed, Green stuck to the facts. "Did you see anything tonight?"

"No, just shadows rushing in front of the blinds. As if a fight was going on."

"Do you know if there are firearms in the house?"

There was a chorus of denials from the neighbours who had clustered around. "They'd never have guns."

"Don't believe in them?"

"And with the boys being ADHD and all …"

Green held up his hand. "How many boys are there?"

"Twins. Nice boys, just really busy, you know?" said the tall neighbour.

"And slow," interjected a woman at his elbow, whom Green took to be his wife.

"Well, they were preemies," he countered, "so they started off behind. They've needed a lot of help, poor little guys. They could be real trouble — used to be real trouble — before they got into the right school."

"Jean had to fight like hell for that," added the wife darkly, apparently much less forgiving of the boys than her husband. "Costs a fortune for the two of them. Everything she and Sam make goes towards it."

Green jumped in again. "How old are the twins?"

Husband and wife exchanged uncertain glances. "Ten?"

"Big enough to handle a chainsaw?"

The wife nodded, but the husband looked shocked. "Oh, no. They're skinny little tykes. Behind, like I said."

"Anyone else in the house?"

"Just Jean and Sam and the twins." The man's eyes were big as he strained to see what the police were doing at the house. "Sweet Jesus, I hope they're all right."

Green thanked them and walked over to introduce himself to the patrol sergeant in charge. As they filled each other in, the tactical officers broke in the front door and disappeared inside. Green heard muffled shouts and thudding boots as the unit dispersed through the house. A few seconds later one of them shattered the glass in an upstairs window and screamed out, "Get the paramedics in here!"

More boots thumping, more shouts, and one of the tactical officers staggered out to vomit in the rose bushes by the front door. "Mother of God, it's bad," muttered the patrol sergeant, echoing Green's thoughts. The tactical guys were a tough bunch.

The sergeant headed towards the front door, and Green scrambled to catch up. "We have to protect the scene," he said, absurdly under the circumstances.

The officer who'd been sick straightened up at their approach. He shook his head helplessly.

"What's the situation?" the sergeant snapped.

"Bodies!" managed the man. "All in pieces. Arms, legs, heads … Fuck!"

"Anyone alive?"

The officer kept shaking his head in disbelief. "Don't think so. I don't even know how many there are. I counted two heads. Kids." He began to shake all over.

The sergeant gripped his elbow and signalled to a nearby paramedic. "Go sit down, son."

One by one the paramedics and tactical officers emerged from the house, pale as ghosts and unsteady on their feet. Green heard the same muttered disbelief over and over. "War zone in there. Blood fucking everywhere."

The patrol sergeant looked at Green expectantly, as if to say it's your case now. Your call, and good luck. Green fought his own dizziness and nausea as he tried to think. He needed to get his own partner over here. He had sent Sullivan home for the day, because he had three little kids and a soccer game to coach. Green kept the details to a minimum on the phone as he gave Sullivan the address. The man would know soon enough.

The call seemed to ground him, for once he hung up, he felt his training kick in. "Call Ident, the coroner and the duty inspector," he told the patrol sergeant. "I want everyone out of the house, and the scene secured. Don't let anyone in but Ident, the coroner and myself. And I want the boots of every officer and paramedic who went into the house."

The orders given, he pulled on gloves, steeled himself, and stepped over the threshold. He had never seen so much blood. He knew the human body contained about five litres, and he'd seen much of it spilled on the floors and walls of previous crime scenes, but nothing prepared him for this. The blood was smeared all the way up the staircase, pooled in lakes at the foot of the stairs, and sprayed in a pulsing arterial line across the walls and ceiling of the living room where the husband lay.

He stared at the ceiling, his throat gaping open and his thinning hair drenched in the blood that spread beneath his head. By his outstretched hand lay a long kitchen knife so covered in blood that it was barely recognizable.

Green barely had time to turn away before vomiting on the hardwood floor at the foot of the stairs. He leaned on the bannister a moment, rested his forehead on his arm and tried to suck fresh air into his lungs. But the air stank of death. The stench of urine and feces mingled with the coppery scent of blood and the acrid smell of gasoline. His stomach rebelled again, but this time he fought the bile down.

The rest of the downstairs was surprisingly neat and undisturbed. The small kitchen was packed with artwork and children's toys. Yellow post-it notes were stuck on the fridge, the microwave and the cork board, containing reminders of doctors' appointments, soccer games, homework assignments and even routines for cooking and cleaning up. Pinned to the wall by the back door, which was broken open by the tactical team, was another note. *Remember to take your lunch and lock the door.* At the bottom of the note, as on the others, was *xxoox* and a happy face.

Green backed away, his breath catching, and turned to continue his systematic search of the downstairs. Everywhere he saw evidence of a neat, frugal lifestyle. Scuffed, mended furniture, homemade bookcases brimming with secondhand paperbacks, and child-like drawings on the walls. When he could no longer reasonably put it off, he took a deep breath and headed up the stairs, careful to avoid the blood on the walls and stair treads.

At the top of the stairs, the bedroom doors were ajar, spilling light into the hall. Lamps were smashed, tables overturned, and bedding strewn about. Everything was bathed in blood. He almost tripped over a cast-iron pan in the middle of the floor. Through the half open front bedroom door, he caught sight of the chainsaw, glistening red. He nudged the door back with his toe. Stepped in. And stared at the carnage.

He felt a door swing shut in his mind. Felt its refusal to grasp, to absorb, to comprehend. Aware only of his crumbling legs, the heat and salt of tears upon his cheeks. He didn't speak, didn't move.

Then, very faintly above the sound of his own ragged breath, he heard a sob. He turned. A closet door stood half open in the corner. Instinct flooded him and he dropped to a crouch behind the blood-soaked bed and unsnapped his holster.

"Police. Come out with your hands out."

Nothing.

He edged around the bed and shoved open the closet door.

Nothing.

Then from the interior of the closet, from behind the snowsuits, the hockey gear and the boxes of Lego, a pale face emerged. Eyes huge with shock, greying hair plastered with blood, lips slack with disbelief.

"I killed him," she whispered. "I killed him."

***

Green bolted awake, as he always did, his sheets soaked with sweat. His heart hammered against his ribs as he panted to catch his breath. He drank in the reassuring shadows of his darkened bedroom; the maple tree against the window, the dresser in the corner, the glint of the mirror on the closet door. And his wife's black curls tumbling over the pillow next to him. She opened her eyes, luminous in the dark, and reached for his arm.

"The nightmare?"

He nodded, and she tightened her grip. "You haven't had that in a long time."

"I guess it's this case and worrying about Twiggy."

She sat up, pushing her hair out of her eyes. "Do you want some tea?"

He hesitated. When the nightmares had come every night and the visions of body parts plagued his waking hours, Sharon had been there to comfort him. To listen endlessly to his rants about mental health and legal loopholes, and to try to explain — not excuse — what Sam had done. She had known Sam during his two hospitalizations the previous winter, supported his wife's futile efforts to have him committed. She had watched him struggle in vain to get well, she had even met the two holy terrors who were his sons. They had come to the ward for visits, ricocheting off the walls, racing the length of the corridors, bouncing off the sofas in the sunroom and spinning the chairs in the nursing station like their own personal merry-go-rounds.

"The stress alone of keeping up with them would tax a healthy parent," she'd said. "And you factor in the loss of his job at the university due to his illness, the financial pressures of the kids' private school, the efforts to hang onto the family house … I think he couldn't see any other way out. He couldn't cope anymore, but he couldn't leave his wife with the burden of managing them by herself."

"And he thought killing them would be easier on her?"

She'd shaken her head, looking dissatisfied. "I can only guess, but I think in his delusional state, he thought they'd be better off dead. He felt he had to put them out of their misery."

That was the theory proposed by the trio of forensic psychiatrists when the case finally wended its way through the legal circus. Homicide-suicide was the verdict of the coroner's inquest. Sam Calderone, in the grip of a psychotic delusion, had hacked his twin sons to pieces with a chainsaw, and while his wife hid for her life in the closet, he went downstairs and stabbed himself in the throat.

Green had his own private theory about the mad workings of Sam Calderone's mind. He had been cutting deadwood, hoping perhaps that what was left of his sons' bodies and minds would grow healthy and strong. He had not intended to die that night, he had planned to be around to witness their cure.

With the knife too smeared with blood to yield usable prints, Green had never told anyone what Jean Calderone had said to him in the closet that night. She had faced a homicidal lunatic who had just sawn their two sons to pieces. Whatever she had done to him, whether in self-protection or in retribution, she had already paid dearly enough.

Now he snuggled down into Sharon's arms and pressed her fingers to his lips. "Just hold me awhile," he whispered.

He was grateful that she didn't utter pointless reassurances about Twiggy's disappearance, but recognized the danger was real, and the longer Twiggy was missing, the less hopeful the outlook. He lay awake a long time, feeling the rise and fall of her breasts against his back, thinking about Twiggy. Tomorrow he would put out an APB on her and get all the patrols looking for her. They would visit the hangouts, talk to the homeless, and double-check the community health centres.

And while the patrols did that, he would solve this damn case and bring this deadly killer down before he got anyone else.

He slept finally, dreamlessly, until the first rays of dawn crept onto his bed.

***

August 12. Gracac, Sector South, Croatia.

This is the first time I feel like I'm writing to this diary. Not to Kit, who I haven't had a letter from in two weeks. These thoughts are not for Kit, they're for me, because I've put away a whole bottle of French wine and I still feel like shit. We lost one of our own today. Not by sniper fire or a landmine, which we always thought would happen, but by one of our own stupid trucks rolling on him. What the fuck are we doing over here anyway? The UN can't get their act together and the locals don't want us, they just want us to get out of the way so they can kill each other.

Today at parade there were all the usual speeches about him and about the great sacrifice he made and how proud we should be of the important job we were doing. The CO said we can't let this get us down, we're soldiers and we have a job to do.

Like what?

TWENTY

GREEN WAS UP before seven o'clock the next morning in order to get the APB on Twiggy out in the morning parade. By the time he emerged from his study, both Modo and Tony were clamouring for their breakfast and Sharon was standing in the hallway, fixing him with knowing eyes.

"It's Sunday, Mike."

He kissed the top of her tousled head. "Go back to bed. I'll feed them."

She grunted, wrapped her pink robe around her and headed back into the bedroom. "A coffee in bed might be nice," she tossed over her shoulder.

He had fed the dog and was toasting a bagel for Tony when the phone rang. It was Sullivan, sounding as if he'd been awake for hours.

"I saw the APB on Twiggy, so I knew you were up."

Green chuckled. "I can tell you really hate being back in Major Crimes. You have to drag yourself in to work every morning."

"You're one to talk. Anyway, I was thinking I'd get an early start on Richard Hamm this morning."

The toaster popped up, and Tony crowed with glee. "Daddy, Daddy, Daddy. Get me my bagel!"

Green fished it out of the toaster and set it on a plate.

"Daddy, put cheese on it!"

Green wedged the phone against his shoulder so he could spread the cream cheese. "At this hour, Brian? Nothing like a surprise attack at dawn to catch the guy with his defences down."

"I doubt that. Hamm is probably the jog-at-oh-four-hundred type. I thought you'd like to know that the situation with him just got a whole lot more interesting."

"I'm listening."

"When I turned on the email this morning, there was a very excited report from your Sergeant McGrath in Halifax. You've got her so fired up on the case, she's using exclamation points after every second word."

Green paused, the knife suspended in mid-air. "She got an ID on Daniel Oliver's killer?"

"No, she hasn't got a match on that guy yet. But she got an ID on the man the killer was talking to just before the assault. The man who gave the fake name? It was Richard Hamm."

Green sucked in his breath. "Hamm was the drinking buddy?"

"Without a doubt. She recognized him herself, then got independent corroboration from the bartender. I thought you should know, in case you had any last minute instructions before Leblanc and I go after the guy."

Green glanced at Tony, who was perched on his bump-er seat, watching the bagel preparations eagerly. Tony had Sharon's dark curls and huge chocolate eyes, but his inten-sity and single-mindedness were all Green's. Green hesi-tated, loathe to disappoint him and to miss this lazy Sunday morning family time, but his own single-mindedness gave him little choice. If he stayed home, he would chafe with impatience all morning and drive the whole family crazy anyway.

"Give me an hour. I'll get some things out of the way here and be right with you," he said. He gave Tony his bagel and brewed up the coffee. Then, remembering the warmth of Sharon's arms around him the night before, he slipped a bagel into the toaster for her and headed out into the backyard. A pale morning sun warmed the small flower garden tucked into the corner against the brick wall, and already Sharon's massive fall bulb planting spree was paying dividends. Vivid yellow daffodils crowded the space. He pinched off one, hoping it would cheer her up after the long, ice-bound winter. Hoping too that it would make amends.

A smile lit her face when he walked into the room bearing the breakfast tray, but it faded slightly at the sight of the flower on the tray. She had heard the phone ring, and she was not fooled. He left her snuggling her son next to her as she picked up her coffee for her first sip. With her free hand, she waved him away.

"Go. The sun's shining, and we're all here today. Your loss, Green."

Steeped in guilt, he slunk out of the house. On the drive downtown, he forced his mind to refocus on McGrath's latest discovery about Hamm. It threw his theory about Oliver's killer and the war crimes cover-up out of whack. Hamm had fit the scenario to a T. He had been one of the few men in MacDonald's unit with the knowledge and capability to suppress a war crime. He had the strength and military training to kill Oliver with his bare hands, and he was also one of the few people interviewed by Peters before she was attacked.

This latest discovery did not exonerate him completely from the actual murders that had been committed; indeed ten years ago, he had lied to the police about his identity and very likely about his relationship to Oliver's killer. But he had not been the one to throw the punch. Which meant they had someone else to find.

Sullivan's prediction proved to be uncannily close to the mark, except that Hamm had not only put in an hour-long pre-dawn jog, but he had swum a few dozen laps at the hotel pool afterwards. He was now sitting in the hotel restaurant, his wet hair glistening and his cheeks ruddy with exertion, enjoying the full spread of the breakfast buffet. Our tax dollars at work, thought Green as he eyed the sausage, omelette, waffles, grilled tomatoes and fresh fruit that overflowed the man's plate. Hamm didn't look surprised to see them, only slightly nonplussed at having his routine disrupted.

"Good morning, gentlemen," he said cheerfully, signalling the waiter to bring them all coffee. "I've been expecting a visit from some more senior men. My sincere sympathies about your detective. Terrible to think such a thing could happen in Petawawa, but I guess rapists know no bounds. It's one of the things I worry about with the women under my command. It's an added vulnerability that men don't have, and in some parts of the world, it makes them fair game. What better way to strike at the enemy."

Green inclined his head to accept the sympathies, then waited for the performance to end. Once the man had established his importance in the pecking order, he shook his head as if to chide himself.

"But I won't keep you longer than necessary, because I know you've got your hands full. What can I do for you?"

"Tell us about your relationship with Ian MacDonald."

Hamm frowned as if searching his memory. "Ah. Still barking up that tree, I see."

Green waited.

"Ian MacDonald was a corporal in my platoon overseas in Croatia, as I'm sure you already know. I never saw him before, nor since."

"He killed himself in 1995."

Hamm cut his sausage into meticulous quarters. "I did know that. At least, I assumed it was intentional. He knew how to handle that rifle."

"Why do you think he did it?"

Hamm chewed thoughtfully. "Some soldiers have trouble with what they see overseas, and it colours their trust in people. Yugoslavia was a brutal and dangerous place."

"You did not seem very supportive of his medal for bravery. Why was that?"

"What the devil gave you that idea?"

"Mrs. MacDonald's impressions, and the sympathy card you sent her."

"It seems to me," said Hamm, laying down his fork impatiently, "that this is all ancient history, the details of which have no relevance to your current investigation. MacDonald was a nice boy, but he was not a soldier. He entered a firefight to save local civilians, all of whom were trying to kill each other, and in the process risked his own life and the rest of his section. That is the reason I was less than supportive. Historically, medals have been awarded to honour acts of bravery or heroism on the battlefront. This medal was all about optics, Inspector. The army had just been dragged through the mud over the Somalia affair, so let's pin a medal on the brave boy who risked his own life to save the locals."

Green had seen enough political games in his twenty-five-year career to know the colonel's assessment was probably dead on. "Still," he said, "that doesn't sound like a soldier so disillusioned and tormented that he'd later take his own life. What exactly happened to change him?"

"I have no idea. I don't make it a policy to psychoanalyze my men. I need to know that they have the strength, training and equipment to do the job I ask. Beyond that..." He shrugged. "Sometimes the stress reaction is delayed, when they have some downtime to think about it. That's why I always kept them busy."

Green paused to take a casual sip of coffee. Tried to make his voice neutral. "Daniel Oliver was a good friend of Ian MacDonald."

A contingent of businessmen had just invaded the buffet table, chattering with an animation Green had not thought possible at this hour. So great was Hamm's focus that he didn't seem to notice. He was watching Green carefully, but didn't reply.

"He seemed to think MacDonald's superior officer was to blame," Green added.

"Then you know his thoughts better than I."

"But you were there at the Lighthouse Tavern the night he accused his killer."

Hamm frowned. "The night Daniel Oliver died? In Halifax? I most certainly wasn't."

Green set his cup down. "Before you say anything to dig yourself in deeper, Colonel, I should tell you that I have two independent witnesses who've identified you as the man talking to Oliver's killer just before the altercation took place. So denial is not a wise choice."

In the silence, the laughter of the businessmen and the clatter of dishes filled the room. Sullivan had said nothing, but now he looked up from his notebook with interest. A faint flush crept up Hamm's neck, but his expression was unconcerned. "It may not be a wise choice, but it's the truth. How can anyone possibly have identified me if I wasn't there?"

"Exactly."

"Who are these witnesses anyway? Soldiers so drunk they could barely prop up their chins? Whores with eyes for every part of a man's body but his face? Come on, Inspector, you can't be serious."

Green leaned forward across the table. "At the time, you gave a false ID to the investigating officers. Luckily, they have excellent memories for faces. The question is, why did you do that? Just to save yourself the embarrassment of being caught up in a sleazy barroom brawl? Or to protect the man you were talking to."

Hamm stared at him, his blue eyes icy. His lips pursed in a taut line. "This is absurd. I don't have to dignify this with a response. First you accuse me of being in a bar brawl, then of providing false ID to the authorities. I've been in every filthy, rotten corner of the world, Inspector. I'd hardly lie about the Lighthouse Tavern."

"You would if you knew the killer, and your identity could point us to him."

Hamm thrust his chair back. "We're done here, gentlemen. Obviously nothing I say will change your minds. You'd rather take the word of a couple of police officers who pick my picture out of God knows what, ten years after the fact. There were at least a dozen drunken soldiers in the bar that night —"

"How do you know?"

Hamm's eyes snapped wide. "I guessed, you fool. You said it was a brawl —"

Green smiled and stood up to go. "Nice try, Colonel Hamm. We'll be in touch."

***

"I want a crack at him!" Kate McGrath announced the moment Green phoned to fill her in. He and Sullivan had just arrived at the station. and Sullivan was sifting through reports on the hunt for Twiggy.

"I think it's premature, Kate," Green replied. "The man had the ego of a colossus. He's not going to crack without a good deal more strong-arming, along with some evidence he can't dispute."

"With all due respect, Daniel Oliver is not your case. I've already cleared it with Norrich and I'm booked on the two thirty flight. I'll be there by five." She paused and her voice softened. "So you've got the day to get your additional evidence."

He hesitated. She was right; he had no right to stop her. And perhaps, just perhaps, her knowledge of the players in the old murder case would be useful in helping him put the pieces together. "Okay, I'll pick you up," he said, and he hung up. The smile was still lingering on his face when Sullivan walked into his office and gave him a knowing look.

Even though it was Sunday, Green could see several off-duty police officers milling around in the squad room outside. Everyone wanted to work the case on Peters's behalf.

"No sightings of Twiggy yet," Sullivan said, "but I phoned the hospital, and Peters continues to improve. She's been upgraded from critical to stable."

Green felt his mood lift even further. "That's good news. Has she regained consciousness?"

"No, but she's beginning to show signs, they said. The cop on guard said the doctors were actually smiling this morning."

Good news all around, thought Green. "We should tell Gibbs. And Weiss."

"I've already tried. Neither answered their phone."

"Bob's probably pounding the pavement again, trying to find someone who saw —" Green broke off as the elevator door opened and Gibbs himself appeared. The balding, bespectacled man who followed him out had a distinctively military stride, despite the extra two hundred pounds he carried on his massive frame. At the sight of Green and Sullivan, Gibbs's face lit with a mixture of triumph and anticipation.

"This is Corporal Neil Thompson, sir. The Queen's University student you asked me to locate." Gibbs introduced the two detectives. Thompson dwarfed even Sullivan in size, but the handshake he extended was flaccid and moist.

"Not a corporal anymore, strictly speaking," he corrected with a diffident laugh. "The reserve unit and I have just parted company."

Green didn't ask why, but suspected the poundage might have played a role. "Thank you for getting here so quickly."

"I drove down and picked him up," Gibbs said.

"But I'm glad to come. Glad to help anyway I can. Ian and Danny were my friends."

Green invited them all to pick up coffees and go down to a conference room where they could talk in comfort. He wanted to keep this initial interview conversational rather than formal, so he chose an executive meeting room that had recently been renovated in plush broadloom and leather. During the week, this room was reserved for intimate gatherings of the senior brass, but on Sunday, it was vacant. When they were settled around the table with hot cups of coffee, Green invited Thompson to tell them about Ian MacDonald's experience in Croatia. The man needed no prompting to launch into his tale.

"It was a pivotal point in our lives that changed most of us forever. Do I regret going there? Not for a moment. Would I go again? Not on your life. It's the reason I'm studying history now, because I realized the truth of the old saying. 'Those who don't learn from history are doomed to repeat it.' No one knew what they were doing over there. Not the UN Security Council, not the Europeans or the Americans or anyone else who stuck their noses in there. Not the military commanders and certainly not us lowly grunts patrolling our APCs up and down the road. But at the time we thought we were doing some good. We were keeping enemies apart, trying to make them compromise and negotiate their conflicts, trying to save innocent villagers who were caught up in the middle. And there were plenty of them."

He picked up his coffee in his sausage fingers and took a noisy slurp. "By the end we thought, well, they're not making a hell of a lot of headway on the diplomatic front in Zagreb, but at least on our little stretch of mountainside, we're trying to show them a better way. Being over there sure made me appreciate Canada. I'm telling you all this to give you a sense of what we were thinking while we were over there, alternatively bored, hot, homesick, terrified and exhilarated. We had a lot of laughs and experiences of a lifetime too. Ian was no different than the rest of us in that respect. Like me, he was a bit more intellectual than some of the guys; he was planning to go to vet school, he was quieter, liked time to think and write in his diary ..."

Green suppressed a jolt of excitement. No one had mentioned a diary. A diary might tell them everything! With an effort, he kept his expression neutral as he nodded for Thompson to continue, but mentally he was already composing his phone call to MacDonald's mother.

"Ian always tried to help where he could. He taught the local kids English and adopted this crazy dog. He loved animals and hated it when we came across livestock that had been hurt in the shelling. Anyway, we all got a little tired and worn down, and as time went on and both sides kept dicking the UN around, we got more jaded. Plus by the end, when we were basically ordered to break up this war, it got downright scary. None of us wanted to die over there, and even our commanders didn't believe our lives were on the line."

Green's senses grew alert. "Tell us about that."

"It was when we were posted to Sector South ..." He paused and pushed his glasses back up. Behind them, his tiny eyes peered at them uncertainly. "You guys know about the UNPAs?"

"Give us the highlights, just in case," Green said. He wanted to interrupt the man's recollections as little as possible.

"See, when Croatia and Serbia declared their independence from Yugoslavia, there were all these disputed parts of the country where they disagreed about whose land it was and which country it should be in, because the ethnic groups were all mixed up. Similar to where I'm from in New Brunswick, where the English and the French live side by side. The Croats claimed a whole lot of territory, and they basically wanted the Serbs out. The Serbs, on the other hand, wanted to join their villages together as part of Greater Serbia. And of course there were Muslims stuck in the middle too." He grimaced wryly as if it were all beyond comprehension, then he shrugged.

"So the UN created these four UN Protected Areas in these mixed pockets. Sector South was the trickiest one. It was in Croatia, but the Serbs had a big population tucked into the mountains there, and they could basically cut off all of Southern Croatia if they wanted. There was a bridge, a dam and a few other strategic installations that both sides wanted to control. When we got there, the Croats had captured the bridge and dam, but the Serbs kept shelling from up in the mountains, so the Croats couldn't use them. It was a war, and neither side wanted a ceasefire till they won. But ..."

He paused to catch his breath. His voice was calm, but beads of sweat had formed on his upper lip and temples. The three detectives sipped their coffees and waited in silence. This was an intelligent and co-operative witness, a dream come true, and they knew it was best to let him tell his story.

"The UN had been taking a lot of heat for the mess in Yugoslavia, what with the rumours of ethnic cleansing, the blatant ceasefire violations, the land grabs, and the endless squabbling and double-talk among the various factions. The UN general at the top wanted to prove the UN military force could do something useful besides sell gasoline on the black market and get the local girls pregnant, so he decided to clean up Sector South."

Sullivan leaned forward, suddenly alert. "A Canadian general? Was that MacKenzie?"

"No, it was a guy from France. Of course, I didn't know any of this when we were little blue helmets down on the ground. I learned all this big picture stuff later. Anyway ... Where was I?"

"Cleaning up Sector South?"

"Oh, yeah." Thompson mopped his brow and pushed his glasses up again. "So the general figures the Canadians can do the job, and all our own brass were so eager to hop to it, they ignored the fact none of the belligerents wanted us there. Plus you know, no one's supposed to fire on the UN. We had these shiny white vehicles you can see from miles away and these big-ass UN flags we're supposed to put on our vehicles to tell everyone we're the good guys. Target practice is more like it. We're trying to dig in and build a bunker to hide in, and they're shelling at each other over our heads the whole time. The Croats are trying to scare us away, and the Serbs are practically sitting in our laps, using us as cover to shell the Croats. Our leaders said 'you're soldiers, this is what you're trained for.' Sure, but we've got no air support, no big guns, and we're not allowed to return fire anyway. So day after day, we're hiding in this bunker covering our heads like kids in a sand fight."

"And you think this is what changed Ian MacDonald?"

"Well, it flipped out our section commander, that's for sure. He kept trying to tell command that his men were in danger, and he kept getting told to get on with it."

"This was Sergeant Sawranchuk?"

Thompson's sweaty face lit with a smile. "Yeah, have you talked to him?"

"Not yet," Green replied. "Did others find it as stressful?"

"We didn't have the responsibility he had. And to tell you the truth, you get used to it, and you don't think bad stuff's going to happen to you, eh? You get to feeling invincible when you never get hit." Thompson continued to grin, probably recalling the sheer adrenaline high of those days. "I think that's why Ian did his superman rescue routine. The Croats launched a mortar attack to capture a bunch of Serb villages, catching us right in the crossfire. Our section had the only safe location in the village because we were dug in, right? So Ian brought all these stranded Serbs inside our section house to protect them. It was brave but reckless. He still believed we could make a difference with the locals, even if their leaders were sabotaging the peace at every turn."

"So MacDonald wasn't angry at his superior officers for putting your lives in danger?"

"No, I think he felt sorry for the local people, because they couldn't just pick up and move out after six months like we could."

"What about Daniel Oliver? Was he angry?"

"Oh, no. Danny was the gung ho type, that's why Captain Hamm promoted him. He would have followed Hamm anywhere. Hamm was a true blue soldier."

"What about the higher ups? Senior NCOs and company officers. Did either Oliver or MacDonald have any trouble with them?"

"Not that I ever knew. Ian wasn't the argumentative type. He trusted people. He really believed everybody should do their best, even if the circumstances were difficult." His thick lips twisted in a sad smile that brought dimples to his cheeks.

Green sensed something in the smile, and in his tone. The man was remembering something more. Green kept his voice soft. "What happened?"

Thompson hesitated, his brow furrowing with distaste at having to face the memories. He shifted his bulk in his chair and took a deep breath. "We had this insane operation where we were supposed to get between the Serb and Croat armies and push the Croats back out of the Serb villages. After the Croats withdrew, the CO figured there would be lots of refugees and injured Serb villagers left behind. He also thought — we all thought, from the shooting we heard — that there might be ethnic cleansing. So he created a sweep team with different types of expertise. Doctors and medics to treat the wounded, military observers and forensic experts to collect evidence of war crimes. And regular soldiers, of course, to help with the refugees and with body recovery. Ian was picked because of his expertise with animals. There were always lots of starving and injured livestock, and I guess you pick up a lot growing up on a farm."

Thompson took a noisy slurp of coffee, which by this time must have been stone cold. "You could smell the stench for miles. Ian came back after two weeks of that ... and he was a different man."

Green absorbed this information, trying to see if the explanation fit with what they knew. Had something awful happened during those two weeks? Across the table, Sullivan laid down his notebook and leaned forward, his blue eyes intense. "You said there were forensics experts. From the military?"

"No, civilians. Both forensic specialists and UN civilian police were brought in to interview witnesses and document crimes."

"Do you remember any names?"

Thompson shook his head. "No, the sweep team was in another unit. None of us met the cops."

"Except Ian."

"Well, yeah. I suppose Ian would have met them."

Green felt Sullivan's eyes upon him. If MacDonald and Weiss had served together in that sweep team, it was an extraordinary coincidence. Surely this had to be the core of the mystery. But was it enough simply to have served together? Was the trauma of that assignment sufficient to have derailed the lives of two young men so completely?

Green felt a niggling dissatisfaction. Something was missing. Oliver had used the word "betrayal" when he confronted his assailant in the bar. Betrayal was a powerful word, usually reserved for when a trust is truly shattered.

Suddenly the implication of the rest of Thompson's statement struck him. "You said the sweep team was in another unit. Do you remember the leader's name?"

"That I do remember, because his name has been plastered all over the news. It was John Blakeley."

TWENTY-ONE

Aug. 19, 1993. Maslenica Bridge, Sector South, Croatia.

The whole Canadian Battalion has taken over this sector and we're quartered at the old school again, waiting for the withdrawal agreement. I feel like we'll be stuck here forever, ducking the shells, while the UN plays with itself and the Croats get ready to wipe the Serbs off the map. I can't wait to go home. Only a month to go, if we don't get killed. Every day the artillery shells fly over our heads. The Serbs are trying to snuggle up as close as they can to use us as cover while they attack, but the Croats blast back at them anyway.

The company commander figures both sides are trying to drive us away so they can have a clear shot at each other. But he's decided we are going to stay put, so all night long, when the Serbs can't see us, we fill sand bags and hump them up the hill to build the biggest bunker you've ever seen. The soil is really red, and Sarge is afraid it's radioactive from some old mine that's near by. But the OC says "you want to die now, or later?"

Aug. 22, 1993. Maslenica Bridge, Sector South, Croatia.

Today all hell broke loose inside the camp. We got blasted by this shell fifteen metres from the bunker while we were asleep. It blew up a whole wall of sand bags and we were all choking on the red dust. Sarge says "that's it!" and he grabs his rifle, jumps in the Jeep and goes off. Word is he threatened to blow the company commander's head off and it took three guys to restrain him. Anyway, a few hours later the Hammer comes up, pins a master corporal maple leaf on Danny and says he's the new section commander. Just like that. I'm glad for Danny, but I'm worried about Sarge. He was only trying to look out for us.

***

JOHN BLAKELEY'S CONDOMINIUM was not at all what Green had expected, given what he had learned about the man. It was on the twelfth floor of a glass and steel spire on Laurier Avenue West, and had a spectacular view of the Ottawa River, the copper roof of the new War Museum, and in the distance across the river, the rounded hills of the Gatineau. The taxes and condo fees alone, even without a mortgage, would have put the average enlisted man in the poorhouse, but Blakeley also had a riverside estate in Petawawa, where he and his wife presumably spent most of their time.

As soon as they had finished with Neil Thompson, Green and Sullivan headed straight over to see Blakeley, wanting to catch him by surprise and give him little time to plan a defence strategy. Atkinson had almost certainly warned him that they were making inquiries about the past, but neither the sweep team nor MacDonald's and Weiss's names had been mentioned before. Green hoped that gave them at least a small element of surprise.

Standing outside the steel and glass high rise, Green was no longer sure what to expect. A man as tall and remote as the place where he lived? To his surprise, Blakeley buzzed them in cheerfully, and when they emerged from the elevator on the twelfth floor, he was standing in the hallway with a hearty grin on his face. In person, even more than in his photo, the ridged white scar across his left eyebrow gave him a warrior's air. He was dressed in ratty jeans and a red Ottawa Senators T-shirt. His white hair, so well tamed in his campaign poster, flew about in wild disarray and his grin revealed a chipped front tooth. He was shorter than Green, with a thick, muscular body.

He shook Green's hand with a vigour that made Green's teeth rattle.

"You caught me in my Sunday best, boys," he exclaimed as he ushered them inside. "But I've been expecting you. Roger said you'd dropped by. I've asked Leanne to put on a pot of coffee. Terrible thing about your detective, and I'll do whatever I can to help. I have some contacts with the police up in Petawawa."

He led the way through a brightly lit hall into an enormous living room banked by an entire wall of windows. The view was unobstructed by curtains, as if inviting the vast open skies into the room. The floors were acres of blond wood and, again surprisingly for the rugged warrior who lived there, the furniture was white leather. The only strong colours came from the vivid framed photographs that lined the walls. Close-ups of nature — a gnarled tree, a rusty tugboat at sunset, a snake coiled in a tree. Not the nature of postcards and tourism brochures, Green noted, but the underbelly. A reflection of the man himself, perhaps?

Green sensed immediately that he was in the presence of a powerful man. A man of strong emotion, vast intellect and a charisma that pulled people in his wake. No wonder the Liberals wanted him. Green chose the leather armchair by the window, so that he was facing into the room and backlit by the sun. It was a small advantage, but he suspected he was going to need every one he could get. Sullivan folded himself into a loveseat at the opposite side of the room, leaving Blakeley no choice but to sit between them, unable to keep both in his sights.

A woman glided into the room with the grace of a cat, bearing a tray with coffee and a plate of scones. She sized up the situation and her lips drew a thin, tight line. "Perhaps you'd prefer to sit at the table," she said, gesturing to the adjoining dining room, where a heavy white table was encircled by plush suede chairs. "It'll be easier that way."

Remind me not to underestimate this woman, Green thought. "Oh, this is no trouble," he replied blandly.

"Gentlemen, this is my wife Leanne," said Blakeley. "Put it over here, honey."

Leanne shot a brief glance at Sullivan before setting the tray on the coffee table between them. She looked at least twenty years Blakeley's junior, as lithe and fine-featured as he was rugged, but Green sensed a will equal to his own.

"Yes, your wife and I met yesterday," said Sullivan. "She runs a very efficient campaign office. Nice to see you again, Ms Neuss."

Leanne inclined her head gracefully, then turned and walked from the room without a backward glance.

Green launched the interview while Sullivan quietly extracted his notebook. "We really appreciate your offer of help, Mr. Blakeley —"

"Please call me John. No formalities here. How do you take your coffee … Mike, is it?"

"Cream and sugar, thanks." Green ignored the familiarity. "I know you're a busy man, so I'll get straight to the meat of the inquiry. Our information is that in September 1993 you headed a sweep team over in Croatia which included a young reservist named Corporal Ian MacDonald. Is that correct?"

If Blakeley was surprised, he betrayed no sign. His brown eyes looked thoughtful, then sad. "That is correct. I remember him well."

"Why is that?"

"Because he'd been recommended for a medal of bravery — and subsequently got it — and I was expecting a damn fine soldier. In fact, I requested him."

"Why?"

Blakeley didn't hesitate. "Because he sounded like the kind of soldier that I needed for the job. He had strength, courage, but most importantly heart. When we walked into the villages after the fighting, I wanted the first Canadians those poor people met to be men like Ian MacDonald."

"And was he what you expected?"

This time Blakeley did pause, ever so slightly before he nodded.

"Why the hesitation?"

Blakeley handed coffee to Sullivan, then tended to his own, drawing out the silence. "It was a difficult mission. Most of the boys struggled with it one way or the other."

"What was MacDonald's struggle with it?"

"He went in, as we all did, expecting to help relocate and bring medical aid to the local population, and also in his case to the animals. He ended up bagging bodies, burning dead livestock to prevent disease, and putting cruelly injured animals out of their misery."

"Our information is that this sweep mission changed him in a way all his previous operations had not. He became depressed and remote, dropped all his plans for vet school, and eventually killed himself."

Blakeley nodded grimly. "I heard. I was appalled."

"What happened to him?"

"Beyond what I've just told you, I don't know."

"Come on, John, it isn't enough to talk about trauma and disillusionment." Hoping to unsettle him, Green speculated further. "Something very real happened to MacDonald. Something he couldn't reconcile himself to, and ultimately couldn't live with."

Blakeley looked from one to the other as if gauging the threat and the appropriate response. He set down his coffee. "Boys, we were at war. Make no mistake about it. Forget all the peacekeeping rhetoric. Half the time there's no peace to keep, and we Canadians are the only ones who believe in it. The rest of the world solves conflicts by war, and it's only the losing side that calls in the UN. We get over there, with our heads filled with peacekeeping fluff and both our hands tied behind our back by the UN, and we're told to take care of things. Don't come whining for hardware, because there isn't any; don't try defending any civilians or fighting back, because that's taking sides. And then when the whole operation goes down the toilet, everyone including our own military and political leadership says what the hell were you boys playing over there, tiddlywinks? Well, yeah, because that was the only game in town."

"Mr. Blakeley — John, we're talking —"

"I'm getting there! But you know how it is, Mike. On the street day after day, you cops make judgement calls that you hope like hell you'll never have to defend to the press, or to your superior officer. A little entrapment here, undue force there … It isn't pretty, but it gets the job done." He held up a hand. "I'm not condoning it. And I'm not condoning any wrongdoing a soldier does in the heat of the moment either. But they're out there halfway around the world, laying their lives on the line twenty-four seven in somebody else's war, and if for two or three seconds they're less than exemplary soldiers —"

"Are you saying Ian MacDonald did something wrong in the heat of the moment?"

"No, I'm not. I'm talking about the standards we demand of our boys —"

"I don't want a campaign speech, Mr. Blakeley. I want to know what really happened with Corporal MacDonald."

Blakeley's face flushed, accentuating the angry white scar. He calmed himself by reaching for a scone, which he buttered with care. "Why? Will it bring him back? Ian MacDonald was a hero. If we put all our boys under a microscope and dissect their every move, we won't have any more heroes. And whether you care or not, we need heroes in the military. We need inspiration and glory, and all the things that are no longer in fashion, or we won't find anyone willing to go out and fight these dirty little wars on our behalf. And the victims of this world will be the worse for it. Look at Afghanistan —"

"So you're saying we should sweep this all under the carpet as a small price we pay for the help we provide to the world?"

"No, I'm saying our boys are human. When we send them into these hell holes, we have to understand that. If we expect them to be God, we'd better not send them."

Green leaned forward, his eyes fixed on Blakeley's. "I might be willing to do that, John, except that in this case his friend Daniel Oliver died because of what happened to Ian MacDonald on that sweep team. And that's not something we cops are prepared to sweep under the rug."

Blakeley had just taken a bite of scone, and his hand froze in mid air. "What are you talking about?"

Out of the corner of his eye, Green had been aware of Leanne moving quietly about in the kitchen, and she chose this moment to glide back into the room. She slipped onto the sofa next to her husband and took his hand in hers.

"I don't think my husband is suggesting you should sweep anything under the rug, gentlemen."

To Green's surprise, Blakeley did not object to her interference, nor pull his hand away. "Of course I'm not, and I know that's not what the inspector means. He's saying that a young man died — two young men if we count Ian MacDonald — and finding out why is more important than personal reputations or public trust."

"Not just finding out why," Green said, "but who. Because the killing hasn't stopped —"

"You're not implying my husband had anything to do with that!"

Since she was running such effective interference, Green decided perhaps she was the one he needed to reach. "He knows something, Mrs. Blakeley. He was the leader of the mission where Ian MacDonald's troubles began. He can't pretend ignorance when the victims keep piling up. First Ian MacDonald, then Daniel Oliver, his fiancée Patricia Ross, Detective Peters, and the latest, a homeless woman whose only crime was to be in the vicinity when Patricia Ross was killed."

Blakeley looked shocked. Almost stricken. He looked at his wife searchingly, and she tightened her grip on his hand. For a moment neither spoke, then Blakeley shook his head. "I don't know what happened. I wish I could be more help."

"Where were you on April 9, 1996, ten years ago?"

Blakeley frowned. "I have no idea. In 1996 I was posted here in Ottawa from January to August."

"Did you travel to Halifax during that time?"

"Not that I recall."

"That was just before our wedding," Leanne said. "You proposed to me in April, remember, darling?" She smiled at the detectives. "I don't think we spent a single night apart for nearly a year."

"You're absolutely sure?" Green asked. "No business trips, brief consultations? Because we will be verifying this."

Blakeley was shaking his head back and forth, but Green thought he looked distracted. Even pale.

"How did you get on with Corporal MacDonald?"

Blakeley shrugged. "He was no trouble. As I said, he was that fine balance the Canadian military needs for our peacekeeping role — a warrior with heart — because we are both fighters and humanitarians."

"Did Ian MacDonald have any conflicts with anyone else on the team?"

"Most people liked him."

"Well, there was that police officer," Leanne said.

Green leaped at the remark. "Who?"

Blakeley gave her a sharp look, but she ignored it. "The one you told me about. It may be important, John."

"It's ancient history, honey. A trivial disagreement, that's all."

"Didn't you say they disagreed about a cause of death or something?"

"Or something."

"Whose death?" Green interjected.

"I don't recall." Blakeley shook his head grimly. "God knows there were enough deaths to argue over."

"Still," she said, "if the police think there's a connection, and if people are still getting killed, then maybe —"

Abruptly Blakeley stood up. "No. This is a fishing expedition, and I will not continue this speculation any further. Innocent people are being maligned."

"Innocent people are being killed," Green retorted. "I need the police officer's name, Blakeley. Was it Jeff Weiss?"

Blakeley strode to the apartment door and yanked it open without a word. As Green and Sullivan rose to go, Leanne moved quickly to their side. "He was from Ottawa, I know that much. You can figure it out."

TWENTY-TWO

"BASTARD!" SULLIVAN EXCLAIMED as soon as they were in the elevator out of earshot. "If that sonofabitch did that to Peters, I'll personally string him up by the balls!"

Green leaned against the faux marble wall and looked across at him, puzzling over the final moments of the interview. "Which sonofabitch?"

"Weiss, of course! That's obviously the cop the wife was referring to. He was the one MacDonald had the beef with."

"But he wasn't in a position to cover up anything. He was a civilian cop, he had no power over MacDonald."

"Doesn't matter. We're fishing in the dark here, Mike. All we know for sure is that something upset MacDonald. It could have been Weiss accusing him of some wrongdoing, which got under MacDonald's skin. Then, when he killed himself, Oliver accused Weiss and got killed for his big mouth. Weiss had the strength and the training to deliver the blow, and we know he had the temper. He thought he got away with it, and then ten years later along comes Patricia Ross threatening to blow the lid off."

The elevator stopped, and they headed outside towards the Malibu. As he scrambled to keep pace with Sullivan's purposeful stride, Green weighed the idea dubiously. "But why would Hamm cover for Weiss? Hamm is a military bigshot, Weiss is nothing but a low-level cop. And where does Atkinson fit in?"

"Maybe nowhere. Maybe his story about the military contact in supplies is the truth."

Green snorted. "And Hamm?"

Sullivan yanked open the door. "I don't know, Mike. Maybe he and Weiss have a history somewhere." He started the car and revved the engine impatiently. "I say we bring Jeff Weiss in and lean on him."

"But he's a cop, Brian. We can't go accusing one of our own when we're still missing half the pieces."

Sullivan pulled a U-turn and squealed the car back down Laurier Avenue towards the police station. "But maybe he can give them to us. He's the weakest link here. Weaker than Blakeley or Hamm."

Privately, Green knew he was right, and usually it was he who was itching to plunge ahead and Sullivan who was the voice of restraint. But at the moment, Green's mind was elsewhere; not with Weiss and his betrayal of his badge, but with Blakeley and his peculiar behaviour during the interview. Of all the men on their list of potential suspects, Blakeley had means, motive and opportunity in spades. He had the most to lose if his complicity in war crimes, or his murder of Oliver, ever came to light. Not just his hard-earned reputation but his promising future at the very centre of government. He was a decisive, physical man trained to size up a threat and eliminate it. He was skilled enough to kill Oliver and Patricia Ross with his bare hands. And with his frequent commuting between Ottawa and Petawawa, he could easily have come to Ottawa to kill Ross, returned to Petawawa to attack Peters and come back in Ottawa to abduct Twiggy.

He made a damn compelling suspect, and his demeanour during the interview had been decidedly suspicious. He had spent the first half giving a campaign speech and the second half dancing evasively around Green's more pointed probes. When that failed, he had pretended offence and abruptly terminated the interview.

Yet it was his behaviour rather than his words that puzzled Green. At the beginning he had been chatty and collegial when lecturing them on the pitfalls of peacekeeping, but when Oliver's death was mentioned, he suddenly lost his hearty charm. As the names of more recent victims piled up, he became visibly shaken and distracted, as if the news had shocked him.

Yet if he was the killer, why the shock? Why not a defensive parry or the well-practised evasion he had displayed earlier? Even odder than the shock was his wife's behaviour. It was astonishing enough that she had interrupted her husband's meeting with the police in order to come to his rescue, but even more astonishing that he allowed it. Furthermore, at the end of the interview, she had essentially handed them Constable Weiss over the protests of her husband. This was not a stupid woman. She had a reason for what she'd done, and she had obviously thought giving up Weiss would help her husband, whether he wanted it or not. The question was — why?

By the time Sullivan pulled into the parking lot of police headquarters, Green still had no answers, but at least he had a plan. He glanced at his watch, which read noon. No time to spare. He jumped out of the car before Sullivan had even brought it to a stop.

"Okay, we're going to lean on Weiss," he said. "But first we're going to make sure he's got no room to weasel out. So I want you to round up all the available detectives in the squad room and meet me in the incident room in ten minutes."

Sullivan smiled. "Are you going to tell Superintendent Devine about this? Otherwise, she'll have your balls."

"I know. That's partly what the ten minutes is for." He started for the door.

"It'll take more than ten minutes!" Sullivan yelled.

"Just watch me!" Then he sprinted inside the building, took the stairs two at a time and was dialling his office phone in less than thirty seconds. Kate McGrath was not at her desk, and he wasted several minutes badgering the duty clerk before remembering that he had her home number in his book. She picked up on the second ring.

"I need you to check one last thing before you come," he said.

"I'm just packing to go, Mike. My taxi will be here in half an hour."

"I'm emailing you two more photos. Just check them out with the Lighthouse bartender."

"But I'll miss —"

"No, you won't. Have you got a laptop at home? I'll send them directly to you, and you can bring your laptop by the Lighthouse on your way to the airport. Ten minutes, tops."

"It won't be a proper line-up."

"So I'll email you a whole photo array. Kate! We've lost another person up here, this time an innocent old lady."

She fell silent, and he could almost hear her calculating the time. Then she rhymed off her email address. "Just make it quick, Mike, and pray the bartender is there. It's Sunday."

After he'd sent the photo array, he grabbed his address book again and flipped through it for another number. While he waited for the MacDonalds to answer their phone, he took deep breaths to slow himself down. This next call was going to be delicate work.

After over half a dozen rings, Mrs. MacDonald's quavering voice came on the line. Defeat seeped into her very cadence, a defeat so profound that nothing could ever lift it, except her son's return to life. Green hated the part of his job which required him to probe the unhealed wounds of survivors.

He introduced himself and reminded her of their last visit. He heard a little gasp of dismay, but she said nothing. He wondered if her husband was in the room.

"Can you talk?" he asked.

A wary "Yes."

"I'm told Ian kept a diary of his months in Yugoslavia. It may be very helpful to our investigation here. The man who killed Daniel Oliver has tried to kill again, this time one of our police officers." He paused, debating how deep to poke the knife. She waited in silence. "He may also have killed an innocent bystander. I think the key to the man's identity may lie in your son's diary."

Still silence.

"I'm really hoping you'll let us have the diary for a day or two. I could send someone from the local RCMP to pick it up."

A slight moan.

"I promise we'll handle it with care and send it back as soon as possible."

"It's gone."

Green was so startled he wasn't sure he'd heard properly. "Where?"

"It disappeared years ago, and I don't care where," she repeated, her voice gathering force. "I didn't want to ever be reminded of those hateful, hateful times. They killed my boy, as truly as if they'd pulled the trigger. They killed his soul."

Oh, fuck. Green sank back in his chair, listening to her slowly spin out of control. He reached out to stop her.

"Did you read it?"

"No!"

From her vehemence, he suspected she might be lying, but he also knew he was not going to budge her. He forced himself to be gentle. "Did Ian ever mention a Constable Weiss? Or a Captain Blakeley?"

"He didn't talk about those times. He kept them deep inside, as if he was ashamed. And nothing I said ..." Her voice broke horribly.

"I'm sorry, Mrs. MacDonald. I'm so sorry I had to trouble you this way. If you do remember anything you want to tell me, please, please give me a call. Any time."

Green dropped the receiver back into its cradle with a despairing thud and took a moment to collect himself and make sense of this latest news. What had become of the diary? Had Daniel Oliver taken it at the same time he took the medal? If so, had he read something in it that led to his fatal confrontation with Blakeley? And where had it ended up after Oliver's death? In Patricia Ross's apartment, lost among the photos and letters from Daniel's army days?

Green glanced at his watch and was dismayed to see his ten minutes was long over. Reluctantly he picked up the phone, prepared for battle. But Barbara Devine was not answering her cellphone or her phones at either the office or home. Grateful for small mercies, including the fact that Devine's efficient secretary was not on duty Sunday to take up the search, Green left urgent but vague messages on all lines, then grabbed his notebook and headed to the incident room.

When he walked in, seven detectives were assembled around the table. Only Gibbs was missing. They were casually dressed but sat upright in silent attention. Notebooks were open, and a sense of anticipation hung in the air. Green stared at them all gravely. A good bunch, seasoned and level-headed. They would need both those qualities in the next few hours. He walked up to the head of the conference table and slipped a fresh disk into the laptop which was used to collect and organize all the reports on the case. He dreaded the task ahead.

"The Ross/Peters investigation has reached a highly sensitive and confidential point, and I'm going to ask you not to tell anyone — anyone! — what we're looking at. We're going to be investigating a fellow officer. Anyone uncomfortable with that had better leave now."

Eyes widened, but no one moved.

"Has the officer been charged?" Leblanc asked.

"No, he has not been charged." Green summarized the latest developments in the case, including the disappearance of Twiggy and the involvement of high profile Liberal candidate John Blakeley. The energy around the table was electric, until Green came to Weiss's role. As they listened, Green could see the outrage and disbelief on their faces.

"This is all just coincidence and speculation," Charbonneau protested. "You don't actually know anything."

Green nodded. "That's right, and that's why you're here. To clear him, or to expose him. Let's hope I'm wrong, but remember, if he's guilty, he betrayed Sue." He waited a moment for that message to sink in, then resumed quietly. "We have five tasks to complete. First, we have to find something more than coincidence to tie him to the case. Charbonneau and Leblanc, I want you to prepare a photo line-up with Weiss in it, then pay a visit to a witness named Hassim Mohammed, a manager at the Tim Hortons on Bank Street." He handed over the photo he'd taken from Weiss's file. "Ask Mr. Mohammed to ID the man who was asking about Twiggy. And get going, because the next steps hinge on that ID."

The tension in the room eased as the detectives focussed on the job. Charbonneau and Leblanc jotted some notes and rose to go. "Have you got a home address? It's Sunday."

Green read off the address. "Nice co-operative guy with a soft spot for Twiggy, but he's a bit jumpy, so go easy on him."

The two detectives rolled their eyes before hustling from the room.

"Second, search warrants —"

The door burst open, and Gibbs rushed in, his face flushed and his eyes shining. "Sorry I'm late, sir. I was just waiting to confirm something up in Petawawa. That mystery cellphone? I just got the phone log on it, and it received a call about two minutes before the call went to the bartender at the King's Arms —" He stopped, looking flustered. "I mean, whoever called the Petawawa bartender to set up Sue? He got a call two minutes earlier from another phone."

"We got that, Bob," Sullivan said patiently.

Gibbs grinned sheepishly. "That other phone? It was a payphone in a convenience store just down the street from Sue. One of the places Jeff Weiss would have been canvassing at the time she was attacked."

Silence descended as the grim implications set in. Had one of their own really set her up for the kill? Or received instructions to do it himself?

Green spoke first. "Good work, Bob. We'll have to tie Weiss to that call, so send the Petawawa OPP the same photo line-up and get them to follow up with the staff at the store. Meanwhile, it's more ammunition for our search warrants. We need two — one to access Weiss's phone records, both cell and landlines, and another to search his house. Jones, you're the search warrant genius. You and Wells get started on the paperwork. We'll have to wait till Mohammed's positive ID before we finalize it."

Jones was nodding as he scribbled in his notebook. "What are we looking for?"

"Jean Calderone. AKA Twiggy. And/or evidence she's been there."

Jones stopped writing and looked up in surprise. "He wouldn't be stupid enough to take her to his house."

"No, but it gets us in the door, and we'll have to search everywhere very thoroughly to find evidence of her, like fingerprints and stray hairs. And while we're searching, who knows what else we might turn up."

Soft chuckles rippled through the room.

"You should also add stuff like clothing and shoes, for traces of blood, dirt from the crime scenes, you know the drill. We'll seize every stitch of clothing he owns if we have to."

For a few minutes they ironed out the contents and timing of the search warrants. Both detectives recorded everything in their notebooks, but Green didn't make a single entry to the official case file. Too many eyes had access. Once the detectives had headed out to complete their job, Green entered a short note on his own disk. Sullivan watched him in silence, and Green was grateful he made no comment. He needed no reminder how fragile a limb he was climbing out on. He looked up at the remaining detectives.

"Next, we need to keep track of Weiss while we get all these pieces in place. Wallington and Connors, I want you to locate him and keep him in your sights at all times. And whatever you do, don't tip him off till we're ready to bring the bastard in."

After the two had left, Green looked across at Gibbs, who was now alone with Sullivan in the room. Gibbs was looking at him expectantly.

"What's the news on Sue?" Green asked.

"The nurses say she's the same. But I think she knows I'm there. I'm sure she squeezed my hand." Gibbs flushed and shifted his lanky frame restlessly. "What's my assignment, sir?"

Gibbs looked as if he hadn't slept in days. In his time off, he'd kept a vigil at Peters's bedside, never giving up hope that she'd open her eyes. Green knew he should send the young man home to bed, but he also knew Gibbs needed to be here, fighting on Peters's behalf. Green told him about his fruitless conversation with Ian MacDonald's mother. "After you send the OPP Weiss's photo, I want you back on the computer finding out the name and location of every member of Blakeley's sweep team. Soldiers, medics and police. We need to confirm the connection between Weiss and MacDonald, and if possible find out what the hell happened over there."

***

Results began to pour in very fast. First to report in were Charbonneau and Leblanc, so excited with their success that they phoned in from their car outside Hassim Mohammed's house.

"He nailed him, sir!" Leblanc exclaimed. "Took a good long look at each one, hesitated only a few seconds, and picked out Weiss."

"Even with the sunglasses?"

"Even so. It was the wide forehead and the cheekbones, he said."

Green felt a peculiar surge of emotion. Part triumph that they were closing in on the culprit, part outrage that he was proving to be one of their own. He realized that he'd been hoping against hope that Weiss would be exonerated, and that it would prove to be just one of those crazy coincidences that plague detective work from time to time. But there was no imaginable reason why Weiss would be inquiring about Twiggy unless he was somehow connected to the case. Moreover, Weiss was the only one of their suspects who would have known that Twiggy was a potential witness to the murder, because he had seen her at the scene that morning, giving her statement to the police.

"What did you do with her, you bastard?" Green asked himself after he'd thanked the detectives. Twiggy had apparently dropped off the face of the earth. The uniformed patrols had turned up no sign of her, and the questioning of street people at her favourite haunts had yielded nothing. Among her usual hangouts, the only place she could have gone without anyone seeing her was the art gallery, because no one had dared return there since the murder. It was the one place she would have gone to wait for Green. It was also the one place, however, where Weiss would have known to look for her.

Green cursed the twist of fate that had intervened to prevent him from meeting her. If he'd gone there Friday at sunset as she'd asked, she would be safe today. On Friday Weiss was in Petawawa, his whereabouts accounted for until well into the night. Therefore, if he'd snatched her, he had not done so until some time Saturday morning. When the bastard had called in sick and was supposedly at home recovering from his trauma.

The trauma of setting up his partner to be killed.

The call from the Petawawa OPP came in fast on the heels of Leblanc's call. The convenience store owner remembered

Weiss coming in to ask questions about a woman, whom the store owner claimed he never saw, then using the payphone on his way out. Asked about Weiss's demeanour, the store owner said he seemed distracted, and he'd glanced out the window several times during the interview. The phone call was brief, no more than two minutes, after which he had headed next door to the pizza restaurant.

To his credit, the OPP investigator had pressed for further details about the call. Had Weiss known the number by heart, or had he looked it up? If so, in what? The store owner recalled that he'd consulted a piece of paper from his breast pocket, which was hardly surprising, Green thought, since it was a private cell number not found in any book. Had Weiss made more than one call? No, the owner assured him. A two-minute call, tops, and he'd gone on his way.

Two minutes was plenty of time to tip someone off and set the assault in motion. Green still had that nagging suspicion that Weiss was merely a bit player, a conduit whose strings were being pulled by the real villain in the case. Who? And why was Weiss co-operating? What did the killer have on him that he could coerce an otherwise dedicated officer to betray his oath of service and the very colleagues he worked with?

In less than an hour, Wallington and Connors phoned in to report on their surveillance efforts at Weiss's home. Green already feared what they were going to say. The curtains were drawn, the doors were locked, and the pick-up truck registered in his name was missing from the drive. Weiss was not there.

Of course he's not, thought Green in frustration, because he's gone into hiding somewhere. The question was whether he had Twiggy with him, or whether her body had already been dumped.

"We've checked with the neighbours on all sides, and no one has seen him since early Friday morning," Connors said. "One of the neighbours phoned his home and his cellphone at our request and got no answer."

"What about mail in the mailbox?"

"It was empty, sir."

So either he received none on Friday, or he picked it up sometime after returning from the hospital Friday night, Green thought. Had he received orders to snatch Twiggy at that time, or had he been trying to find her since Thursday and had struck it lucky at the art gallery on Saturday morning because she'd still been waiting for Green?

Stop going there, he chided himself. It serves nothing but to cloud your objectivity, which is already clouded enough.

"Do you want us to set up a stake-out, sir?"

Wallington's question stopped his spiralling thoughts. Weiss had to be found, even if they had to look under every rock. "Yes. Get that neighbour's co-operation to do surveillance on the QT from his place, and interview all the neighbours again to see if any of them know where he might go to get away from things. Relatives, a fishing lodge, a cottage … anything like that. Also work up a list of known associates. I'll put some guys on that from this end as well."

"And if Weiss comes back?"

Green thought about that for less than five seconds. Weiss had proved too elusive to risk losing him all over again, along with all chance of finding Twiggy and catching the other players in the game. "Apprehend the bastard and bring him in."

"On what charges?"

"I'll be working on that."

After he hung up, Green sat at his desk a moment, pondering that very question. He was about to arrest a fellow police officer and bring him in. All hell would break loose at that moment, from the police chief and Barbara Devine on down to the Police Association. He needed to know what was going on before he committed himself to an action that would be dissected for months, possibly years to come. He needed to know whether Weiss was the ruthless mastermind, or some small player caught in a web way beyond his control.

Green had always prided himself on his intuition, and after twenty years in the trenches, he'd witnessed human distress in all its varied guises. Weiss's behaviour at the hospital on Friday had been unusual in its extreme, but his distress had seemed real. Only a very gifted actor could summon up the pallor, the trembling and the tears on cue.

Whatever part Weiss had played, however willingly he had played it, something was tearing him up inside. He was not the cold, calculating person Green had imagined the killer to be. He was conflicted, desperate and unpredictable, which made him dangerous not only to himself and to the Twiggy, but to the ruthless killer who was pulling his strings.

And that killer was almost certainly smart enough to realize that.

TWENTY-THREE

Sept. 1, 1993. A beach somewhere in Sector South, Croatia.

Dear Kit … It was good to hear from you finally. We've been moving around a lot, so I'm not sure where we are, or what we're doing here. Mostly keeping an eye on Serb troop movements, counting artillery fire, and waiting for the order to move when the Croat withdrawal agreement is signed. The Hammer has us doing a lot of PT, humping up and down the mountain with our packs so we won't get soft. And drills. Man, am I sick of drills and cleaning the guns.

We're in a town on the coast that's pretty deserted, so we have our choice of houses. Danny moved our section into this big old mansion. Most of the furniture's been looted, but there are beds for all of us. Beds! The first night I slept on one, I didn't sleep a wink. I still feel like I'm in that bunker on the hill. It's hard to shake that, and just relax.

I've been thinking about home a lot, now that it's getting close. I'll have lots of money saved when I get back, but I think I'd like some time off, just to hang out at the farm and help my folks. Maybe I'll be ready for vet school next year, but it all feels a long way off.

***

GREEN YANKED OPEN his office door and scanned the squad room to see who might be available to join the search for Jeff Weiss. He spotted Charbonneau and Leblanc back at their computers and was about to call them over when the elevator slid open and George Nelson lumbered out. The staff sergeant's bald dome was bright red and shiny with sweat, and even from across the room, Green could hear his wheezing.

When Nelson saw Green, his eyes sparked. Without a word, he gestured Green back into his office and slammed the door. "I hear you've got half a dozen officers going after Jeff Weiss."

Green forced himself to sit down behind his desk with a serenity he did not feel. Jesus, the last thing this delicate operation needed was a leak that brought the entire police service down on his back. "Who told you that?"

"Is it true?"

Green met his belligerent stare with silence. Finally, Nelson wagged his heavy head back and forth with disgust. "Jesus H., Mike, what are you doing?"

"You know I'm quietly looking into Weiss's possible involvement, George. You yourself talked to me."

"An off-the-record discussion between supervisors is one thing. You've got guys out there watching his house and checking his phone records!"

Damn, Green thought, one of my men is blabbing. Some of his anger crept into his voice. "I'm tracking a killer, and I'm also trying to prevent him from killing again. I have to tell you, the evidence against Weiss is piling up."

Nelson absorbed this in silence, his breathing loud in the tiny room. "Have you told the brass yet? Or Professional Standards?"

Green hesitated. He had made one effort to contact Devine, but had been relieved she wasn't there.

"Jesus H.!" Nelson said. "You've got to tell them. This has to be by the book."

"It will be. Nothing has been done yet, and so far all I want to do is locate Weiss so I can keep an eye on him till I put the pieces together."

Nelson raised a skeptical eyebrow. "It's going to blow up in your face, Mike. If I found out, half the force will know by dinnertime."

Green didn't appreciate being reminded of the obvious. He tried again. "Which one of my men told you?"

"It wasn't one of ours. It was a neighbour of Weiss's who's in the RCMP. He knew I knew Jeff, and he wanted to know what was going on." Nelson paused to wipe the sweat that had trickled down his cheek. "Law Enforcement's a small community. Everybody knows somebody, nothing stays a secret very long. Weiss is going to find out."

Green tried to imagine the fall-out. "That's not necessarily a bad thing. It might force his hand."

"Weiss is a scrapper. If he's innocent, he'll come after you with every regulation in the book."

"And if he's guilty?"

Nelson's eyes narrowed behind the bags of bruised flesh as he concentrated. Gradually worry crept into them. "You know the type of cop who eats their gun?"

Green leaned forward urgently. "Then help me find him, George. Where would he go? Who would he turn to? Is he married?"

"Divorced."

"Kids?"

Nelson nodded. "Three, but they're still pretty young."

"Is he close to his ex-wife?"

Nelson sucked his jowls into a scowl and shifted his bulk in the chair. "The break-up was on my watch, when he had that bit of … disciplinary trouble. It was hard on him, although the decision was mutual. To answer your question, I think they're amicable."

"Would he turn to her?"

"He might. He doesn't have many friends."

Nelson couldn't remember the wife's name, but he tested his vague recollections against the listings in the phone book until they had narrowed down the most likely Weiss. A quick phone call to see if she was home netted only her voice mail, but Green didn't leave a message. He didn't plan to do this interview over the phone; he wanted to see her in person so he could interpret every pucker of the brow or blink of the eyes.

After he'd escorted Nelson to the elevator, thanked him for his help and asked him to try to quash the rumours, he dispatched Charbonneau and Leblanc to check the wife's house and to set up a stake-out from an inconspicuous place on the street. Then he returned to his office, bracing himself for the task he could no longer put off. Devine was not in her office, but this time she picked up her home phone on the second ring.

"Green!" she snapped before he could get more than a word in. "What's going on down there?"

He cast about, unsure which crisis she was referring to. Good God, could she too have heard the news that he was investigating Weiss? "Lots of things," he countered cautiously. "Why?"

"Turn on the television, CBC. See for yourself! Then call me back. I want to listen now."

He hung up and dashed out of his office down to the coffee room, where a small TV sat in the corner, almost never used except for the Stanley Cup playoff games. He turned it on and flipped channels until suddenly, to his surprise, John Blakeley's grim face filled the screen. He was standing at a microphone, soberly attired in a navy suit and tie. His wife stood at his side, her gaze expressionless, but her lips pulled in a tight slash.

"I am eternally grateful to the faith that the Liberal Party and the people of Renfrew-Nippissing placed in me, and it is with a heavy heart and much soul searching that I have made this painful but necessary decision. Public office is an onerous and awesome responsibility, and those who accept it must be able to devote their full attention and energy to it. Public office is also an honour, and those who accept it should be worthy of the trust placed in them and serve as an example of all the best ideals our country embodies."

He glanced at the ceiling, as if searching for inspiration in the phrasing of his dilemma. "As long as our armed forces and the missions they have accomplished are under scrutiny, I do not feel I can serve the Liberal party nor the Canadian people with the attention, energy and honour they deserve. Therefore, at fourteen hundred hours today, I notified the Chairman of the Liberal Party of my intentions and submitted a formal withdrawal of my candidacy to the Chief Electoral Officer."

Blakeley had been standing rigidly still with his hands clasped behind his back and his gaze fixed straight ahead, like a warrior facing his execution. Throughout the speech, his voice rang clear and firm, but now he paused and Green could see the fine quiver in his jaw.

"I sincerely apologize for the inconvenience and disappointment my withdrawal will cause for the Liberal Party, the voters of Renfrew-Nippissing, and my hard-working staff. I wish to assure you all that, had there been another way, I would have taken it. Thank you."

Barely were the words out of his mouth than the press peppered him with questions. A reporter jostled another to get his own microphone closer, and cameras flashed. John Blakeley did not stay for questions; he took his wife's hand and the two of them hustled out a door at the far side of the room, which Green recognized to be the marble lobby of the Chateau Laurier.

Immediately, the CBC news commentators began scrambling to analyze the speech, which had apparently caught everyone by surprise. A spokesman for the Liberal Party, hastily reached on the Sunday, called the loss of John Blakeley's candidacy regrettable but by no means insurmountable, as there were many other fine Liberal candidates in area ridings. Which translated, meant that the Party brass was already distancing itself from John Blakeley and whatever mud he might have stuck to him.

Green listened impatiently for the crucial detail he had obviously missed — the connection between Blakeley's withdrawal and the scrutiny of the military. What scrutiny? The analysts were asking that very question as well. Apparently, Blakeley was expecting an imminent revelation in the news that would put the military under scrutiny, but he'd given no specifics. Speculation ranged widely from more equipment failures in the aging naval fleet to mistreatment of Afghan prisoners by our troops in Kandahar. Only one reporter wondered whether the recent beating of an Ottawa police officer in Petawawa might be connected. Considering that Green had left an interview with the man less than three hours earlier, he thought that extremely likely.

Green's cellphone rang.

"Did you see it?" Devine demanded.

"Yes."

"So? Is it connected to the Ross case?"

"I don't know." Strictly speaking, that was the truth.

"I'm not a fool, Mike. In about two minutes flat, I expect the press to be on the phone, asking what the connection is and whether we're investigating John Blakeley. Are we?"

"Well … yes."

There was a brief pause. "My office, fifteen minutes. I want the media relations people there too."

He sensed she was about to hang up. "Barbara!"

She came back on the line. "Damn it, Mike! The Chief is already on the other line. He'll have to be included."

Green groaned. He knew she was right, but he felt the whole delicate investigation spinning out of his control. "Okay, but you and I need to meet privately first, so I can tell you where we really are and figure out what the hell to release for general consumption. Because it's explosive, Barbara. Really explosive."

For the next fifteen minutes Green paced his office and jotted notes on a pad of paper. He was so busy figuring out exactly how much he was going to tell Devine that he had no chance to consider the significance of Blakeley's announcement. He needed Devine's co-operation to keep the investigation of Weiss under wraps, but when she finally summoned him upstairs, he discovered she had an entirely different concern.

When he walked in, she was on the phone talking to the Chief himself. "Absolutely not, sir," she was saying. "Inspector Green has just arrived, and I will keep you well apprised of any actions we plan to take … Of course, sir."

When she hung up, she pivoted on her stiletto heel and walked to the door to close it firmly behind him. Despite her haste, she'd managed to arrive at the office impeccably packaged in the latest spring colours. Her green linen suit hadn't a single wrinkle in it, and every black hair on her head was lacquered into submission. She waved peach-tipped fingers at the group of chairs in front of her desk.

"John Blakeley," she announced without preamble. "I've just been on the phone with the Chief. You're not to go near him again without our approval."

In his astonishment, he froze midway into his chair. "Barbara, that's ridiculous. He's a prime suspect —"

"Do you have concrete evidence?"

"Not yet, but —"

"Then you won't touch him. The media will be all over this. They'll have a field day with his connections to the Liberal Party brass, and the opposition parties will grab any chance to smear the Liberal leadership. They'll say it's another example of their poor judgement, if not their outright criminal connections."

He thought about the call he'd overhead between her and the Chief. Who in the Liberal Party had the power to call in favours from the police? And why?

"Is there something I don't know?" he asked. "Some other player who has the ear of the Chief? Because I don't want to be blindsided by someone's secret agenda —"

"Of course not, Mike. It's just a media jackpot. Blakeley's wife is the daughter of Jack Neuss, who's been a senior policy advisor for the Liberals since the days of Trudeau. You know how it works, Mike. It's two weeks to the election, and the public has never been more fickle."

He paced in outrage. "So you're saying if I'm planning to arrest Blakeley, I should wait two weeks?"

"Are you planning to arrest him?"

He forced himself to slow down and think of how he might persuade her. "Not yet. But I will need to talk to him again, and you can't seriously suggest we go easy on the guy when one of our officers is lying in the ICU, possibly because of him."

She stared up at him unblinking for several seconds. "All right, tell me about it."

"If you promise not to interrupt. We have very little time to waste."

Her eyes narrowed at his bald insubordination and her mouth opened as if to protest, but in the end, she snapped it shut. "Go ahead. But for God's sake, sit down."

He sat, and for fifteen minutes he gave her an executive summary of the case to date, starting with the suicide of Ian MacDonald and the fatal beating of his friend Daniel Oliver by a man he and MacDonald served with in Yugoslavia. He described Oliver's fiancée's arrival in Ottawa with a newspaper clipping about Blakeley and his campaign manager, who coincidentally just happened to have been a witness to Oliver's death. He traced her movements in Ottawa as they knew them, from her trip to Petawawa to her date with a mystery man only hours before her death.

Finally, with some trepidation, he broached the subject of Weiss, including his connection to MacDonald and Blakeley in Yugoslavia, his request to be put on the case, his inquiries about Twiggy, and most damning of all, his phone call from the convenience store that set up Peters up.

Devine's lips grew tighter as the evidence against Weiss added up. When Green mentioned Weiss's recent disappearance along with Twiggy's, she shook her head in outrage.

"There's more than enough there to bring him in."

"I agree. And we will, as soon as we can find him."

"I don't see how you have a single thing on Blakeley, however."

"Only a theory —"

"We can't destroy a man's reputation or torpedo an election on a theory."

Green clenched his teeth and prayed for patience. "Blakeley was MacDonald's and Weiss's superior officer. Whatever wrongdoing occurred in Yugoslavia, he had to have been involved. And I think the fact he withdrew today is the most damning evidence of all. It's tantamount to admitting we're going to turn up something rotten."

"But maybe nothing more than a poor judgement call or a superior officer's desire to protect his men. That's not a good enough reason to flush a man or the election down the toilet."

Green stared out the window, weighing his options. Devine's office, like all the senior administration, had a spectacular view of the Museum of Nature, that sat like a Medieval Scottish Castle in the middle of the park across the road. Green had always found it soothing in an other-worldly way, but today he felt his blood pressure climb. Eventually he figured out a way to manouevre.

"All right, I'll give you fair warning before I move on Blakeley. I have a number of leads to pursue first, which may give us more concrete evidence against him. Or exonerate him, for that matter."

"And you'll keep me informed?"

Hating it, he nodded. She leaped to her feet, moved behind her desk and reached for her phone. "Fine. We'll go see the Chief and hammer out what we're going to say when the media come calling —"

Green's cellphone rang, startling them both. It was Gibbs, stuttering with excitement. "S-sorry to interrupt, sir. I didn't know i-if I should, but I thought you'd want to know this."

"Where are you, Bob?"

"D-downstairs in the squad room, sir."

Green considered the alternatives. Devine was already looking at him questioningly, and he knew she would demand an update, which meant he would waste precious time playing middleman. Instead he told Gibbs to come upstairs. When he'd hung up, Devine slowly put her own phone down.

"I think Detective Gibbs has found out something important," he said.

"That would be a first," she replied as she sat down behind her desk, her shoulders squared and her hands folded, the picture of authority. Green bit back a retort. As usual, Devine never saw behind appearances.

Less than a minute later Gibbs arrived, flushed and sweaty. The same suit had hung on his lanky frame for the past two days, and it looked as weary and bedraggled as he did. But despite his exhaustion, his eyes shone.

"The canvass, sir! It finally paid off."

"Which canvass?"

"L-looking for the man Patricia Ross had a drink with? One of the uniformed officers finally hit paydirt. And you were right, sir, it was an upscale bar in the Delta Hotel."

Green scanned his memory of the city quickly. The Delta Hotel was a boutique hotel at the western edge of the downtown business district — discreet, elegant and most importantly only a few minutes' walk from the aqueduct where Patricia Ross was murdered.

"Someone remembered her and her companion?"

Gibbs bobbed his head up and down. "The bartender. It's a s-small bar, sir, mostly business people having a quiet drink. It doesn't really get many girls in the game — that's what the bartender thought she was, although she wasn't really high-priced enough for a place like that. But he remembered her sitting with a man at a corner table, talking quietly for at least an hour."

"Did he hear any of the conversation?"

"A bit, sir, but mostly the woman's. He said sometimes she'd get angry and raise her voice, and he heard things like 'I have needs, you know' and 'It hasn't been a picnic.' That's when he wondered if maybe she was a girlfriend instead of a hooker."

"What about the man? Did the bartender hear any of his answers?"

"No. He says the man never raised his voice. He kept checking around him, and it looked like he was trying to calm her down."

Green tried to visualize the interaction. It did not sound like an angry confrontation or a demand for vengeance, but rather a quiet discussion punctuated by Patricia's occasional flare-ups. "I have needs too," she'd said. Blackmail? Could that be what she'd been after all along?

"Good work," he exclaimed. "Did the bartender get a good look at this man?"

"Mediocre, sir. He'd chosen the darkest table."

"Well, I suggest you get over there and show the bartender a photo line-up. Maybe it will help jog his memory."

Bob Gibbs broke into a broad grin. "I already did that, sir. I took the photos of all our suspects, plus some neutrals. I just got back."

Green took in the big grin and the dancing eyes. He felt his own pulse begin to race. "You got a hit."

"I did, sir. Colonel John Blakeley."

TWENTY-FOUR

Sept. 10, 1993. Serb village in Sector South, Croatia.

Dear Kit ... A wild day yesterday! Just as our section was getting dug in at this little village near the new cease-fire line, the Croats suddenly went nuts and started firing on the village. Our section house is in this solid stone hall, and we're just getting the coffee on when kaboom! A shell blows a hole in the street right outside. And then kaboom, kaboom, right down main street. We hunker down under the stairs and between each shell we take turns going out-side to see where it hit and we write it down. When I go, I see this woman running towards us, screaming, and she grabs my hand to pull me towards this house on fire. I finally figure out that her family is inside, so I go back in the section house and grab some guys, and we go out in the APC and get four people out of the house.

I knew the safest place in town was our house, so I brought them back. Danny yelled at me a bit before he agreed to stash them in the basement. I guess what I did was a little crazy, but it didn't seem right that they were out there while we were nice and safe. That was the begin-ning. By the time the arty stopped at nightfall, I'd been out ten times, sometimes in the APC and other times just running out to grab people, and now we have forty-two Serbs in the basement, chattering up a storm. There are fifteen little kids all chasing each other around the basement like it was a church picnic. I guess people can get used to anything.

***

"IT'S NOT ENOUGH, Mike."

"What are you talking about, Barbara!" Green couldn't believe his ears. Devine was standing by the door, having just ushered Gibbs out and shut it again. Now she was shaking her head stubbornly. What would it take to convince this woman that Blakeley was implicated up to his eyeballs? "He was the last person to see her alive!"

"He could have been meeting her as an old friend, or a friend of her fiancé's. For that matter, you have absolutely no proof that she came up here looking for Oliver's killer in the first place. Your entire case is a house of cards. She could have been coming up to reconnect with his old friends."

"Then why did she end up dead?"

She drew her peach lips in a stubborn line. "That could have been random misfortune."

"And the attack on Peters? Come on, Barbara!" He almost added "Where's your brain?" but he stopped himself.

"I'm not saying I believe it, Mike. I'm saying that's how Blakeley's lawyers could play it, so I'm not authorizing a move on this guy till we have him nailed down six ways to Sunday."

He thought of the precious time running through his fingers, time when Weiss could get further away, Twiggy could be slipping closer towards death, and Blakeley could be booking a flight to some Caribbean island without an extradition treaty. He didn't have time to nail things down six ways to Sunday, even if he had the leads. Speaking of which …!

He glanced at his watch. Fuck! Unless he broke all the speed limits between here and the airport, he was going to be late for Kate McGrath's flight. He jumped to his feet.

"Fine, we'll do it your way," he said as he dived out the door. "But can you keep Professional Standards apprised? I won't have time."

"As long as you keep me apprised!" he heard her yell at his retreating back just before he reached the stairs. I'll try, he muttered to himself. With any luck, Professional Standards will keep you too busy to answer your phone.

He hit every red light going down Bronson Avenue and screamed into the airport fifteen minutes late. He nipped the car into the front taxi space, put a police sticker on the dash and ignored the chorus of objections from the cabbies in the queue as he ducked inside. He nearly ran straight by Kate McGrath, who was standing by the exit door with a compact suitcase in tow and a garment bag slung over her arm. Her blue eyes twinkled as she grabbed his arm.

"Whoa, sailor! I would have waited for you."

He turned in surprise. She was wearing a royal blue jacket that did fabulous things to her eyes, and a pair of tapered jeans over boots that made her legs look ten feet long. Her silver hair was tousled and soft, and her eyes twinkled as she smiled at him. Arousal scattered his thoughts, and he hastened to avert his eyes.

"Long day," he muttered as he grabbed her suitcase. "I've got a lot to tell you."

"So do I," she said, following him out to the car. He hoisted her bag into the back seat and walked around to open her door. Giving him a peculiar look, she yanked it open herself and slipped lithely inside. The cabbies were still cursing in a colourful array of languages as they drove away.

"So who goes first?" he asked as he merged the car into the existing traffic.

"I do," she replied without hesitation, flashing him a triumphant smile. "Because whatever you've found out, I can trump it."

He chuckled. "Dangerous lady. You haven't even seen my hand yet."

"No, but unless you've identified the murderer, I've got you beat."

He almost drove off the road. "You got a hit on those photos?"

"I did. Lucky for both of us the bartender was in the place early, cleaning out the fridges. It took him all of ten seconds to look at all the pictures and pick out the man who killed Daniel Oliver." She looked across at him excitedly. "The shit is really going to hit the fan, Mike. It was John Blakeley."

"Hot damn! He's sure? It's a long time to remember a face."

"Absolutely positive. He remembered the scar on the guy's eyebrow."

Green slapped the steering wheel with triumph. "Now we've got him six ways to Sunday, and we're not wasting one more second doing this little off-limits dance that my super, the chief, the Liberal party and God knows maybe the queen wants me to do." He drove one-handed as he groped in his pocket for his cellphone. Devine snapped up the phone before the first ring was over.

"Barbara," he said, "you'd better warn the Chief. John Blakeley has been positively identified by an eye witness as the man who killed Daniel Oliver in Halifax ten years ago. The officer from Halifax is here now, and we're going to swing by the station to pick up Brian Sullivan, then we're going after him."

"Mike!" Her shriek nearly hit high C. "Wait for the warrant. Do it by the book."

"No! That little press conference was his farewell speech. He's internationally connected, and I'm not letting him get on a plane and take all his secrets with him while I'm hunting down some justice of the peace at his Sunday dinner. We'll bring Blakeley in for questioning, and we'll get the paperwork in order while he's there."

"But —"

"I know the book, Barbara. Give me some credit."

"All right, but you control it. Not Halifax. They observe, nothing more."

Green glanced at McGrath, who was watching him expectantly. She had come two thousand kilometres, she had broken open the case …

Devine broke into his thoughts. "Do you hear me? Inspector?"

"I need to phone Sullivan," he muttered and hung up. Before McGrath could get any questions in, he dialled Sullivan to set the wheels of justice in motion.

When he and McGrath arrived at the station, Sullivan was already waiting in the incident room with Detective Jones, reviewing the paperwork for the nationwide warrant on Blakeley. Sullivan greeted Kate McGrath with a broad smile and a hearty handshake, but he flicked a sideways glance at Green that spoke volumes. Green busied himself looking over the paperwork.

Once they had completed their instructions to Jones and dispatched him to finalize the warrant, they argued over their approach strategy. Until the warrant was completed and a justice of the peace tracked down to sign it, which might take hours, they hadn't the legal means to apprehend Blakeley. Since it was a Halifax case and McGrath was the officer of record, she needed to swear the affidavit before the JP. Technically, nothing stopped them from dropping by for another informal chat with Blakeley in the meantime, but his lawyers and the courts would cry foul if he was questioned without being informed of the pending changes and given the chance to consult his lawyer. Yet Green feared that even now, two hours after his press conference, Blakeley was already long gone.

In the end, they settled on a compromise. Jones would write up the warrant and accompany McGrath to the JP while Green and Sullivan, along with a couple of plain clothes teams, would keep Blakeley's condo under surveillance. A discreet call also went out to the head of security at the airport to delay Blakeley should he try to board a flight.

"Don't you dare start the interrogation without me!" McGrath warned as they all prepared to leave. "Ten years this guy has been inside my head, Mike. I want a chance at him!"

Green faced her reluctantly. Her eyes glowed, and her cheeks were flushed. He understood her hunger, but the interview would be delicate enough without Devine barging into the middle of it. This was not about closure or settling the score. More than nailing the guilty, this was about keeping the innocent alive.

"I know," he said as he and Sullivan headed out the door. They took the stairs two at a time down to the basement parking lot.

"She's quite the woman," Sullivan remarked ambiguously as they signed out a car.

"That she is."

"Are you going to wait for her?"

"Devine vetoed it."

"She's going to be pissed."

"I assume she'll be professional."

Sullivan chuckled as he started the car. "Don't count on it. Where the two of you are concerned, you're way past professional."

Green busied himself with the seatbelt, hoping Sullivan couldn't see his scarlet face. How the hell had the man figured that out in the brief hour since he met her? They pulled out of the parking lot in silence and headed up Catherine Street, both of them staring at the road ahead.

"Nothing is happening."

"Oh. Right."

Green risked a glance. A smile played at the corner of Sullivan's mouth. "I mean, nothing is happening."

"As long as you keep it that way. Sharon is way more than you deserve."

"Oy, my conscience. It's good to have you back." Green gestured as they neared the intersection of Kent Street. "Now can we keep our minds on this case, before we stumble upon this guy totally unprepared?"

Ablaze in the slanting rays of the sinking sun, Blakeley's condominium high-rise looked deceptively serene as long as one ignored the three media vans parked outside. Green and Sullivan slipped out of sight on a side street and coordinated the surveillance as unobtrusively as possible. They placed an officer at each of the exits, including the underground parking garage. A check inside revealed Blakeley's Lexus SUV still parked in its spot, but Green dismissed it as irrelevant. If Blakeley was leaving the country, he would hardly leave his car at the airport as a billboard announcing his travel plans. He would leave it at home, hoping it would serve as a decoy for at least a day or two.

As Green predicted, a phone call to Blakeley's apartment from an unlisted number went unanswered. Even if the man was at home, he would be crazy to answer his phone with all the media camped outside. Green and Sullivan accessed the high-rise across the street and selected an apartment on the twelfth floor.

"You're the third person in the past hour who's asked to get into my place to spy on them," the tenant replied when they knocked on her door. She was shouting through the door over the blare of the television, but she sounded more intrigued than distressed.

"But we're the police, ma'am," Sullivan said. "We won't take long."

"We just need to ascertain that the Blakeleys are safe," Green added, ignoring Sullivan's frown.

She let them in finally. Wrapped in a ratty pink sweater over her pyjamas, she led them into her living room, which was stifling hot and smelled of cat urine. A quick peek through binoculars revealed no signs of movement in the apartment opposite, but the balcony door was open.

"They're there," Sullivan said.

"Not necessarily. This is a military man. Creating a diversion would be second nature to him."

Sullivan snorted. The tenant was listening with unabashed fascination. "Do you want to station a policeman to watch from here?" she asked. "Just in case?"

Green had to fight a smile. The woman has been watching too many cop dramas, he thought. But to his surprise, Sullivan nodded. "That would be very helpful, ma'am. I'll send someone up shortly, and I'd like to thank you for your co-operation."

She batted her eyelashes. Sullivan, at six foot four with broad shoulders, merry blue eyes and a full head of bristly blond hair, cut a commanding figure that still attracted women, even when he didn't turn on the Irish charm. Unlike Green, however, his own gaze had never strayed from the farm girl he had loved since he was sixteen.

Back out on the street, they settled into their car to wait for word that the warrant had been signed. Green chafed at the forced inaction, his thoughts racing over the case. What had he missed? What else should he be doing in the meantime?

He phoned in to Gibbs, who had drawn the unfortunate task of remaining at the station to coordinate the flow of information. "Any word from Wallington and Connors about Weiss?"

"Nothing, sir. No one is home at the ex-wife's house, and they've batted zero with all his known associates. He doesn't have many friends, it seems."

Or those he does have aren't talking to us, Green thought grimly. "Anything else new?"

"We're still waiting for Weiss's phone records, but Charbonneau and Leblanc have the search warrant for his house. They want to know if they should go ahead."

Green stared out the car window at the front door of the condominium. No one remotely interesting had passed in or out in the last fifteen minutes. God, he'd forgotten how tedious stake-outs were! He would give anything to join the search of Weiss's house, to poke around in the man's private closets and get a glimpse of the man's secrets. But the warrant for Blakeley's arrest could come any second, and this was where his skill and authority were needed.

Besides, he wouldn't miss Blakeley's arrest for the world. Reluctantly, he said "Tell them to go ahead and keep me posted every step of the way."

When he hung up, Sullivan cocked a questioning eyebrow at him. "Anything important?"

"The search of Weiss's house."

Sullivan rolled his eyes. "Control freak."

Green opened his mouth to defend himself, but the ringing of his cellphone interrupted him. Jones's voice came through. Two simple words. "Got it."

"Meet us at the station," Green said, and before Jones could mention Kate McGrath, he hung up and nodded to Sullivan. "Time to rock and roll."

"Are we going to notify Devine?"

Green was already out of the car and activating his radio to alert the others on the stake-out. "Once we have him in custody."

They were just heading across the street towards the front door when a cab pulled up, partially blocking their view. At the same time, the front door opened and a man emerged wearing a baseball cap, sunglasses despite the sunset shadows, and a bulky raincoat that hid much of his shape. But there was no mistaking his squat, powerful frame and the white hair sticking out beneath the cap.

"Shit, it's Blakeley!" Sullivan sprinted back to the car, revved it up and hurtled it forward across the lawn to block the cab's exit. Simultaneously, Green dashed towards the back of the cab, yelling into his radio for the officers to converge. Blakeley stopped with his hand on the rear door handle and looked up, surprise changing to horror at the sight of Green.

The media leaped out of their vans and raced across the lawn, scrambling to get their cameras and microphones in position. Green cursed. What a goddamn circus, all to play out on the six o'clock news. Devine's worst nightmare.

He grabbed Blakeley's arm and leaned in close to his ear. "John, for your own sake, please come with me to the car up ahead. The less we give the media to talk about, the better."

He felt Blakeley stiffen and pull away as if to resist. Then the man sized up the descending hordes, glanced at Sullivan's unmarked car, and all colour fled from his face. Wordlessly, he acquiesced. Heads down, the two of them hurried down the drive, dodged the microphones and ducked into the back seat of the car. Once they were inside, Green slammed the door and heard it lock into place. Sullivan hit the accelerator, and the car slewed out into the street, leaving the media behind.

Blakeley whipped off his sunglasses and stared out the back window. "Animals!" he snarled. "I haven't had a moment's peace since the press conference, and just when I'm trying to give them the slip, you show up! That's going to look just great."

"Where were you headed?" Green asked. Surreptitiously, he was studying Blakeley's clothing, trying to determine if he had a weapon hidden. This operation was going fabulously. The abduction of Blakeley by the local police was going to lead on the national news, and here he was stuck in the back with a known killer who had been neither searched nor handcuffed, and who possessed more than enough skill and nerve to shoot him and take Sullivan hostage to make good his escape. Sullivan's eyes met his in the rearview mirror, telegraphing the same thought.

"Back to Petawawa," Blakeley replied, oblivious to the interchange. "Leanne has already gone."

"They'll find you there."

"Yes, but at least there I feel as if my prison has more space." He swung on Green as if the word prison had triggered an association. "What were you doing at my place?"

"Actually ..." Green leaned forward, thinking fast. They were just nearing the turn-off onto Elgin Street. Traffic was light, and there were few people around. "Brian, could you pull over when you get a chance? There's something I should do."

Sullivan's gaze caught his again in the mirror, and he nodded slightly. Just before Elgin, he turned into the drive behind Friday's Roast Beef House and stopped the car in the alley, effectively hemming Blakeley in between the stone wall of a Church and the brick building next door. Both detectives climbed out, and Green saw Sullivan's hand move towards his gun. Blakeley remained in the back seat, suddenly wary.

"Could you step out too please, John?"

He didn't move, and for one brief moment Green feared they were going to have a gun battle in the middle of downtown Ottawa on a Sunday afternoon. Another great lead for the news. Then Blakeley climbed out and backed away uncertainly, his fists clenched in an instinctive fighter's stance.

"What's going on, fellas?"

"Turn around and place your hands on the vehicle," Green said.

Blakeley stared at him, first with incomprehension, then horror and finally resignation, His hands fell limply to his sides. "Sonofabitch," he muttered. "You're arresting me."

"Hands on the vehicle, John."

Blakeley turned to lean against the car and stood impassively as Sullivan searched and handcuffed him, then began his recital. "John Blakeley, I have a warrant for your arrest for the murder of Daniel Oliver on April 9 —"

To Green's surprise, Blakeley shut his eyes and bowed his head. "Daniel Oliver. Yes."

"I am required to warn you that —"

"I always knew that would come back to haunt me."

"John," Green interrupted, "it would be better if you didn't speak until you've been formally processed and had a chance to consult an attorney."

"I don't need an attorney. I want to explain."

And I sure want to hear your story, Green thought, but not like this. Not standing in a back alley where you can later claim you were threatened or coerced into admitting a pack of lies. "The faster we get through the formalities, the faster you can explain the whole story to us," he said.

When they reached the police station, the media had already arrived and were lying in wait outside the entrance to the police parking lot. Blakeley ducked his head as the car zipped past and drove down the ramp into the prisoner's bay, where Green handed Blakeley over to the duty sergeant for fingerprinting and processing. Blakeley looked wan and beaten, a shadow of the warrior they had met only hours earlier. He complied with orders like an automaton.

"Bring him up to the video interview room as soon as possible, Sergeant," Green said before heading upstairs to prepare for the interview. He was expecting to do battle with attorneys, political spin doctors, the military and his own superiors in his attempt to get the truth out of John Blakeley, but he was wrong.

Nothing could have been easier.

TWENTY-FIVE

Sept. 14, 1993. On the road, Sector South, Croatia.

I'm trying to write in the APC and it's noisy and hot as hell. We're on the move again and this time it's big. The whole company is together and we're going to a place called Medak, where the Croats grabbed a whole lot of land inside the UN pink zone and nearly got a bunch of our guys in Charlie Company killed. It was the same offensive we experienced the other day but even worse up at Medak because they rolled their tanks in and took over a bunch of Serb villages. Now the politicians are at the table again, making up another new ceasefire deal.

Danny got the word to pack us up and in less than two hours we were rumbling down the road. The OC dropped by for a pep talk to tell us this was the real thing. This was going to be war and we should be prepared for anything. Some of the guys are really pumped, but I don't know. I'm wondering how long all of us can dodge the bullet.

***

BLAKELEY DIDN'T WANT a lawyer, he didn't want all the protections the Charter of Rights and his political handlers thrust at him. He wanted to tell his story. When they finally began, seated opposite each other at a small interview table in the windowless recording room, Green realized why.

"I've lived with this for ten years," Blakeley said. He was seated at attention, his back rigid and his gaze fixed on the wall behind Green. Sullivan sat in the corner, quietly taking notes. "It was a moment I could never take back, a moment of shame and weakness that I could never live down. All that I accomplished afterwards and all the good I did, could never make amends for that second when I lost control and killed a man. I don't deny it. I don't excuse it. And I always knew that somehow, someday, I'd be called to account."

Green waited.

"When I told you this morning about the danger and brutality of the Yugoslavian mission and about how one momentary lapse in behaviour shouldn't be allowed to destroy all the good that a soldier accomplishes, I wasn't only talking about Ian MacDonald. I was talking about *me*, and trying to justify *me*. As I've done for the past decade."

He flicked his gaze at Green as if gauging his response, then returned to his spot on the wall. Green kept his face neutral.

"I've worked hard for peace, doubly hard since that incident. I believe in peacekeeping and in providing support to the weak and victimized of the world, and I know more than most when and how that support should be deployed. I would have had something important to contribute at the cabinet table, an expertise that could save countless lives not only of those victims, but of our own soldiers as well. I believed that might balance the scales."

Still Green waited, but his impatience with the rhetoric must have shown, because Blakeley glanced at him again, this time with a ghost of a smile.

"That's what I told myself, and most times in the bustle of the day, I believed it. But in the dead of night, the truth comes calling. I had heard about critical incident stress, of course. It had been drummed into us at staff briefings and by the army padres all the time. I knew I was supposed to watch for signs of it in my men, and I knew what I was supposed to do to help them. Encourage them to talk about it, give them a few days of light duties, and refer them to the padres. But you know, we have hundreds of years of military conditioning working against that. There's a tradition of soldiering on, of hiding the pain behind bluster and stoic good cheer, of sharing a cathartic belt of whiskey — or two or half a dozen — at the end of the day. The military still measures success by how well a soldier can do that, not by how well he asks for help or confesses to panic and sleepless nights."

He paused and took a sip from the water glass on the table, licking his lips as he considered his next move. "I was ambitious. Croatia was my first real field command, and I was determined to prove myself. I accepted every mission and earned myself a reputation as a can-do guy. If you have a really tough assignment, and you want it done, give it to Johnnie Blakeley. I thrived on the challenge and came back from my first tour there raring to go back and prove myself again. And the military were only too happy. They were spread really thin, and they needed experienced field commanders, so they promoted me and sent me back, this time to Bosnia. More brutality, more danger."

As he spoke, his eyes began to shine, and his hands swept in broad gestures, but Green sensed a manic edge to his excitement. "Again I sailed through it. I had endless energy and confidence. I volunteered my unit for every dangerous, gut-wrenching mission there. We worked against impossible odds, and we were stretched so thin on the ground that sometimes all we had were a couple of Iltis Jeeps and a lot of bluff against militias fifty men strong. A few of my men cracked, but by God, not rock-solid Johnnie Blakeley. I slept like a baby, drank only my two beers a day, and got so used to the sound of shelling that I didn't even hear it anymore."

He shook his head in wonder and reached for his glass again. The glow had died from his eyes, and this time his hand shook slightly. Ah, thought Green, we're finally getting to it.

"But when I returned home to Edmonton, I couldn't come down. I was bored and out of sorts. I felt useless running drills and playing fake war games. I couldn't relate to any of the concerns of my family; they felt trivial and extraordinarily petty. My wife —" he corrected himself, "my first wife said I'd changed. I had. I had bonded to a world outside my family. To my men, to the villagers of Yugoslavia, and to the harsh mountainous beauty of their land. My wife and I fought. She complained, and I told her most of the world had it far worse. When I was posted to Ottawa, she refused to move. I didn't consciously leave her, I just ignored her ultimatum. In Ottawa, away from my unit and my family, I began to unravel, but I still didn't see it. I met Leanne, who was working in communications in DND at the time. She was ambitious, adventurous and fearless — all the things my wife wasn't. And more importantly, she admired my accomplishments. We kept it low-key, because our relationship could have jeopardized both our careers, until my wife got wind of it and filed for divorce. I didn't think I cared."

He stopped and looked directly into the camera. "Is that thing going to run out of tape?"

Green shook his head. He didn't tell Blakeley that there were half a dozen people watching the digital image from the room down the hall, including Kate McGrath, who had been nearly apoplectic when she found out she was excluded. "I have a history with the guy," Green had told her. "It's me he's expecting to talk to, me he feels a connection to." "Oh, I see," she'd retorted. "Man to man?" He'd said nothing, reluctant to be drawn into a dispute, whether over jurisdiction or the old boys' club. In response, she had pointedly turned her back.

Blakeley pulled his gaze away from the camera with an effort and began to massage his forehead near his scar. He wet his lips. "But the next thing I knew, I'd booked myself a week off, ostensibly to return to Edmonton to work out the separation with my wife. But instead I flew to Halifax at the other end of the country, where no one knew me and no one would judge me if I drank myself into a stupor for a week. I hit the Lighthouse Tavern on my fourth night, hung over and plagued by nightmares and flashbacks. There in the Lighthouse was another officer from Yugoslavia, also quietly getting drunk, and on the TV in the background that damn witch hunt called the Somalia Inquiry. We commiserated about the lack of understanding and respect we'd encountered back in Canada, especially among the military's senior admin and JAG staff, who'd never set foot in a foreign battle field in their entire careers."

"You're talking about Dick Hamm."

Blakeley looked beyond surprise. He nodded with resignation. "You know that? Of course you do. Dick and I hadn't been in the same company, but we'd still shared a lot of briefings together. Meeting him at the Lighthouse was like walking into the arms of an old friend. I started to let all my frustrations out, and at the height of it, I felt this dam inside of me begin to break open. I got up to relieve myself, and to get a grip too. Hamm was a tough soldier, and I had a feeling he'd never come apart the way I was close to doing.

"Anyway, that's when Daniel Oliver accosted me and accused me of killing his friend."

"How?"

"Not literally, obviously. By not giving him the support he needed when he was over the edge."

"Was that true?"

Blakeley nodded reluctantly. "We had a difficult mission to do, and as it was, I had young, green kids puking their guts out as they dragged these bodies down for the medics. Men unable to sleep because of the stink and afraid they were bunking down on top of a mass grave. I told them all we had a job to do."

"Where did Constable Jeff Weiss fit into this?"

Blakeley looked momentarily dismayed but seemed to resign himself to the fact Green had tracked the police officer down. He shook his head wearily. "He was a kid too, only five years on the job before they sent him over to help monitor and train the local police in Sarajevo. He was bright enough, and he spoke some Serbo-Croatian, so when our CO asked for police and forensic support during the Croatian withdrawal, they included him. He asked to go, if I recall, a request I'm sure he regrets to this day. He didn't expect to be piecing together body parts."

"Your wife mentioned a dispute between him and MacDonald over a cause of death?"

Blakeley looked impatient. "Two Croatian soldiers had been shot. Our unit was documenting and mopping up dozens of Serb deaths — combatants and civilians alike who'd been shot by the Croats — so frankly if a Serb got in some retaliation, I wasn't going to lose sleep over it. Weiss was going around questioning Serb villagers, and naturally they lied. Why wouldn't they?"

"They said it was MacDonald?"

"They said it was a blue helmet — that's a UN peacekeeper. They didn't say who, but Weiss narrowed it down to MacDonald."

"And he came to you with this information?"

Blakeley nodded.

"What did you do?"

"I told him in no uncertain terms that this did not happen."

"You told him to bury the report?"

Blakeley stiffened. "I told Weiss that before he impugned the reputation of the UN peacekeeping force, the Canadian army and a brave young man who was about to get a medal for rescuing civilian lives, he'd better be damn sure of his facts. That was the end of it."

Green sat back, frowning at the blustering man sitting opposite him. "But if that's what happened, why did Daniel Oliver accuse you of not supporting MacDonald?"

"I requested MacDonald in the first place. Oliver was his section commander and tried to veto the request. He didn't say why, and I thought it was just because they were friends, so I went over his head to Hamm. I realize now that he vetoed it because he knew how close to the edge MacDonald really was."

The explanation seemed credible enough, and yet the story felt incomplete. MacDonald had come home from Croatia haunted by something he had experienced there and unable to get beyond it, until he took the only way out he could think of. And Weiss, more than twelve years later, was implicated in some as yet unknown manner in the cover-up of Patricia Ross's death.

Blakeley must have seen the skepticism on Green's face, for he leaned forward intently to bolster his case. "I didn't even see the warning signs in my own behaviour, let alone MacDonald's. I believed in our capabilities and in getting on with things. That was the pride of the Canadians there. But in Halifax, it all caught up with me. I was waking up in a sweat, buried in body parts and gagging on the stink of corpses, fighting the haze of smoke and gunpowder from the burning villages. The Lighthouse bar stank, the smoke hung like a pall … Next thing I knew, I reached across the table, grabbed Oliver by the throat, and gave him a jab to the head. Just one. Before Hamm and Oliver's buddies pulled me off."

He broke off, dropping his gaze. In the quiet of the interview room, his breath grew ragged as he stared into the abyss of his memory.

Green shifted gently forward. "But one was enough."

Blakeley managed a brusque nod. His jaw clamped and tears brimmed in his eyes. He jerked a desperate hand toward the camera. "Jesus, can we turn that thing off?"

Green didn't reply, but watched in silence as the man struggled against the long buried past. After a moment, he resumed.

"I haven't had a really restful sleep since it happened. I caught the first flight back to Ottawa, swore off booze, and tried to bury the fact that I'd ever been to Halifax. Nobody knew I'd been there, nobody connected me to Daniel Oliver whatsoever. Leanne helped me through it."

"You told her?"

"I had to tell someone. I came back to Ottawa a basket case. I couldn't eat or sleep. Everyone else thought it was the divorce, but Leanne knew something terrible had happened. She sat with me those endless nights, she never judged or pried. Without her, I would never have pulled myself out of the tailspin."

Green thought about Leanne's behaviour during the interview earlier in the day. This explained her protective interference and his acceptance of it. It also provided a plausible explanation for her mentioning Weiss, even over Blakeley's objections. She had been anxious to divert suspicion away from her husband because she knew the explosive secret that lay in his past.

As Green had noted before, not a woman to underestimate.

Blakeley squared his shoulders and took a deep, weary breath. "What happens to me now?"

Green looked across the table at him expectantly. "That depends on what else you can tell me."

"About what?"

Does the man think I'm an idiot, Green thought, but he kept his voice dispassionate. "About Patricia Ross and Detective Peters."

Blakeley stiffened. "Good God, man. You don't think I had anything to do with those, do you?"

"Don't pretend ignorance, John. That's where the evidence points."

"But Daniel Oliver was a drunken flash of anger. It wasn't premeditated. I could never intentionally go out and kill someone!"

So what were the years of military training all about, Green was tempted to ask, but he stuck to the facts. "We have an eyewitness who places you in the Delta Hotel having drinks with Patricia only hours before her death."

Blakeley sat back with a thud. "Lord help me," he muttered.

"Perhaps the truth will," Green said drily. "What happened."

"I didn't kill her. I didn't do anything wrong."

"Did Patricia Ross contact you?"

Blakeley glanced around the small room as if hoping for answers or rescue from its shadowy corners. His gaze flicked to the camera. Eventually, seeing no other escape, he gave a faint nod. "She phoned me."

"Where? At your campaign office?"

"No," he said quickly. "At my Laurier Street condo."

"How did she get the number?"

"She didn't say." His expression cleared as if he'd come to a decision. "She said she had something to discuss with me about Halifax, and she wanted to meet for a drink. I suggested the bar at the Delta because it was nearby and discreet."

"What was the date and time of this call?"

Blakeley paused. "Friday night, April 21st. Two days before the meeting. I was going home to Petawawa for the weekend, and I wanted time to think."

"Why?"

Blakeley shot him a scowl, his first display of spirit in some time. "The woman was obviously planning to blackmail me, Inspector. I needed time to arrange my assets and figure out what my response should be."

"Maybe she just wanted to confront you and get an apology. And maybe some gesture of compensation."

"I was on the brink of a high-profile career. She was a drink-ravaged, hard luck girl looking for the brass ring. My instincts told me blackmail."

"Did you tell anyone about the phone call or your meeting?"

"Absolutely not."

"Not your wife or your campaign manager Roger Atkinson?"

Blakeley shook his head vigorously. He thrust his chin out and looked at Green in open challenge. "I deal with a lot of classified material, as I'm sure you do, and I've learned to be a good poker player."

Not good enough to fool Leanne ten years ago when you returned from Halifax, Green thought, and not good enough now either. "So what happened at the meeting?"

"As I thought, she wanted money. Not a reasonable amount as compensation for Oliver's death — which I would have given her without hesitation, by the way — but ten thousand a month for the rest of her life. A sum I couldn't possibly raise."

Green thought of the man's two luxurious homes and exquisite white leather couches. Patricia Ross had lived her final years in a dingy room furnished in Sally Ann rejects. "Couldn't or wouldn't? You have some significant assets."

"I didn't kill her! I left her waiting for a cab."

"What time was this?"

"Ten thirty."

"And what did you do afterwards?"

Blakeley cast about, looking uncomfortable. "I walked around for a few minutes to clear my head, then walked back to my condo."

Green calculated rapidly. Ten thirty was just outside the limits of MacPhail's estimated time of death. The pathologist wasn't foolproof, but he'd seen a lot of dead bodies in his time. "Can anyone verify that?"

"My wife."

Blakeley must have seen Green's disbelief, for he flushed. "It's true!"

"But you said you told no one about this meeting with Patricia, so you see my dilemma. Patricia is dead. If no one but you knew about the blackmail, who else could have killed her?"

"I don't know! That's your job, not mine."

Green raised his hands innocently. "And my job points to you."

"That won't get far in a court of law."

Green stared him down for a moment, wondering what leverage he could use. The old warrior was back in form. "I'm quite prepared to proceed with the evidence we have, sir. But that's not what concerns me now. There is a woman who witnessed Patricia Ross's murder and who has now disappeared. She's probably already dead. That's a lot of bodies piling up as a result of your ill-advised punch to Oliver's head. A lot more bodies to hide from your conscience. But we haven't found hers yet, and as long as that's the case, there's a chance you can save her. What can you tell me about her disappearance?"

Blakeley had grown pale at the mention of a witness, and now he lowered his head in his hands and shook it despairingly back and forth. "I … don't … know. Nothing. I didn't have anything to do with the Ross woman's death."

"Then someone else killed her on your behalf, John. Because without a doubt she was killed to stop her from revealing what she knew about you."

Blakeley remained with his head in his hands.

"I'd say the list of people who fit the bill is pretty small," Green said. "How many people know you killed Daniel Oliver? I can think of three." He held up three fingers and ticked them off. "Dick Hamm, Roger Atkinson, and by your admission, your devoted wife."

Blakeley's head shot up, his jowls darkening with rage. "Don't … don't —!"

"Am I missing someone, John?"

"How do I know? There were lots of people in the bar that night!"

Green kept his three fingers in front of Blakeley's face. "And of those three, how many care enough to commit murder for you? Hamm, Atkinson or Leanne?"

Blakeley knocked away his hand with a lightning fast swipe. "This is nothing but the most outrageous speculation!"

Green's hand stung, sending a spike of anger shooting through him. He fought the urge to seize the man's wrist. "Let me tell you about this innocent witness whose life hangs in the balance," he managed evenly. "She was once a school teacher, married to a history professor and the mother of twin boys. When the boys were ten, their father chopped them into pieces with a chainsaw. That's what Twiggy lives with every day as she scrounges out a half-life on the riverbank. You talked earlier about how much our society needs heroes, John, and I can tell you there have been precious few in Twiggy's world. So you have a choice here to put your money where your mouth is."

Blakeley stared at him in stony silence. Green held his gaze and let the silence lengthen until he could no longer trust his dispassion. Shoving back his chair, he stood up. "Think about it, John. Wherein lies honour?"

TWENTY-SIX

"IT WAS A good try, Mike," Sullivan said, after Green had stalked out of the recording room. He had left Blakeley slumped at the table, still resolutely silent.

"Oh, I'm not done," Green snapped as he headed for the situation room with Sullivan and McGrath on his heels. "I've planted some thoughts in his head, and we'll just let them germinate for a while. Meanwhile, we're a lot further ahead than we were. At least we know where to look next."

"I don't believe for one minute that he didn't kill Patricia Ross," McGrath said as they entered the room. She was obviously still smarting from being excluded from the interview, because her tone was glacial. "Just look at the guy's temper."

"His temper is why he killed Daniel Oliver," Green said. "But Patricia Ross wasn't killed by temper. She was killed by premeditated ruthlessness."

"I disagree." Her tone dropped ten more degrees. "They could have had an argument about the blackmail money, and bang — before he knows it, he strangles her."

Green crossed the room to the blackboard and drew three vertical lines down it. At the top of each resulting column, he scribbled a name. Hamm, Atkinson, Leanne and Weiss.

"These are our suspects. Barring some unknown twist —"

McGrath stalked to the board, screeched the chalk down a fourth line, and wrote Blakeley at the top before returning to her seat.

Green felt a flush creep up his neck. "You're right," he said in what he hoped was a conciliatory tone. "We should keep all possibilities open."

"I don't see why Weiss is up there," she countered. "He didn't even know about Daniel Oliver's death."

"But he's clearly involved somehow, and as Brian said earlier, he may be our best hope of breaching the code of silence. Brian, can you check if surveillance has had any sighting of him yet?"

They waited in chilly silence while Sullivan called Charbonneau and Leblanc. The conversation lasted barely a minute, and when Sullivan hung up, he shook his head. "No luck tracking Weiss down, and so far no sign of his ex-wife either. They're going to keep an eye on both premises for a few hours yet, and call if anything develops."

"Is Gibbs still in the squad room?"

Sullivan shook his head again. "He went off to see Sue. The lad's almost dead on his feet anyway, Mike."

Sullivan's expression was deadpan, but there was an ominous edge in his voice which Green recognized all too well. He was warning Green to put the brakes on before he let his own impatience and single-mindedness trample over everyone else's views. Green forced himself to nod in agreement. "How is Sue? Any change?"

"Apparently she's conscious for short periods, but that's about all. The doctors will be running more tests in the morning." Sullivan stifled a yawn. His hair was standing in tufts, and his eyes were red-rimmed with fatigue. "It's probably about time we called it a night ourselves, Mike. There's not much that won't wait till morning, when we'll all be much sharper."

Green glanced at his watch. It was now past ten o'clock, and night was settling in. But with every passing hour, the hope of finding Twiggy dimmed.

"I'd like us to run through what we've got on these suspects, to make sure we're not missing anything and to see if there's anything the night shift guys can follow up on in the meantime."

Sullivan groaned and reached for his cellphone. He punched in a number on his speed dial.

"What are you doing?" Green demanded irritably.

"Ordering us pizza and coffee. If we're going to be here half the night, I want food."

Green stole a sheepish glance at McGrath, who returned it with a stony stare. *Oy*, he thought, this is going to be a tough sell. Maybe food will help. Once the pizzas were ordered, he turned his attention back to the blackboard.

"Let's ask a few basic investigative questions here. First of all, if we assume the killer was protecting Blakeley, then he or she had to have known about Blakeley killing Oliver —"

"Why?" McGrath demanded. "The killer could be any of Blakeley's friends or staffers, for example, who found out about the blackmail and decided to eliminate the threat to him even without knowing the cause."

Green mustered some patience through his fatigue. "That's an outside possibility but unlikely, because only a few hours elapsed between the blackmail attempt and the murder. Not much time to learn about it and react, particularly if Blakeley told no one."

"If you believe that."

"Good point. So let's rank these five. Who had the strongest motive for protecting Blakeley?"

"His wife, Leanne," Sullivan said.

McGrath thrust her chair back and crossed her arms, mentally withdrawing herself from the discussion. Green pretended not to notice. "Absolutely," he said. "She's very protective of him anyway, and her fortunes are irrevocably tied to his."

"And I'd say Hamm has the least motive," Sullivan added.

"He does have a motive, though. Both of them are military men, and we don't know enough about their relationship. That's something for the night shift to look at." Green jotted down some notes before returning to the list.

"Atkinson is a behind-the-scenes man whose fortunes are also linked to Blakeley's," Sullivan said. "If Blakeley gets a cabinet portfolio, imagine how high Atkinson could fly. And for an ambitious lad from Sheet Harbour, that's pretty heady stuff."

"But hardly on a par with what Leanne has to gain or lose. I'd put Atkinson in the middle between the wife and Hamm."

Sullivan eyed the board dubiously. "I don't know where Weiss fits in."

"No. Until we know what his connection is, we can't know his motive." Green put a question mark under Weiss's name.

McGrath shifted irritably in her seat. "I still say Blakeley is number one," she muttered. "No one had more reason to protect his secret than the man himself."

Green nodded. Within the context of the question, she was right, and at this point he was glad for any participation. He didn't dare mention the gut feeling he'd had staring at Blakeley across the table as the man denied point blank that he was the killer. Either he wasn't the killer, or he was a damn good liar.

"Next question," he said instead. "Which one has the physical strength to do the job? Crushing Patricia Ross's vertebrae and beating Peters within an inch of her life both require considerable strength. My money's on Hamm for this one."

"Yeah," said Sullivan. "Although beneath his suit and slick manner, Atkinson has a lot of muscle. I'd say he works out."

"Leanne ... Well, as tough as she is, there's no way a woman —"

McGrath nearly shot out of her chair. "And who was huffing and puffing up the hills in Halifax?"

Sullivan laughed, and Green felt his cheeks grow hot. "I'm the first to admit I'm no basis for comparison. But between a fit man and a fit woman —"

"Both of these victims were women themselves," she shot back. "And a fit woman can be a match for many men, especially if she's had martial arts training."

Green regarded her ruefully. Her cheeks were pink and her eyes blazed. He forced himself to separate her anger from her message. "You're quite right, and we need to check that out. In fact, we need to know much more about her background, her health and even her political activities. Superintendent Devine mentioned that her father is a Liberal bigshot, and getting her husband into that inner circle may be a big deal for her." He jotted down another note for the night shift. "In the meantime, Hamm and Weiss earn the highest score, Atkinson next and Leanne last."

McGrath sat back, a stubborn scowl on her face. "You're forgetting Blakeley again. I think he'd rate at least with Hamm and Weiss."

Reluctant to add further fuel to her anger, Green cast a silent plea for assistance at Sullivan, who seemed to read his mind. "He's older, so that's a factor, but he's probably on a par with Atkinson."

Green ploughed on before McGrath could object further. "Third question. Opportunity. Who could have been in Ottawa on Sunday night and up in Petawawa the following Friday?"

All three of them studied the list of suspects in silence. Sullivan spoke first. "Weiss obviously was in both places at the times in question, and on the face of it, the four others all have good mobility and legitimate reasons to travel back and forth without attracting attention."

"But we have gaps in our alibi information," Green said. "So far, what do we know?"

"We know Hamm was in Petawawa when Peters was attacked, but ..." Sullivan activated the incident room computer and clicked through boxes. "Hamm said he was in Petawawa with his wife when Ross was killed. Corroborated by the wife."

"Which doesn't mean much, but at least it's an alibi," Green muttered. "Leanne will probably back up Blakeley's statement about what time he got home, but we still have to substantiate that."

Sullivan rubbed his face wearily. "More work for the night shift." Unexpectedly, his cellphone rang and his face lit up. "Ah! That will be our pizza."

When a duty officer brought the pizza up, Sullivan dived in with gusto, but Green didn't know which he needed more, food or sleep. A wave of exhaustion crashed over him halfway through the first slice. Small wonder, he though, when he realized he'd been on the job now for nearly eighteen hours, with little more than a fitful few hours the night before to tide him over. Half an hour later, they called it a night, handed over the notes to the night shift for follow-up and packed up to leave. McGrath, who had barely taken a bite of her pizza, headed towards the door without a backward glance.

"Do you want me to pick you up when we're ready to get started in the morning?" Green asked.

She swung around. "This part of the investigation isn't really my case. Not that it would make any difference if it was."

She leaned against the door frame and crossed her arms. Even though her eyes were hooded with fatigue, the tilt of her chin was defiant. Green didn't know how to placate her and hadn't the spare energy to think about it. He tried for a sympathetic tone.

"Do you want me to drop you off at your hotel on my way home?"

"What I want is a shot at interviewing Blakeley in the morning."

He considered her request. They had left Blakeley in the holding cell overnight to contemplate his future, and his conscience. A little extra nudging might be just what he needed after a long night. If Devine and the Chief went ballistic, tough.

He nodded. "I'll leave word. Now let's get some sleep."

Green felt as if his head had barely hit the pillow when his cellphone rang on the night table beside him, prompting muffled curses from Sharon's side of the bed. He groped to silence it before the second ring and croaked a greeting through the fog in his brain.

Leblanc's voice came through uncertainly. "Sorry to wake you, sir, but Sullivan said you wanted to be informed. We just checked on the status of Weiss's wife."

Green sat up, the fog clearing abruptly. "And?"

"Her car's in the drive now, sir. There are no lights on, but I figure she's probably asleep. Do you want me to ring the bell and see?"

Green peered at his clock radio. Three a.m. Jesus! What maniac goes out on the streets at three a.m. He thought about it for all of two seconds. Me.

"No, don't do anything. We'll be right there."

***

Sept. 16, 1993. 3 a.m. Middle of no-man's land, Sector South, Croatia.

We're sitting in our APC on a stretch of deserted road, in the middle of the combat zone. I'm a million miles from sleep. Two rows of tanks are pointed straight at us, and I'm listening for every sound. A few hours ago we had all-out war with the Croats, who have machine guns, rocket grenades, 20 mm. cannons and at least twenty tanks. Apparently nobody told them about the withdrawal agreement their president signed in Zagreb, and they didn't want any part of it. We were told that we could fire back if fired upon, so we were giving them everything we had. The noise was unbelievable. Our first real combat. Some of the guys were like 'yeah, finally!'.

The miracle was, we didn't lose a single soldier. After it was over, we ran around checking that we were all okay, then Danny and I went across to their position for a look. There was blood all over, and a little ways away, a Croat soldier lying all by himself. A kid, really. I wonder if he took a long time to die, and if he was scared. It bothered me, thinking it might have been my bullet.

Later, the CO and a few officers went over to the Croat side to prove there was an agreement, and the CO said we were going to put two APCs at the crossover point just to keep our foot in the door till morning. So here we are, like sitting ducks with tanks staring at us from both sides. We're flying the biggest UN flag in the battalion and we're hoping nobody over there gets trigger-happy after a snootfull.

Sept 16, 1993. 6 p.m. Croatian front line, Sector South, Croatia.

The next day started off bad and got worse. We were stuck inside the APC, trying to get some sleep, when this huge explosion shook the ground and blasted our ears. I poked my head out of the hatch and saw a massive column of dust and smoke up ahead, behind the Croat line. There's supposed to be a ceasefire, so what the hell is this? There's the stink of gunpowder and smoke everywhere. I'm so sick of this shit, people who just fucking destroy for the hell of it.

Soon the CO and the rest of the company came up to join us and we set off in a convoy down the road to the Croat side. That's when the trouble really started. Another fucking Croat roadblock. Anti-tank mines across the road, tanks and missiles pointing at us and some tin-pot general saying we're not going through. The orders come down from the CO to pick a target, so Danny points the C-6 at this missile that's pointing at us. Talk about playing chicken. I thought, this is it, I'm going to die over here. Two weeks left till the end of my tour and I'm going home in a body bag. Two hours later, I'm still shaking, even way down deep in my gut.

***

The suburb of Orleans was a mushrooming tangle of crescents lined with cookie cutter houses and big box malls that had gobbled up the vast plains of farmland sloping up from the Ottawa river. It owed its name to the tiny French Canadian farming village that had once been its core, but beyond the ornate, silver-roofed stone church on St. Joseph Boulevard, very little remained of its village roots.

Green could never get in and out of Orleans without becoming lost, so he was counting on Sullivan to navigate their route to 1765 Appletree Court. Sullivan had not offered a word of protest about being roused at three in the morning, and had arrived at Green's house bearing two extra large Tim Hortons double-doubles. These were almost gone by the time the car had looped endlessly through Applefield Drive, Applewood Avenue and Appleglen Crescent, past identical vinyl-sided houses with minivans in the driveways and juniper beds under the front windows. Rounding yet another bend, they spotted a familiar beige Malibu parked discreetly at the curb.

"Ahah!" Green exclaimed. "That's got to be Charbonneau and Leblanc."

A moment later Leblanc and Charbonneau had joined them in the back of the car, where Sullivan thoughtfully provided them with yet two more double-doubles from a box on the seat.

"It's that house with the green Dodge Caravan in the drive," Leblanc said between grateful gulps.

Green studied the townhouse, which was dimly lit by a street light across the way. He could see a couple of bicycles and a spindly sapling on the front lawn, but the house itself was masked by curtains. A light shone from a window upstairs, and he thought he could see a faint glow through the front door.

"The lights are on," he said.

"Yeah, they just went on a few minutes ago," said Leblanc. "After we called you."

Green frowned. It was not yet four o'clock. What could have roused her in the middle of the night? News of Weiss? Maybe even his arrival? Weiss would have recognized the beige Malibu a mile away and slipped into the house unseen through the back yard.

Green opened the car door, his mind made up. It was time to find out what she knew, and who she might be hiding.

Frenzied yapping erupted inside at the sound of the bell, followed by a flurry of footsteps and a hoarse "shut up!" which did little good. He waited a minute and rang again. This time above the din he heard the slap of shoes upon the floor, and a pair of bloodshot eyes glared through the small glass panel in the door. Sullivan held up his badge to the glass, and the eyes grew wide. A predictable enough reaction at this time of the night, Green thought, trying not to read anything more into it.

Locks clicked, and the door swung warily open to reveal a tiny woman wearing red flannel polka dot pyjamas that hung on her scrawny frame. Her bleached platinum hair was piled haphazardly on top of her head, and her thin face was pinched with worry. Smoke curled from the cigarette in her hand, causing her to squint as she peered at them.

"What's wrong?"

"I'm Inspector Green, and this is Sergeant Sullivan from the major crimes unit. Are you Eleanor Weiss?"

She recoiled, reaching to steady herself against the wall. A faint whiff of whiskey drifted around her. "Yes. Why?"

"May we have a word inside?"

"No. I don't know. What's happened?"

"Is your husband at home?"

She hadn't moved, and now she shook her head vigorously. "He doesn't live here anymore. We're separated."

Sullivan stepped forward and loomed over her, taking her arm to soften the impact of his size. "Mrs. Weiss," he said gently, "it's very important that we speak with you. Please, let's go inside."

She looked up at him, her pale eyes blinking with alarm. Something in his gaze seemed to reassure her, for she nodded and stepped aside for them to enter. "We can talk in the kitchen. The children are asleep."

A black terrier swirled around their feet as they followed her down the hall. Green cast a quick glance around, not really expecting to spot Weiss hiding behind the curtains or Twiggy stashed in the corner. The living room and the hallway were strewn with clothes and children's toys. A peek into the open hall closet revealed a jumble of clothes, including a pair of men's boots and a beige parka far too big for Eleanor Weiss. There was no proof they belonged to Jeff Weiss, but if so, he still had a toehold in the family.

Inside the kitchen, cigarette smoke choked the air. On the table sat an overflowing ashtray and a half glass of amber liquid, which she hastily cleared into the sink. "I was having a bit of trouble sleeping," she said as she fluttered around the kitchen like a restless moth, avoiding their gaze.

The day's dishes were still piled in the sink, and out of the corner of his eye, Green counted the dinner plates. There were four, just enough for the mother and her three children. Eleanor Weiss was clearly agitated about something, but it didn't appear that her husband had been in the house. At least not at dinner time. He nodded to Sullivan in a silent invitation to take the lead. Like many anxious, overwhelmed women, she seemed to draw comfort from Sullivan's bear-like presence.

"Mrs. Weiss," Sullivan said gently, "we have to speak with your husband. Can you tell us where he is?"

She scrubbed at a stubborn spot on the table. Grease caked much of the stove and counter, in Green's experience a sign that the woman was barely coping with the demands of daily life. If late night forays into the liquor cabinet were common occurrences, it was small wonder.

She shrugged defensively. "As I said, we're separated."

"But very few people know him as well as you do. He's been under a lot of stress at work. If he was trying to get away from things, where do you think he'd go?"

She turned and leaned against the counter to study Sullivan as if she were trying to size up the threat. Still, she shook her head. "I don't know what Jeff's been up to."

"Have you noticed any signs of stress recently? Restlessness, short temper?"

"I haven't seen him."

The woman's not as fragile or as obtuse as she pretends, Green decided. He hooked his arm over the back of his chair and affected a casual pose. "I've been speaking to his superior officer. He said Jeff is still getting over his experiences in Yugoslavia. Did you ever notice that?"

She shifted her attention from Sullivan to Green, and her eyes narrowed. "If Jeff is involved in something, I want to know what it is. So stop pussyfooting around."

Green nodded. At four o'clock in the morning, straight talk was refreshing. "Your husband is in a lot of trouble, Mrs. Weiss, and the best thing he can do for himself is come clean. He faces disciplinary charges and possibly even criminal ones. You are aware that his partner was nearly killed in Petawawa while investigating a case involving the military. There's evidence that Jeff set her up."

Her jaw dropped. "He would never do that."

"There's more. You're probably aware that John Blakeley, a Liberal candidate from Petawawa, withdrew from the campaign today." Her eyes widened at the news, but still she said nothing. "John Blakeley is a former military officer who was your husband's unit commander in Yugoslavia. Did he tell you that?"

The colour drained from her face. "He … he didn't talk much about those days. And I avoided them."

Green sensed a vulnerability in her tone. Beneath the defiance, she was frightened. He felt a twinge of guilt for harassing her. He leaned forward, trying to sound gentler. "Why was that?"

"Because it worked him up. It was better for everyone if he didn't get worked up."

"You mean safer for everyone?"

Her chin quivered. "His temper … I know it was a struggle for him, and he hated himself afterwards, but it was like he couldn't help himself."

"And that's why you left him?"

"I didn't want to. I know he needed us. I felt terrible turning my back."

"But he needed more help than you could give him."

She nodded. A touch of anger hardened her jaw. "The police force didn't help. They never noticed how stressed he was. He hid it well, and none of his superior officers saw past his front. Just said he had an attitude problem. And now you say he's in trouble, and you're going to blame him for what happened to his partner."

"That's just the way it looks, Mrs. Weiss," Green said. "But you're right; he's been a good cop, and I'm sure there's another explanation. Did he ever mention Captain Blakeley or a soldier named Corporal Ian MacDonald?"

She hesitated and he could see her hovering on the brink of revelation. After a moment, she sighed as if releasing a great burden, and gave a faint nod. "Jeff's been working on John Blakeley's campaign."

Green nearly choked on his surprise. He struggled to sound casual as his mind raced over the implications. "On his campaign? So Jeff knew him here as well? What did he say about him?"

"He said Blakeley would sure stir things up at the Liberal caucus table, because he fought for what he believed in and said what he meant. Jeff said those mealy-mouthed, two-faced Liberals wouldn't know what hit them."

"So Jeff liked him?

"He thought the world of him."

"Enough to cover up evidence in order to protect him?"

She froze as if realizing the trap too late. "That's not what I meant."

"I can't give you details, but the evidence suggests that Blakeley has done something wrong, and Jeff has been helping him cover it up. Perhaps even committed a crime on his behalf."

She pressed herself back against the counter, as if trying to retreat. Her head whipped back and forth. "He wouldn't do that! He admired Blakeley, but he would never, ever, commit a crime."

"Even for some greater good?"

Hesitation flickered across her face. It lasted only a fraction of a second, but it told Green what he needed to know. She had doubts. In fact, perhaps she was beginning to put some puzzle pieces of her own together.

He leaned towards her gently. "For Jeff's sake, he needs to come in, before he digs himself in any deeper and someone else gets hurt."

She groped her way to a chair and sank into it as if her legs could no longer support her. "I … I don't know."

Green eyed her thoughtfully. She had been away most of the day, then in the dead of night she'd been awake, a bundle of nerves. Who else but Weiss could tie her into such knots? He took a wild guess. "Did you go to see him this evening?"

She stared at the table, her eyes slowly filling with tears. Faintly, she nodded.

"Please tell us where he is."

"It's too late."

Green felt a sick dread rising in his throat. "Why? What happened?"

"He wanted his passport. He phoned and asked me to bring it to him."

"And did you?"

She nodded wretchedly. "I didn't even dare ask questions. I'd never heard him so tense."

"Where is he?"

"He's probably not there anymore." She glanced at the clock on the wall. "He's on his way out of the country."

Out of the corner of his eye, Green saw Sullivan reach for his cellphone. "How? By air?"

"I'm not sure. That's what he said, but …"

Sullivan was already slipping into the hall to alert security at the airport. If they could lock down the exit routes, they might still have a chance of catching him.

"But what, Mrs. Weiss?" Green asked.

"I don't want him in trouble. I know, no matter what he's done, he'd never hurt anyone. He's a good man, he's just not thinking straight right now."

"Then for his sake, you have to be strong for him. He may be in too deep to see a way out. But his best chance is us. If he's all alone on the run from us and —"

"He's not alone."

Green stiffened. "What do you mean?"

"He has a friend helping him escape."

"Who?"

"Another police officer."

Green hid his shock. "Jeff told you this?"

"No. The man called a little while ago. Woke me up. He said he was supposed to pick Jeff up and help him get across the border, but he was lost and needed directions again."

Green's stomach knotted with dread. "Did you get a name?"

She must have heard the alarm in his voice, for her own voice rose. "No. My caller ID just gave a number."

"Is the number still on your phone?"

She rose and disappeared into the hall for a moment, reappearing with a cordless phone in her hand. "I gave him directions. Oh, my God, I hope I did the right thing." She found the number and held out the phone. Green had only to glance at it to confirm his fears.

It was the same number that had phoned Patricia Ross at her Vanier Hotel and the same number that had called for Sue Peters at the bar in Petawawa before she was attacked.

TWENTY-SEVEN

THE NIGHT WAS just beginning to lift when Green and Sullivan left Eleanor Weiss's house and raced back to their car. Green was grateful to see the dark smudges of treetops and roof lines etched against the faint grey of the sky. A search in the countryside would have been nearly impossible in the pitch dark.

Once Weiss's wife realized the error she'd made, she had held nothing back. "The man sounded so nice!" she'd exclaimed.

"You're sure it was a man?"

"Yes. Well —" she paused, her eyes frantic as she raked her memory. "I thought so, but the connection wasn't good. Oh, God, Jeffie! What have I done!"

"We don't know that there's anything wrong," Green lied without much conviction. "But you have to tell us where Jeff is."

"He was at his trailer in Quebec. He has a little trailer on a river up past Wakefield that he uses for fishing. And for peace and quiet when things get too much."

He nodded toward the phone. "Can you reach him there?"

She shook her head. "There's no electricity or phone. And his cellphone has no service there."

"Then how did he get in touch with you earlier?"

"There's a payphone at the general store in the village."

"What village?"

"Brennan's Hill." She grimaced in dismay. "It's up near Low, Quebec, at least twenty minutes' drive from the trailer."

Green's thoughts were already racing ahead. "Can you show us where the trailer is on a map?"

She dashed out of the room. As soon as she was out of earshot, Sullivan shook his head grimly. "That cellphone call came in at 3:49, which means that our killer, assuming he called her from Ottawa, has about a half hour's head start. Low is about an hour north of here by car, which means our guy's not there yet."

Green nodded. "We'll have to get the Sûreté du Québec on it ASAP, and at least get some uniformed officers out to the trailer to check what's going on." *Just what I need*, he thought. *Not only another jurisdiction and another province, but another language to add to this intricate mess.*

Eleanor reappeared clutching a map and a page of directions. She was flushed and breathing hard, but the task seemed to focus her. "I'm afraid the trailer is really hard to find. It's on a river at the back of a farm owned by a Claude Theriault, and the lane isn't marked from the road."

Green took small comfort from that as he thanked her, grabbed the material and headed towards the door. He paused in the open doorway for a last look at the worried woman. "We'll find him, Mrs. Weiss, but if he calls, warn him to stay away from the trailer and to report in to the station."

Out in the car, Sullivan did a rapid U-turn and headed back towards the main road while Green called the communications centre to explain the situation. "Get hold of the Sûreté du Québec's Outaouais District and patch me through to the commanding officer," he snapped.

While headquarters worked on that job, Green spread out the map and bent his head over it, tracing the thin, squiggly roads deep into the Quebec bush.

"It sure is out in the boonies," he grumbled. "But I suppose that cuts both ways. The killer may have trouble finding it too."

Sullivan squealed around a curve. "You know, Mike, it seems to me more likely what he told Mrs. Weiss is true. That he's an accomplice who is supposed to meet up with Weiss to get out of the country. We know from the call to Peters in the bar that this has been a two-person job all along. And now that we know Weiss was working for Blakeley, we've got his motive for protecting him."

Green pondered the idea. Sullivan's scenario was possible, even likely given this latest discovery about Weiss, but something didn't feel right. If this had been a planned rendezvous between the two men, surely the man would have had proper directions and some sort of back-up means of communication. It made no sense for him to phone Weiss's ex-wife, who not only knew nothing about the escape, but who was not even married to him anymore.

The main streets of Orleans were still dead quiet as Sullivan accelerated onto Jeanne D'Arc Boulevard. Activating the emergency lights, he sped down onto the Queensway. En route, Green called the comm centre again to order bulletins at all the border crossings in southern Quebec and Eastern Ontario, as well as APBs on Weiss's vehicle in both provinces.

The roads were empty, but narrow streets slowed their progress as they wove through downtown to the MacDonald-Cartier Bridge. Just after they'd crossed the Ottawa River into Quebec, Green's cellphone rang. It was Sergeant Fortin of the Low Detachment of the Sûreté du Québec, speaking in a rapid, broad vowelled French. Green had taken the usual obligatory French courses at school, but had learned more from the rival French gangs in the inner city neighbourhood of his youth than he had ever learned memorizing conjugations in class. Over the years, he often used this limited repertoire when dealing with Ottawa's francophone community, but Fortin's Outaouais version of the language was almost more than he could decipher. He stumbled through a basic explanation of the situation.

Sergeant Fortin's voice rose in excitement, and his French became even more indecipherable. Theriault was his wife's uncle, Fortin said. He'd never been to the man's farm, but he'd seen him at family affairs. He was a frail old man, and even the arrival of squad cars with sirens and guns might give him a heart attack.

Oh, wonderful, Green thought. What else could possibly go wrong? Lots, he amended on second thought. Hanging onto the overhead strap, he struggled to talk Fortin through the directions.

"No problem," said Fortin cheerfully. "We have lots of experience with this area. We can have a team there in less than half an hour."

Fuck, Brian and I will be there ourselves in less than that, Green thought. "How many officers?"

"Two." There was a silence, during which Green kept his protest in check with an effort. Seconds were ticking by. "*Ben*, it's the middle of the night."

"Then wake some others up, pull them from other detachments. We need all available units."

More silence on the line. "Okay, I'll check with —"

"Don't check, do it! Get out to that farm and lock it down. But no lights, no sirens."

He hung up before the sergeant could object, and turned to find Sullivan grinning at him. "I understood most of that," Sullivan said. "I think those French lessons are paying off. Next thing, I'll be gunning for your job."

Green snorted. "You wouldn't want it." He filled him in on the gist of Fortin's information and Sullivan grew sober again.

"Jesus, Mary and Joseph," he muttered. "Those guys aren't going to get there much ahead of us."

"And we have absolutely no idea what they're going to face when they do." Green cursed and slapped the dash. "Push it, Brian!"

Sullivan stepped on the gas, and Green felt the car surge forward. They were racing along Quebec's divided Highway 5 now, climbing high into the Gatineau Hills which rose in pine-jagged silhouette against the greying sky. Green welcomed the light with relief. Dawn was still more than an hour away, but at least they would no longer be bumbling around the backwoods in utter darkness.

Sullivan was frowning. "We could be way off-base, you know. Maybe Weiss doesn't have Twiggy with him. Maybe she's hiding out in the city somewhere, and Weiss is just laying low while he puts together a plan to get out of the country."

"Except there's that damn cellphone call to Weiss's wife. No, Brian, someone is after Weiss. I agree Twiggy is a question mark, but I'm damn sure Weiss is a target. I just wish I knew who. And why."

"Well, our list of suspects is shrinking. Blakeley's in jail, and if Weiss is the target, that only leaves —"

A blur of grey flashed in front of the car. Sullivan slammed on the brakes and the tires screamed as he fought to keep the car on the road. Green barely registered the deer before it leaped gracefully over the roadside ditch and disappeared into the trees. In its wake, Sullivan shook his head, his knuckles white as he eased forward on the gas again.

"Holy Mary, that was too close. I forgot this is prime deer hour."

Green's heart gradually slowed, and they pressed on in tense silence, focussing on the road. When they reached the end of the autoroute, Sullivan slowed to navigate the turn onto the two-lane highway that followed the Gatineau River up towards Low. Green chafed at the narrow, twisting road.

"Brian, we have to go faster."

Sullivan scowled as he pressed the accelerator cautiously. "One near fatal encounter not enough for you, Green? How about I do the driving, and you keep your eyes glued to the shoulders of the road up ahead."

They drove in silence again, past the scattered settlement on either side of the highway. A gas station, a building store, a lone house … Green's thoughts drifted back to their list of suspects. Who would they meet at the end of the road? Hamm was his greatest worry. He was a professional soldier trained in tactics and combat, tough and disciplined, perhaps to a fault. But that very professionalism gave Green pause. Hamm had three generations of war heroes to live up to. Would he disregard the military tradition and chain of command he revered so much, simply to protect a colleague's name?

Atkinson, on the other hand, had shown himself to be the king of expediency and sleaze. John Blakeley was his meal ticket, and there was no telling how high Atkinson's own star would rise if Blakeley got himself into the Liberal cabinet. Atkinson would waste little regret on the likes of Patricia Ross or Sue Peters if they got in his way. But the question was whether he had the physical savagery to actually kill them himself. Green wished he had met the man; old-fashioned instinct often told him more than a dozen well-crafted reports.

That instinct played a large part in his assessment of their third suspect. Gibbs's background report on Leanne Neuss had painted a picture of a strong, capable woman used to taking charge and getting the job done. With her mother dead from cancer and her father addicted to backroom politics, she had run his household and raised her four younger brothers almost singlehandedly. All of this had certainly been good training for her role as a saviour wife, but on the face of it, not for cold-blooded murder. Yet Green had met the woman and seen first hand her strength and her protectiveness. Had she inherited her father's passion for power as well? Blakeley was her mission, whether as a wounded warrior in need of healing or as a promising star of the Liberal Party. Could she assault two women with her own bare hands, if his future was at stake?

Green's cellphone blasted into the middle of his thoughts. It was Fortin again, announcing that another unit had been dispatched and that he himself was on his way to the farm.

"What about the first unit?" Green demanded.

Fortin's cellphone crackled ominously. "Not yet arrived, sir. But it should be any time."

Not yet arrived, Green thought, glancing at his watch. What were they driving? Horse buggies? He peered outside at the passing landscape. On his right lay the broad silver ribbon of the Gatineau River, and on his left the rugged rock face. No lights winked through the pallid dawn, no signs of life. Nothing but pasture and scrub, blurred in places by a pale mist that hung over the ground.

"Where are we?" he asked Sullivan.

"Some navigator you are. I think we must be almost at Brennan's Hill. Keep an eye out for a restaurant on the left. That's the entrance to McDonald Road."

McDonald Road, according to Eleanor Weiss's directions, was a long, winding dirt road that led deep into Quebec farmland. A side road branched off it about ten kilometres inland, followed by another ten-kilometre stretch to the Theriault farm. Even at a risky sixty kilometres an hour, they were probably still twenty minutes away. Too long!

He turned his attention back to Fortin. "When do you expect to arrive?"

"I'm just on Chemin McDonald now. Maybe fifteen minutes?"

"We're right behind you. When you get to the farm, proceed with caution. Check with the farmer for signs of strangers before making a move. We need to know what we are dealing with."

"No problem," said Fortin. "I'll handle this, sir."

After signing off, Green turned to Sullivan. "Step on it, Brian. Our Quebec colleague sounds a little too sure of himself."

A cluster of buildings emerged from the gloom up ahead, and a small highway sign announced "Brennan's Hill." At the last minute, Green spotted a narrow road snaking up behind a building on the left.

"That must be our turn!" he shouted. Sullivan executed a rapid emergency turn, swerving the car with a shriek of rubber and heading onto the side road. The tires thudded over potholes and tossed a shower of stones in their wake as he stepped on the gas again. The sky had lightened almost to white, and Green could see the silhouettes of village houses bleached pale grey with the dawn. But mist hung thick over the passing fields and swirled in the headlights up ahead, forcing Sullivan to slow even further.

"This is great," Green muttered. "Now we've got fog to complicate things even more."

"Yeah, but remember, it's more difficult for our bad guy as well," Sullivan replied, jerking the wheel to avoid a large pothole in the road. The Malibu fishtailed on the crumbling pavement, but Sullivan wrestled it under control with an expert hand. They drove in silence through the rolling countryside past squat little homes and desolate farms. Puffing chimneys poked up through the fog, and the scent of wood smoke and manure clotted the dank air. An endless ribbon of rocks and grass swept by in their headlights. After a few minutes, the pavement gave way to bone-rattling gravel.

Occasionally, Green caught a glimpse of red taillights in the fog far ahead. "That could be our man," he said.

"Or the Sûreté," Sullivan said. "Either way, it's good news."

For the first time, Green relaxed a little in the seat as he scanned the passing signs for the side road on Eleanor Weiss's map. Chemin Lyons, Chemin Murray, Daly …

"Gee, Brian, you'd be right at home around here."

Sullivan grunted. "It was probably settled by the same tough Irish peasant stock as the Ottawa Valley. Same hardscrabble life too, from the looks of it."

They turned north and followed the side road deeper into green, rolling pastureland. Ten minutes farther along, a small laneway cut into the cedar brush on their left. Sullivan skidded to a stop, and Green eyed it dubiously.

"There's no road sign," Green said.

"But it's the right distance, and it's the only road around." Sullivan climbed out and went to peer at the muddy ground at the entrance. When he returned to the car, he nosed it into the lane. "There are several fresh tire tracks. This is it."

They proceeded cautiously down Theriault's drive, which became little more than a wagon track rutted by tires and awash in mud. The third time the Malibu bottomed out on a rock, Sullivan winced and slowed to a crawl. They lurched across a cow pasture, through a copse of scruffy cedars and into another clearing. Finally up ahead the tall stack of a silo loomed out of the fog, followed by a barn, several out buildings and a rambling old stone farmhouse. A dog barked as they slithered to a stop behind two Sûreté du Québec SUVs parked haphazardly in the mud outside the house. Four men stood on the porch, surrounded by excited dogs.

A lean, wiry SQ sergeant bulked up by his vest and utility belt leaped off the porch and strode towards them. Beneath the peak of his cap, Green could see sharp blue eyes and a pencil-thin mustache. He and Sullivan climbed out of the Malibu, casually letting their jackets fall open to reveal their guns. They knew that technically, they had no official standing in Quebec, and if Fortin wanted to be a hard-ass, he could disarm them and park them in the farmhouse for the duration of the operation. Fortunately, the sergeant took one brief look at their Glocks and gave a barely perceptible nod before extending his hand in greeting.

"Gilles Fortin," he said cheerfully. "I was just getting information from my uncle."

He led the way to the porch, where a shrivelled old man stood leaning on a cane. He had sunken cheeks, a tattered eyepatch and no teeth, but his one good eye danced like a young boy's. He began to rattle away in French incomprehensible to Green, waving his claw-like hands excitedly towards the far side of the barn. Green held up both hands to halt the flow.

"Speak more slowly," he said.

The man rattled away again, the absence of teeth making all his consonants dissolve into *f*'s. After a bewildered moment, Green appealed to Fortin, who was laughing. Fortin then proceeded to speak for the first time in accented but fluent English.

"He says the owner of the trailer went down there on Saturday, which was a surprise this early in the season. There's a back lane down to the river. He's still there, my uncle thinks."

"Did he have someone with him? A woman?"

Fortin posed the question and Theriault erupted into another flurry of hand gestures and incomprehensible French.

"My uncle says he saw his white pick-up in the back pasture Saturday afternoon, and there was no one else in the cab with him."

But a pick-up has plenty of room in its truck bed to hide a person tied up, Green thought. Or dead, for that matter. "Has he seen anyone else around?"

Theriault had been watching Green shrewdly through the web of wrinkles that encircled his good eye, and Green wondered how much English he really understood. Now he began to speak again, shrugging his bony shoulders expressively. This time Green managed to decipher *"sheh pas."* I don't know.

Once again, Fortin obliged with the full translation. "There are six trailers down there, but normally no one goes at this time of the year. However, he thinks he heard a vehicle in the far field when he went out to milk the cows this morning. His dogs barked, but there were no headlights, and he couldn't see anything through the fog."

No headlights … Green didn't like the implications. On this rocky, unpredictable terrain, driving without headlights was suicidal unless stealth and surprise were paramount. "How recently?"

The old man shrugged and gestured to the sky. Green didn't need a translation to know that the farmer judged time not by a clock but by the rhythm of the day. Green knew enough about cows to know they were usually milked by dawn. Which could mean a mere five minutes ago, or as much as an hour ago. Green's heart sank. An hour was plenty of time for their bad guy to set up his ambush, kill Weiss and make good his escape. But then another thought struck him. Given that time frame, surely the man would have encountered Green and Sullivan coming along Chemin McDonald the other way. But they hadn't met a single car since turning off the main highway.

He felt a dawning of hope and excitement. "I think the bastard's still here! Either he's biding his time waiting for a chance to get by us, or he still hasn't accomplished what he came for. Maybe Weiss has managed to hold him off. We may still have a chance to save him."

He scoured his brain for everything he knew about emergency tactical response, which was limited to a few videos and powerpoint presentations by the Tac Team over the years. Combined with whatever expertise Fortin could offer about SQ procedures, it would have to be enough. There was no time to reconnoitre the surroundings or develop a sophisticated system of signals to coordinate an attack. Somehow, they had to storm the trailer, overpower the killer and secure everyone's safety, all within the shortest time possible.

He sent Theriault into the house to draw a quick map of the trailer camp, and while the old man was busy, a third SQ cruiser bumped down the lane. Green looked on while Fortin gathered the officers to check out their equipment, training and radio systems. Between them, the SQ had their four service revolvers, plus two semi-automatic rifles and long-range field binoculars in the back of their SUVs. The two Ottawa detectives pocketed an extra ammunition clip and pulled their body armour out of the trunk. It wasn't a tac outfit, but it might keep them alive.

Leaving Fortin to ready his officers and discuss the operation, Green hurried into the house to examine the map the old man had drawn. After only a brief glance, a rough plan of attack began to coalesce in his mind.

TWENTY-EIGHT

September 17, 1993. Medak, Sector South, Croatia.

I'm dead on my feet. I'm sitting out here in the woods with my shovel. I said I needed to take a shit, but the truth is I needed a break. The stink here is unbelievable. Rotting bodies, gunpowder, smoke, burning cows ... I don't think I'm ever going to barbeque again.

So much has happened the last day, I don't know what to write. Yesterday the Croats finally let us in to take over the Serb villages, and what a mess we found. The Croats had blown up or torched everything to hell. We were still looking for a place to dig in when Danny tells me I've been assigned to another unit to take care of the Serb civilians we liberated. Temporary, and if I don't want to go, he'll try to fix it. I figured maybe it would be a nice change to do some good instead of fighting with assholes, so I tell him I'm good to go.

They pair me with this reservist from Regina and assign us a section of houses to look for survivors. We're walking along watching for mines and calling out that it's safe to come out. But nobody comes. It's eerie. We know there are two, three hundred Serb civilians in the area, but all we find are dead animals. Cows, goats, horses. Shot, set on fire, thrown into the wells to poison them, or just left to rot. By the end of our shift, the only people we find are these two dead Serb soldiers shot through the eye like an execution.

We figure the villagers are hiding in the mountains, not ready to trust the UN because we just sat on the tarmac yesterday waiting politely for the go-ahead while the Croatians wiped out their homes. So tomorrow we'll extend the search further up the mountains.

***

ACCORDING TO THERIAULT'S map, the trailer park was just a string of six trailers plunked along an unused stretch of riverbank. The trailers sat empty most of the year, propped on cinder blocks about thirty feet apart along the water's edge. Weiss's trailer was third from the end, a one-room box measuring about eight feet by ten with a window on each side and a door at the rear. As far as Theriault could remember, Weiss kept his locked but hid the key under the back step.

Theriault had originally cleared the shoreline of the thick cedar swamp that hemmed it in, and had provided access roads in and out, but over the years a tangle of weeds, raspberry canes and sumac had grown up in the clearing, making access more difficult. Theriault apologized for the state of repair.

"I'm alone now, and at my age ..." he said, gesturing to the cane clutched in his gnarled hand.

"Pas de problème," Green reassured him. "The brush will provide some cover for our approach."

Considering the state of Theriault's main road, Green suspected the lane down to the trailer park would be little more than a cow path. It started in the back pasture, dipped down the hill to the river, then looped through the row of trailers before climbing back up the hill at the other end. Theriault said the track was fairly level until the last hundred yards or so, when it dropped steeply down to the river, but even the SUVs might find it hard to get back up the hill. The last thing Green wanted was a couple of SQ vehicles spinning their wheels in the muck in the middle of a crime scene.

With the camp hemmed in by river on one side and cedar bush on the other, there were only three avenues of approach — both ends of the access route, and the river. Green looked at Theriault and tried his French again.

"Have you got a boat?"

"Ah, ben ouais!" The man broke into a broad grin and mimicked rowing. The others laughed, but Green announced that a sneak approach would be perfect. With Fortin officially in command, they created three teams of two, and coordinated their watches and plans of approach. Fortin and one of his men went off with Theriault to get his boat, which was pulled up on the shore below the farmhouse. Green paired Sullivan with the SQ constable who spoke English and dispatched them in one of the SUVs to find the far access route to the camp. He chose the closer route for himself, wanting to get there ahead of the others so that he could size up the situation and adjust their final plan of attack. He took along the almost unilingual officer who made up for his lack of English by smiling a lot and adding an enthusiastic "okay!" after every comment.

They drove across the back pasture as far as they dared, jolting over rocks and potholes until the SUV was splattered with mud and scraping its undercarriage ominously. The SQ officer, who introduced himself as Jacques Langlois, finally stopped the car and studied the foggy terrain ahead, shaking his head dubiously. Nearby, a couple of cows stared at them with disinterest.

"We walk, okay?" Langlois announced, opening his door.

Green eyed the muddy manure that surrounded them and was grateful at least for his vinyl Payless shoes. $49.99 on special. Langlois, he noted, sported spit-polished, black leather boots. His brown uniform blended perfectly with the mud and scrub of their surroundings, whereas Green's shiny grey polyester was like a beacon. Terrific, Green thought, if there's anyone down there lying in wait, I'm the one who's going to get shot.

Seemingly oblivious, Langlois slung his rifle over his shoulder and strode off at a rapid pace that left Green scrambling to catch up. They slipped and slithered along the track as fast as they could, dodging the worst of the potholes and manure. As they reached the top of the hill, Green signalled Langlois into the trees at the edge of the track and crouched down to search the area ahead through the binoculars. The air was cold and dank with the smell of cedar loam. Fog still lay thick in the river valley and clung in patches to the hillside, but on the higher ground the sun was making some headway. Above him, crows flapped in the treetops and the chirps of early songbirds filled the air. In the distance Green could hear the sibilant rush of what he assumed was the river.

Apart from the sounds of wakening nature, the woods were still. He motioned Langlois to move forward, and together they crept down the hill under cover of the thick brush, all the time scanning ahead for signs of movement. Despite their best efforts at stealth, twigs snapped underfoot, and spiky branches tore at their clothes, so that by the time the first trailer materialized through the fog, Green feared that anyone hiding in the trailer park would be on full alert and waiting for them.

He stopped at the edge of the clearing to train the binoculars on the scene again. Still nothing. They ducked into the clearing and ran along the side of the first trailer. Green thought he heard a distant rattle, but when he strained his ears to listen, the rush of the river drowned out all other sound. They passed the second trailer and came upon a mud-splattered white pick-up truck tucked in between the second and third trailers, almost as if trying to hide from view. Green glanced at the license plate. Weiss's truck.

He crept up to it, peering first into the cab, which was empty, and then into the back. His heart leaped into his throat, and for a second he couldn't breathe. Bunched in the corner was a tattered garbage bag with its familiar contents spilling out. Twiggy's bag.

So the bastard had her after all.

Anger settled in his gut. He unsnapped the holster of his Glock and crouched in the tall dry brush to survey the surroundings. Langlois followed suit. Together, pressed against the side of the truck, they listened. Heard a thump, so muted it could have been his over-active imagination. Or the beating of his own heart. His blood pounded in his ears. The next trailer was Weiss's, and the moment they moved to the other side of the truck, they would be visible to him, and to anyone else who was lurking around.

From up ahead came a sharp snap followed by a hiss that sounded like a gasp. Now there was no mistaking it. Someone was sneaking around. Who? And where were they? Green hugged the side panel of the pick-up and slowly edged forward until Weiss's trailer came into full view. It was faded to a blotchy silver colour and surrounded by dessicated raspberry canes that looked as if they'd been trampled numerous times. The windows and doors looked shut, and no lights shone in the window. If Weiss and Twiggy were inside, they were in the dark.

Somewhere in the fog ahead came a louder thump and a metallic squeak that sounded like a door opening. Yet the door to Weiss's trailer, which was directly ahead, remained firmly shut. Something was wrong. Had Theriault been wrong about which trailer belonged to Weiss?

Green had only a split second to make a decision. He had no idea what was happening, but someone was prowling around, attempting to move soundlessly as he or she searched the area. Too soon to be Sullivan. It had to be the killer. Green knew he had mere seconds before the killer found what he was looking for. No time to wait for back-up or plan a coordinated attack. Jesus!

He took out his Glock and signalled to Langlois to stay put. "I'm going to Weiss's trailer. Cover me."

Langlois looked surprised and bewildered, but fortunately had been trained not to question a superior's folly. Obediently, he crouched behind cover of the truck and took out his revolver.

Green scurried through the ten feet of scrub that separated the truck from Weiss's trailer and pressed himself against the back wall of the trailer, trying to stifle his panting. His heart pounded and sweat slicked the gun in his hand. What the fuck am I doing, he thought in a brief moment of clarity. Who am I, Rambo? I've never done anything like this in my life. Twenty years on the police force, and I've never pulled the trigger on this thing outside the qualifying range. Here I am in my polyester grey suit and Payless shoes, ass deep in fog and mud, without a plan or even a clue who the bad guy is.

But then from somewhere up ahead came a soft thud, and a duck burst from cover with a flurry of wings and squawks.

Through his own panic, Green heard again the soft hiss over the rush of the river. This time it sounded like a curse. Green pressed his ear against the wall of the trailer but could hear nothing from within. He was about to reach under the step for the door key when he noticed that the padlock on the door hung open. The door was unlocked.

Cautiously, he reached up and pushed it open an inch. Nothing. Another few inches. It rattled. He froze. Waited a few seconds, expecting a volley of gunfire through the gap. When nothing happened, he readied his gun and peered around the edge of the door. The interior was dark and musty, but a faint odour of cooking oil hung in the air. A quick glance into the Spartan interior was enough to tell him it was empty.

Too much time, he berated himself as he ducked back outside. People would be dead by the time he found this guy!

Beckoning to Langlois to follow him, he raced along the side of Weiss's trailer and looked around the far end. Nothing but more raspberry canes. Further away, light footsteps swished through the dry grass. Jesus! He needed another pair of eyes! Where the hell was Sullivan?

He and Langlois dashed through the raspberry bushes to the back of the fourth trailer. It was a much larger one and its door gaped open. Inside, Green could make out at least two rooms. He hesitated. He thought he heard stifled breathing. Was someone hiding in there? On the other hand, the prowler might be outside, and if he and Langlois went inside, they would both be trapped. Sitting ducks. Nowhere was safe, but on balance they had more escape routes outside.

He gestured to Langlois to check one side of the fourth trailer while he inched over to peer around the other. He nearly gasped aloud, for barely fifteen feet in front of him, huddled against the side of the trailer, were Weiss and Twiggy. Their backs were to him, and their attention was riveted on the fifth trailer, which loomed fuzzily in the fog ahead. Weiss held his Glock in one hand and to Green's surprise, Twiggy's hand in the other. They were tiptoeing backwards towards Green as slowly and silently as they could.

Suddenly the door to the fifth trailer slammed open and a figure stepped out, dressed from head to toe in black from his cap to his steel-toed boots. He held a massive semi-automatic pistol in his hand and he stood on the top step, his feet apart, unafraid.

"Well, well, the birdies are flushed," he said and raised his pistol to sight along the barrel.

Jesus H. Christ! Green thought with no time to react. I'm dead, Twiggy's dead, we're all dead in seconds with that weapon. He thrust himself into the open with his own gun outstretched, screaming a distraction.

"Police! Freeze!"

Weiss whirled around, but the gunman didn't flinch. Green saw his finger squeeze on the trigger, and barely registered Twiggy's move as gunshots exploded the silence. One, two, three. Then from behind Green a different sound. Five shots in rapid, disciplined succession. Green hit the ground, Weiss screamed. The gunman on the porch hurtled back against the trailer door and toppled sideways off the steps to fall face down in the tall grass.

Green scrambled to his feet and spun around to see the SQ constable still in a shooting stance with both hands on his gun and shock on his face. Weiss uttered a guttural wail and when Green turned back to check the damage, he saw Twiggy sprawled on the ground, blood pumping from a wound at her neck. Weiss flung himself at her side and pressed his bare hands over the wound in a futile attempt to stem the flow.

Green raced to the killer's side, snatched his gun from the grass where it had fallen and pulled out the clip. Weak, choking sounds caught in the man's throat. Green was about to check his pulse when Langlois laid a restraining hand on his shoulder. The young SQ officer swayed on his feet, his eyes huge and his face grey with shock, but he nodded towards Twiggy bravely.

"You take care of the woman. I'll deal with him, okay?"

Green's French deserted him. "Thank you. And thank you for ..." he nodded to the downed gunman.

"Is okay," replied Langlois in fractured English, pointing to his SQ badge. "Better I do."

Green peeled off his suit jacket and hurried over to Twiggy. Weiss was still bent over her, cursing.

"She took the bullet for me," he said over and over. "She said she was slowing me down." He struggled to hold her together but Green saw at one glance that it was futile. The bullets had blown off half her neck and chest. Blood from her carotid artery shot high into the air, drenching the trailer wall.

"Twiggy," he murmured, pressing his jacket over the spray. "What the hell? Why the hell?"

In the distance, he heard running footsteps and Sullivan's frantic call, but his throat constricted and he couldn't answer. He looked down at Twiggy and saw the light fading from her eyes. Between tremors, she managed a final quirky smile.

"Debt repaid, Mr. G."

***

September 19, 1993. Medak, Sector South, Croatia.

I have become them. Not an animal, because an animal doesn't kill for revenge. A savage.

I could blame the Croats. Three days of guts and maggots and bodies so burned they fall apart when you try to get them in body bags, but not a single villager to save. They are gone. Hundreds. Where? Buried in mass graves? Carted away to hide the evidence of their slaughter?

Yesterday all day long Reggie and I bagged bodies and lugged them down the mountain to HQ for autopsy. This morning at parade the captain told us we aren't going home for another month because our replacement unit — called Operation Harmony, for fuck's sake — isn't ready yet. Four more weeks of hard rations, maggots and mud. I'll never get the stink of bodies out of my combats. The captain can see we're down, so he gives us a pep talk. He says even if there aren't any villagers to rescue, we're going to find all the bodies and make sure we document every single crime the Croats committed. Let's make sure the bastards pay, he says.

So this morning I'm covering the grid behind a burned out barn, looking for bodies, and I find this pair of draught horses. One's dead and just beginning to bloat, and its mate — a big bay mare — bends over to nudge it. I get goosebumps all over. Finally a live animal. I'm going to get her to bring her back to camp when suddenly I hear laughter and these two Croat soldiers step out from the barn. One of them sees the horse and stops. Raises his brand new American-made assault rifle and shoots her five times in the head. When she falls, the other one leans over to check if she's dead, presses the muzzle to her head and fires again.

I tackle them. Smash the first guy in the face with my

rifle butt, then rip the other one's rifle from his hands and throw him to the ground. It's like I have the strength of ten men, like the spirit of that mare poured into me. I shove the rifle in his face. The bastard's so freaked I can see the whites of his eyes. I pump six rounds into each of them. Turn their heads into a bloody pulp.

TWENTY-NINE

GREEN LOOKED UP through a mist of tears as Sullivan and his SQ sidekick burst onto the scene, guns ready. He struggled up from Twiggy's side and raised his hand in a restraining gesture.

"It's over." He jerked his head at Weiss, who was sitting back on his heels in stunned disbelief. "Search him and cuff him."

Sullivan waved his gun and pulled out his handcuffs. "Palms against the wall. You know the drill."

"I need to explain," Weiss began.

Anger billowed up in Green's throat like bile, burning him. "You bet you do, but not right now."

Weiss stumbled to his feet, cast one last look at Twiggy and bowed his head in resignation. Once he was safely cuffed, Green turned his attention to Langlois, who was still bent over the gunman. To Green's astonishment, the gunman was gasping for breath and struggling to sit up.

As Green drew closer, he saw some blood spreading from a wound on the man's shoulder, but across his chest there were only a few telltale nicks in his flak jacket. The SQ constable had pulled the black cap from his head, revealing a bristly grey crew cut. As Green looked into the man's blue eyes, defiant even in pain, he felt not the disgust or rage he'd expected, but sadness.

"So, Colonel," he said. "I'd say the battle is over."

Hamm fought back pain and snarled at him. "You don't know what you've done!"

Green looked at the carnage. At Twiggy sprawled on the ground and Weiss slumped against the trailer. He shook his head in wonder. "Do you?"

"John Blakeley could have saved thousands, soldiers and civilians alike! He could have changed the face of peacekeeping across the globe!"

"You may be right. But he also killed a man."

"An accident," Hamm replied. "And in the scheme of things ..."

Green had squatted down by Hamm's side to check his injuries. Belatedly disgust and rage bubbled up inside him. Even now, the man didn't grasp the significance of what he'd done! Green turned away to look at Langlois. Colour was beginning to return to the young officer's face. It's always nice to know you haven't killed a man, Green thought, even one as inhuman as the one before us.

"Put the handcuffs on him and read him the Charter warning," he said. "We have him dead to rights on Twiggy's death at least."

***

Fortin arrived when it was all over, strenuously rowing against the spring-swollen current of the river. So much for my carefully coordinated tactical response, Green thought in a moment of absurdity. He was grateful to hand over the operation to Fortin, who radioed his superiors to get the wheels of justice in motion. Since Weiss's crimes, whatever they might prove to be, had occurred on the Ontario side of the river, Green and Sullivan were eventually able to bundle him into the back of the Malibu and head back to town, leaving Fortin to deal with the removal of Twiggy's body, Hamm's evacuation to hospital, and the mountain of paperwork facing them all regarding what had transpired.

Sitting in the back of the Malibu on the ride back, Weiss seemed to retreat into shock, and Green hadn't the strength to browbeat him. All he wanted to do was crawl home to bed. Once they'd delivered Weiss into the duty sergeant's custody, with a promise to return later to lay formal charges, he dragged his exhausted body toward the parking lot.

Where he ran smack into Kate McGrath, leaning against the side of his Subaru with a triumphant smile on her face and two steaming cups of Tim Hortons coffee in her hands.

"I heard a rumour you were in the building," she said.

"A woman after my own heart." He plucked the coffee from her hand and unlocked the car. "I thought you'd gone home."

"I postponed my flight. After I heard the excitement you had this morning, I wanted another go at Blakeley." She circled the car and slid gracefully into the passenger seat. Her triumphant smile broadened.

He put the keys in the ignition but didn't turn it on. "And?"

"He didn't know about Hamm. He suspected someone was committing murder in order to conceal his old crime, but he was afraid it was his wife."

"Well, she was certainly high on our list, too. What made him think it was her?"

"Because she knew something was wrong that night when he came back from the meeting with Patricia, and he said he may have let something slip. The poor man's been beside himself."

"Poor man!" Green snorted as he ventured a cautious sip of the hot liquid. "The asshole started this whole damn mess."

"Anyway, he finally sang like a bird when he realized it wasn't her. Hamm always scared him a bit. Too dedicated a soldier, too determined to succeed. Not ambitious in the usual sense like most up-and-coming commissioned officers, but for the good of the corps. Blakeley always figured that Hamm backed him up that night in the Lighthouse Tavern not so much because of their history together, but for the sake of the army's reputation. Another Somalia-style scandal might have destroyed the entire force."

Green thought of Hamm sitting in the grass that morning, ranting about the lives Blakeley could have saved. For Hamm, the army came before all else. "I wonder how much Hamm will be willing to talk once we finally get him into our custody." He glanced across at her. In the confines of his little car, she seemed uncomfortably close. A mere finger touch away. "Are you going to stick around to talk to him?"

A faint pink tinged her cheeks before she shook her head. "No. The case is over. Blakeley's given a formal confession, and I expect he'll plead. I'm going to make arrangements to have him transferred to Halifax court. Less of a media circus for him to contend with."

"Don't count on it." He paused. An unspoken feeling hung between them "I'm sorry I had to handle it the way I —"

"You were an asshole." Her eyes twinkled as she looked at him. "But you were probably right, and in the end I did get the confession." She glanced at her watch. "But now I've got to hightail it. My flight is in an hour."

"Oh!" He was surprised at his disappointment. And his relief. He started the car. "Then let me drive you to the airport."

"That was the general idea. And if you're ever down east again ..." She stole him a mischievous side glance. Despite his fatigue, his senses tingled. "I'll take you to the Rock and treat you to the best cod tongues in the world, bar none."

Then she laughed, a marvellous musical laugh that lingered in the silence as he accelerated out of the lot.

***

By the time Green arrived home, it was five o'clock in the afternoon and Sharon's car was not in the driveway. He'd forgotten she was at work. He'd called her earlier in the day so that she wouldn't panic when the news broke about a fatal shooting in the Patricia Ross case. But with a dozen officers milling around, he'd kept his personal comments to a minimum.

Now, the sight of the empty driveway filled him with gloom. So much had happened in the past week that it felt like a lifetime since he'd really talked to her. God, he needed to talk.

Hannah was sprawled on the living room sofa, ostensibly babysitting Tony, but she was deep in conversation on her cellphone, and Tony was fast asleep on the floor. A MuchMusic video of gyrating guitar players blared on the television.

She looked up at his entrance without the slightest hint of guilt. "Are you making dinner?"

He dumped his keys on the hall bookcase, too weary even to pick up the mail. "No, I'm not. I have to go back to the station to interview a prisoner soon."

"Oh." A faint scowl marred her innocent pixie face, and she returned to her phone conversation. His anger flared, and he opened his mouth to voice it, but stopped himself. Fighting with Hannah took far more energy and emotion than he could muster at the moment.

Instead, he dragged himself upstairs, stripped his clothes, and stood under the pulsing shower, hoping to gather strength from its heat. He emerged more depressed than ever. He'd experienced this feeling often enough in the past to recognize what was happening. After a week of subsisting on adrenaline and sheer force of will, he'd hit the wall at the end of the race. Usually he had enough elation and triumph to carry him through the aftermath, but today he had neither.

He crawled into bed and pulled the duvet up to his chin. Desperately he willed his body to relax and his mind to go blank. He had only two hours before all hell would break loose over Weiss's detention, and he needed to wring the truth out of the man before the lawyers and the union threw half a dozen gag orders in his way.

There was a knock on the door, and to his astonishment Hannah appeared, carrying a tray with a pot of tea and some dubious-looking lumps of dough. An uncertain smile twitched at the corners of her mouth. "Tony and I baked peanut butter cookies. Since you have to go out again, I thought you might like some tea."

He sat up in bed, surprised to find he couldn't speak around the sudden lump in his throat. She laid the tray on the bed and stood over him, fiddling with his cup. "I guess you had quite a day, eh? I caught part of it on the news."

It was on the tip of his tongue to deny it. To protect her — and himself — from the gruesome imagery of his job. But in the end he sank back among his pillows with a sigh. "Yes. I lost a friend today."

"That homeless woman?"

He nodded. A facile platitude sprang to his thoughts, that maybe the homeless woman had finally found her home. She had clearly chosen her end, trading her life for Weiss's, as if it somehow paid for the life she herself had taken years ago. Yet anger drove the easy answer from his mind. She had not deserved the murder of her children, nor the bullet at the hands of Hamm. It had all been a senseless, goddamn waste of one of the good souls in this world.

Hannah poured his tea and held it out. He looked at her veiled eyes. "Will you join me?"

She shot him a glance and edged to the door. "No, I …" She examined her painted toes, scarlet now instead of black. Progress. "Well, I guess maybe a minute. Then I got a call to make."

A minute may be all either of us can handle, he thought as he shifted over to give her a place to sit. They could talk about rock music, and maybe that minute would give him the strength to go back into battle for the final round.

***

September 22, 1993. Medak, Sector South, Croatia.

It's 2 a.m. and it feels too heavy to keep inside. I imagine it growing and swelling 'til I think maybe the only way to relieve the pain is to plunge a knife in my gut and burst it.

Captain Blakeley came to me today and told me the conversation we were about to have didn't happen. He told me the OC is recommending me for a Medal of Bravery for my civilian rescue. Then he said he knew about the Croat soldiers and by all rights I should be thrown in detention or slapped in the psych ward. I was a disgrace to the uniform, a traitor to Canada's peacekeeping ideals and a menace to those we're sworn to protect. We're not the judge, jury and executioner over here, he said. We don't have any idea what these people have been through and we have no right to play God with their lives.

But the army really needs the morale boost of a successful mission and the example of my medal, he said, so he wasn't going to put anything on my record. It's our secret, he said, and unless you want to see the whole Second Princess Patricia Light Infantry Battalion hung out to dry in the press, you'll never reveal it to a living soul.

Then he walks out. What the hell is this traitor and menace crap? What ever happened to the guy who promised only three days ago that we'd make the bastards pay?

THIRTY

TO HIS SURPRISE, when Green arrived back at the station, Weiss was ignoring the advice of his lawyers and his association rep and was clamouring to talk to him. Sullivan had gone home to treat himself to a well-earned Senators play-off hockey game, but Gibbs had returned to the station, eager to get at the man who had betrayed Sue. When he came down to the video room, where Green was supervising the set-up, he was vibrating with an energy Green couldn't quite interpret. Part rage, part triumph, part pure testosterone.

"I know you want this, Bob," Green said, "but that's a good reason for you to stay out of it."

"I won't interrupt, sir. I just want to be there, to watch you and — and to hear what the bastard has to say."

"But Weiss knows how you feel. Having you there ..." Staring him down, Green wanted to add, but thought better of it, "... is going to colour his statement. It may even shut him down."

Gibbs took a deep breath, as if to galvanize himself. Anger glinted through his excitement, and for a moment Green thought he was actually going to lash back.

"You can watch from the video room," he added, to forestall an outburst the usually diffident Gibbs would later regret. "Sue would appreciate that."

The mention of Peters seemed to deflate Gibbs, and he looked at his feet awkwardly. "She doesn't remember wh-what happened. I suppose that's a good thing."

"Probably," Green said. On balance he thought so. Amnesia seemed to be nature's way of shielding the mind from terrors too great to bear. Given the alternative — years of nightmares and flashbacks — he wished it was something he could invoke at will. "I heard she was talking today. I bet she'll be back on the job in no time."

Gibbs shuffled his feet. "I hope it … it hasn't changed her. Taken away her nerve."

"Sue Peters? Not on your life!" Green spoke with more confidence than he felt, but for now it was what they all wanted to believe. "Now let's get at that sonofabitch who put her there."

Green had seen so many faces of Weiss over the past week that he wasn't sure who was going to walk through the interview door, but he prepared himself as best he could. He stationed Jones unobtrusively just inside the door and placed two molded chairs at right angles. A notebook and pen lay on the small, square table between them. Simple, intimate, yet professional.

Weiss was wearing nondescript cellblock scrubs that hung on him, several sizes too big, but he'd been allowed to shave and comb his hair. Green suspected he had not received the most compassionate treatment from the guards in the cell block — stabbing your partner in the back would not earn you points among your fellow officers — but at least they had allowed him to salvage some of his dignity.

Even so, he looked as if he had precious little dignity left when he shuffled into the room. His blue eyes, only last week so cocksure, were red and puffy, and his shoulders sagged as if the world weighed heavily on them. Green hoped it did. He felt a flash of anger at the man, and he waited in silence until it receded. Then, summoning up a dispassion he didn't feel, he gestured to a chair.

"Sit down, Jeff."

Weiss sat and only then raised his head to look around. His eyes passed over Jones as if he were invisible, then came to rest on the camera lens in the corner. "Do we have to do that?"

"You know the drill, Jeff." For the record, he explained the legalities of videotaping, repeated the Charter warning, and made the formal introductions for the tape.

Weiss gripped his head in his hands and shook it slowly back and forth. "I just need you to believe me." He flicked his hand at the camera. "They won't. The fucking brass won't."

"This is not a private confessional, Weiss. Just so you know, the OPP has connected you to the call that tipped Hamm off about Peters. The Petawawa convenience store owner ID'ed you. And the Tim Hortons manager here on Bank Street picked you out as the one asking about Twiggy last Thursday. It's looking pretty bad. Obstruction of justice, kidnapping …"

Weiss jerked his head up as if stung. "I didn't kidnap Twiggy! I took her to keep her safe!"

Great job you did, Green thought drily. He softened his voice with an effort. "Okay, maybe it would help if you start at the beginning."

"With Patricia Ross?"

"With Ian MacDonald."

He glanced at Green in bewilderment. "I don't see what MacDonald has to do with it."

"Weiss, stop dicking around. I know about MacDonald's actions in Croatia. I want to know your part in it."

For a moment, Green feared his loss of patience would jeopardize the interview, to say nothing of the case if Weiss's lawyer got hold of it. But it seemed to focus the man. He stared at the table and ran his tongue around his parched lips. "Croatia. Fuck. I was way over my head in Croatia, but the UN needed police who could speak the language, and my mother was from Sarajevo. I grew up in the Croatian community in North York, and I figured it was a chance to see my roots." He shut his eyes and winced as if at the memory. "They should never have put Macdonald on clean-up duty in Medak. The fucking Croats … They wiped out everything. Over three hundred homes destroyed, almost two hundred animals slaughtered, not to mention the mutilated people. So when I came across the dead Croat soldiers, I didn't know what to make of it. I mean — this wasn't just some combatants shot in a skirmish. The guys' heads were obliterated. Then a couple of local Serb villagers who'd been hiding in the hills told me it was a blue helmet. I was afraid one of our guys was maybe going off the deep end, so I reported it to my unit commander."

"Blakeley."

Weiss nodded. "The best commander I've ever had. A take-charge, buck-stops-here kind of guy who stood up for his men. Blakeley told me the Serbs were probably lying to protect one of their own, and who could blame them anyway? He told me to leave it with him."

"So you never knew how he handled the situation?"

"No, but whatever he did, he backed MacDonald up. Not like the kind of chicken shit superior who leaves you hanging out to dry when things get rough for you."

Green pondered the story. It corroborated what Blakeley had said, but if it was true, why had Daniel Oliver accused Blakeley of betrayal? Something didn't make sense. "Did you know MacDonald killed himself two years later?"

"Dick Hamm told me."

"Did you know Hamm back then?"

"Just by reputation."

"Which was?"

"A hardass, but another guy you want in your corner when the bullets start flying." Weiss's jaw tightened, and tears brimmed in his eyes. "Shows you how fucking wrong I was."

Green sensed they were finally hovering on the brink of the real story. He leaned forward and lowered his voice. "So tell me how you got into this mess, Jeff."

"What's the use? I'm going down. I deserve to go down."

"Maybe. But I have some discretion here. You said you wanted someone to understand. Try me."

Weiss brushed his hand through his blond hair, which now hung in strings rather than curls. Sucking in a deep breath, he began. "I volunteered for John Blakeley's election campaign, that's how it started. I hadn't seen the man since Medak, but like I said, he was a real leader. The Liberal Party and the senior military brass have been jerking the army around for years because no one understood what peacekeeping missions were really like, and the public hasn't got the balls to pay the price, either in taxes or lives. Oh, everyone is paying lip service right now to funding the military, because of the dangers in the Afghanistan mission, but when it comes to forking out the money so the guys can do the job properly, nobody wants to pay. And the first time we get into a firefight over there or suffer a few casualties, suddenly the public and the politicians are screaming 'Oh this is not the Canadian way.' They just don't understand you have to fight for right.

"Usually I vote Alliance and Conservative, but you know, one sleaze bag is much like another. When I read about Captain Blakeley putting his hat in the ring, I thought there's a guy we really need on Parliament Hill. I know Blakeley wasn't too happy to have me on his team, but I just put it down to our disagreement in Croatia. But Dick Hamm persuaded him to let me work with him —"

"Hamm was working on Blakeley's campaign?"

"Yeah, but in the background, so the military looked like it was keeping out of politics. Hamm did most of the private security work, watched Blakeley's back, that kind of thing. And that's where he thought I'd be useful."

"How did you make contact with Hamm initially?"

"I went to Blakeley's campaign headquarters to volunteer. Met his wife Leanne, who kind of ran things behind the scenes there. She said I could really make a contribution doing security. She introduced me to Hamm."

"Did Hamm know about your past history in Croatia?"

"Oh yeah, I told him that's why I really admired the man." Weiss shook his head in disgust. "Fuck. I was suckered every step of the way, by both of them."

"So you did security work with Hamm?"

"On my days off. Just bodyguard stuff, working the crowds at rallies … I thought that's all it would be. Until …" Weiss broke off.

Green leaned in. "Until what?"

Weiss tried to take a sip of water, but the glass trembled so violently he put it down untouched. "Politics can be dirty. The Conservatives were running scared, because they saw there was a chance they could lose the riding, so a lot of people wanted to bring Blakeley down. I don't know how else to explain ... what I did."

Green let the silence lengthen. He was not about to help the man with his unburdening. The seconds ticked by in the claustrophobic room. Finally, Weiss sucked in a deep breath and began to recite, like an officer giving a report. "At seven a.m., last Monday, Dick Hamm placed a phone call to my residence just as I was heading out for work. He said there was a situation that could compromise John Blakeley's election. He said a woman had been found dead by the aqueduct in Ottawa and that Blakeley's name might get dragged in, because he'd had a drink with the woman the night before."

Seven a.m. Green wracked his memory. The 911 call had come in at 6:37, less than half an hour before. "Did he say how he knew about it?"

"He used to follow Blakeley whenever he was concerned for his safely. This woman had called Blakeley for a meeting. Hamm told me it was for old times' sake because Blakeley had known her fiancé years ago. At the time, I thought it was a crock. I figured he'd picked up a piece of ass in the hotel, and now we had to do damage control."

Weiss's bloodshot eyes held a hint of the old defiance, as if he were willing Green to call him naive, yet the explanation was just plausible enough to work. Green retrieved the thread without comment. "So Hamm was tailing Blakeley?"

Weiss nodded. "Blakeley called a cab for the woman, who was Patricia Ross, of course. Then a few hours later the woman turns up dead not five minutes from where he left her. Hamm asked if I could keep an eye on the investigation so that he could handle any of the fallout if Blakeley's name came up."

"And you agreed to that?" Green allowed incredulity to creep into his voice.

Weiss rubbed his hands through his hair again. "He didn't ask me to interfere in the investigation, just give him a heads up."

"Didn't it ring any alarm bells that Hamm knew who she was and what had happened to her barely half an hour after her body was discovered?"

The defiance faded from his eyes. He shook his head wretchedly. "Hamm is so focussed, he sucks you right in. He said he'd thought she was up to something, so he'd kept her under surveillance as a precaution."

"And watched her die?"

"He told me he'd seen her leave the hotel with some other guy as soon as Blakeley left and head towards the aqueduct. Then he checked back in the morning when he saw the squad cars arriving."

As an explanation, it was just barely credible, but Weiss had been a fool not to be suspicious once the facts began to emerge. To judge from the man's distraught expression, he agreed.

"So you got yourself on the case and kept Hamm informed," Green said.

"Just if it might have an impact on John Blakeley."

"Which it did, once you and Peters went up to Petawawa."

"Hamm said Patricia Ross had been up to Petawawa trying to see John, but he wasn't there. He'd heard she was blabbing in bars around town, and when she'd had too much to drink, she might have mentioned Blakeley's name. So Hamm wanted me to let him know if Sue and I uncovered anything. He gave me his private security line." He broke off, his jaw working. "I never dreamed ..."

"What did you think Hamm was going to do with the information?"

Weiss flushed. "I don't know. Create a diversion? Interrupt Sue?"

"You phoned a person of interest in the investigation, and told him what the detective was doing and where. Did you not ask yourself what his motives were? Did you not think maybe you'd put her in harm?"

"No!" Weiss shoved his chair back against the wall. "Fuck, do you think I would have done that if I knew what he'd do?"

No, you were just going to screw up a police investigation, Green thought, allowing his eyes to convey his disbelief. Come on, you idiot, you've been on the streets, you've even been overseas. You can't tell me you're that naive.

"Why did you obey the request, Jeff? Hamm had no rank over you."

"Because I believed in Blakeley! I thought Patricia Ross was just a drunken hooker, and that because some random sicko killed her, a good man's political career was going down the toilet."

And what's one washed-up whore compared to the good of the country, Green thought. He shook his head in slow disbelief. "You've been a cop now what? Almost twenty years?"

Weiss thrust back from the table and jumped up. "I knew this was a waste if time! Just get the charges over with!"

Green gestured calmly to the chair. "Sit down, Jeff. We're not done yet. I want the whole story. How did Hamm explain the request?"

Weiss hesitated, staring at Green through reddened, defiant eyes. Slowly he righted his chair and sat back down. "He said all he wanted to do was protect Blakeley."

"When did you realize Hamm himself was guilty?"

"When Sue Peters was attacked. That's when I realized I had truly and royally fucked up."

"Why didn't you tell us then?"

"I had no time. The OPP and the paramedics were all over me, and all I could think of was getting Sue to hospital."

"Then why didn't you tell me that night at the hospital?"

Weiss shifted. "Because by that time I'd remembered that homeless woman."

Green hadn't been expecting an honest admission that Weiss was simply protecting his own ass, but nonetheless his bizarre answer startled him. "Twiggy?"

"I knew Hamm had her in his sights. He said she'd seen Blakeley with Patricia outside the hotel, and he was afraid she'd recognize him from the papers. She hoarded papers, he said. He asked me to find out more about her. Once I realized the truth, and how ruthless he was, I knew he'd come after her. I couldn't think how else to protect her but to get her away from here."

Green gritted his teeth. "Why didn't you inform us, Jeff? We could have picked her up."

"I needed time to think! I knew you wouldn't believe I had nothing to do with the attacks. My career was down the tubes … my pension, my benefits, all the stuff I've put nearly twenty years of my life into. And while you were busy throwing the book at me, he'd get to her."

"You don't give us much credit, Jeff. You could have brought her in yourself, and kept her safe."

Weiss jerked his head up and his eyes flooded. "Do you think I don't know that? That if I'd had the guts, she might still be alive? But you don't give him enough credit! He's fast, he's deadly, and he strikes before you even know he's there."

Green remembered Hamm that morning, slipping silently through the trailers like a cougar stalking its prey. Undeterred by police, unflinching in his goal. Green didn't want to believe Weiss; he wanted instead to despise the man for his treachery and his self-serving cowardice, but in truth he might be right. Maybe Twiggy's fate was sealed the moment she first laid eyes on Blakeley talking to Patricia at the hotel that night.

Whether it justified Weiss's actions in spiriting her away was a question for the courts to decide.

THIRTY-ONE

TUESDAY MORNING GREEN awoke to the steady drum of rain upon the roof. He opened one eye to squint at the clock radio by the bed. 11:45. Half the day was over, but every muscle in his body refused to move. Mentally he reviewed his schedule, which had been shot to hell in the past week.

Blakeley was awaiting the paperwork on his transfer to Halifax, Weiss was facing arraignment on the one criminal charge they'd decided to fling at him — obstructing a police investigation — but Professional Standards would handle that. Green suspected Weiss would plead to something even more innocuous in exchange for giving them Hamm. The real villain in the piece was still on the Quebec side while the two provinces squabbled about who should have first go at him.

Green also had a routine committee meeting on the RCMP's new information sharing system and a long-overdue briefing with Gaetan Larocque about what had been happening in the rest of his department in the past week. And there was also a meeting with Devine, about the inter-provincial mess he'd embroiled her in.

All of it was expendable, all of it deadly dull. Downstairs he could hear Sharon humming a Raffi tune and laughing at some antic their son was performing. Without a second thought, he rolled over, reached for the phone, and called in sick.

Wednesday morning, he was back at his desk, sorting through the extraordinary backlog of messages, memos and emails that had accumulated in his absence, when a bulky package arrived in the mail. It was bound completely in scotch tape and addressed only to "Detective Green, Homicide Department, Ottawa Police." By some miracle it had survived Canada Post.

There was no return address. Curious, he unwrapped it carefully so as to preserve the packaging as much as possible, and extracted a well-worn student notebook. On the cover was the name "Corporal Ian MacDonald, West Nova Scotia Regiment" and attached to it with a paper clip was a simple note.

Dear detective, Danny sent this back to me before he died, and I decided you should have it after all. If it can help save other people's lives, I think Ian would have wanted it. Please don't judge my boy too harshly.

Sincerely, Mary MacDonald

Green opened the notebook. Tight, spiky handwriting crammed every wrinkled page. With a racing heart, he began to read.

***

Two hours later, Green closed the notebook and sat staring into space, fighting a sense of overwhelming defeat. He still hadn't moved when Sullivan stuck his head into his office.

"Richard Hamm is on his way over from Gatineau. Do you want a go at him?"

Anger and disgust swept through Green, chasing out the despair. He picked up the notebook and jumped to his feet. "You bet I do."

Richard Hamm looked none the worse for wear, in body or spirit, for his flesh wound and his short stint in the Gatineau jail. He strode into the interview room two hours later with his shoulders squared, his head high and his gaze sharp with defiant pride. Green half expected him to salute as if he were greeting a fellow officer on the battle front.

"Sit down, Mr. Hamm," Green said brusquely, to disabuse the man of any notion that he was among equals. Hamm perched on the edge of the plastic chair, poised and alert. Green let a full fifteen seconds elapse while he pretended to study the notebook.

"You're in serious trouble here," he said finally.

"I am aware of that."

"You are charged with two counts of premeditated murder in the deaths of Patricia Ross and Jean Calderone, and one of attempted murder of Detective Susan Peters. You're going to prison for a long, long time."

Impatience flickered across Hamm's face. "Inspector, I've been in theatres of war all over the world. Death was always a stray bullet away, but it was a risk I embraced without hesitation."

"This was not a theatre of war, Hamm. Two innocent civilians were killed."

"Innocence and guilt are all in the breadth of your vision, sir. I don't expect you to understand. Those people were threats to the future of our country."

Good God, Green thought with disbelief. The man is delusional, like the SS commanders who went to their executions steadfastly defending the necessity of their actions for the good of the Reich. Green had a sudden fear that Hamm's lawyers would defend him on the basis of Not Criminally Responsible for his actions. But on second thought, he realized that Hamm would never permit it. He believed himself blessed not with madness but with an intellect and vision far greater than ordinary mortals.

Green wondered if it was even worthwhile asking the man about the death of one lowly, expendable corporal in his command, but before he could broach the subject of Daniel Oliver, Hamm gave a tight, patronizing smile.

"I'm not crazy, Inspector. Merely trained to accept that every mission worth achieving may require casualties along the way."

"The mission being the election of John Blakeley?"

"No. The mission being to place a spokesman for the Canadian military and for the defence of this country into the chambers of government."

"Even though that spokesman was himself guilty of murder?"

Hamm splayed his fingers on the table and aligned them in a perfect arc. "Blakeley made one mistake that was at worst unintentional homicide. His potential for good far outweighed that."

"Just as Ian MacDonald made one mistake? A mistake for which he had a good deal more provocation, but for which neither you nor Blakeley were prepared to excuse him."

"MacDonald was reckless, not heroic."

Green tossed Ian MacDonald's diary down on the table. "I'm referring to the time he shot two Croatian soldiers six times in the head."

For the first time Hamm looked off-balance. He drew his elbows in as if to protect his flank and pursed his lips mutely.

"I see John Blakeley didn't even tell you," Green said. "Yet it's the root of all this, Hamm. All this started with MacDonald's momentary lapse and Blakeley's unwillingness to forgive it."

Hamm's lips tightened further. "Forgiveness has no part in the military, Inspector, except in the chaplaincy."

"On the contrary, it underlies everything. When we ask our soldiers to take a human life, there has to be a tacit recognition that the killing, although regrettable, is forgivable. Not just sanctioned, but forgiven. Otherwise, as in MacDonald's case, it would haunt the soldiers for years afterwards."

"Riddles!" Hamm replied shortly. "If MacDonald shot Croatian combatants after the ceasefire, he deserved whatever discipline Blakeley chose to impose. There are rules which form the basis of any military engagement, and they determine whether a killing is sanctioned, as you put it."

"Blakeley's punishment was to tell a young man who'd been pushed beyond his limit that he was a disgrace to the uniform, and that if news of his actions ever leaked out, it might cripple the military. He sentenced the boy to keeping the shameful secret inside for the rest of his life, with no hope of resolution or understanding."

Hamm smiled, a tight, humourless smile that didn't reach his eyes. "You've obviously never heard a regimental sergeant major at morning parade. As reprimands go, that was pretty mild, and hardly justification for taking the coward's way out at the end of the day."

Green wanted to beat the arrogant self-assurance from his face. Did nothing touch the man? "Perhaps. But you may find living with murder a great deal more difficult than you think."

Hamm looked straight at him. "This isn't about me, Inspector. This is about the future defence of our country. I admit the killings I carried out were regrettable and personally distasteful, but they were undertaken with that greater goal in mind. As an officer, I am prepared to accept the full consequences for my part in the mission."

As he absorbed the colonel's words, Green had an eerie feeling that a deeper meaning lay hidden beneath. *His part in the mission* ... As if the elimination of witnesses had been a covert operation complete with orders, rules of engagement, and a proper chain of command.

Jesus, he thought, are we still missing something?

***

In ten seconds, Green was down the hall, sticking his head into the recording room. On the video, he could see Hamm still sitting in the interview room with his arms crossed and his eyes closed, trying to look bored. Tension radiated from every carefully controlled muscle.

"Brian, do we have the records of that secret cellphone yet?"

Sullivan swung around in surprise. "Yeah. The OPP sent it yesterday. What's up?"

Green was already heading further down the hall, leaving Sullivan scrambling to catch up. "I have a hunch."

In the situation room, they found Gibbs painstakingly inputting information into the major case file. The bags beneath his eyes were gone, and he sat upright, smelling of lime aftershave and fresh clothes. He abandoned his data the moment he heard Green's request. It took him less than a minute to locate the printout of phone calls made to Hamm's covert cellphone. All three detectives bent over it eagerly.

There were only a handful of calls made or received over the past ten days, supporting the theory that it was only used for clandestine communication. Hamm likely used his official cell or land line for normal calls. Green scanned the dates back to April 23rd, and his heart leaped in triumph as he found what he wanted. He stabbed an entry near the top of the page.

"I thought so! Hamm received a phone call at 11:03 Sunday night. That's about half an hour after Blakeley claims he left Patricia Ross getting into a cab." He traced his finger down the column. "The next call was one he placed at 7:04 a.m. That would be the one Weiss says he received." Green spoke more to himself than to the others as he wrestled with the implications. "So Hamm communicated with no one between eleven p.m. and seven a.m. If I'm right, this eleven p.m. call is the crucial call. Bob, find out whose number it is."

While Gibbs clicked through computer links, Sullivan looked at Green questioningly. "What are we looking for?"

"The mastermind. It was staring us in the face all along. Hamm is a soldier; he's not a lone wolf or a psychopath. He's a little warped, a little obsessed —"

"A little!"

Green hesitated. "Okay, a lot. But his assignment was security. I don't think he would expand his operation to include murder without an order from above."

Sullivan stared at him in bewilderment while he traced Green's logic. "Jesus, Mary and Joseph! You think it was Blakeley after all?"

"We should know soon enough." Green nodded towards Gibbs as new text filled the screen. "Is it one of Blakeley's numbers?"

"No, sir," Gibbs said. "It's a payphone in a bistro on the corner of Laurier and Bay."

"That's only a two-minute walk from Blakeley's condo," Sullivan exclaimed. "Holy Fuck! Blakeley ordered the hit after all!"

Green's mind was racing. Half an hour. It would have taken Blakeley a mere five minutes to walk home from the Delta Hotel, where he'd left Patricia Ross, and at most two minutes to walk from the condo to this bistro. That left more than twenty minutes unaccounted for. What had he been doing for that time? Pacing in panicky circles? Figuring out what to do?

Kate McGrath's words came back to him. She'd said Blakeley had been talking to his wife. The rock of his life, the woman who stepped in to rescue him every time he floundered.

"Not Blakeley," he said. "His wife Leanne."

Both detectives stared at him. Gibbs looked utterly baffled, but Sullivan's eyes narrowed thoughtfully. He hasn't lost his instincts, Green thought. He's met the woman too.

"Why her and not him?" Sullivan challenged, testing the theory. "I'm not sure Hamm would take orders from a woman."

"Not just any woman, Blakeley's wife. Perhaps even more importantly, the daughter of Jack Neuss, Liberal backroom kingmaker." Green rose to scribble his points on the blackboard. "Look at the evidence. She's fiercely protective, and she doesn't hesitate to run interference. Blakeley talked to her after his meeting with Patricia Ross; he himself was afraid she was the killer, and who knows better than him what his own wife is capable of?"

"Just because she's capable doesn't mean —"

"The call was made from a payphone away from the condo. Why?"

"So no one could trace it back to him."

"Possibly," Green said. "But at that point neither of them knew we'd ever latch on to this phone number. I think it was made from the bistro so that Blakeley wouldn't overhear the conversation. He knew Leanne went out shortly after he told her, and that's why he was so afraid she was guilty."

Silence fell in the room as the detectives considered the points on the board. Gibbs had flushed with anger, and finally he spoke. "Are we ever going to be able to get her? Blakeley will never give her up."

Sullivan nodded gravely. "Neither will Hamm."

"We can try," Green said. "We should be able to connect her to the bistro and the phone call to Hamm."

Sullivan shook his head. "She'll just say that she phoned him to discuss the Patricia Ross situation and to get his advice. That she never, ever dreamed he would take the action he did. Which could be true, Mike."

"It could be, but I'd bet my whole career it's not. In fact, I bet if we check the payphone records for the time just before that 11:03 call, we might find an outgoing call to Daddy Dearest to get his advice. Leanne learned power politics at her father's knee. She learned about ruthlessness and determination when most girls were still playing with Barbies. Blakeley is not only her whole life but the future of the Party she loves. Patricia Ross threatened to destroy them both."

"Maybe," Sullivan said. "But if her defence lawyer put that loyal, devoted wife in front of a jury, we wouldn't have a chance."

Gibbs had been scribbling in his notebook, and now he looked up, his eyes flashing. "That doesn't mean we won't try! Maybe someone at the bistro overheard something. I'll check the bistro phone records, I'll dig into her background, speak to campaign workers, put her life under a microscope —"

Green walked over and laid a restraining hand on the young detective's shoulder. He had his own thoughts about how to crack the case. A brief word with Kate McGrath to plant a thought in Blakeley's ear. At heart, Blakeley was a decent man. He'd lived for ten years with one death on his conscience, and it had nearly destroyed him. How long could he keep silent with two more deaths on his conscience, knowing that the woman he considered his saving angel had been responsible for both?

Gibbs could dig all he wanted, but for once, Green thought, time and patience might prove their greatest ally. For the first time since Twiggy died, despite this bewildering and unsettled end, he felt some hope that justice would have the final say.

He squeezed Gibbs's shoulder. "Tomorrow, Bob. We've all had a rough week, but Sue's had the worst. Why don't you and Brian go tell her the news, and then take the rest of the day off."

Gibbs looked at him. "Are you coming, sir?"

Green hesitated. He thought of the pale, wan figure surrounded by tubes, machines, and the smell of disinfectant and death. "Soon," he said. "I just have to wrap up some paperwork."

He walked back to his office and sat at his desk, staring at the blinking phone and the jumble of papers on his desk. He should write up the Hamm interview, he should check with Larocque about the Byward murders, he should update Devine …

He stared into space with Macdonald's diary still in his hand, thinking about death, forgiveness, and the human soul.

About why Twiggy and MacDonald had been unable to make peace with their crimes, no matter how provoked and justified they seemed. And why Hamm had walked away from the calculated killing of two innocents with his conscience unscathed.

God, I'm getting too old for this, he thought. He set down the diary, left his phone messages and his memos unanswered, and headed off to see Peters.

***

September 10, 1995.

I haven't looked at this diary in two years. Got home from Croatia, stuck it in the bottom drawer, and tried to forget about it. Just like I tried to forget about Croatia.

Dad's really proud of my medal, and everybody down home wants to talk to me about it. But what the hell can I say? It's a lie. I'm an imposter, and I can hardly stand to listen to praise of what I did, let alone talk about it. The army paraded me in front of the other units and the press, but the guys who really mattered — Blakeley, the Hammer — were never there.

So my medal sits with this diary in the bottom of the drawer, and I thought today would be a good day to look at them. Two years to the day since I rescued those Serbs. Almost two years since we beat the shit out of the Croats and moved into Medak, only to find they'd already destroyed the place. Three hundred Serbs killed without a trace.

Almost two years since I made those Croat soldiers pay the price. These past two years, I've hoped that maybe some good came of what we did. That maybe we'd helped them all feel more secure and find a better way to get along. Yesterday I read an article in the paper about Srebrenica, a village in Bosnia that the Serbs invaded while the Dutch UN peacekeepers stood by and watched. Over eight thousand Muslim boys and men have vanished without a trace.

Fuck it.

ACKNOWLEDGEMENTS

THE THEME OF *Honour Among Men* is a timely one as Canada searches its soul for its place as peacemaker in the modern world. The characters and the story are entirely fictional, and any resemblance to persons living or dead, is purely coincidental. However, the historical places and details are based on fact, and I am indebted to two authors, military historian Sean M. Maloney and journalist Carol Off, for their detailed and compassionate books on our peacekeepers' experiences in the former Yugoslavia, which provided much of the background information for my story. Any errors or distortions, whether accidental or intentional, are mine alone.

Writing a novel is a solitary, uncertain journey, but as always I am grateful to the many people who provided information, inspiration and constructive criticism along the way. As always, a very special thanks is due to Mark Cartwright of the Ottawa Police for his technical expertise and critical eye for realism. Second, thanks to Paul Fiander and my cousins Sally, Ed and Jeff Goss for their colourful insights into Halifax. Third, writers need a mirror to see the images they create, so I'd like to thank the members of my critiquing group, Joan Boswell, Vicki Cameron, Mary Jane Maffini,

Sue Pike and Linda Wiken, who held up the mirror for me by diligently wading through the first draft. Fourth, I am grateful for the ongoing belief and support of my agent Leona Trainer, my editor Allister Thompson and my publisher Sylvia McConnell, whose efforts brought it to final fruition.

And last but not least, a very special thanks for my family. For everything.

ABOUT THE AUTHOR

BARBARA FRADKIN WAS born in Montreal and worked for more than twenty-five years as a child psychologist before retiring in order to devote more time to her first passion, writing. Her Inspector Green series has garnered an impressive four Best Novel nominations and two wins from the Crime Writers of Canada. She is also the author of the critically acclaimed Amanda Doucette Mysteries and the Cedric O'Toole series, and her short stories have appeared in mystery magazines and anthologies such as the New Canadian Noir series and the Ladies Killing Circle series. She is a two-time winner in *Storyteller Magazine*'s annual Great Canadian Short Story Contest, as well as a four-time nominee for the Crime Writers of Canada Award for Best Short Story. She has three children, two grandchildren, and a dog, and in whatever spare time she can find, she loves outdoor activities like travelling, skiing, and kayaking, as well as reading, of course.